PRAISE FOR THE NOVELS
OF A. L. JACKSON

Come to Me Recklessly

"A. L. Jackson writes with so much raw emotion. My heart was invested in Christopher and Samantha's story from the first word to the last."
—Mia Sheridan, *New York Times* bestselling author of *Archer's Voice*

Come to Me Quietly

"As always, A. L. Jackson knows how to tap human emotion. Every word she writes bleeds meaning. *Come to Me Quietly* is a riveting tale . . . simply breathtaking."
—Gail McHugh, *New York Times* bestselling author
of *Collide* and *Pulse*

"A devastatingly beautiful story of love, grief, and healing. Every emotion on the page will grip at your heart and leave you stuck in the characters' lives for days after."
—Molly McAdams, *New York Times* bestselling author
of *Stealing Harper*

"*Come to Me Quietly* is raw and real. It's an achingly beautiful story about a man with a ravaged soul and his chance at a life he never thought he deserved. A. L. Jackson has written . . . an emotionally impactful story that grabs you right from the start."   —Kim Karr, author of *Torn*

"Exquisite, beautiful, poignant—A. L. Jackson is in a league of her own! [She] has a way with words that makes the pages come to life. You'll live with these characters, feel their ups and downs, their loves and losses. You'll bleed *with* them, and *for* them. . . . Heartbreaking and heartwarming, this book made me ache, made me cry, made me think, and made me fall in love."
—S. C. Stephens, #1 *New York Times* bestselling author of *Reckless*

continued . . .

Lost to You

"Oh Lord! Amazing doesn't begin to cover it. Beautiful. Heartbreaking. Passionate . . . that's a little more like it. . . . And A. L. Jackson . . . oh my word, I can't begin to describe what she makes you feel in this book. She has a talent for bringing out emotions, and I could literally feel every one of them throughout the book. The love, the passion, the adoration, and even the heartbreak gripped me."

—*New York Times* bestselling author Molly McAdams

"I was completely hooked from the second I opened *Lost to You* . . . a beautiful and powerful love story."   —Flirty and Dirty Book Blog

"I loved this! Absolutely fantastic! A. L. Jackson is one of the most talented authors I've ever read. Her words have a way of reaching deep into your heart and not letting go."   —Aestas Book Blog

"Can A. L. Jackson write anything but excellence? . . . She always finds a way to get my insides twisted into so many emotions that I feel like it is all happening to me. . . . 5-star perfection!"   —Madison Says

"A beautiful, heart-stopping love story. . . . You will sigh happily, swoon, smile, cry, and get pissed off. What a great range of emotions."   —The Book Enthusiast

When We Collide

"A great read. . . . The intensity in the novel is extraordinary and I look forward to reading other books by A. L. Jackson."

—Reviewing Romance

"Reading *When We Collide* was like a slow, agonizing torture, but in the best way. . . . I felt so much love and hope for these characters. It was an amazing read."   —The Book List Reviews

Take This Regret

"An incredible, touching love story that will have you on the edge of your seat needing to know what happens next. . . . *Take This Regret* is one read I won't soon forget; it still haunts my thoughts . . . a truly amazing, beautiful read." —Flirty and Dirty Book Blog

"Absolutely amazing! . . . I felt love, hatred, joy, sadness, pain, betrayal. . . . This is truly a great read." —My Secret Romance

"There are no words that could begin to explain how wonderfully powerful this story is. It wasn't your typical romance. No fluff stuff here! It was an emotional roller-coaster ride from the beginning till the end!" —Crazy Four Books

Pulled

"There are not enough words that could possibly describe how I feel about this book. It is hands down one of the most amazing love stories I've ever read. . . . Thank you, A. L. Jackson, for allowing me into the world of these characters."
—*New York Times* bestselling author Gail McHugh

"What an emotionally intense and addictive story . . . and I loved every minute of it! This is what I look for in a romance book."
—My Secret Romance

Also by A. L. Jackson

The Closer to You Series
Come to Me Softly
Come to Me Quietly

Come to Me Recklessly

The Closer to You Series

A. L. JACKSON

 NEW AMERICAN LIBRARY

New American Library
Published by the Penguin Group
Penguin Group (USA) LLC, 375 Hudson Street,
New York, New York 10014

USA | Canada | UK | Ireland | Australia | New Zealand | India | South Africa | China
penguin.com
A Penguin Random House Company

First published by New American Library,
a division of Penguin Group (USA) LLC

First Printing, April 2015

 REGISTERED TRADEMARK—MARCA REGISTRADA

LIBRARY OF CONGRESS CATALOGING-IN-PUBLICATION DATA:

Jackson, A. L.
Come to me recklessly / A. L. Jackson.
pages cm.—(Closer to you series)
ISBN 978-0-451-47201-4 (softcover)
I. Title.
PS3610.A25C67 2015
813'.6—dc23   2014042396

Printed in the United States of America
1   3   5   7   9   10   8   6   4   2

Set in Bell MT
Designed by Spring Hoteling

To love and faith.

COME TO
ME RECKLESSLY

PROLOGUE

There are few things that hurt so much as a broken heart.

It's physical.

Intense.

Real.

It doesn't matter which way you slice it, analyze it, or add it up, you'll always come up with the exact same sum. The worst part is there is no antidote for this affliction.

They say time mends all things.

I say they are liars.

Maybe time subdues, burying the pain beneath all the new memories we make, tucking it under the burdens and joys and new experiences that life layers on over the years.

But that broken heart?

It's always right there, lying in wait. Ready to crush you when you're slammed with that errant, unexpected thought.

But nothing could have prepared me for this—what it would feel like to look up and find him standing inches from me.

From the moment we met, he always had the power to bring me to my knees. I should have known his control over me would never diminish or dim.

I should have known it would only intensify.

Maybe I should have run.

But somewhere inside, I knew he'd never let me get far.

ONE

Samantha

My phone rang with the special chime, the one reserved just for my brother Stewart. I rummaged around for it in my purse while I was browsing the aisles of Target. The grin taking over my entire face was completely uncontrollable. I just couldn't help it. Talking with him—seeing him—was always the highlight of my day.

Running my thumb across the screen, I clicked the icon where his message waited. I'd never even heard of the app until he'd convinced me I *had* to get it, teasing me that I was living in the Stone Age, which to him I was pretty sure would date all the way back to 2011. I couldn't begin to keep up with all the tech stuff he loved.

I held my finger down on the new unread Snapchat message from gamelover745.

An image popped up on the screen, his face all contorted in the goofiest expression, pencils hanging from both his nostrils as he bared his teeth. I choked over a little laugh. The joy I felt every time I saw his face was almost overwhelming as it merged with the twinge of sorrow that tugged at my chest.

Quickly I shoved the feeling off. He told me he couldn't stand for me to look at him or think of him with pity. I had to respect that. He was so much braver than me, because seeing him sick made me feel so weak.

I forced myself not to fixate on his bald head and pale skin, and instead focused on the antics of this playful boy. The little timer ran down, alerting me I had only five more seconds of the picture, so I quickly read the messy words he'd scrawled across the image.

I'm sexy and I know it.

On a muted giggle, I shook my head, and I didn't hesitate for a second to lift my phone above my head to snap my own picture. Going for my silliest expression, I crossed my eyes and stuck my tongue out to the side.

So maybe the people milling around me in the middle of the busy store thought I was crazy, or some kind of delusional narcissist, but nothing inside me cared. I'd do anything to see him smile.

I tapped the button so I could write on the picture.

Love you, goofball.

I pushed SEND.

Seconds later, my phone chimed again. I clicked to receive his message. This time he was just smiling that unending smile, sitting cross-legged in the middle of his bed, radiating all his beauty and positivity, and that sorrow hit me again, only harder.

Love you back, he'd written on the image.

Letting the timer wind down, I clutched my phone as I cherished his message for the full ten seconds before our Snap expired. The screen went blank. I bit at the inside of my lip, blinking back tears.

Don't, I warned myself, knowing how quickly I could spiral into depression, into a worry I couldn't control, one that would taint the precious time I had with him.

Sucking in a cleansing breath, I tossed my phone back into my purse and wandered over to the cosmetics section, browsing through all the shades and colors of lip gloss. I tossed a shimmery clear one into my cart, then strolled into the shampoo aisle.

Apparently I was in no hurry to get home. It was sad and pathetic, yet here I was, twenty-three years old and passing away my Friday night at Target.

Ben had texted me earlier saying he was going out to grab a beer with the guys and not to wait up for him. All kinds of warning bells went off in my head when I realized that his leaving me alone for the night only filled me with an overwhelming relief. That realization hurt my heart, because he'd always been good to me, there for me when I was broken and needed someone to pick up the pieces, making me smile when I thought I never would again.

But with Ben? There had always been something missing. Something significant.

That flame.

The spark that lights you up inside when *the one* walks into the room. You know the one, the one you can't get off your mind, whether you've known him your entire life or he just barreled into it.

Was it wrong that I craved someone like that for myself?

Maybe I'd be content with Ben if I had never felt the flame before. If I'd never known what it was like to need and desire.

But I had. It'd been the kind of fire that had raged and consumed, burning through me until there was nothing left but ashes. I'd thought that love had ruined me until Ben came in and swept me into his willing arms.

He'd taken care of me, a fact I didn't take lightly. I honored and respected it, the way Ben honored and respected me.

So maybe I never looked the same or felt the same after *he'd* destroyed something inside me. But I'd survived, and I forced myself to find satisfaction in that, willed it to make me stronger instead of feeble and frail.

I tossed a bottle of shampoo I really didn't need into my cart, but it smelled all kinds of good, like vanilla and the sweetest flower, and today I didn't feel like questioning my motives. In fact, I tossed in a bottle of body wash for good measure. I rarely treated myself, and I figured I deserved it. The last four years had been spent working my ass off, striving toward my elementary education degree at Arizona State University, and I'd finally landed my first real job a month ago.

Pride shimmered around my consciousness. Not the arrogant kind. I was just . . . happy. Happy because of what I had achieved.

I bit the inside of my lip, doing my best to contain the ridiculous grin I felt pulling at my mouth.

Finally . . . *finally* . . . I'd attained something that was all on me.

Ben was always the one who took care of me. But he also had a bad habit of taking all the credit. Like my life would fall apart without him in it.

Slowly, I wound my way up toward the registers. I needed to get out of here before I drained what little I had in my checking account with all my *celebrating.*

I rolled my eyes at myself and squashed the mocking laughter that rolled up my throat.

Yep, livin' large and partyin' hard.

My life was about as exciting as Friday-night bingo at the retirement home down the street.

But hey, at least my hair would smell good and my lips would taste even better.

Scanning the registers, I hunted for the shortest line, when my eyes locked on a face that was so familiar, but just out of reach of my recognition. Curiosity consumed me, and I found I couldn't look away.

She was standing at the front of her cart, her attention cast behind her. Obviously searching for someone.

I stared, unabashed, craning my head to the side as I tried to place the striking green eyes and long black hair. She was gorgeous, enough to make any supermodel feel self-conscious, but she was wearing the kind of smile that spoke a thousand welcomes.

Two feet in front of her, I came to a standstill, which only caused her warm smile to spread when her gaze landed on me. My attention flitted to the empty infant car seat that was latched onto the basket, then darted back to her face. My stomach twisted into the tightest knot as recognition slammed me somewhere in my subconscious, my throat growing dry when her name formed in my head before it swelled on my tongue. "Aly Moore?" I managed, everything about the question timid and unsure. Well, I wasn't unsure it was her. There was no question, no doubt.

What I wasn't so sure about was whether I should actually stop to talk to her. My heart was already beating a million miles a minute, like a stampeding warning crashing through my body, screaming at my limbs to go and go now.

Still, I couldn't move. Short gusts of sorrow were a feeling I was well accustomed to, dealing with Stewart and all the sadness his illness brought into my life.

But this?

Pain constricted my chest, pressing and pulsing in, and I struggled to find my absent breath.

God, she looked just like *him*. I always did my best to keep him from my thoughts, all the memories of him buried deep, deep enough to pretend they'd forever been forgotten, when in reality, everything I'd ever shared with him was unrelentingly vivid.

Seeing her brought them all flooding back.

His face.

His touch.

I squeezed my eyes shut, trying to block them out, but they only flashed brighter.

God.

"Samantha Schultz." My name tumbled from her mouth as if it came with some kind of relief. She stretched out her hand, grasping mine. "Oh my gosh, I can't believe it's you. How are you?"

I hadn't seen her in years. Seven, to be exact. She was only two years younger than me, and she'd always been a sweet girl. Sweet *and* smart. Different in a good way, quiet and shy and bold at the same time. I'd always liked her, and some foolish part of me had believed she'd always be a part of my life. I guess I'd taken that for granted, too.

But that's what happens when you're young and naive and believe in promises that turn out only to be given in vain.

I swallowed over the lump in my throat and forced myself to speak. "I've been good. It's so great to see you." It was all a lie wrapped up in the worst kind of truth.

I dropped my gaze, my eyes landing on the diamonds that glinted from her ring finger where she grasped my hand, and I caught just a peek of the intricate tattoo that was woven below the ring, like she'd etched a promise of forever into her skin.

A war of emotions spun through me, and I wanted to fire off a million questions, the most blatant of them jerking my attention between the empty infant carrier and her ring. My mind tumbled through a roller coaster of memories as it did its best to catch up to the years that had passed.

"Oh my God . . . you're married? And you're a mom." I drew the words out as I finally added up the obvious, and a strange sense of satisfaction at seeing her grown up fell over me. It seemed almost silly, thinking of her that way, considering she was only two years younger than me. Now the years separating our ages didn't seem like such a big deal. Not the way they had then, when I'd thought of her as just a little girl, a hundred years and a thousand miles behind me. It seemed now she'd flown right past me.

With my words, everything about her glowed. She held up her hand to show me the ring I'd just been admiring, her voice soft with a reverent awe. "Can you believe it?" She laughed quietly. "Some days I can't believe it myself."

The joy filling her was so clear, and I chewed at my bottom lip, both welcoming the happiness I felt for her and fighting the jealousy that slipped just under the surface of my skin. Never would I wish any sorrow on her, or desire to steal her happiness away because I didn't have it myself. I wasn't vicious or cruel. But seeing her this way was a stark reminder of what I was missing.

Happiness.

I bit back the bitter feeling, searching for an excuse to get away, because I was finished feeling sorry for myself, when Aly's face transformed into the most radiant smile, her attention locked somewhere behind me. There was nothing I could do but follow her gaze. I looked over my shoulder.

All the surprise at finding Aly Moore amplified, spinning my head with shock when I saw who she was staring at.

Jared Holt strode toward us.

My knees went weak.

The grown man was completely covered in tattoos, every edge of him hard and rough. But none of the surprise I felt was caused by the way he looked, because I'd been there to watch his downward spiral. Part of me was surprised to see he was still alive.

He held an adorable, tiny baby girl protectively against his chest, the child facing out as they approached. She kicked her little legs when she caught sight of her mom. A soft smile pulled at his mouth and warmth flared in his eyes when they landed on Aly.

My heart did crazy, erratic things, and the small sound that worked up my throat was tortured. Someone was trying to pull a sick joke on me, dangling all the bits of my past right in front of my face.

It just had to be Jared.

No, he hadn't been responsible for any of the choices Christopher or I had made. Still, he'd been the catalyst that had driven the confusion.

The overwhelming feeling rushing over me was altogether cruel and welcome at the same time, because God, how many times had I lain awake at night, unable to sleep because I was thinking of Christopher Moore, wondering where he was and who he'd become? And suddenly here was his world, our world, his sister and his best friend, the people who had been with us and were part of what defined that time—standing in front of me at Target with their little baby girl.

Aly must have sensed my panic. Again she reached out to squeeze my hand. "You remember Jared Holt, don't you?" She obviously knew I did. There was no missing the look that passed between the two of them, a secret conversation transpiring in a glance.

"Of course," I whispered hoarsely.

"Samantha," Jared said as a statement. He handed Aly the little tube of diaper rash ointment he must have gone in search of while she waited at the front of the store. He turned his attention right back to me. "God . . . it's been years. How are you?"

"Good," I forced out, wondering where in the hell that word even came from, because right then, I was definitely not feeling *good*. I was feeling . . . I blinked and swallowed. I couldn't begin to put my finger on it except to say I was fundamentally disturbed, as if the axis balancing my safe little world had been altered. "How are you?"

The concern that involuntarily laced my tone was probably not needed, because he smiled at Aly as he situated his daughter a little higher up on his chest and kissed her on the top of her head.

"I'm perfect," he said through a rumbled chuckle.

Aly took a step forward and lightly tickled the tiny girl's foot.

The little black-haired, blue-eyed baby kicked more. Her mouth twisted up at just one side, as she was obviously just learning how to control her smile, and she rolled her head back in delight. She suddenly cooed, and her eyes went wide and she jerked as if she'd startled herself with the sound that escaped her.

Aly's voice turned sweet, the kind a mother reserved only for her child. "And this is our Ella . . . Ella Rose."

Ella Rose.

They'd named their daughter after Jared's mother, Helene Rose.

Affection pulsed heavily through my veins as I looked on the three of them, so happy to see their joy. As strong as that emotion was, it wasn't enough to keep my own sadness at bay, and my mind reeled with the questions I wanted to ask about Christopher.

But those questions were dangerous. It wasn't that I didn't want to know. I *couldn't* know.

Instead I reached out to let their baby girl grip my finger. I shook it a little, and that sweet smile took over her face again, this time directed at me as she tried to shove my finger in her mouth.

I just about melted. I was pretty sure this little girl had the power to single-handedly jump-start my biological clock. "Well, hello there, Ella Rose. Aren't you the sweetest thing." I glanced up at Aly. "How old is she?"

"She just turned two months yesterday," she answered. "It feels like she's growing so fast, but I already can't remember what it was like not to have her as a part of our lives. It's such a strange feeling."

My head shook with stunned disbelief. "All of this is crazy." I eyed them happily as some of the shock wore away, as if being in their space was completely natural. "The two of you ending up together."

Aly blushed, and Jared watched her as if she was the anchor that kept him tied to this world. Then he slanted his own mischievous grin my way. "Don't be too surprised, Sam. This girl was always meant for me."

Good God. How Aly wasn't a puddle in the middle of the floor, I didn't know. His words were enough to leave me all swoony and light-headed and they weren't even intended for me. And I wanted to laugh, because he'd always called me Sam, almost like a tease, a dig at his best friend, Christopher, who refused to call me anything but Samantha.

It instantly took me back too many years, and I was there, feeling flickers of that flame that had been missing from my life for so long. But those kinds of flames had burned me right into the ground. Those kinds of flames hurt and scarred.

"So what about you?" Aly asked, stepping back. "What have you been up to? Do you live around here?"

"Yeah, I live with my boyfriend in the neighborhood right behind the shopping center."

"You're kidding me. We do, too." She laughed at the coincidence. "We're neighbors."

Here we all were, standing in the same store in this huge city, miles away from where we'd all begun. I almost had the urge to look behind me, fully expecting to see Christopher sauntering toward us, an apparition sent to taunt me in a ruthless twist of fate.

"How is your little brother? I heard he was doing really well after your family moved across town."

After being thrown headfirst into all these tumultuous memories of Christopher, my walls were down, and this time I wasn't prepared for the sadness that sliced straight through me. I attempted to steady my voice. "He was in remission for five years, but the cancer just recently came back."

Aly sobered, and genuine sympathy edged the curve of her mouth. "Oh my God, I'm so sorry," she murmured, and it didn't hurt to hear her say it. Instead I felt comforted.

"Me, too," I agreed, shaking my head as a saddened smile twisted up my mouth. "He's the sweetest kid." Well, he wasn't so much a kid anymore. Really, he was almost a man, but it was hard to look at him that way when he was so frail. "I just keep praying for him, and I spend as much time with him as I can to keep his spirits up. He's been pretty sick with the treatments, so he hasn't been getting out of the house all that much lately. I couldn't imagine having to go through my junior year of high school online, but he doesn't complain."

Stewart was now seventeen, the youngest in our family. My brother Sean was two years younger than me, in the same grade as Aly had been, and my sister, Stephanie, was nineteen. My parents had us in quick succession and had had some kind of overindulgent lovefest with our names since theirs were Sally and Stephen. It used to bother me when I was young.

Not anymore.

We'd been a normal, rambunctious family until Stewart had gotten sick when he was nine. When I met Christopher, Stewart had been at his worst. Well, at his worst . . . until now.

Ella released a shrill little cry and squirmed in Jared's hold. Gently, he bounced her, shushing her in a soft whisper against her head. "I think someone is going to need their mommy soon." Soft affection flowed from Jared's laughter. "She goes from completely content to starving in five seconds flat."

"Oh, well, I better let you two go," I offered, hating that it sounded almost reluctant. "It was really nice to see you again."

Aly hesitated, glancing at her husband, before she tipped her head and studied me with intent. "Would it be weird if we . . . I don't know . . . had coffee or something? I totally understand if you're not comfortable. I get it. But I'd love to really catch up with you if you're up for it. I could use a friend around here."

Maybe that's what I liked about her most. She just came right out and said it, gave voice to that huge elephant that was snuffing out all the air in the room. That and she was genuine and kind.

I refused to allow myself to believe I was agreeing because she was Christopher's sister.

"Yeah, I think I'd like that."

"Good."

She dug around in her huge bag for her phone, while Jared just stood there swaying Ella, his mouth seemingly pressed permanently to the side of her head as he showered her with small kisses.

Aly thumbed across the screen. "What's your number?"

I rattled it off while Aly entered it into her phone. Two seconds later, my phone dinged with a new message.

"There, you have my number, too."

This time, Ella's cry was a demand.

"We'd better get her home so I can feed her. I'll call you soon."

"That would be great."

She hugged me, only glancing back once as she followed Jared into a lane to pay.

I hurried to one of the express registers, all of a sudden feeling guilty, like I'd committed some sort of mortal sin by giving my number to a Moore.

Christopher had broken me, shattered my belief and trust. But more important than that, I had Ben to think about. Ben, who had stood by my side. Ben, who even with all his faults, truly cared about me. He was my father's best friend's son, and basically we had grown up together. My parents had raised me with the impression that someone like Ben would be the right kind of guy for me, and with my demolished heart, it hadn't taken him all that much to convince me I belonged with him.

I paid and rushed outside. The blistering Phoenix summer was in full force. Suffocating heat pressed down from above, taking everything hostage, the evening sky heavy with dense clouds building steadily at the edge of the horizon.

My feet pounded on the scorching pavement as I made my way up the aisle to my Ford Escape.

Funny, that suddenly felt like exactly what I needed to do.

Escape.

Take this whole afternoon back.

Leave the classroom of the tiny private school where I'd taken a job as a teacher during their summer program, and instead of coming here gone straight to the small house I shared with Ben—where I was safe and memories of Christopher were buried and hidden in the hope that one day they would finally be forgotten.

I slumped into the driver's seat, my gaze drawn to the little family that came bustling out of the store.

My heart rattled in my chest.

"Shit," I cursed, gripping the wheel. "What am I doing?"

The sick part was I knew the answer to that.

TWO

Christopher

Outside the bedroom door, the party raged on. Timothy's house was splitting at the seams, the way it always was on a Friday night. Music blared and voices lifted above it, echoing through the thin walls. Distorted sounds pounded heavily against my skin, my eyesight hazy in the deep shadows of the darkened room.

I felt completely weightless and somehow still pinned down by the pungent fog clouding my brain.

Every elemental part of me slowly became detached. Floated away. All of my emotions. All of my thoughts. It was like they hovered somewhere overhead, just out of reach. My entire consciousness faded away, right along with my conscience, leaving me with nothing but the physical.

It's what I craved. Needed. The relief of feeling nothin' but skin on skin.

Even though some part of me hated it at the same time.

Slouched back on the worn-out couch in the spare bedroom,

I lifted the half-drained bottle of Patrón to my lips, idly watching the dull mop of brown hair obstructing the face of the girl who was on her knees, sucking me off.

The only things I could discern were the pleasure of her hot, needy mouth and the burn of tequila as it roared through my system to settle in a scorching pool in my gut.

She looked up from under her thick veil of hair, brown eyes wide as they searched for a connection but instead met with the apathy in mine.

That was the fucking problem. I was on disconnect.

That plug had been pulled a long time ago.

Never would I allow someone to have that kind of control over me.

Not like *she* had.

Not ever again.

Monday morning, I rolled up in front of Jared and Aly's house at the ass crack of dawn. I squinted against the bright rays of light burning my eyes as the sun climbed over the horizon, chasing the last of the night from the sky.

I cut the ignition and jumped from the cooled cab of my truck. Heat swallowed me whole. You'd think at five thirty in the morning we'd get a little reprieve. No such luck. Summers in Phoenix were fucking misery.

That didn't stop the eager smile that tugged at my mouth as I ambled up their walkway.

So what if I had to leave my man card at the door every time I walked into Jared and Aly's place. Call me a pussy, I didn't care. My niece had me wrapped around every single one of her tiny fingers.

I rang the doorbell and rushed my hand through my hair,

listening for movement inside. A shadow passed behind the draped window before metal slid as the lock was unlatched. My sister grinned at me when she opened the door.

"Christopher, aren't you looking chipper this beautiful morning," Aly teased as she lifted a knowing brow, stepping back to let me inside.

So yeah, I'm sure I looked like hell. Both Friday and Saturday nights, I'd been over at Timothy's house, *living* it up. Funny how all that *living* made me feel like death warmed over. Every weekend left me just a little more hollowed out. I was pretty sure I was slowly killing myself, week by week losing just a little more of who I was, carving away more and more of what had been important to me.

Pretty soon there would be nothing left.

But there was no way to get any of it back.

Ancient-history bullshit, anyway.

I shoved all the unwelcome thoughts off, rolled my eyes as I ruffled Aly's messy hair. "Yeah, yeah, yeah. You don't have a whole lot of room to talk there, Aly Cat. You look like you got about as much sleep this weekend as I did. Livin' up to your name?"

Dark bags sat heavily under her green eyes, and her near-black hair was all tangled. She was wearing an old stained-up T-shirt that had to be Jared's, because the girl was swimming in it. Still, my sister was beautiful. Inside and out. No wonder my dumb-ass best friend couldn't keep his hands off of her.

She groaned a little, but somehow the sound was filled with pure affection. "Ella decided she was hungry every twenty minutes last night. I have no clue how I even got out of bed this morning. I feel like a walking zombie."

Jared suddenly appeared behind her, wrapping his arms around her waist as he tugged her against his chest. He buried his face somewhere in her neck. "Apparently Ella likes her mommy as much as I do."

I'd just about lost my goddamned mind when I found out these two were hooking up. Not because I didn't like Jared. He'd been my best friend since I was a little kid. Sure, we'd fought like brothers, messed with each other until one of us was crying, but bottom line, we were thicker than blood. Brothers. We were always the first to have the other's back.

Until the day Jared caused that car accident. The one that stole his mother's life. That accident had stolen my best friend, too.

An old kind of pain hit me, and my chest tightened. That car accident had stolen everything. Changed everything. None of us had come out looking the same.

Afterward, the guy had fucked away his life, landed himself in juvie, then disappeared for years. I never expected to see him again. When he showed up here last summer, there was no question he was still haunted. I recognized it immediately, because I recognized the same bullshit in myself.

Then he'd gone and taken a liking to my little sister, and all hell broke loose. He and I were too much alike, and I wasn't about to let him bring my sister down. She deserved so much better than that.

Of course the guy had proven me wrong in every way. He loved her. Wholly and completely. Loved her in a way that girls like Aly deserved, with respect and care and devotion.

How could I stand in the way of that?

Didn't mean it didn't make me a little sick to my stomach. I took it upon myself to razz the asshole every chance I got. "Watch yourself, man. No matter which way you cut it, that's still my little sister."

He nuzzled her more, this time lifting his gaze to meet mine, the mischief in his blue eyes meeting the challenge. "And no matter which way you cut it, she's still my wife. This girl belongs to me."

Aly grinned wildly and leaned back into his hold.

My chest tightened more, because it made me happy to see her this way. Happy she got to have this. Not many of us did. Love like that didn't come around often, and she'd snatched it up when she saw it, even when it'd seemed dangerous and impossible. But she'd known it was worth it.

I'd been the fool who'd let that kind of crazy love go. Didn't matter that I'd been just a stupid punk kid, barely sixteen, or that the girl and I were nothing alike and the entire world was against us.

None of it mattered. Not at fucking all. The only thing that mattered was it'd been real.

Cringing, I put a cap on those thoughts, because I wasn't about to go there. Stupid shit that I couldn't deal with. Nor did I want to. All it did was leave me feeling pissy and sorry for myself, scorned by a girl I'd always thought would be mine.

Leaving Aly and Jared all wrapped up in each other, I headed for Ella, who was lying on her back on the cushioned play area Aly had set up for her in the family room between their huge-ass overstuffed couch and the fireplace.

"There's my girl," I sang as I wound around the couch and knelt down in front of her. Her blue eyes were all bugged out as she watched the lights flashing on the infant play gym set up over her. Five brightly colored stuffed animals hung down from it, teasing her. She didn't come close to being able to touch them. Yet she had her tiny hands all balled up in fists, her arms flailing and her legs kicking as she stared, fixated, making it clear how badly she wanted to reach out and touch one.

A tiny sound escaped her pursed lips, and my heart throbbed a wayward beat.

Yep, man card at the door.

This little girl owned me.

"Don't worry, angel . . . Give it a few weeks, and that monkey is yours," I promised as I bent down and maneuvered her from under the play gym and into my arms. "Come give Uncle kisses before your daddy drags me off to a grueling day of work."

"Grueling my ass," Jared shot from the other side of the room. "You're in the air-conditioned office while me and the guys are out doing the grunt work. I'd say you have it pretty easy there, my friend."

Laughing it off because what he said was nothing but true, I brought Ella's face close to mine. She offered me one of those little grins that I felt right in the center of my chest. She reached out, her nails digging into my bottom lip as she grabbed for me. I kissed them. "You take care of your mommy while we're gone."

"She always does," Aly said, watching us with a soft smile on her face. Something shifted in her expression, and she bit at her lip and quickly turned her face to the floor.

I felt the frown crease my forehead. I knew my sister pretty damned well, and that meant I was pretty damned sure she was holding something back. "What?" I asked, my eyes narrowing as I pinned her with a stare.

She lifted her head, blinked, looked away. "Nothing."

At the same second, Jared tensed up a little, like he knew exactly what was running through Aly's mind.

Nothing my ass.

My frown deepened. "Nothing?" I challenged, my brow rising.

Aly shook her head and looked almost repentant. Unease slowly snaked its way through my senses. My gaze darted between the two of them. Something was up. Something they didn't want me to know. A silent tension filled the room.

COME TO ME RECKLESSLY

"Nothing," she reaffirmed in what I knew was a lie. "I just . . ." She shrugged. "Seeing you with Ella like that makes me happy."

"Come on, man, we need to get a move on," Jared cut in, obviously putting an end to my questioning. He walked to the kitchen island and grabbed the small cooler he kept stocked with food, water, and sodas. "It's going to be a busy day and an even busier week. You may just find yourself on the job. Then I'll let you complain about work being grueling." He tossed me a mocking wink, then sauntered up behind Aly, hugging her as he whispered something in her ear.

Below her breath, she laughed and nodded.

Three months ago, my brother-in-law, aka best friend who bagged my little sister, had somehow managed to persuade me into starting a new venture with him. I went straight from a lazy college student, one who gave little thought to what he was going to do with his life after he graduated—because the truth was, he really didn't give a shit—to business owner in a matter of weeks.

I mean, fuck, me being part owner in the remodeling business with Jared and our other partner, Kenny? All signs pointed at a no-go. I wasn't exactly what most would consider the ambitious type. But somehow Jared convinced me to team up with him, said he didn't want to do it without me. Jared and Kenny had fronted the money, and now I was doing my all to live up to it. Turned out I was pretty damned good at it, too, basically running all the business shit that didn't deal with the hard labor, all of the accounting and paperwork that needed to be dealt with in the office, although the company was growing so fast there'd been a couple of times Jared had hauled me out on a job when he was shorthanded. It was crazy going from scrimping every month to having more money in my bank account than I knew what to do with. I wasn't loaded by any means, but it sure felt nice not to have to check my bank balance anytime I wanted to buy something.

Truth was, I liked having a reason to drag my ass out of bed in the morning. And I had two. The other one cooed, grabbing my attention. I kissed Ella at the corner of her mouth. "Stay sweet, little one."

I passed her off to Aly and followed Jared out the door and into the approaching day. Jared climbed into the passenger seat of my truck.

Each week, we traded off driving. We figured after I moved into my new place a couple of miles away, there was no reason for both of us to hike it across town separately since Jared checked in at the office every morning before he headed out to the job sites in a work truck.

After Aly moved out, the apartment we had shared near the ASU campus had felt all wrong. Lonely. I knew it was time to make a change. Plus being so near to them gave me an excuse to stop by all the time so I could hang out with Ella.

I glanced across at Jared as I hopped into the driver's seat of my brand-new truck, the leather already heating up with the rising sun blazing through the window. He smirked at me, lifted his chin. Guess it wasn't so bad hanging out with him, either. Honestly, it'd been good watching him come back to life, over-coming the darkness that had plagued him since his mother's death.

A flash of resentment twisted through me, and I quickly tamped it down. I didn't blame him. Couldn't. He'd been through more than I could ever imagine. What had happened wasn't his fault. I'd made those mistakes all on my own.

I started the truck and shifted into gear. "So what was that back there?" I asked.

His face lifted in a clueless expression. "Don't know what you're talking about."

I cut my eyes toward him, watching the little twitch of his jaw when he gritted his teeth. He averted his gaze to his tablet and clicked into his schedule, asshole acting like he was all too busy to look my way.

Right.

He knew exactly what I was talking about.

And whatever it was, I wasn't really sure I wanted to know.

THREE

Samantha

My eyes popped open to the blaring of my alarm clock. I flopped over, smacking at the little button on top to silence it. Groaning, I squeezed my eyes shut and wished for five minutes' more sleep. But all those little kids were waiting for me.

Working at a private school summer day camp hadn't exactly been my dream when I'd gone to college to get my degree, but it got my foot in the door, and I was all too happy to jump on the opportunity.

I'd always wanted to be a teacher, and if this job meant I got to be around a bunch of kids with eager minds, their little brains sponges, sucking in all the information around them, then sign me up. It was at a small private Christian school about five miles away, and a few of the regular teachers hadn't been available to work during the summer program, so there'd been an opening.

My insecurities had screamed at me that I wasn't qualified

and that I might not want to work in such an intimate setting, but somehow I'd built up the courage to apply.

I'd loved it the second I stepped through the doors.

Beyond that, it made my parents happy. They loved the idea of me working at a small, conservative school, where I'd be safe and maybe some of that *conservative* would rub off on me. I was no wild child, like they'd chalked me up to be, and I'd spent the last seven years trying to prove that to them.

Funny how they'd accused me of conspiring with the devil when I was with Christopher yet they'd had nothing but praise for us when Ben had announced we were moving in together.

Warily, I looked over at him where he slept on his back on his side of the bed.

That announcement had come as a big old surprise to me, too. I'd done everything in my power to backpedal, giving up explanations that Ben was only joking around, because he had to be *kidding*. No sane man would just rent a house and announce to his girlfriend's parents that they were moving in together without consulting her first.

But that had always been Ben's way. Making decisions that weren't his to make. Up to that point, they'd always been small and I'd just shrugged it off. Attributed it to his protective way. Our whole relationship he'd taken care of me. But this? It was the first time I'd begun to question his motives, this elaborate announcement that had made him look as if he were some kind of exaggerated hero, doing all of this for me, and cornering me so that any hesitation I showed just made me look like the unappreciative jerk.

What no one knew was that he'd asked me to move in with him the month before, and I'd told him I wasn't ready for that.

Yet here I was.

Sighing, I climbed out of bed and headed for the en suite bathroom. I turned the showerhead to high and let the small room fill with steam as I peeled my tank and flannel sleep pants from my body.

That was just Ben—something I had to accept. He always thought he knew better than I did. And maybe he did.

He'd been right about Christopher.

I guarded my heart from the ache that flared at the thought of *him*, his black hair and searing green eyes, blocked the distinct memory of his laughter, a sound that struck me all the way to the core.

Thoughts of him had been all too frequent over the last week, since I'd run into Aly. A feeling of anxiety and dread had steadily built up in my gut as I thought of how close she was, somehow knowing that made him close, too. Like at any moment, I'd walk out the door and he'd be standing there, that potent smile at the ready to crush me all over again.

The worst part was that the anxiety and dread were growing into something that felt like anticipation, a sweet taste on my tongue that warned that something was to come.

But that's what I needed to take it for. A warning. Not a promise.

Stepping into the shower, I closed my eyes and let the soothing water rush over me, the warmth washing me of all my pent-up thoughts and regrets, the hurt of Christopher and the worry over Stewart. If I let it, it'd all be too much to bear, and I had twenty-three other obligations waiting for me who all needed my undivided attention today.

Washed and shampooed, I managed to feel refreshed as I shut off the faucet, grabbed my towel, and began to dry off. I wrapped my towel snug under my arms, brushed my teeth, then ran a brush through the long sheets of my light blond hair. So maybe I felt a little too self-satisfied being dowsed in the smell of my brand-new yummy shampoo and body wash. As if maybe using them was just like lifting a big ol' middle finger, one directed at Ben, one I'd never be brave enough to give him.

One that told him to stop acting like my father and more like my partner.

My lover.

But I'd started to question whether I still wanted him to be either of those things.

An unwelcome cringe assaulted me with the thought, followed by a wave of guilt. I knew I shouldn't be in this place and with this man if it didn't make me happy. If my heart wasn't committed to this relationship. But my heart belonged in a place it should never go, to a man it never should have known, to an entity who was just as callous as Ben and my mother had promised he would be.

This . . . this was where I belonged.

I headed into the walk-in closet that lined the back of the bathroom, the space jammed full of both my and Ben's things. The house was quaint but nice, a little on the small side, what most new families would consider a starter home.

No doubt it'd be scorching out, so I dressed in a flowy white skirt that went just past my knees, a cute pink top to match, and white sandals to top the outfit off. My pedicured red toenails peeked out, the color almost as red as the natural color of my lips. I brushed on the same clear lip gloss I'd picked up over the weekend.

I never put color on my lips.

For very foolish reasons.

But it was something that had stuck with me all these years.

I was almost tempted to grab one of the lipsticks Ben had surprised me with over the years, all of them left unopened, just to mute the vibrant color out. But doing so felt wrong, like a slap to the perfect memories I had of him, the ones I cherished before everything had gone right down a festering drain.

Hearing the shuffling behind me, I glanced up through the large mirror above the sink to find Ben lumbering into the bathroom, scratching his bare stomach while his mouth was wide with a yawn that was turned toward the ceiling.

He wasn't an unattractive man. Quite the opposite.

And he definitely knew it.

His dark blond hair was a morning mess and his chocolate eyes watched me with appreciation as he approached.

I shuddered, and he smirked.

This was the part I hated, Ben watching me like he wanted to eat me when I had a hard time thinking of him as something beyond a friend.

"I see someone has left me with quite the invitation this morning . . . can't say I don't like it." His voice was rough with the innuendo, and he went right for the hem of my skirt. He ran his hands up the outsides of my legs, gathering the material as he went, gripping my thighs.

"Sorry, but that's not going to happen. I have to be at work in fifteen minutes."

He ground himself against my ass. "I can make it fast."

I resisted the urge to roll my eyes. No question he could.

Wriggling out of his hold, I sidestepped him, mustering the best smile I could find. "Sorry, babe, but I really have to go. You'll have to take a rain check."

Annoyance twisted his face into a scowl. "Those rain checks just keep piling up. You owe me big. One of these days I'm going to keep you in bed the entire day so you can pay up."

Right.

I always owed him and he never let me forget it. But this was the one debt I was always loath to pay.

His eyes softened, and he grabbed my hand and pulled me into his chest. "I just miss you," he whispered at the top of my head.

Another pang of guilt ribbed me, and I sighed into his hold, remembering how good he'd always been to me. Even though he pulled so much of this overbearing crap, I knew he really cared about me. "I know . . . I'm sorry I've been so busy lately. This new job is exhausting, so by the time I make it home at night, I'm completely spent."

He kissed my temple. "Just as long as you're coming home to me at night, that's all that matters."

Nodding weakly, I pulled away. "I'll see you later."

I hadn't been lying when I told Ben I was spent by the end of the day. Late Friday afternoon, I turned the key to the lock of our little house, my feet dragging as I went inside. I dumped my purse and keys on the side table next to the door. Blowing an exhausted breath from my lungs, I flopped back on the couch.

As much as I loved those kids, they were filled with more energy than any one person should have. And I swore, every time they touched me, they zapped a little of my own energy and used it for themselves. *Hyper* didn't come close to describing a room full of five-year-olds.

From the table, my phone chimed with *that* ring. I smiled and dragged myself up, never too tired for him. I grabbed my phone and settled back onto the couch.

I opened Snapchat and pressed my finger to the waiting message.

Stewart's face lit up the entire screen, the biggest puppy-dog eyes begging from the image he'd captured.

Coming to see me Sunday?

Grinning, I snapped back an even bigger, eager smile, pretending it didn't hurt to see him this way, instead showing him how excited I was to hear from him.

I wouldn't miss it.

Stewart and I had a standing Sunday date. He rarely felt up to getting out of the house, so I brought over his favorite foods, praying something would seem appealing to him. I'd just hang out with him all afternoon, sitting on his bed and watching funny videos on his laptop or playing video games, even though they weren't exactly my thing and I was terrible at them.

But for Stewart?

Video games suddenly became my very favorite hobby.

I dropped my phone to the floor and sank into the comfort of the plush cushions of the couch, my legs stretched out and propped up as I closed my eyes and let myself drift away.

When my phone dinged from the floor, I jumped, my eyes blinking rapidly as I tried to make sense of my surroundings. The room had dimmed as the sun had declined, evening filtering in through the loose, shimmery drapes hanging across the window.

I rubbed my face. Guess I'd been more tired than I'd thought. When I ran my finger across the front of my phone, I saw I'd been out cold for two hours. Then something inside me went *cold* when I saw the waiting message that had stirred me, but it was the kind of cold that burned and flamed, a warning of something unknown that I felt approaching like a building storm.

So maybe the text was just from Aly.

It still stopped my heart, as if her words were an extension of him, a tether that led me right back into the past.

Coffee tomorrow morning? 10ish?

I clutched my phone, warring with my decision though it had already been made. It was foolishness to the extreme, I knew, putting myself in this position, but I couldn't stop my fingers from tapping across the screen.

Would love to. Where?

Five seconds later, my phone dinged with her reply.

Cory's? Great coffee and even better pastries ;)

Nerves twisted my stomach, and I quickly typed my response.

Sounds perfect to me.

Perfect and completely ludicrous.

Great! C U then.

For a few seconds, I held my phone out in front of me, trying to convince myself to text her back, to tell her something had suddenly come up, some ridiculous excuse that she would know was exactly that.

An excuse.

Something like I'd suddenly moved out of state, never to return again.

Instead I jumped when my phone suddenly lit up with a message from Ben. I grimaced as I read it.

Picked a place for dinner. At Firebird's by the mall. Will be waiting.

Reluctantly, I stood, gathered myself, and forced my feet to carry me out the door.

The next morning, I slowly pulled into the parking lot where the small mom-and-pop coffee shop rested in a tight corner of the popular plaza. The entire shopping center was packed on a Saturday morning, and I cautiously made my way through the crowded parking lot, searching for a spot. I pretended that I wasn't relieved, that I wasn't thankful for those few extra minutes that bought me a little more time.

Why I was so nervous, I didn't know.

I eased into the first spot I found and cut the engine. The moment the air conditioner was off, heat engulfed the entire cabin. Yet there I sat, unable to propel myself out the car door.

Okay, so maybe the reason I was nervous was glaringly obvious. Because some huge part of me knew this was wrong, that I shouldn't be here, and that I should run far, far away. The fact that I'd lied to Ben about where I was going this morning was evidence enough.

But the whole brokenhearted side of me, the one that was hoping to gain a measure of understanding? Her voice was just much louder than the one that whispered reason.

Opening the door, I stepped out into the sunshine. I'd pulled on my favorite jean shorts and a cute little tank, flip-flops on my feet. Rays of warmth hit my skin, and I relished the feel. People constantly asked me how I could live here, but I wouldn't trade the heat for cold. Not for anything. It took someone growing up here to appreciate it.

For a second, I lifted my face to the sky and sucked in a breath of resolve, reminding myself that I actually *liked* Aly. I truly cared about her and wanted to catch up on her life. Meeting her wasn't just a messed-up manipulation to bring me closer to Christopher.

With that resolution set firmly in place, I tucked my purse strap tight up on my shoulder and strode toward the coffee shop. I jogged across the busy lane right in front, hopping up onto the concrete landing.

Little metal tables with big red umbrellas were set out in the outdoor patio area in front, pots of flowers strategically placed around them. Misters cooled off the patrons who rested leisurely around the space, enjoying all the deliciousness the place had to offer.

I pulled in a deep breath through my nose as I headed for the entrance, the heavenly aroma of coffee wrapping me up and drawing me forward. I was a coffee whore and I wasn't ashamed to admit it.

"Samantha," a voice called from behind me, and I shifted my attention over my shoulder to see Aly working her way toward me, the infant car seat handle tucked in the crook of her elbow, the carrier bouncing at her side and her other arm weighted down by an overflowing diaper bag and a huge purse. She rushed across the busy lane I'd just crossed, her smile wide as she approached. A phone rang out from within the depths of her bag, and she lifted the entire load she had on her arm, as if she were contemplating how in the heck she was going to maneuver to reach it.

Awkwardly, I stretched out my arms and giggled as my hands flapped all around, searching for something to take from her. Then I laughed outright, feeling completely useless, standing there with a tiny little purse while Aly looked as if she'd taken on the world. "Can I help you?" I asked, reaching forward again.

Aly released a relieved laugh, one that was completely filled with ease and harmony, as if she found no burden in lugging all of this stuff around. "Oh gosh, thank you," she said as she shifted the carrier into my hold and turned to dig through her purse.

I was almost surprised by her passing her daughter off to me so quickly, but I was quickly distracted by the sweet baby girl nestled in the seat, wearing the cutest onesie with tiny pink flowers all over it, all the hems edged in a satiny pink. Twisting the carrier around, I held it in both hands, the bottom of it pressed into my stomach, bringing her the closest I could get her. "Good morning, little Ella. How are you today?"

Her wide blue eyes latched onto mine, and she did one of those squirmy smiles where her head rolled back and her mouth lifted just at the side.

My heart swelled, and I cooed softly, murmuring all of her sweetness back to her.

I barely registered Aly's conversation, though it was clear she was speaking with her husband, her voice lilted in a tone that was obviously reserved for him, playful and affectionate, edged with a hint of seduction. "You can't do anything without me, can you?" she provoked him, smiling over at me and mouthing, *Sorry.*

I just shook my head, not offended or annoyed for a second, and instead I turned back to have a little more me time with Ella.

A thud of panic hit me when I realized I'd already claimed a little part of her as my own.

Foolish, foolish girl, I chastised myself. *Watch yourself.*

This wasn't my family. Was it wrong that that fact hurt me? That I felt as if there was a huge missing piece in my life?

Yeah, it was probably very, very wrong.

Aly ended her call and tossed her phone back into her purse. "Sorry about that. The second I leave Jared at home by himself, he always needs something."

My tease was knowing. "He just can't stand when you're gone."

She grinned like a crushing schoolgirl. "Pretty much." She shook it off and reached for the seat. "Here, let me take that. I didn't mean to make you a babysitter."

"Oh, I've got her. Let me give you a little break while we order. I want to eat her up, she is so cute." Adoration filled my voice as I turned back to Ella, who had her sight set on her mom.

Aly shook Ella's hand, her words soft. "She does have that effect on people." Aly gestured to the entrance. "Come on, let's get something to drink. And I'm dying for one of their apple strudels."

I followed her inside. We ordered and found a little spot in the shade outside. Aly unfastened Ella and pulled her into her arms, relaxing back and sipping from her iced decaf latte. It didn't matter to me how hot it was outside, I liked my coffee the way nature intended it, piping hot, warming up my body from the inside out.

For a few minutes we rested in the comfortable silence between us. Birds chirped from the tree that grew up close to our table, and there was a distinct calm out on the patio as people took a break from the hustle of their lives, couples chatting quietly with each other, some absorbed in a book, others looking off into nothing at all.

Finally Aly sighed in contentment and smiled across at me. "Thank you for meeting me today. After we left you last weekend, I was a little worried I had put you on the spot."

I shook my head. "Not at all. I was excited when I got your text."

Completely freaked-out and panicked, but excited. She really didn't need to know that, though.

She rested back against her chair, slowly rocking Ella, who she'd shifted up to her shoulder. "So tell me all about you. What have you been up to all these years?"

A soft chuckle fell from me, and I shook my head as I thought of the last seven years, realizing not a whole lot had happened, all the day-to-day stuff that made up a million memories, though very few of them stood out.

"I guess there isn't a whole lot to tell. I finished up college here this last May, and I got a job for the summer at a small private school not too far from here . . . Which I love," I added quickly.

"That is wonderful." She smiled. "I remember you telling me you wanted to be a teacher."

I nodded, a self-conscious blush landing on my face. "Thank you . . . I did always want it. It feels incredible to finally be finished with school and get started. All the kids are great."

I took a sip of my coffee. "Sean and Stephanie are both doing really well. Stephanie's going to school out in California, and Sean is here at ASU." I swallowed hard. "And Stewart . . ." I trailed off, the lump in my throat growing solid and thick. "He did really great for quite a few years, but he got sick again about six months ago." Moisture filled my eyes, and I swiped at the wayward tear that slipped free. "I'm sorry, I didn't mean to get all weepy on you."

Aly reached her hand across the table, taking mine. "Hey, don't apologize. I asked about your life because I wanted to know how you are . . . how your family is."

A swell of gratitude got all mixed up with my sadness, thankfulness that Aly was willing to be there, even after I hadn't seen her in years and years, thankfulness that she was so kind and seemed willing to just listen.

I didn't have a whole lot of that in my life.

I nodded a grateful acceptance and continued over my choppy explanation. "God, Aly . . . I thought he was out of the woods and we didn't have anything to worry about. Then he started feeling weak and developed a cough. My mom took him in to the doctor just to check it out, and in the matter of days, our worlds were turned upside down again."

Sympathy wet her own eyes. "I'm so sorry, Sam. I hate hearing he's going through this again . . . that you and your family are going through this again."

We sat in a few minutes of silence, Aly letting me gather my staggered breath, before she shot me a playful stare. "And . . . ," she drew out, prodding for something that was so plain to her while I sat there without a clue.

My brow quirked in question.

"Your boyfriend?" she asked, as if it should have been natural that I would first have blurted everything about him, swooning like I should be after I'd met the man of my dreams. A frown crossed her face when she took in my expression, which I guessed to be verging on numb. Her frown deepened. "You did tell me you lived with your boyfriend, right? Did I misunderstand?"

Fidgeting, I laughed off the unease. "Oh no, sorry," I apologized again, feeling like an idiot. "I do live with my boyfriend. Do you remember Ben Carrington?"

Aly seemed to sift around in her memories before she shook her head. "I don't think so. Should I?"

I lifted an indifferent shoulder. "Probably not . . . He's four years older than me and went to high school across town, but he used to hang out with some of the guys from the old neighborhood sometimes, so I thought you might have met him."

She pursed her lips. "Nope, can't place the face." Her green eyes gleamed with a warm mirth. "You'll have to introduce me sometime."

"Yeah, sure . . . of course. He's sells health care policies to small companies. Travels a lot. He's a good guy." I described him with all the enthusiasm I could muster, which this morning was about zero. My gaze wandered off to the side because I was afraid it was completely obvious, the lackluster response to her interest in my boyfriend up against the flagrant way my heart hammered with the questions about Christopher that continually swirled through my mind. Inside, I was begging her to mention him, to give me just a hint of what he was doing or where he was.

How he was.

The dimming in her eyes told me she'd caught on to it. She pulled in a deep breath, hesitated, then dropped her voice to a

mere whisper as she leaned in closer to the table, careful to protect her daughter's head. "You can ask about him, you know."

I lifted my face to her, and that lump from earlier was back
in full force, knotting up my throat with unspent emotion. "I'm
not sure that I can."

A war raged inside me, one side desperate and destitute, the
other rigid and strong. Funny how the damaged side felt so
much more powerful than the fortified.

That scared me.

I was sure that fact was written all over my trembling face.

Aly managed to lean in closer. "Let me ask you something.
Are you here because you wanted to hang out with me or because I'm Christopher's sister?"

That rigid side reared its head, and I met the curiosity in
her gaze. "Let me ask you something. Are you here because you
wanted to hang out with me or because I'm Christopher's
ex-girlfriend?"

Aly sat back with a wry laugh. "Touché." Her head shook as
if she were trying to make sense of it, to find the straight truth
in her answer. That was one thing I was sure I would get from
Aly, something genuine and without condition or expectation.
It was the thing that kept me sitting in this chair even though I
felt more vulnerable than I had in a long, long time.

Apparently the Moores had that way about them.

"Honestly?" Chewing at her lip, she stared across at me, her
eyes kind and open. "I was really excited to run into you. But
seeing you definitely did make me think about my brother and
the way he is."

I cringed.

The way he is.

Of course I knew what she was talking about, but a piece of
me had been holding out hope that he'd become a different man

from the one I'd left in that room staring at me without remorse while I stood frozen in outright horror. The night he'd broken every ounce of trust I'd had.

"I won't pretend that I know all that much about your relationship or what happened between you two. All I know is my brother was the happiest he's ever been when he was with you."

Another stake right through my failing heart.

Remorse took up the whole of Aly's face. "And I know it all fell apart when everything went down with Jared. Watching his best friend lose his mother and then himself. Christopher basically lost Jared at the same time."

I remained mute, unsure how to respond. She had so much of it right, though there were holes all over her assumptions, all of them punched out by my insecurities and Christopher's callousness.

Sighing, she hugged her daughter close, as if she were protecting her family as she drifted into the past. "My husband has been through a lot and has overcome so much, Samantha, and I'm pretty sure Christopher got lost in the shuffle. Believe me, he hasn't said a word about what happened between you two, and I'm going to be truthful and tell you I've often thought about it . . . wondering about everything that happened with Jared and how it affected Christopher . . . how he just kind of lost it after. And I've thought about you," she admitted quietly, "wondering if you were okay or if he'd left you broken, too."

My mouth twisted up with pain, remorse and regret and guilt spinning through my being. That breaking had gone both ways.

Aly flinched, just the smallest fraction, but it was there, the woman insightful. Her head pitched just to the side. "Judging by the look on your face, I'm going to take a wild guess and say it went a whole lot deeper than what happened with Jared."

It did. It went so deep that it'd cut me right in two. But I wasn't ready to tell her that. Offering a halfhearted shrug, I issued the lamest excuse I could find. "We were young." As if our ages had diminished anything we'd felt.

Puffing out a knowing breath, Aly softened. "I love my brother. He's truly amazing. He constantly makes me laugh. But it goes far beyond that. He's caring. Loves with everything he has. This little girl?" She patted Ella's back. "He'd do absolutely anything for her. He is one of the best guys I know when it comes to us . . . to his family. But I know he doesn't see the rest of the world that way, and he most definitely doesn't see himself that way. It makes me sad. I worry about him. He's messed up, but I won't judge him for anything he's done in his past . . . just like I won't judge you."

I cut my attention away. God, she could see right through me. Finally I lifted my gaze and shook my head in surrender. "It doesn't matter, Aly. What's done is done. And neither me nor your brother can undo it."

Even if either of us wanted to.

She looked like she was going to object, so I interrupted. "Enough about me. Tell me about you. How in the heck did you end up with Jared Holt?"

I sat back and listened to what had to be the most heartbreaking story I'd ever heard, but my saddened spirit warmed as she spoke of glimpses of light, of a hope that was slowly breathed into a man who'd thought he'd lost everything and deserved nothing. Right up to the point where they brought that precious little girl into the world.

"Wow," I said.

"Yeah," she agreed, the word filled with awe.

"And what are you doing now?" I asked, taking a sip of my coffee, which had gone lukewarm.

For the first time, Aly looked self-conscious. She bit her lip. "I went to art school and I started drawing some portraits for families, but I haven't done quite as much with it since Ella was born. I really hope to get back into it soon. It's nice because I can do a lot of it from home."

"That's incredible."

"Thank you."

I glanced at my phone. We'd already been at the coffee shop for two hours. "I'd better get going. I'm taking up your entire Saturday." I looked at her with a sincere and happy smile. "It was really great catching up with you. I'm so happy for you. I hope you know that."

She returned my smile with a warm and honest one of her own. "I think I do know that." She paused, seeming to waver, before she rushed out, "Don't say no before you hear me out, but we're having a small get-together tonight at our house, just a barbecue with a couple of guys from Jared's work."

I immediately started to protest, but she held up her hand. "Christopher won't be there. He already had plans with one of his other friends and said he couldn't make it. I'd love for you to come."

My mouth snapped closed. I wasn't sure if it was in disappointment or relief.

Victory glinted in Aly's eyes.

Yep, she could see right through me.

"Come over at seven. I'll text you our address. I'm betting you could walk over if you wanted to."

Quickly I stood, flooded with a sudden and overwhelming need to escape again. Still, there was no stopping the surrender that rushed from my mouth.

"Okay."

FOUR

Samantha

I scratched out a quick message to Ben and stuck the little pink sticky note to the refrigerator. He was out with the guys. Again. And again, it'd only filled me with relief. When he'd called to tell me he'd be out, a silent *thank God* had come like a fierce whisper, whipping through my consciousness, a voice that was quiet but almost terrifying because it spoke with honesty. Without warning, piercing my thoughts. And more and more, it came too often.

Went to hang out with some friends. Be back soon. I smoothed my finger over the top edge of my note, making sure it was secure. Guilt tickled along my ribs before it spiraled down into a dark pool of foreboding in my stomach.

Tomorrow, I'd tell Ben where I'd gone tonight. I wasn't a liar, and I wasn't about to become one now.

My feelings shifted just about as quickly as the guilt came on. Almost indignant, I stamped my foot as I turned and headed for the door, grabbing my purse from the table. I wasn't doing anything wrong, and I didn't have to give Ben an explanation. I didn't owe him or have to stick to his rules.

The sick part was, I was having trouble convincing my heart of that.

Probably a whole lot of that had to do with the way I trembled as I stepped outside into the evening. Color slashed across the horizon, blazing pinks and purples and blues as the sun cast sharp rays of light into the sky, the bright orb squatting low as it eased away. Heat saturated the air, hot and heavy, though it'd waned from the harsh intensity of the blistering day.

Still, I shook as a roll of cold chills slipped down my spine.

Foolish, foolish girl, I chastised myself for the hundredth time in just the last five minutes, adding to the millions of other times I'd berated myself for agreeing to go to Aly's since I'd left her at the coffee shop earlier today. Everything about this was foolish. I knew it in my gut, felt it strongly as the anticipation that had simmered all week threatened to rise to a boil.

But no matter how foolish it was, there was no stopping myself from lifting my chin and marching in the direction of her house.

Of course I'd figured out where she lived long before she'd texted me her address, my fingers too curious after I'd seen Aly and her family at Target not to dig, searching out the names of the homeowners in the little family neighborhood we lived in.

It took me less than two minutes to find Jared Holt.

All I had to do was make a right at the end of my street and travel three houses down. Less than a five-minute walk.

And here I was, traversing that distance, my sandals pounding the sidewalk as if they had every right to take me to this careless destination.

Aly had told me the get-together was casual, so I still wore my favorite jean shorts, though I'd traded out my plain tank top for a dressier one, red and satiny with a pretty lace cutout at the back. I'd ironed my hair into long sheets of blond, my straight bangs cropped low across my forehead.

I felt pretty, confident, and completely brainless at the same time.

When I rounded the corner, I found a few cars lining the street just ahead, right where I knew Jared and Aly's house would be. I sucked in a breath and increased my speed, unwilling to back out now, even though my ears were ringing with a chorus of warning bells that I couldn't shut off.

I headed up the walkway and rang the doorbell. Biting at my lip, I fidgeted with the hem of my shirt while I waited.

Foolish. Foolish. Foolish.

The door swung open so quickly I almost gasped.

Aly was there, and she immediately leaped for me, squeezing me in a welcoming hug. "You're here!" She pulled back, mischief playing all over her face. "I was beginning to think I was going to have to come down to your house and drag you over."

I laughed and stepped inside. "Sorry I'm late."

She shook her head. "Not to worry. We're just getting ready to eat."

The layout of Aly's house was almost exactly like mine, although everything had been flipped, the master bedroom to the left when mine was on the right, their kitchen on the right when mine was on the left. Their house was decorated much differently, though, modern and sleek, yet warm at the same time.

Home.

I knew in Aly's eyes, that's exactly what this was.

She took my hand. "Everyone's out back. Come on, I'll introduce you to our friends."

She led me through the spacious family room, through the

open area that separated the dining room and kitchen, and out the sliding glass door into their backyard.

Just off to the left, two outdoor table sets took up the patio, umbrellas still lifted to block the remnants of the day. My eyes swept over the people there, three men and two women. One of the women held Ella, smothering her in kisses, while the other watched a little brown-haired boy playing from where she sat in her chair. The little guy, who couldn't have been more than two, tottered around on the . . . grass.

They had grass.

"How in the world do you get grass to grow?" I asked. "I've tried for the last year. I was pretty sure it was impossible here."

Aly laughed and waved an indulgent hand at her husband, who was manning the grill set up off to the right. "Oh, Jared has his ways . . . he's out here pretty much every day, loving it and sweet-talking it, showering it with so much affection and water it has no choice but to grow. I'm starting to get jealous."

Jared flipped a couple of burgers, slanted a playful eye at his wife. "Baby, you know all I do, I do for you."

Slinking up to him, she lifted on her toes and pressed a kiss to his jaw. "It'd better be."

She began to back away, but he caught her around the waist and buried his face in her hair.

My first instinct was to drop my gaze, to look away, because everything about them was so intimate. But I got the distinct feeling they were always this way, and if I was going to be in their space, it was probably something I should get used to.

Jared lifted his chin toward me in a casual *hello*.

Proof enough. This was them, sweet and good, and I couldn't help but sink more and more into their comfort, more and more feeling as if I belonged, even though seeing it ate at me, and somewhere inside, the broken part of me flared with pain.

I pushed the thought aside and smiled. "Can you come and sweet-talk some grass into growing at my place? I don't think weeds even attempt to grow in the wasteland that is my backyard."

Jared laughed, wholehearted and free. "You'll have to take that up with my wife. If she's jealous of her own grass, not sure how she's gonna take me going over and lovin' on yours."

Aly's green eyes glinted, and she hugged his arm tighter against her stomach. "I have to admit, I'm not so good at sharing him. Even with old friends."

Untangling herself from his hold, she crossed back to me, led me over to the tables, and introduced me to their other guests. I shook hands with James and his wife Livette, James a friend of Jared's from work. The little boy, Cayden, belonged to them. Two single guys, Kurt and Simon, were also both friends of Jared's. The second woman, Megan, was Aly's best friend.

"It's so nice to meet you all," I said. Every second I spent here put me a little more at ease, and I began to wonder what it was I had been so freaked-out about when I stepped out my door. I liked Aly. There was nothing wrong with that.

"Beer, wine, soda?" Aly asked, pausing before she went back inside.

"Oh, go for the red," Megan cut in, lifting her near-empty wineglass. "It's delicious."

"Yeah, and if you have any more of it, your auntie duties are cut off for the night," Jared called out from the grill, wielding his spatula in her direction.

Megan chuckled and shook her head, her hold protective as she rocked Ella on her chest. "I've had half a glass."

"Exactly," he returned.

Megan widened her blue eyes as she looked at me. "He's not overprotective or anything."

I giggled. Apparently not at all.

She inclined her head to the empty seat next to her. "Come sit and keep me company."

Rounding the table, I settled down into the free chair. "Thanks."

Her smile was genuine, a lot like Aly's. I had a hard time trusting women, always putting up a wall, never quite believing they wouldn't turn around and sink their teeth into me. High school had been rough, all the taunts and teases for no apparent reason other than the gang of mean girls decided they didn't like me. Didn't like my family or what they stood for, since my father was a pastor. Because of them, I tended to keep most people at arm's length. Real friends were hard to come by, and truthfully, I had none of them, no one except for my mom and Stewart.

"I'm glad you're here," Megan murmured almost conspiratorially. "This place is always overrun with men. I'm not sure how much more testosterone I can take."

"Hey," Kurt shot out, taking a swig of his beer. "I'm sitting right here. I can *hear* you."

She slanted me a smile. "See what I mean?"

I just sat back, fighting a grin, happy to accept the glass of wine Aly offered me, more than happy when Megan finally gave up her claim and passed Ella to me.

My heart did that crazy thing again, pulsing with affection for a little girl I really didn't know but somehow felt an affinity for, all the same.

She was a Moore. A piece of *him*. Like Aly. Like Jared. Jared might not have been blood, but he and Christopher were bonded in a way few ever got a chance to experience. I knew firsthand how much Christopher loved Jared. How devastated he'd been. How it'd made him desperate and broken and lost.

Emotion fisted my throat, pressing on my deflated chest as I stared down at the perfect face of the slumbering girl.

What was I doing? Wedging myself into their lives? It was as if I was trying to carve out a spot for myself in a place where I'd always believed I belonged, forcing myself to fit when that place had been cut off long ago.

Slowly, I rocked Ella, loving the feel of her tiny body curled up on my chest.

Maybe it was pathetic and dangerous, being here. That didn't mean it didn't feel right.

"All right, I think dinner is ready. You all better be hungry. Aly might have overdone it at the grocery store this afternoon." Jared balanced a huge platter of burgers and brats as he went inside. We all followed him, filling our plates with too much food before coming back out to the patio, where we ate and drank, enjoying the descending night. Laughter rolled through their yard, voices free and kind.

I allowed myself to relax into their peace, for once letting myself go.

Three glasses of wine and a full plate later, I was stuffed and satisfied.

"Dinner was delicious, Jared. Thank you."

He smiled over at me from where he rested on his chair, his booted foot casually tilting him back as he sipped at a beer. "It was good to have you here." His expression shifted, searching, as if from across the table his ice blue eyes could see right through me, working to define my intentions, figuring out if I was the same girl Christopher had rescued and then destroyed.

Sometimes I thought if Christopher had just left me for the vultures who flocked around me in high school, I would have fared better.

Maybe Jared recognized that I was not the same—simply

because it was Christopher who had changed me—because his eyes narrowed infinitesimally, as if maybe he was just now asking himself all those questions I'd been silently asking for so many years.

But deep inside me, pieces of that shy girl remained, the one who'd so stupidly fallen hard and fallen fast.

A crush, my mother had said.

But crushes didn't last for years. They didn't tear you up and rip you apart.

On a heavy exhale, I stood, for a moment needing to remove myself. "Can I use your restroom?"

"It's right down the hall," Aly answered.

"Thank you," I said as I excused myself, hating the bipolar mess I seemed to be, one second getting all cozy in their house and the next again having that overwhelming urge to run.

In the guest bathroom, I freshened up, hoping to clear my head. Studying myself in the mirror, I dug in my pocket for the tube of lip gloss. I smeared the clear, shimmery gel over my red lips, puckered them before they spread out into their natural pout. My blue eyes were sad and soft, as if they were letting me glimpse the state of my heart after spending the evening with these amazing people.

I blew back my bangs and tucked my lip gloss away, unlocked the door, and ventured out.

Stepping into the hall, I froze, and my heart lifted to my throat in the same moment my stomach completely bottomed out. My feet faltered and I reached for the wall with my shaking hand, catching myself before I fell to the ground.

Because being here had done exactly what I'd anticipated it would do, what I'd secretly hoped would happen even if more and more being here had become about spending time with Aly and her family.

It had brought me face-to-face with Christopher.

Only he hadn't seen me in the shadows of the darkened hall, and he had no clue I was there. I watched him, my fingers digging into the textured wall to keep from falling to my knees.

God, how many times had I imagined this? Seeing him again. What it would feel like, if it'd feel the same or less or more, if I'd burn up with desire or if I'd realize the years had only exaggerated the memories of him, building him up into something he was not.

What I never imagined was he would crush me anew.

As much as I wanted to look away, my gaze was locked on the boy who held every piece of my heart. There was no question of it now. No denying what I felt or the way he affected me.

Only now he was no longer a boy, but a man. From my vantage I watched as he smiled his cocky smile, predatory, both warning and promising his prey of the plunder and pillage he was getting ready to unleash on her. He oozed danger and menace, all of that wrapped up in one big, playful bow. His perfect jaw clenched as a tease fluttered all over his full lips, his green eyes gleaming as they prowled over some girl he'd brought with him. She faced away from me, facing him.

He gripped her by her bare thigh, her shorts so short every inch of her long legs was exposed, and he pulled her flush against his body.

He wore jeans and a tight, tight tee, it clinging perfectly to the span of his wide chest, every defined muscle flexing below the thin dark gray fabric. Bold, colorful ink curled out from under one shirtsleeve, and another black tattoo was stamped on the inside of the opposite forearm. He was lean but strong, taller than any man had the right to be, the power of his presence imposing and enough to steal every breath of air from my lungs.

He dipped down and burrowed his face in her neck, his black

hair wild and mussed, sticking up in every direction. She squealed and drove her fingers into it, tugging on the length as he bent her back, kissing her up and down.

My heart squeezed so tight I could feel it splintering, disintegrating into dust.

Coming here hadn't just been foolish.

It was reckless, plain and simple.

Still I stared, unable to look away from the man who had meant everything to me. One I should hate and blame, for the way I let myself give up and give in. But I knew I was crumbling only because I couldn't stand to see him this way, wrapped up in another woman's arms, when every *whole* part of me wanted that girl to be me.

How sick was that?

My mouth went dry when he suddenly stilled, the corded muscles of his tanned arms rippling as he slowly lifted his head as if he sensed my presence. His green eyes met mine, widening with shock, before they flashed with something dark and fierce. Then his face twisted in arrogance, those green eyes narrowing as if he knew he had me trapped.

Just like he had that night.

I was helpless to look away, and he held me captive as he went back to work on her neck, his mouth at her jaw and at her chin. The entire time he never released me from the prison of his contemptuous glare.

It was the *wrecked* pieces of me that were wise, ones that already knew Christopher Moore had the power to destroy me. He'd done it before, and by the way he was looking at me now, I knew he'd gladly to do it again.

Not because he wanted me. But because he wanted to play with me. Like he'd done all those years ago. I'd believed him—that he loved me and cared about me, that he cared about my brother—that he hadn't just been seducing me into becoming an unsuspecting pawn in his sick, twisted game.

It didn't take me long to realize that's exactly what I was.

It took everything I had to compose myself. I steadied my feet and shaking hands, but there was nothing I could do about my bleeding heart. Thankfully it was safe and hidden away, in a place I'd no longer allow him to see.

I lifted my chin in nonchalance, as if seeing him meant nothing at all, all the while praying to God my legs were strong enough to carry me out back so I could give Aly and Jared my thanks, grab my purse, and go on my way.

Because really? All I wanted was to run.

But I wouldn't be giving Christopher that satisfaction.

I wound around him and the girl, who'd just come to recognize that Christopher wasn't giving her his full attention because his eyes were pinned on me. I smirked a little, catching her surprise, and immediately felt bad because this girl probably had no idea what an asshole he was.

She probably was just as naive as I had been.

I stepped outside, where the night had taken hold, a few bright stars breaking through the glow of the city lights, Aly and her family and friends still completely relaxed and enjoying each other.

"There you are," Aly said with a casual smile, before her eyebrows creased together when she caught the expression on my face. "Are you okay?"

"Yep, perfect," I lied, grabbing my purse from where I'd tucked it under the chair when I first arrived. "But it's getting late, so I'd better get home." I looked between her and Jared. "Thank you so much for inviting me. It really was great catching up with you."

My attention jumped around the tables at the people who

I'd been foolish enough to somehow think of as friends. Of course Christopher would snuff that out, too.

"It was nice to meet you all."

"Nice to meet you, too," went up as a chorus, and I wound back around the table, leaned in close to Aly, and brushed my fingers through her daughter's soft hair.

Aly frowned and I gave her the best smile I could manage, hoping she understood how much I truly appreciated her and hoped for her happiness.

I knew I wouldn't see them again.

Then I turned and rushed to the sliding glass door. I went to duck inside, when my path was obstructed by an imposing figure at the doorway, the man a full foot taller than my five foot four. I didn't want to look up, but I couldn't stop myself from being drawn, and his warm breath washed over my face.

Chills cascaded in a dizzying wave down my spine, before the venom in his voice lifted the hairs at the nape of my neck, the words cold and deathly quiet. "What the fuck do you think you're doing here?"

Lost in the searing anger blazing in his green eyes, I stammered for an answer. "I . . . I . . ."

I swallowed hard and he leaned in closer, his nose brushing mine, and I was suddenly drowning in everything Christopher Moore—the way he smelled, clean, like a breath of the morning's freshest air, but still something else entirely intoxicating, like sex and lust and everything I'd ever wanted but knew I shouldn't have.

My thoughts went fuzzy as I got lost in it, before that wicked voice snapped me back. "Stay away from my family." Like a caress, he trailed his finger along the line of my jaw, lifting a line of goose bumps in its wake, before he hooked it under my chin, bringing his mouth a centimeter from mine.

There was no stopping the way my lips parted on instinct, as if they'd forever been waiting for his. His heat spread across my face, and I felt myself leaning forward.

"And stay the fuck away from me."

Stunned, I stared, my mouth gaping open with offended shock and my body reeling from the need he'd spun up in me.

Aly's frantic voice penetrated from behind. "Christopher, what are you doing here?" The metal legs of her chair screeched as she pushed it back to stand. "You said you weren't coming."

I grasped for clarity, berating myself for my stupidity, for my foolish reaction. That's all I'd been since the second I'd spotted Aly in that store. Foolish.

What in the hell is wrong with me?

Christopher jerked his attention up and outside, and I took the opportunity to push around him, a shock of breath wheezing into my burning lungs when I was freed from his hold. The girl he was with stood in the middle of the room, arms crossed over her chest, looking pissed off, as if I had ruined her entire evening.

I wanted to laugh in her face, because she had no clue.

Shouldering by her, I ran for the door, fumbled with the lock, and threw it open. Outside, beneath the summer's night, I grasped my head, gasping as I fought back angry, broken tears.

When it came to Christopher, foolish was all I'd ever been.

Just a foolish, foolish girl.

And I swore I would never be her again.

FIVE

Samantha

Late August, Seven Years Earlier

I cringed, my shoulders held up protectively against my ears, wishing I could hide. I ducked farther into the safety of my locker as I dug around for my math book. Of course, I already knew exactly where it was, but I was delaying, doing everything I could to ignore the taunts Jasmine hurled my way.

She edged in close to my back and leaned over my shoulder, the caustic smell of her thick perfume making me recoil. Jasmine laughed, obviously thinking it was her face all up in mine that had me shrinking away.

Anger burned deep in my spirit, a feeling I despised, but one I'd been experiencing more and more lately.

"Aren't you praying hard enough, Sam? Is that why your brother is sick?" she taunted. Jasmine glanced behind her to the pack of snarling girls staring me down, all of them at the beck

and call of their vicious ringleader. "Maybe the little prude isn't
as innocent as she leads us all to believe," she said to incite her
little crowd.

The Bitch Brigade laughed and threw in their own jeers.

I wanted to spit in her face. Maybe wrap my hands around
her neck. Worse yet, I wanted to wish my brother's sickness on
this girl instead. But I kept my mouth pressed tight, holding in
all the harsh, evil words I wanted to set free.

My parents taught me never to match this kind of provoca-
tion, warning that people would always judge me for who I was.

The pastor's daughter.

It was something I had discounted, never believing my parents'
caution, until Jasmine and her crew had somehow set their sights
on me toward the end of last year. Every day it got worse and
worse, as if the insults they slung were never enough. Or maybe it
was just that I never gave them the satisfaction they craved.

Jasmine grabbed me by the shoulder, her fingers digging
painfully into my skin. She jerked me around and pushed me
back up against my metal locker. It rattled behind me.

My eyes went wide as they all closed in on me, and fear
slithered under the surface of my skin. I'd never been frightened
of them before, but there was something on Jasmine's face that
told me maybe I should be.

Because it was filled with pure hatred. A hatred I had neither earned nor understood.

"Prissy bitch . . . such a little cock tease, prancing around
here like you're God's gift to the earth."

The shake of my head was flustered, confused. I'd never come
close to *teasing* anyone. People rarely even talked to me or gave
me a second glance. For the most part I was invisible . . . until
word had spread about my brother, and for a fraction of a moment,
I'd become the center of attention, as unwelcome as it'd been.

That's what this is about?

"You're pathetic." I whispered my anger around my dried tongue.

That flicker of fear grew stronger when Jasmine edged in closer, but I didn't care. I wouldn't stand silent and listen to them slander my brother, my family, even if it spurred Jasmine on.

I could take it.

A loud crash of metal caused me to scream, and the lockers shook with the force of the bash that came just above my head. Pinching my eyes, I waited for a lance of pain, for the strike to register on my face, but none came. Slowly my eyes flickered open to find Jasmine stumbling back when she met with the face of Christopher Moore, who had wedged himself between me and the girl who'd taken it upon herself to make my life a living hell.

"Don't you have something better to do? I heard the entire basketball team is in the locker room. They should be expecting you. Or have you already grown bored of the taste of sweaty dick in your mouth?" His taunt was just as thick as the one Jasmine had used on me.

"Fuck you," she slurred, clenching her fists at her sides, her hands extending lower than the scrap of a skirt she wore. "You didn't seem to mind when it was your dick."

Jasmine had a reputation. I knew all about it. The worst part was Christopher Moore had one, too.

Like her words didn't even faze him, Christopher glanced over his shoulder at me. "You okay?"

I tried my best to catch my breath and clear my head, but his expression muddied my thoughts all up again. The dread I'd felt in the face-off with Jasmine had transformed into a wave of dizziness that started in my unsettled belly and swirled all the way up to spin my head.

Christopher Moore was talking to *me*.

He frowned, still guarding me, but twisting enough so that his torso was facing me, concern strewn all over his gorgeous face. "Did this bitch hurt you?" he demanded.

I swallowed, searching for words that were all locked up in my tightened throat. Spastic and jerky, I shook my head. A shock of embarrassment rushed to my face, splashing crimson all over my pale skin. "No," I whispered low when he continued to stare me down, waiting for an answer.

"What the hell do you care?" Jasmine had regained her composure, all the haughty bitchiness back in full force.

Because just like Christopher had called her, she was exactly that.

A bitch.

Jasmine tossed her hip to the side, going for a sexy, seductive pose that made me want to hurl.

A voice rumbled from the side. "He obviously cares nothing about you, Jasmine, so why don't you be on your way."

I tore my attention from where it was fixated on Christopher to the origin of the voice.

Jared Holt.

Here I was, surrounded by two guys who commanded attention wherever they went, Christopher Moore and Jared Holt. I couldn't tell which of them was better-looking. Any of the girls at the school would have died to have either one of them.

But there was something about Christopher's dark hair and the overt mirth and tease that gleamed bright in his emerald eyes that just about brought me to my knees. He was gorgeous. Beautiful. And a little bit terrifying. He was trouble with a capital *T.*

And I didn't do trouble.

Jasmine ignored Jared and instead backed an inch away, glaring at Christopher. "You're an asshole."

Christopher edged in closer to my side. As if he was taking up *my* side.

My head reeled again.

"Yeah?" His nose curled with distaste. "And I can smell your nasty cunt from over here."

My eyes went wide with shock. I couldn't believe he'd just used the C-word. That was the dirtiest of dirty words. But it just rolled off his tongue as if he used it all the time.

He probably did.

My skin zinged when he gathered me up close, tucking me under his arm to shield me from the stifling hostility radiating from Jasmine.

"Let's get you out of here," he whispered, moving to shuffle me toward the school's outdoor hallway.

With his arm slung over my shoulder, he shifted enough to look back, lifted his free hand high in the air to flip Jasmine off. "Stupid bitch," he shouted out, before he turned and whisked me away.

I shook my head, staring at my feet as I rushed to keep up with Christopher's long, confident stride, trying to make sense of what had just gone down. I blinked and attempted to slow down, whispering the words from my raw throat. "You didn't have to do that, you know."

Christopher scoffed, still taking up his protective stance at my side. "Yeah, I did."

"Why?" I couldn't stop the question from escaping my mouth. It was a genuine question with an answer I wasn't sure I could really understand.

Christopher just shrugged. "Because I'm tired of watching that rabid bitch treat everyone around her like shit." He glanced at me, all that bold arrogance playing around his face, but something serious blanketed his eyes. "And I sure as hell am not gonna stand around and watch her messing with you."

The nerves rolling around in my stomach got confused with the attraction I'd always felt toward him.

But that attraction had always been from afar.

"Come on . . . let's grab some lunch. I've worked up an appetite putting Jasmine in her place." Christopher tossed me a casual wink and turned me toward the cafeteria.

Overwhelmed by it all, I allowed my wary feet to drag me to a standstill. "You don't even know me."

A step ahead, Christopher stopped when he realized I was no longer at his side, his pivot slow as he turned to face me. His expression pinned me to the sidewalk and left me without breath, the sudden burning intensity of his green eyes branding me.

He erased almost all the ground between us, swallowing up the personal boundaries I had so firmly set in place. Everything lit inside of me. Places that I'd had no idea existed flamed to life in front of this beautiful boy.

Cocking his head to the side, he captured my dumbfounded gaze. "I know your name is Samantha Schultz. I know you sit one row over and two seats in front of me in English literature because I can't stop watching you."

He lifted his hand, the pads of his fingertips fluttering along my jaw. A flash of nerves pebbled my oversensitive skin. He hooked his finger under my chin, bringing his lips a fraction from mine.

"And I know you have the prettiest mouth I've ever seen."

SIX

Christopher

I fisted my hair in my hands, doing my best not to lose my shit, trying to keep from coming unglued right here in the middle of my sister's quiet house. This place was supposed to be a sanctuary, where I could come and leave all the bullshit I got myself into behind. Where I could pretend like I was living for something instead of admitting that I was wasting my life away.

Never had that fact been more glaring than now.

A waste.

A total fucking waste, because my entire life had just gone running out Aly's front door.

That mouth.

That fucking mouth.

I was one second from losing my goddamned mind, one second from losing sanity.

When I'd confronted her at the sliding door, Samantha had been no more than one staggered breath away. So close I could almost taste her. Everything that was sweet filled up my nose and invaded my senses. My heart stumbled, and all that rushing blood decided it was a good idea to travel straight to my aching cock.

After all, I was just a man, and that girl was single-handedly responsible for who I was today.

It'd taken just about every ounce of power I had inside me to keep from leaning in and taking what should have always been mine—that mouth that was all red and perfect, twisted up like a tiny little bow, taunting me with what I couldn't have.

Like only a minute had passed instead of years, she'd managed to suck me right back into the endless blue of her expressive eyes. Just like she always had. But this time they were all dark and turbulent and wounded, as if she had no idea what she'd done to me, as if just her setting foot inside this house hadn't brought the walls closing in and the ground crumbling beneath my feet.

Like maybe she thought it should be me apologizing to her.

And damn if it didn't piss me off.

Did she have no fucking clue how bad it hurt to even think about her? And there she'd been, standing there in all that glorious flesh, luring me forward like she was some kind of forbidden fruit.

Anger clenched my jaw, that emotion in an all-out war with the relief that had come barreling in like a freight train when my body had trembled with awareness, all my nerves set on high alert, as if they could sense some kind of impending change in the air.

And that change had been standing right at the end of Aly's hallway.

At first I'd thought I was hallucinating. I mean, how many times had I imagined her? Saw myself touching her. Loving her.

Too many times I'd wondered what she'd look like now with all these years passed. Would she still be good and sweet and innocent, or had I damaged her so much that she'd become just like the rest of the girls I could barely stand?

Should've known those fantasies wouldn't come close to doing her justice.

She'd always been beautiful. But in a soft sort of way, all of it subdued by her modesty and kindness, her shy smile and bright eyes filled with the excitement of the future and a genuine kind of innocence that had knocked something loose inside me the first time I saw her. No doubt that's what had drawn me to her in the first place. I liked that she didn't know how pretty she was. Like maybe I was the only one who recognized it and I'd be the one who got to convince her of it.

Or maybe it was just that she really didn't care. She didn't make it the center of her world or wield it like power to garner herself attention or manipulate those around her.

But God, there was no hiding that striking beauty now.

She was still petite, probably a full foot shorter than my six foot four, but time had cut away the roundness of her cheeks. Now they were high and defined, accentuating the sharp line of her jaw. It only drew attention to the delicate skin that graced the soft slope of her neck. Skin I'd do just about anything to get lost in. Those deep blue eyes were keen with an understanding that came only with loss, but still wide and pure and enough to see straight through me, like with just a glance she could crush every wall I'd ever set in place.

And that body . . . God, that body was just too much. Every kind of perfection. She was thin, but not skinny, her hips curvy and her chest full. Her legs were strong and toned, almost defiant in their stance when she faced me, even though I'd seen the way her knees had rocked when my gaze first locked on her eyes.

Her blond hair, so light it was almost white, had been cut in long sheets that fell around her slender shoulders to the middle of her back, and her bangs hung across her forehead to form a frame around that beautiful face that had haunted me for years.

Which brought me right back to that mouth.

Good God, that mouth. I didn't know how I stopped myself. Overwhelming desire had taken me like a damned prisoner. It'd taken my all not to crush myself to those lips that were so red and lush.

Instead I'd uttered the worst kind of profanity—pure and blatant blasphemy—as I demanded that she stay out of my life and out of my family's lives.

Because there was no piece of me that could handle her here.

"What the hell is your problem?" With the venomous voice, I jerked to look over my shoulder.

Kristen stood with her arms crossed over her chest, her tits making a bid to climb right over the top of her collar. She was all ruffled and pissed and offended, her face twisted up in a sneer.

I'd forgotten she was even here.

Of course, I'd used her like a goddamned prop when I'd found Samantha there, and a second was spent feeling guilty for employing her as a tactic in some kind of defective defense mechanism. But really, that pang of guilt was all wrapped up in the expression that had slurred across Samantha's face, reflecting back betrayal and disloyalty.

Which was exactly what it'd been.

"Christopher, what do you think you're doing here?" Aly demanded from behind, stepping inside.

Awesome.

I was getting assaulted on all sides, by Kristen, who thought I owed her something, and by my sister, who I was feeling just a little bit pissed off at. All week I'd known something was up.

Aly had been acting all sketchy while Jared's mouth had remained locked up tight. Neither of them had said a word or thought it'd be wise to give me a warning. Like they didn't have a single clue how seeing her would mess me up.

I had to admit, that was probably the truth. None of them had a single clue. Because over the years, I'd remained just as tight-lipped as the two of them had this week.

It was much easier to live up to my reputation, give myself over to being a lecherous asshole, than admit I'd gone and let myself get crushed up by a tiny girl who shouldn't ever have had the power to turn me inside out.

I turned and glared at my sister, who passed Ella off to Jared. Jared stood right behind Aly, watching me over her shoulder, his eyes digging deep, as if he were trying to search through my thoughts. Aly fretted, looking behind me toward the door, clearly more concerned for her guest who had fled than for me.

That kind of pissed me off, too. "What the hell was she doing here?" It came as a harsh rasp.

"I invited her," Aly shot back on a hard whisper, like she had every right in the world to summon Samantha back into our lives.

I laughed, the sound humorless and mocking. I drove my hands through my hair and looked toward the ceiling. I leveled my eyes back on her. *"You invited her."* I drew out the words, testing out just how angry I was against the roaring in my ears that was screaming at me to run after Samantha, just to get a taste.

Just one more taste and maybe I could wipe all the pent-up memories away. Regrets that I'd always thought I could cover up with the delirious rush of numbness I felt when I was buried in a vacant, willing body. All that greedy nothingness I found myself seeking day after day.

Maybe I could make Samantha that.

A body.

Maybe she'd feel like nothing, just like everyone else.

Maybe then I'd be okay.

Maybe then I could let all this bullshit go.

"Yes, I invited her. I like her and I always have. Do you have a problem with that?"

Sarcastic, incredulous laughter erupted from my throat. "Did you really think I wouldn't have one? Isn't that what you've been hiding this entire week?"

Instantly, remorse creased the corners of my sister's eyes. She stretched out her hand and gently set it on my forearm. I didn't know how badly I was shaking until she tried to still me. "God, I'm sorry, Christopher. Honestly . . . I didn't mean to upset you or try to trick you. You said you weren't coming, so I thought it was safe to invite her. I'd never hurt you on purpose. You have to know that."

Of course I knew that. But that didn't change the fact that Samantha had been here, in my space, a place I couldn't allow her to invade.

"What were you doing talking to her in the first place, Aly?"

She should have known better.

She dropped her gaze to her feet before she looked up at me. She seemed to hesitate, wavering on what she wanted to say, how much she wanted to admit. "She lives here in the neighborhood with her boyfriend. Just a street down. Jared and I ran into her at the store last week and we exchanged numbers. I just . . . I wanted to catch up with her. She told me her brother was sick again, and I'm pretty sure she needs a friend. So I invited her."

Bile burned a hole in my gut. I choked over the acrid taste as it rushed up my throat. I couldn't hear anything beside the fact that her brother was sick again and that she had a boyfriend. That she was living with him. Vile images corrupted my already beat-up mind, and I wanted to claw my eyes out. The idea of someone touching her made my skin crawl.

And Stewart. Memories of his smile swelled as I pinched my eyes closed, that kid . . . that fucking awesome kid who was supposed to be okay.

Goddamn it.

I wanted to punch something. I couldn't do this. I had to get out of here, away from everything I didn't want to face, away from what was supposed to be long forgotten, brushed right under a tidy little rug and trampled underfoot, squashed into nothing.

Obliterated from my mind.

Kristen laughed a bitchy little laugh. "I'm not sticking around for this shit, Christopher. Why you had to drag me over here for this, I don't know, but I'm obviously not welcome and I have better things to do."

I turned back to her. "Then go."

Her eyes narrowed, and something like disappointment filled them before she headed toward the door, mumbling, "Guess you really are an asshole, aren't you." Kristen stormed out the door and slammed it behind her.

There went my ride.

The walls shook, evoking a small cry from a startled Ella.

Damn it.

I turned back to Aly, my attention darting between her, Jared, and Ella, who Jared was now trying to calm, and then to some of the guys from work and Megan staring at me from where they sat out back, all of them getting mixed up in my mess.

I felt on the spot. Caged. Like there was something inside me savage and untamed, fighting to be unleashed. I glared across at Jared. "I need a ride."

Without a second thought, he lifted his chin in consent,

handed Ella back to Aly, and kissed my sister on the top of the head. "I'll be back in a bit."

Aly nodded against his mouth, cradled her daughter to her chest as she looked on with worry and questions and all the shit I didn't want to deal with.

"Sorry," I blurted out, not sure what I was apologizing for, but I was pretty sure that everything that had just gone down had ruined everyone's night.

Especially mine.

"Christopher," Aly attempted, taking a step forward, and I lifted a hand to stop her.

"Not tonight, Aly. You said you were being honest with me. I can accept that. But I have to be honest with you. I'm really pissed off at you right now. You should've told me."

She cringed. There was no question Aly hadn't done it maliciously, because there was nothing in her that was bad. But she had this thing about her, keeping secrets from me when she thought she was protecting me, when she thought she was protecting what was important to her.

I didn't appreciate it when she pulled it when she started hooking up with Jared, and I sure as hell didn't appreciate it now.

Jared clapped me on the shoulder as he passed. "Come on, man, let's get you home."

I hated the guilt that was etched in deep lines across Aly's forehead, so I went to her. As I approached, she lifted her head, and I dropped a swift kiss to the frown marring her forehead, going for the light that I always used, the fuckup who was always laughing because he didn't give a shit about anything.

Tonight it wasn't so easy to pretend.

"Don't worry about it," I tossed out, doing my best to convince her it was nothing when we all so obviously knew it was something. I turned to walk away.

Her soft voice hit me from behind. "There's never a time when I don't worry about you, Christopher."

I slowed but didn't look back. I stepped out into the night. Gusts of wind whipped along the desert floor, stirring up dust and leaves. The high-pitched trill of bugs echoed from the dense trees Jared had planted out front.

I slowed, breathing fresh air in while I fought against the pull begging me to look in the direction I knew Samantha had to have gone, like I was being drawn into the darkness.

That same suffocating tightness got all locked up in my chest, and I wanted to lash out, because I hated feeling this way. Hated feeling out of control. Hated feeling like I was quickly losing my grip.

A long time ago I learned how to be comfortable.

One second of Samantha? There wasn't one cell inside me that was comfortable, every single one of them trembling with some kind of unease. Funny how I'd been the one who was supposed to be *trouble*, the one everyone warned her to stay away from, guarding that sweet little heart from whatever destruction I would bring.

And maybe she should have stayed away.

I knew I wasn't good for her, that I was being selfish taking from something that was so pure and good.

But what I never anticipated was how I should have protected myself from her. I had never expected that she'd come ripping through my life just as fiercely as I'd gone ripping through hers, both of us tearing everything apart, leaving us wrecked.

Jared clicked the fob to his truck. The running lights flashed in the driveway and the locks popped. Climbing in, we slammed the doors shut in unison, the overhead lights dimming slowly, leaving the two of us sitting in a charged silence, staring out the windshield.

"Sorry, man," he finally said, slanting his gaze in my direction. "That was messed up. Should've said something, but really, I didn't think it would matter all that much."

I shrugged, grunted. "It doesn't."

Low, disbelieving laughter rumbled from him, and his mouth twisted up in a wry smile. "Really? Sure doesn't look that way to me."

"Just caught me off guard, that's all."

"*Right.*" Sarcasm dripped from the word, laced with an undertone of sympathy. "I don't think I've seen you so spun up since the night you found me with your sister. And we all know how that ended."

I shot him a warning glare. "Fuck you, man. Don't even start on me. I don't need your two cents when it isn't welcome."

Releasing a low chuckle, he turned over the ignition, and his giant truck rumbled to life. He dug for the stash of gum he kept in the door side pocket and stuffed a piece into his mouth. Dude had gone and given up his bike the day he married my sister, crumbled up his last pack of cigarettes the day Ella was born. Guess he realized he had something to live for, after all.

"Funny, 'cause you never hesitated to give me yours when I didn't ask for it."

Somehow I managed a grin. "That's because you were in dire need of it, my friend. Always going off the deep end, pulling all that emo crap on me. Figured it was on me to intervene."

Jared had been through some major rough patches. We always gave each other a hard time, tearing each other down when in reality we were just building each other up. But not on the serious shit—not until now, when he could look at it all in a different light. I'd gotten into his business because I really fucking cared, wanted him to be better and to have a good life after all the shit he had gone through.

He flashed an almost challenging smile and backed out onto the street, turning down the path I knew she had taken. "So maybe it's my turn to intervene."

"Don't need it, man. I'm just fine, so don't you and my sister go and start scheming up any plans to rescue me, because I'm not in need of rescue, as much as she might think I am."

Aly had been hounding me lately, making comments that it was time to settle down, that I needed to find someone who really made me happy. Apparently she thought that came in the form of her digging up my ghosts.

No, thank you, little sister.

"So what brought you to our house in the first place?"

Blowing out a breath, I shrugged. "Nothin' really. Kristen texted, offered to pick me up before we went out. Thought I'd stop by really quick and get a little taste of normal before I gave myself over to another night of debauchery." I lifted a telling brow, and Jared just shook his head, because he knew exactly what a night of that entailed.

I should've known better than to bring Kristen there, though. That was stupid in itself. I didn't like mixing my worlds, and I sure as hell didn't want Ella growing up watching me parading one girl in just as quickly as I kicked another out.

Guilt throbbed deep in my chest.

That little girl didn't need to witness that shit, didn't need that kind of influence, and the last thing I wanted was for my niece to look at me in a negative light. But as strong as that need was, it hadn't stopped the words from tumbling from my mouth when I'd suggested to Kristen that we stop by my sister's really quick.

Fucking brilliant idea.

Jared headed out onto the main road toward my house. "You could have called."

Even though his eyes were trained ahead, watching the road, I could still feel them searching me, all his questions perfectly posed to get inside my pounding head.

"Do I ever call?" I defended. "I do seem to recall the two of you saying I was welcome anytime."

He hefted out a regretful sigh. "Yeah, you are, and you're always gonna be." Silence fell between us, before he glanced toward me, then shifted his attention right back to the road. "Listen, I'm sorry for the way things went down. Bottom line, we should have said something, whether we thought it mattered or not. The fact that we had to think about it at all should have told us that what we were doing wasn't cool."

Jared pulled to a stop at the curb in front of my house. Headlights splayed out across the pavement ahead of us, and I looked to the side, where the face of my house was engulfed in darkness. Agitation curled through me, and I gripped the door handle, wanting to fucking run from here just as badly as I'd wanted to run from Aly's house, knowing there wasn't one place in this world where I'd find relief for what I was feeling tonight.

Seeing her had ripped those old wounds open wide, leaving me raw. Hearing about her brother?

That *killed* me.

I thought if just one good thing came out of it all, it was that Stewart was finally healthy, that he could live and Samantha could go on. Then maybe I could, too.

But I hadn't. I'd gotten stuck in that moment, lost to that memory of how fucking bad it'd hurt when she'd looked at me that way. Like she was terrified of me. Like she didn't recognize who I was. Then her words confirmed that she believed everything her parents had been spewing my way.

Maybe they'd been right all along.

But all I'd wanted was to prove to her that I was different.

"You okay?" Jared's voice broke into my thoughts, and I shook my head, staring at my lap as I unlatched the door.

"Sure," I said, knowing it sounded just as weak as I felt, and I forced myself from his truck and into the dark.

Overhead light poured down on his face, and I watched as Jared's brow knitted, concern forming a line between his eyes as he looked across at me standing in the open door.

Without a word, I shut it, dragging my feet as I headed for my front door. Jared's engine rumbled as he shifted into gear, seemingly reluctant when he finally drove away.

Inside my little house, I flicked on the light to the main living area. My place was nice, the space decorated in blacks and grays and reds by my mom and my sister, who'd clearly hoped to make it some kind of upscale bachelor pad that still felt cozy and homey.

But I was pretty sure one person couldn't make a home.

Tonight, that loneliness screamed back at me, a crude reminder that I was wholly and utterly alone. It didn't matter how many friends I had or how many girls I took to my bed.

And it was my fault. I knew it. Accepted responsibility for it. But that didn't mean it didn't suck.

I went straight for the updated kitchen. Speckled green-and-black granite graced the countertops, compliments of the new business. The appliances were also new and sleek and for the most part unused. I opened the top cabinet, rummaged around for the bottle of Patrón I had stashed there. I fumbled for a shot glass, filled it to the brim, and tossed it back.

The amber liquid burned a roiling path down my throat, hitting my raw stomach like a fiery stone. Another roll of nausea writhed in my gut.

I felt sick.

Unsettled.

Unsound.

Because everything was wrong.

I slammed another four shots. Taking in deep, even breaths, I braced my hands on the counter and dropped my head between my arms, forcing the alcohol to stay down, before I hauled myself up long enough to stumble down the hall. I flung myself face-first onto my unmade bed, the gray and black and red theme from the living room duplicated here.

In my darkened room, memories spun and spiraled, and as hard as I fought to keep them away, they firmly took root in the forefront of my mind. Tonight, there was no hiding from the expression that had haunted me for years, when every hope I'd ever had for us was erased in the desperation of one incoherent second. When I'd pushed too far and Samantha had cut me loose.

It was the first time I'd truly hated myself, the moment I made Samantha cry, after I'd promised her again and again that I wanted to be the one to dry her tears, to hold her up when she was falling apart. I'd wanted her to need me just as badly as I'd needed her.

But just like her parents had said, like what that asshole Ben had said, I couldn't live up to it, couldn't ever be good enough— even when every piece of me wanted to be.

Wrapping myself around a pillow, I pulled in a deep breath. I could still smell her. All that sweet innocence filled up the well of my lungs. Immediately I was assailed by that picture from earlier tonight, that perfectly wretched instant when her mouth had parted when I'd traced along her jaw, like she was silently begging me to give in to what I so desperately wanted.

I squeezed my eyes tighter.

That mouth.

Every sick part of me had sought out the feel of it through

an endless string of girls, hoping just one of them would make me feel an ounce of what a mere brush of hers did. A physical replacement for the hole Samantha had gouged out right at the center of my chest, a festering pool feeding the asshole I'd let myself become.

But that had always been the problem.

With Samantha, it had never been just physical.

SEVEN

Christopher

Early September, Seven Years Earlier

Soft moonlight filtered through the trees. Above, a gentle, cool breeze rustled through the branches, and the limbs lightly scratched along the eves of Samantha's slumbering house. Inside, all the windows were darkened, shadows playing across the walls where I knew she slept.

Like I was drawn, I edged forward, my heart racing and my insides curling.

No matter how hard I tried, I couldn't shake her. And God knew, I'd been trying.

Samantha wasn't close to being my type.

She was too shy. Too sweet. Too good.

I always went for easy and the promise of a good time.

Not for complicated and complex, not for someone who came with worry and concern and effort.

Yet here I was, making an *effort*.

In the dark, I dug the toe of my tattered-up Vans shoe into the desert floor. When I unearthed a tiny rock, I leaned down and picked it up. Running the smooth, small pebble between the pads of my fingers, I hesitated, searching inside myself for some kind of resolve, for a measure of courage—the courage to just go and leave this innocent girl alone.

Funny, it was the first time in a long time that I'd had the urge to do the honorable thing. The crazy thing was, I wasn't quite sure what that meant—walking away or moving forward.

Somewhere deep inside of me, a foreign feeling fluttered in protest.

Moving forward felt like the only option.

Sucking in a breath, I flicked the rock. It pinged against her windowpane before it ricocheted back and skittered along the dirt. Impatiently, I waited, shifting my feet as I yanked at my unruly black hair.

God.

What was I doing?

Whatever it was, I couldn't stop.

Patience wasn't exactly my strong suit, so when there was no movement after thirty seconds, I grabbed another stone and tossed it at her window. This time a little harder than the last.

The anxious breath I was holding blew from my lungs when the drapes suddenly parted at the side. Moonlight glinted against the glass, and I could barely make out the subdued lines of her silhouette as she squinted out into the night. Taking two steps forward, I slowly revealed myself, locking eyes with the girl I couldn't get off my mind.

What it was about her, I didn't know.

So maybe patience wasn't my forte. But confidence? I wore it around like a second skin, though even I was wise enough to know that arrogant way came with the assurance that I really didn't have all that much to lose.

When not a whole lot matters to you, the chances you take come with little risk.

Somehow tonight, standing there, watching her in the thick silence of the night sky, I knew I was putting myself on the line.

Everywhere inside of me, I knew it *mattered*.

My chest tightened, and I clenched my fists at my sides and tried to make sense of this girl. One I shouldn't be giving a second thought to, but instead, she seemed to be taking up residence in every single one.

Samantha's window screeched when she cracked it an inch. Cringing, she slowed, carefully pushing it open the rest of the way. She braced herself on the ledge, her blond hair falling around her face and brushing down over the spaghetti straps of the white tank top she wore.

Desire curled in my stomach and I bit back a groan.

Fuuuck.

She was so sexy it physically hurt.

"What are you doing here?" she asked on a hard whisper, obviously straining to focus on me.

In a helpless shrug, I lifted my hands out in front of me. "Couldn't sleep."

Speculation and worry narrowed her blue eyes. Still, there was no mistaking the flare of excitement that blazed in their depths at finding me.

"Are you crazy? You're going to get me in trouble," she hissed quietly, though she was chewing at the hint of a smile on that pretty little mouth.

And that's really what I wanted. To kiss her. To see if that perfect mouth that reminded me of a silky red Christmas bow made of candy could possibly feel as good—taste as good—as I imagined it would.

Ha. Get her in trouble?

Without a doubt, I was the one who was in trouble.

Deep trouble.

I kept my footsteps light as I closed the distance, stopping less than a foot away from her open window. I yanked at her hand, making her gasp and lurch forward. When I placed her palm flat across my thundering chest, I wondered if she could feel the turmoil she'd spun up inside of me.

I fought off all the intense feelings and instead quirked her a flirty grin, that same half smirk with a wry flash of teeth that always won me what I wanted.

And what I wanted was her.

I pressed her hand closer, the heat of her palm burning me through. "Crazy for you."

A rush of redness blossomed on the snowy flesh of Samantha's neck, flaring hot as it headed north and flooded her cheeks. Still, she rolled her eyes and attempted to yank her hand away.

Silly girl. I wasn't about to let her go.

"Cheesy words aren't going to win me over, Christopher."

"Then what *will* win you over?"

I'd been chasing her for the last two weeks and I couldn't seem to catch her. Ever since the day I'd intervened in the altercation between her and Jasmine. It wasn't as if I wouldn't have broken it up anyway, even if Jasmine's vitriol hadn't been aimed at the same girl who stirred up something foreign inside of me every time she breezed by, the mere passing of her presence like she was washing me in something good when I always seemed to be delving into the bad.

Jasmine was a bitch. Through and through. Not for a second

did I mind putting the slut in her place. I did it happily and with a huge-ass grin on my face.

What I'd been unprepared for was the surge of protectiveness that had shot through me when I'd rolled into the hallway and found Samantha backed into a corner. The welling of possessiveness that filled up all the dead space inside me the second I'd tucked her against my side.

Still, it didn't matter what I did or what kind of move I made. Samantha was skittish to the extreme. Shy and strong. And apparently that combo didn't work so well for a guy like me. In what'd seemed like some sort of miracle, I'd convinced her to sit with me twice at lunch, and once she'd gone as far as letting me walk her home from school. But even then she'd been distant, all on guard, with a fortified ten-foot wall barricading her, like she was pretty sure all of my motives were ulterior and she was determined to shut me out.

Probably showing up at her house in the middle of the night wouldn't convince her otherwise. But hey, a guy had to try.

She frowned. "What are you really doing here, Christopher?"

I dropped the facade, because around her, I couldn't seem to front it. My voice lowered in sincerity. "I just wanted to see you. That's it."

Her frown deepened, but it seemed more in confusion than anything else. "Why, Christopher? Why me?"

"Because I like you," I chanced, going for honest, because I realized I didn't have all that much more to give.

She hesitated before she huffed out a breath of surrender. "Hold on a second."

She disappeared behind the drape. A sharp, short gust of wind sent it billowing into her room, stretching out, like it was seeking her in the same way I was.

Relief hit me hard when she popped up, now wearing a black

tank top over the flimsy piece of material she'd been sporting earlier, the white straps still peeking out from under the scoop neck. She hoisted herself up and over the windowsill, a second's distress tripping her up when she landed on her feet on the ground. She glanced behind her, then warily back to me.

"My dad's gonna kill you if he finds you out here with me."

"I'm willing to take the risk."

"You haven't met my dad."

Grabbing her hand, I hauled her back through her front yard and onto the sidewalk, getting her away from the possibility of prying eyes, all the while relishing the feel of her hand in mine. I gave it a squeeze. "No, you're right, I haven't, because you haven't invited me over." I gave her a teasing hard look. "Maybe we should fix that."

She barked out a laugh, then clamped her free hand over her mouth, her blue eyes going wide. She jerked her attention back over her shoulder and toward her house, looking for any sort of movement her outburst had stirred within. She turned back to me, those stormy eyes going wild, as if she couldn't believe for one second she'd just pulled this stunt, couldn't believe she was getting away with it, couldn't believe she was out here with me.

Guess I was pretty surprised myself. Part of me expected her to tell me to get lost.

"Come on, let's get out of here," I urged, breaking into a run, dragging her behind me. At the end of her street, Samantha started laughing. This uncontained, near-hysterical sound that bubbled up from her stomach, only to grow as it was freed.

Like maybe something inside of Samantha had been freed.

"Oh my gosh . . ." She bit down on the soft flesh of her bottom lip, the biggest smile bursting from under it. "You really are crazy." She shook her head. "I can't believe I'm doing this."

"It's not like I'm whisking you off to elope or somethin'."

She laughed again. This time it wasn't so carefree. "Oh, this is worse . . . way worse. Me sneaking out in the middle of the night with a boy?" She shuddered. "You don't even know."

"Then tell me."

Mellowing, she leaned into my arm as we walked under the cover of night. We rounded the corner and headed up the next street. All the while I kept her hand secured in mine. "I'm not even allowed to date, Christopher. If I got caught sneaking out with you? I'd probably be grounded for the rest of my life."

"You've never had a boyfriend?"

"Nope." She peered up at me, and the moonlight lit up her face in a way that made my breath get locked up right in the center of my throat.

God. She was pretty. Beautiful, really, because I was coming to understand the difference. Beauty radiated, and it was surrounding her like some kind of halo of light.

"Don't you already know that, though? . . . The stuff those girls say about me?" There was both sadness and defiance in it, the way her voice hardened the slightest fraction as she slowed.

"I don't listen to a word that pack of bitches say, Samantha. Not. A. Word. You shouldn't, either, because everything that comes out of their ignorant mouths is nothin' but bullshit and lies."

She flinched at the harshness of my tone before she settled her weight a little deeper into my arm, like maybe she found some sort of comfort in the outright hate I felt for all of them.

Especially Jasmine. Should've known better than to have gotten mixed up with her.

"Whether they're right or not, that doesn't change who I am," she emphasized, so clearly trying to convey something to me, something that was already so obvious.

"Think I already have a pretty good handle on who you are, Samantha."

"Do you?" She looked to the ground, letting me guide her across the street and into the family park that took up the space between our two neighborhoods. Here, the grass grew thick, and tall, lush trees lined the lot, all of it well kept, mowed and shaped right up to the sand that filled in the playground.

Not a soul was around, and I'd be lying if I said I hadn't been dying to get her alone.

And not for the reasons I knew everyone would place over my head like some kind of presumed verdict. I wasn't half as bad as everyone chalked me up to be, but I didn't waste my time trying to deny it, because God knew I was guilty of the other half.

We stopped at the fringe of the playground. Samantha gravitated to me, coming to face me, her expression shifting so fast I couldn't latch onto one emotion. I lifted our hands between us. Samantha gasped and I felt her pulse pick up when I pinned them between our chests.

I tilted my head, searching the intensity in those sincere blue eyes. "I know you're supersmart. I know you're sweet and kind. I know you'd go to the end of the earth to protect and defend your family, because I've seen it myself."

With my free hand, I rubbed my thumb along the hollow beneath her eye, and her mouth parted on a sigh as I stared down at this girl who was undoing something inside of me. "I know you're sad."

I saw it there. There was no missing it. And fuck if it didn't make me sad, too.

A choked sound strained in her throat, and she reached up and wrapped her hand around my wrist, like she couldn't allow me to get any closer but she refused to let me go. "I am," she admitted through a pained whisper. "So sad."

"Your brother?"

I knew all about that. The whole school did. We might live in a big city, but that didn't mean the gossip didn't fly here just as fast as it did in some small-time town.

She nodded. "I can't stand it, Christopher. Seeing him that way. Hurting and scared. It kills me."

Emotion ran hard and fast in my veins. I pulled her into my arms, her face buried in my chest while I just held her. I pressed a tender kiss to the top of her head. "I'm sorry."

She didn't say anything, just pulled away, and I knew she was warring with something inside of herself when she kept her attention on me as she slowly wandered around the playground. She ran her fingers over the metal chains of the swings, pitching them in a slight sway. The whole time I stared at her, wondering just how hard and fast this girl could cause me to fall.

At the last swing in the row of four, she took hold of both chains, her face framed in them as she pinned her honest gaze on me from across the lot. "You scare me, Christopher."

"Why?"

Rough laughter ripped from her, and she dropped her head, shaking it, before she cut her stare back up at me. "Because I don't know how to handle someone like you. More than that, I don't want to be one of those girls."

I didn't want her to be, either.

Didn't she get that?

"You could *never* be one of those girls, Samantha. I promise you that. I just want to be with you. And yeah, I know I have a reputation, but that doesn't mean I earned all of it."

Her brows dropped down in a probing scowl. "What about what Jasmine said the other day? About . . ." She trailed off, clutching the chains tighter.

I swallowed over the lump that suddenly got lodged at the base of my throat. "That was true," I admitted.

Thing was, my fame had preceded itself, and what Jasmine had tossed out was as far as I'd ever let things go. I never confirmed or denied any of the rumors because it wasn't anyone's fucking business who I'd been with, even if I hadn't really *been* with anyone.

Frustration infiltrated her long, hard blink. "That's what I'm talking about. I don't know what you want from me . . . because if that's it? You're after the wrong person."

Did I want her? Yeah. For sure. I was a sixteen-year-old boy. No one could blame me. I *wanted* her. Really wanted her. This wasn't about me getting my cock sucked by some girl I could barely stand. This was different.

"I want whatever you're willing to give me."

Releasing the swings, she moved to the slide and slowly began ascending the steps, like each one she put her foot to answered another question posed somewhere in the recesses of her mind. At the top, she just stood there, hanging on to the handles while she stared down at me. The moonlight had her all lit up again, showcasing all her modesty, maybe showing off the woman who wanted to work her way out.

Edging forward, I waited at the bottom of the slide.

She lowered herself, gave a little shove, and slid down. I stopped her descent at the bottom, her back pressed into the metal. I grasped the sides, holding myself up, my nose an inch from hers as I hovered in her space. Her eyes were doing that wild thing again, a raging sea that churned with all that shyness, but flamed with bold strikes of courage, a storm that didn't know which way to turn.

"Anyone ever kiss you before, Samantha?" I murmured low, letting my nose do a little exploring along her jaw.

She shook her head no.

"Didn't think so," I whispered, before I took a chance I was pretty damned sure was worth taking, and brushed my mouth against hers. And was I ever right. She tasted like sugar and all things sweet, like a spoonful of pure honey. A remedy.

Her kiss was every kind of timid, cautious in her inexperience, but it didn't take a whole lot to convince me that this kind of kiss was my favorite.

I let her get accustomed to me, to the way my lips pressed and pulled, opened then closed over hers, just savoring this second. When a little moan rumbled up her throat, I let my tongue graze along the rim of her bottom lip. In a blink, her hands were in my hair, desperate to draw me nearer, and she was suddenly kissing me like that storm had taken an abrupt turn and hit land.

I kissed her back, going for soft and sincere, but I was unable to hold back the quick lashes of my tongue against hers.

I wanted to eat her whole.

My hands cinched down on the metal. It cut into my skin, but there wasn't a chance I was letting go because there was no way I was pushing her, and I was pretty sure if my hands got free they were gonna have a mind of their own. No way would I let my actions even skate in the direction of affirming the fears that had been keeping her back.

The bad news was I was gonna have a case of near-fatal blue balls for days. But there wasn't a chance in this godforsaken world that I'd go looking for a cure for this growing issue in someone like Jasmine. Not anymore. Not ever again.

Turned out my mom was right, after all, encouraging me to hold out even when I might not want to, because there was going to be a day I wished I had.

Today was that day.

And I knew it down deep. It didn't matter at all that we were nothing but kids. Didn't matter that she was scared and I was stupid.

Nothing else mattered except for the way this felt.

Finally I pulled back. Samantha licked her swollen lips, then let go of a lazy smile and traced her fingers down my face.

"So that might have won me over, crazy boy."

I coughed out a laugh.

Yeah.

Crazy.

All kinds of crazy for her.

EIGHT

Samantha

I knocked lightly at the door, cracking it open at the same time. "Stewart?" I called quietly.

I peeked inside to find my little brother asleep in the middle of his small bed, on his side and facing away. At the sound of my voice, he slowly stirred, groaning as he rolled over. He blinked incoherently before he sat up and rubbed his sleepy eyes. When he dropped his hands, he quirked up the most radiant smile. "Samantha."

It didn't matter how terrible I was feeling inside, there was no stopping my smile, which spread out to match his. Stewart was my happy place.

I pushed his door open the rest of the way and stepped inside and set the bags of three different kinds of fast food down on his messy desk. I'd made a mad dash, doing rounds through the drive-throughs of all his old favorite places.

Taking the four steps to bring me to the side of his bed, I

dropped a swift kiss to his temple, ran my hand over the top of his bald head. "Hey there, Stew. Sorry to wake you."

He didn't hesitate to lean into me, hugging me fiercely around the waist, or as fiercely as Stewart could in his weakened state. I wrapped my arms around his frail shoulders. I was both swept away in sadness and bolstered in spirit.

My little brother just had something about him, something magical and kind, as if he understood things long before they happened, as if he knew when someone needed an extra smile or a tighter hug.

He must have known it now, because he held on to me for the longest time while I clung to him.

"Nah," he mumbled softly, "I'm just bored out of my mind. I don't have anything better to do, so sleep it is."

I winced, knowing it was only half the truth. On the phone this morning, Mom had told me his last round of chemo had really knocked him flat, zapping him of all his energy, and he'd either been sick in the bathroom or curled up in bed for the last three days.

He released me, and I edged away, but not far enough away that I couldn't cup his cheek. I searched his face. "How are you feeling? I mean, really feeling? Not what you tell your doctor and Mom and everyone else you don't want fretting over you."

A short chuckle rocked from him, and for a second, his blue eyes gleamed with mischief. "Like shit."

"Hey, watch your mouth," I warned through a giggle.

He pressed his lips into a thin line, trying not to laugh out-right. "What? You asked for the truth, and the truth is that I feel like shit. There's no other word for it."

I knew I sheltered him too much, treated him as if he were years younger than his seventeen. But it was so hard to let that little boy go, because he'd missed so much of his childhood that it seemed impossible he was almost eighteen.

"We need to get you past that, don't we?"

His face fell a little, flattening into something too bleak for my taste. "Hope so."

I forced a bigger smile. "Know so," I promised.

He reached up and squeezed my hand, which was still on his face, a silent conversation transpiring between the two of us. I knew he was scared and just all around sick of being sick, but he also didn't want to waste his days complaining about it. We both smiled knowing smiles, before we seemed to let go of a heavy breath, putting all of this aside.

Which would have been a whole lot easier for me if I wasn't still reeling from what had happened last night. If I wasn't feeling raw and wrong and completely unsettled. Inhaling, I made a valiant attempt at tucking all of those unbearable thoughts into the quiet corners of my mind. Because this was Stewart's time, and I didn't want to waste it on my stupidity and foolishness, on that reckless and impulsive move I'd made that set me on a collision course with a man I would have done well to have long forgotten.

I gestured to the greasy bags sitting on his desk. "Are you hungry?"

He shrugged. "Maybe later. Mom made me drink one of those milk shake things a couple hours ago. Not sure I can force anything else down right now."

I nodded, though I hated to hear it.

He rested his elbows on his knees, his legs crisscrossed in front of him. "So tell me something... anything... I need gossip... drama. I'm about to lose my mind here. It's pretty sad when I have to live vicariously through my twenty-three-year-old sister, who acts more like a forty-seven-year-old crazy cat lady."

My mouth puckered in offense, and his deep laughter ricocheted around his room.

"You are such a punk," I accused through a tease, before I went for a look of sophisticated arrogance. "I'll have you know I went to the store three times this week. And I drank an entire bottle of wine. *By myself.*"

Did I leave out all the stuff about Aly? About Christopher? About how incredibly pathetic and sad and heartbroken the whole situation made me feel? Yes. Yes. And yes.

I wasn't about to go there with him. It wasn't prudent and it most definitely wasn't important.

Or at least that's what I was trying to convince myself.

"Really . . . three whole trips to the store, huh? You are such a rebel." He considered me when I fidgeted, and his blue eyes narrowed. "You sure there isn't something more exciting you want to share with me?"

"No. Of course not," I hurled out way too fast.

In an attempt to hide the cringe that pinched my face with that blatant lie, I turned away from him and crossed my arms over my chest as I studied the rows and rows of wood shelves that were bracketed on his walls. All of them showcased his prize possessions, trinkets, memorabilia, and character dolls from all his favorite video games and books. My chest tightened when my attention landed on his most cherished keepsake of all—the signed copy of his favorite childhood book.

I'd never forget the day it'd arrived in a padded package all the way from the UK. Mom and Dad had both been skeptical when a deliveryman had shown up needing a signature for something that was from out of the country and addressed to Stewart.

Forever I'd cherish the expression that had taken over Stewart's face when he'd ripped into that box and came to realize the significance of what he held, that it was signed to him with an inscription telling him to *Never stop believing in magic.*

It wasn't just happiness.

It was a deep-seated joy, something so precious to him that it'd stolen his breath and sent silent tears streaming down his face.

It was a survivor's prize.

God, I was so thankful he'd been given something so special, the gift so thoughtful that it'd crumbled the last bits of my resistance.

After I'd asked around, Ben had admitted he'd been the one who had it sent, and it was that book that had finally won me over.

"What's up with you today?" The concerned voice shook me from my faraway thoughts, and I looked over at Stewart, who was watching me with too-keen eyes. That was the problem when you were this close with someone. It was really hard keeping secrets from them.

"Have my Nerd Lair powers taken you hostage and that too-smart brain of yours is being held captive in another realm? Because you definitely aren't acting like yourself."

I coughed over the abrupt laugh that found its way out, because only Stewart would name his room after one of his favorite games. Apparently I had been sucked away to another realm. A realm that had always been a fantasy, impossible, wrong, because Christopher had always been wrong for me.

Bad for me, really.

That knowledge didn't really matter, though, did it?

I'd already known the end result of hanging out with Aly. Had wanted it even, somehow thinking that seeing Christopher again would shut that chapter in my life that had never seemed to close.

He'd left something gaping inside of me, and stupidly I thought seeing him would close it.

I should have known it would only rip it open a little wider and pour on a fresh layer of pain, one that was blended with a whole ton of confusion and mixed with zero clarity. His words had been a harsh contradiction to the temptation of his touch, and every single thing about the encounter had left my head spinning and my heart hurting.

Oh, and my body burning.

Uncontrolled redness flared to my cheeks.

So intense I could feel it heating up my insides.

That was the reaction I'd hated most, that Christopher could control me with just a brush of his hand. *Never* again would I allow him that, the power to sway me physically.

I knew better than that.

I *was* better than that.

Ben's face flashed like an errant bolt of lightning in my mind, striking me in the most loyal place in my conscience. Lying next to him last night had seemed unbearable, because it was the last place I'd wanted to be. When he came stumbling into our room after two this morning, he'd rained a trio of sloppy, drunken kisses to my cheek, my jaw, and then my mouth.

Guilt had almost cut me in two, and I hadn't even done anything wrong.

I bit back a bitter laugh. I could just keep telling myself that and continue pretending it wasn't a lie. Because Ben still had no clue where I'd been or what I'd been up to, had no idea that another man had again broken my heart when he should have had no dominance over me to do it. He had no idea that I'd muffled my cries in my pillow as I mourned someone there was no question I wanted, one who with the slightest touch had left me bound by unseen chains, burning from the inside out, wishing for his touch even when I knew that touch would ruin me.

Blatant worry screwed Stewart's face up in concern. "Seriously . . . what's up, Samantha? You're acting weird."

I lifted both shoulders to my ears, held them for too long before I dropped them helplessly. "Just tired and trying to get settled into a new routine with work."

"I thought you loved your job."

"I do."

"And you look like you have enough energy that you could run a marathon."

I huffed in frustration. He was too perceptive for his own good. Or maybe for my own good.

"It's nothing. I'm fine."

His smile was smug. "You're about the worst liar I've ever met." He leaned back against his headboard. "But if you don't want to tell me what's bothering you, that's fine. I'm here for you whenever you do, though. I mean, if you can take all my awesomeness and profound advice."

I grabbed a pillow and chucked it at him. His boisterous laughter was unrestrained, and he deflected my attack by lifting his arm up to protect his face. Cautiously, he let his arm drop. He grinned victoriously at me when he found me unarmed, again radiating all that beauty and positivity, a lightness that shouldn't be there after everything he'd been through.

There were few things that made me as happy as seeing him that way.

My movements were slow as I went to him, lay down at his side, and curled up next to him. I rested my head on his shoulder. "I know you're always here for me, Stewart. You're the best. You know that, don't you?"

He squeezed me around the shoulders, and there was no

mistaking the hoarseness that came with his tease. "Of course I know I'm the best. You really *are* lucky to have such a great brother."

It was funny, because you'd think my standing Sunday dates with Stewart were meant for him, that I was sacrificing my day off to spend time with him, to keep him company and to keep his spirits up. But right then, closed in the quiet of his tiny room, surrounded by collector toys, game consoles, the walls smeared in childish posters, I was pretty sure it was him who was comforting me.

I pulled into the driveway, parking my blue Escape next to Ben's large SUV. I situated the sunshade against the windshield, giving myself a little pep talk before I went back inside.

Yeah, last night had been a mistake, but maybe it was one that had to be made, a lesson that needed to be learned as an adult and not through the eyes of a sixteen-year-old girl. I'd told myself before I went that I just needed to *know*.

Now I did.

Christopher was still an asshole, mean right down to his very core, all too happy to play with me until he squeezed the life right out of me. I hadn't misunderstood. He was just as vicious now as he had been the night he'd completely ripped me apart.

Images slammed me in quick succession—his face, his hands, that body. Brighter than all of them were his eyes. He was devastating, so beautiful it hurt to look at him. That hadn't changed, either. The years had only made it worse.

But all of that would have to be ignored if I was to focus on the moral of the story.

And that was that I had to stay away from Christopher.

I shook my head through my pathetic laughter as I got out

of the car and headed for the front door. *Right*. He'd made it
clear enough he didn't want anything to do with me, anyway.

How absurd was it that his words had stung worse than him
flaunting himself with that slutty girl?

Ludicrous. Ridiculous.

Downright dangerous.

I fisted my hands and marched right through my unlocked
front door. It was quiet inside, the shimmery drapes pulled wide,
allowing the early afternoon sun to slant through the large window, pouring natural light and warmth into the open family
room.

"Ben?" I called. Metal clattered against wood when I dropped
my keys onto the small table under the window, and I slipped my
flip-flops from my feet.

"In the office," he hollered back from down the hall. In reality the *office* was a glorified man cave, replete with blackout curtains on the windows and a leather couch that cost five times my
monthly salary.

In the office meant he was busy, scouring the Internet,
stalking Facebook, or playing a game, all of which took up a
huge chunk of his day.

Good.

That meant I had some time to clear my head and put myself back together.

Before I had even crossed the room, the doorbell rang. I
froze. I stood there, considering not answering it, because somehow I already knew who it would be.

The ring was followed by a soft knock, like the person
standing on the other side of my door was asking for entrance
with a genuine *please*.

A sound of resignation left me, and I turned back to the
door, guarded as I drew it open. Aly stood there with her fist

halfway to the door, and it was pretty clear her next knock was going to come with much more force than the last. Beside her on the stoop, Ella was all tucked and protected from the sun in the comfortable shade of her fancy stroller, lost in the sweet abyss of sleep.

"Samantha," Aly whispered on a sigh. It was pure relief all bundled up with a silent apology.

"Hey," I said, chewing at my lip, not knowing exactly what to say or do. The sane part of me told me to tell her to go away, to just leave me alone and let bygones be bygones instead of dredging up the past, because I didn't think I could handle feeling this way much longer. From the moment I spotted Aly in that store little more than a week ago, a disturbance had settled over my life, my axis shifted and my foundation rocked.

I needed to get back on solid ground.

The insane part of me widened the door.

She fidgeted, dipping her chin as she inclined her head. Those same deep emerald eyes—eyes just like his—that had hounded me in my thoughts and chased me in my dreams since I'd run from her house the night before were doing their best to get a read on me. "I was just in the neighborhood," she finally said, her voice cracking as she went for a joke, and Aly split a pleading, hopeful smile.

And there was nothing I could do. Soft, affectionate laughter trickled up and out.

"You were, huh?"

She swayed innocently, widening unassuming eyes as she went for it. "Figured since I was already nearby and I *just* happened to notice your car in the driveway, not that I was keeping tabs or anything, I should stop in and say hi since I wasn't sure when I'd be in the area again."

My heart did that erratic thing, that quivering tremor that

stoked the anticipation of impending change, a feeling that rang as a promised warning that I knew clearly I should heed.

I *knew* I should.

Instead I stepped out into the heat and pulled the door shut behind me, all the while berating myself for once again being drawn to Christopher's sister. I couldn't help it. There was something good and whole about her, something lacking in all my other acquaintances, something that made me sure she really cared.

Somehow, even under all these nasty circumstances, I knew she was truly my friend.

Sunshine poured down from overhead, and Aly lifted her face toward it, drawing in a deep breath of air, before she leveled the most earnest expression on me. "I am so sorry, Samantha."

Her apology made all the chaos inside me rise to the top. Moisture grew in my eyes, and I did my best to blink it back, but it was no use. I found myself swatting away the tears that slipped down my cheeks.

"You don't have to apologize, Aly. I knew what I was getting myself into, going over to your house." I glanced behind me at the latched door, dropping my confession to a whisper. "Part of me wanted to see him again. I just didn't know it was going to hurt so badly. It was a mistake. One I'm willing to take responsibility for."

One I wouldn't repeat.

She flinched. "Don't say that."

"How could it be anything else?"

But I guessed Aly couldn't have known the way things transpired, the cruelness Christopher seemed to get off on, his words meant to bite and sting.

The guy was a straight-up pig. A deviant asshole.

"Everyone there last night loved you, Samantha."

A mean streak of pettiness pounded through my veins, and I crossed my arms over my chest. "Everyone except for your brother and his girlfriend."

The second I spouted it, I felt bad, because that wasn't me. That was part of the problem. Christopher fueled unnatural things in me, a passion that was too strong. So strong it made me bitter and weak.

I hated him for it.

"Maybe," she admitted with an unsure lift of her shoulders. "I honestly have no clue what was going through my brother's head last night except for the fact that he was just as upset as you were."

Flustered air shot from my nose. "I seriously doubt that. Your brother doesn't care anything about me."

Aly scoffed. "I know Christopher very well, and I can most definitely assure you that he *cares*."

A dispute was on the tip of my tongue, where I let it die, because there was no sense in arguing what I already knew to be the truth. My voice softened. "None of it matters, Aly. Like I told you before, what's done is done. I never should have gone to your house. Your brother broke my heart." I fisted my hand at my chest, allowing myself to be the most honest I'd been in a long time. *"He broke me.* I never should have acted like it was okay to set foot back into his world."

"But what if I want you in my world?"

"Last night Christopher made it perfectly clear he doesn't want me anywhere near you."

And for my own health, I knew I shouldn't be anywhere near him.

It seemed to be anger that pursed Aly's lips. She shifted her feet, her words hard and pleading. "That's not Christopher's decision to make, Samantha. I like you. My entire family likes you,

and so do my friends." I went to protest, and she cut me off. "And
don't say Christopher doesn't. You know I'm not talking about
him." She shrugged as if the rest of the circumstances didn't
matter. "I want us to be friends . . ." Her tone tightened with
strain. "It feels like we need to be." Sadly she shook her head.
"And honestly I don't know how to make that work if Christopher's not a part of that equation, too."

I blinked through my confusion. This time it was my turn
to try to get a read on her. "Let me get this straight. You're
asking me into your life, knowing by doing so I'm making the
conscious decision to get in your brother's line of fire?"

"You have a boyfriend, Samantha . . . who you're *living* with.
Obviously you've moved on. But it's also obvious both you and
Christopher are harboring a ton of resentment toward each
other. I'm asking you to make an effort to let that bad blood go
so both of you can truly move on."

I choked over bitter laughter. "Let it go?"

That was impossible.

Glancing to her feet, she seemed to contemplate what to say,
then lifted her sincere gaze back to me. "I'm not asking you to
hang out with him. But I *am* asking for you to hang out with me
and be okay if that sometimes means he might be there."

This was crazy.

"I don't understand why you care so much, Aly." There was
no outrage in the question. I just needed a straight answer.

"There's just something nagging at me not to let this go.
Last night, I couldn't sleep, worrying about you and how to handle this, because I felt like I lied to you after I invited you over
and promised Christopher wouldn't be there. I felt your good-bye
last night, and I know you meant it to be permanent."

Intently she stared at me, as if she was trying to get me to
see something that was so clear to her. "I have to believe there's

a reason for all of this . . . you living less than a minute away from me. Don't you?"

"Maybe it's a coincidence." A terrible, brutal, breathtaking coincidence.

An ironic smile spread over her too-pretty face. "No. I don't believe in those."

Neither did I. But that didn't mean fate was always on my side.

"This morning Jared and I had a long talk about this." She paused before she drew in a deep breath and continued. "I'm *inviting* you to come back to my house next weekend."

That dreaded anticipation balled up in my chest, making it difficult to breathe.

"Jared's little sister, Courtney, is coming to spend the week with us to celebrate her sixteenth birthday. And before you ask, yes, Christopher will probably be there. But so will the rest of our friends and family, and we want to make this the best birthday Courtney has ever had. We'd love for you to be a part of it. It would mean a lot to me if you were there."

God, for a second I was wondering if Aly might be just as manipulative as her brother, luring me in with kind words formulated to sway my trusting heart.

I felt guilty just for thinking it. Aly was sincere, even if she might be blind, too good to see the bad in her brother. She struck me as the type who refused to see the negative, believing instead that there had to be some sort of positive in every person, in every situation, even when it was so objectively obvious there was nothing there worth redeeming.

I used to see things the same way.

Until her brother crushed all my belief.

"Please, Samantha . . . just give it a chance. If it turns out you and Christopher can't stand being in the same room together, then we'll keep our visits to coffee and, if you'll have me, here at your house."

I chewed at the inside of my lower lip, willing myself to form the correct response.

No.

Instead I said, "I can't handle your brother treating me the way he did last night. It was horrible, Aly."

"I'll talk to him. I promise I won't let that happen again."

And I found myself uttering that fateful word again. "Fine." And again, I wanted to run, to escape inside and never have opened the door.

But what I wanted most was the chance for a redo. To get that answer I'd wanted, because the only thing last night's encounter had done was left me confused.

God, I had to be completely out of my mind.

She threw her arms around me and hugged me. She rocked us as if she couldn't get me close enough. "I always liked you." Her statement was almost urgent.

"I always liked you, too," I whispered hoarsely.

A gust of disquiet whipped straight through me. This time I didn't feel just unbalanced and lost. I felt as if I'd been pushed over the ledge and was in a free fall.

Aly pulled back, all traces of heaviness erased, and she squeezed my upper arms in her hands. "See . . . we were supposed to meet. Target has everything . . . lost friends included."

I giggled in spite of myself, wiped away some of the residual tears I could feel drying on my face with the back of my hand. "You're ridiculous. You know that?"

Deep laughter rolled in her chest. "You have no idea."

Then she took a step back, her brow lifting in question as she released the brake on the stroller. "Saturday?"

COME TO ME RECKLESSLY

It wasn't so much a question as she was looking for confirmation.

"Saturday."

She swiveled the stroller, ambling casually down the sidewalk.

I watched them until they disappeared, listening to the soft incantation of Aly's voice as she quietly sang to her daughter.

On a weighted exhale, I opened the door and stepped back inside.

Ben stood at the end of the hall. "Who was that?"

"A salesman."

The lie left me before I had the chance to think it through.

Ben harshly shook his head. "You'd think those assholes would get a clue from the NO SOLICITING sign in the window."

I shrugged. "It wasn't a big deal."

"That's because you're too unassuming."

I wanted to laugh. *Unassuming* didn't come close to describing it.

He raked an easy hand over his head. "Let's get out of here and get something to eat. I'm starving."

"Sure."

I was still feeling antsy, and getting out of the house was the best idea Ben had had in a long time. I slipped on my flip-flops, grabbed my keys and bag, and headed out to my car. I slid into the driver's seat, because Ben preferred for me to drive so he could mess with his phone.

Once we were both settled, I turned over the ignition and backed out onto the street, carefully easing through the quiet neighborhood and rounding the corner. I did my best not to bring any attention to Aly, who was still two houses away from her own, the large wheels of the stroller eating up the sidewalk as she took long strides behind it.

Not that he'd notice anyway, the man absorbed in his phone.

Maybe it was time he did notice. Because if I was going next week, then Ben was going with me. I was finished with Christopher making me a liar. He'd always had me lying to those who mattered most.

Not anymore.

A gasp flew from me and I slammed on the brakes. A big monster of a truck squealed to a stop when the driver did the same, and we came to a screeching halt less than a foot away from each other, the truck pointed at the front left quarter panel of my car. I'd been too occupied with my own thoughts to notice the stop sign that intersected the street running along Aly's and the main one that led out of the neighborhood. I'd almost hit this truck, which could probably run right over the top of my hood.

Stupid.

That gasp died in my throat when I locked eyes with the driver—emerald eyes that sparked wild and fierce before they darkened to a dangerous obsidian, deep enough to match the ebony of his hair, harsh enough to make my heart thrum savagely at my ribs.

"Would you watch where you're driving, Samantha?" Ben scolded, shaking his head as he turned right back to his phone. "I swear to God, you're the worst driver I have ever ridden with. Why I even let you drive, I don't know."

I gulped down my shock and completely ignored Ben's assholery, and instead focused on trying to quiet my thundering heart. I pressed down on the accelerator when Christopher didn't seem to be going anywhere. His hard stare was fixed on me, clearly urging me to make the first move and go.

As if he were again demanding that I get out of his life.

A downpour of confusion rained over my head when he refused to break away from my eyes, like he'd done last night, keeping me trapped in this tangled web of a man who I knew would suck the life right out of me.

I drove around his truck, both of our expressions stretched wide in blatant shock and outright hatred, flexing in something else I didn't want to recognize. Something that spread like a wildfire beneath the surface of my skin.

I tore my eyes away and forced myself to focus ahead, trying to ignore the throb that took a straight descent to the juncture right between my thighs.

Foolish, foolish girl.

NINE

Samantha

Late September, Seven Years Earlier

"What are you doing here?" I whispered through a hiss at my front door, wanting to throw my arms around him but knowing I had to tell him to go.

He wasn't supposed to be here.

And he already knew that.

But here he was, standing in my doorway, wearing tight jeans and a fitted tee, every piece of his outfit just as black and disheveled as his hair, which stood out in shock against the canvas of sun that glowed behind his head. Emerald eyes gleamed back at me, a sparkle of mischief that was rooted in a chin set in firm determination. "I wanted to see you."

Nerves spiraled through my body, and I cast my eyes over my shoulder to where Stewart was occupied on the couch, playing a video game. Our house was supersimple and plain. The big family room behind me was where we hung out most of the time, and the kitchen was separated from it by a wall and a swinging door. Off to the right ran a long hallway leading to four small bedrooms, and off to the left of the main rooms was my parents' bedroom.

Five minutes ago, I'd walked out of the kitchen, where I'd been doing my homework and my mom was preparing dinner. I crossed my fingers she was still in there and hadn't heard the doorbell ring.

I turned back to Christopher. "You know you can't be here. Are you trying to get me in trouble?"

It seemed he was always trying to get me in trouble. In the three weeks since he'd become my *boyfriend*, I'd broken more rules than I'd broken in my entire life before then.

Rule number one—having a boyfriend at all. The fallout came with everything that went along with that, like kissing and touching and sneaking out my window almost every night so we could do some more of that kissing and touching.

Come to find out, I liked all of that kissing and touching way more than I should.

Just the word *boyfriend* sent chills flying across my skin. I still couldn't believe he was mine. That he wanted me. He was so beautiful in that *Oh man, this guy is trouble* kind of way, his face so handsome it almost hurt, the man so pretty it almost conflicted with the cockiness he wore around like a crested chip on his shoulder.

But it wasn't hard to see he went deeper than all of that. Underneath his rough exterior, he was caring and kind. Vulnerable. Sweet.

Christopher Moore was his own brand . . . the kind I was pretty sure I wanted to wear forever.

Being with him? I'd never felt so alive. So free. Apparently

I'd happily take any trouble he brought my way if it meant I got to be in his space.

He dragged a hand through the messy locks of his hair, dropped his gaze before he looked back at me. "Of course not. I never want to hurt you," he said, his voice taking on an edge of desperation. "I just can't stand hiding us anymore. I want to meet your parents. Tell them how much I like you and want to be with you."

Quiet, humorless laughter rolled from me. "That's exactly what will scare them."

"Who's here?" My mother's voice crawled over me from behind, and that flash of chills that thinking of Christopher had brought to my flesh rose in alarm.

I shot a pleading glance at Christopher before I stepped back and opened the door a little farther, turning just in time to watch my mom's expression darken in suspicion. "Mom, this is my friend Christopher Moore."

I for sure left off the *boy* part, because that kind of introduction wouldn't go over so well.

As if he'd been invited, Christopher stepped into my house and put his hand out in front of him. For a moment, my mom just looked at it, calculating, her eyes slanting to me before they slipped back to him.

Finally she took his hand. "It's nice to meet you, Christopher."

Christopher smiled his wicked smile. I cringed, because I was pretty sure my mom wouldn't like it nearly as much as I did. "Nice to meet you, too, Mrs. Schultz."

Stewart's attention was drawn away from his video game, and he set his controller aside and climbed down from the couch. "Hi . . . you want to play with me? I just got a new game. It's awesome," he shouted with a little bounce on his toes.

This was about the most excitement we'd seen out of Stewart in months, pretty much since he'd gotten sick at the end of school last year.

Christopher looked at the paused game frozen on the television. "No way, dude. You're playing *Lego Star Wars*? That is just about my favorite game in history."

Stewart beamed up at him. "Mine, too!"

No question, Christopher had done it for his benefit, playing it up to bring out that smile on Stewart's face. One I would do just about anything to see there.

With Christopher's simple gesture, I melted a little, that flame that he ignited in me setting fire to another place inside that he hadn't touched before.

Stewart's tenth birthday had just passed a week before, though there hadn't been a whole lot of celebrating. All of it had been spent with him in the bathroom, sick and sad and crying and not understanding why he had to hurt so bad. Seeing him smiling like this now made my heart want to burst.

"So you'll play?" Stewart asked, tugging at Christopher's hand, excited to have someone to play with who might be better than those of us in his family.

"If it's okay with your mom."

Everyone turned to her, waiting for her reaction. She hesitated, twisting her hands in worried contemplation. A soft warning glowed in her eyes when she leveled them on Christopher. "Of course you can stay. Just not too long. We'll be having supper in an hour."

Christopher flashed that smile again. "I'll be sure to be out of your hair by then, Mrs. Schultz."

My mom and dad were *good*. And I understood all their reservations. I knew they only wanted what was best for me— what was best for my brothers and my sister. But sometimes that concern showed itself with an oppressive force, one that fought to keep us small and sheltered, secluded from the evils of the rest of the world.

I sat down with a two-foot space between Christopher and me on the couch and watched him interact with my brother, listened to his patience and his calm, the carefree way he teased and played, making my brother howl with laughter. Christopher told him stories about video games he'd played, and they shared their favorites, which were so much the same, Christopher shining all this light as he made my little brother feel just as big and important as a man.

As I watched, I realized there was no evil in Christopher Moore.

And if there was, I wanted to be infected with it.

At just after ten, I heard a light tapping at my window.

I was ready and waiting. By now I'd become a pro at gliding my window open without making a sound. I crawled out and hopped onto the ground. Christopher was right there to catch me.

Big, warm hands slipped around my sides to my back, and he brought me flush to his body. In the same second, his mouth descended on mine, gentle yet firm and enough to make my breath hitch.

A thrill buzzed through every single one of my senses.

There was no experience as blissful as kissing Christopher. Sure, he was the only boy I'd ever kissed, but I didn't need anything to compare it to.

It was pure ecstasy.

With a grin, he pulled back, set his hand on my cheek, and ran his thumb along my jaw, which didn't do anything to quiet my excited nerves. His voice was low. "Let's get out of here. I want to show you something."

There was no hesitation when he took my hand. On light

feet, we raced across my yard, trying to contain the laughter that bubbled in our bellies as we stole through the quiet of the slumbering night. Little sparks pricked all over my body, the charge of this adventure filling me with adrenaline, all of it spilling over into my stomach, where a riot of butterflies flapped their chaotic wings.

Christopher made me feel like I could fly.

When we got out of the confines of my neighborhood, Christopher tugged me forward and I found that spot at his side that I loved, and I curled into it, his arm wrapped protectively around my shoulder and holding me tight.

I grinned up at him, not really caring where we were going, because I'd follow him anywhere.

We headed in the direction of his neighborhood, cutting between two houses. He pulled me toward a rickety wooden fence. A thin plank had been torn away from it, the remaining portions splintered and sharp. He dipped down and crawled through the hole, never letting go of my hand as he did. On the other side, he squatted low, and his green eyes coaxed me to follow. "Be careful or you'll snag your shirt."

Cautious not to touch the jagged edge of the wood, I wedged myself through the tiny gateway leading into the unknown. I stood beside Christopher, squinting into the muted darkness of the half-moon sky.

"What is this place?"

Subdued light crept over the empty field, the expanse of it overrun with tall, grassy weeds. Five big trees grew up randomly throughout the lot, the wooden fence we'd just crawled through serving as its border on three sides, rising to back the yards of the houses in the adjacent neighborhoods. The fourth side was the main road that ran along Christopher's neighborhood, boxing in this quiet space.

He lifted a single shoulder as if it didn't really matter, but something significant flashed across his face. "It's nothin' really . . . but when we were little, Jared and I used to tear this lot up . . . playing, digging, throwing shit around." Quiet laughter seeped into the night. "My little sister, Aly, would always follow us out here. This was our place. Hardly ever come out here anymore . . . I don't know . . . I miss it and I just wanted to bring you here."

He led me across the lot, traipsing through the overgrown wild grasses and to the bottom of a tree. Up above was a tree house of sorts, although it was crude and without walls or windows, just a platform that had been hammered into the large branches that spread out from the trunk.

Christopher got behind me. "Up you go."

"Are you crazy?"

He cocked a flirty brow. "I think we already established that."

Laughing, I began the climb, digging the toes of my tennis shoes into the little pieces of wood nailed to the trunk. Christopher's hands wandered all over me as he stood guard in case I fell, probably taking advantage of the situation. Not that I minded all that much.

I sat down on the wooden floor and he hoisted himself up after me. He laid his long, lean body out across the floor, resting his back on a branch. He reached for me. "Come here . . . You're too far away."

On a sigh, I curled into the comfort of his arms, my ear pressed to his chest, where his heart beat hard and fast, like it spoke a different language than the normal arrogance he always exuded, his words sharp and fast and quick-witted when his blood pulsed with his own insecurities.

"I like you when we get to be together like this," I whispered.

He hugged me closer and brushed a kiss at my temple. "I like you always."

I'd been to Christopher's house several times, another rule broken, of course, as I'd gone there when I told my mom I was studying at a friend's.

I'd met his mom and dad, Karen and Dave, as well as his sister, Aly, and his little brother, Augustyn. It hadn't taken a whole lot to get me to fall in love with each of them, the feel of their house so much different than mine. The Moores' place was much more casual, as if he could waltz right into his house with me in tow and his mom didn't give much thought other than to welcome me in with a soft twinkle in her eye.

The first time I'd gone, she'd shot Christopher a telling look, one that warned him to be careful with me. It was something that had made me warm to her instantly, and I always looked forward to the times when I could sneak over there and spend time with them all.

But my favorite times were when Christopher and I could be together alone, when there was no one else watching us, when we could just be.

I lifted so I could look at him and show him a smile. He was quick to lean forward and grab a kiss.

Remorse shifted his expression. "I'm sorry for just showing up at your house today." He grazed the back of his hand along my jaw. "That was impulsive and selfish. I shouldn't have done that to you without a warning. Although I have to say I'm having a really hard time regretting it. Your little brother . . ." He swallowed over the lump that grew in this throat. "He's kinda amazing, isn't he?"

Sadness pressed at my chest, and I settled back down onto Christopher's, my fingers twisting nervously in his shirt. "He's the best . . . so kind and sweet. He's my little angel."

Silence engulfed us, a moment of quiet sorrow offered in respect for my little brother.

"How sick is he?" Christopher finally ventured, cautious and slow, his fingers threading in my hair. "I mean, God, I've seen pictures of kids with cancer before. But that? That's just fucking wrong. No kid deserves that."

If he'd stumbled at Stewart's lack of hair and frail body, he definitely hadn't shown it.

"No, he doesn't," I agreed. "Honestly? It's been awful . . . but things are finally looking up. His doctor told us his prognosis is really good. The tough part of his treatment is over, and he'll be going on maintenance therapy for at least another year, but they said it shouldn't be anything like the last six months has been. The best thing is he's supposed to feel a lot better during that time."

"That's good." I could feel the force of his smile. "Really good."

"Yeah, I just want him better." I shifted so I could look up at him. "You made his day today, you know. He's never that excited."

"I'd do it every single day if he wanted me to. If you wanted me there."

"Of course I want you there."

Hurt tightened his tone. "What about your mom? What did she say after I left?"

I laughed through my discomfort, letting my fingertips trail over his chin and down the deep hollow of his neck as I glanced up to gauge his reaction. "She grilled me about you . . . asked a bunch of really personal questions . . . if we were dating and what you meant to me and what your intentions are."

"Did you tell her the truth?"

"Ha. Am I here?" My eyes widened in emphasis. "If she

knew what I'd been doing, I'd be chained to my bed right now. All she knows is that I like you and that we talk sometimes at school."

In a flash, Christopher moved and had his face buried in my neck. "We talk sometimes, huh?" he murmured as he kissed along my collarbone. My heart rate spiked, and I squirmed as that flame licked at my insides. I gripped his hair, holding on for dear life.

"I think she told my dad you had been there," I admitted shakily toward the sky as he continued to kiss me, nudging my chin back farther and farther to gain better access. My voice came all raspy and coarse. "Ben showed up a few hours later. He took me to my room and started in on me, giving me all these warnings about you . . . the things he's seen you do at parties and stuff." I'd tried not to let those stories hurt. Still, they'd stung. "I know my mom and dad had to have put him up to it. He mentioned you by name."

My parents trusted Ben. His family had been a part of my father's congregation as long as I could remember, and his father and mine had become close friends. It was rare that his family wasn't over at our house at least once a week, and my father was always going on that a boy like Ben would one day make a perfect match for me. Ben had always been nice to me, even though as I'd grown older, he still tended to treat me like a little girl.

"I can't stand that asshole," Christopher whipped out, pulling back far enough that I could witness his scowl.

I knew they didn't like each other. They didn't really run in the same circles since Ben went to another school and was a few years older. But their paths had definitely crossed and the feelings were definitely mutual. Ben had warned me to stay away from Christopher, told me he was trouble and he wanted only one thing. I'd scoffed and told him to mind his own business, and he'd grabbed me, almost pleading as he said I *was* his business.

"I admitted to him that we're together."

Christopher blanched, and he edged back a fraction, his eyes darting all over my face. "Why would you do that if you don't want your parents to know?"

"Because I couldn't stand for him to say one more awful thing about you. Couldn't listen to him telling me about the girls you've been with and how I was going to end up just the same. I told him I didn't care what he or anyone else thought . . . that I just want to be with you." My gaze softened as I looked at this beautiful boy staring at me in the dark. I wet my lips. "I don't care what you've done in the past or who you've been with, Christopher. Just as long as you're with me now."

He pulled even farther away. Discomfort covered him, all of him, and he twitched a little, like he didn't know what to say. My own nerves got all spun up, because I wasn't sure if I could tolerate whatever it was he was getting ready to reveal. I prepared for the worst.

"You know I've never actually had sex with someone before, right?"

The confession slipped out like it was a secret but should have been blatantly obvious, all the same.

He blinked, waiting, and I was blinking, too, because that was not the word around school. I frowned. "Don't lie to me to make me feel better, Christopher."

He took my hand and laced his fingers through mine, contemplated our woven skin as he spoke. "I told you that first night I came to your window that I hadn't earned all of my reputation. Yeah . . . I've definitely messed around . . . taken things with girls much further than I probably should have. But there has always been something that's held me back." He shrugged. "I don't

know . . . maybe it's all those talks my mom had with me, warning me I'd end up regretting it." He cupped my face and inclined
his head. "I think I get what she was talking about now."

Okay, so maybe this news shouldn't have made me so insanely happy. But it did. I wanted him for myself. The thought
of anyone else touching him curled my stomach. Maybe it was
foolish and rash, maybe I'd regret it the same way his mom had
warned him he would. But none of that mattered. I knew he was
the one I wanted to have all my firsts with.

And maybe I couldn't have all of his, but at least I could have
the most important one.

Christopher repositioned us, carefully moving me to lie flat
on the wood, situating himself over me. He kept his weight light,
but he was close enough that I could feel every hard inch of him.
I struggled for my lost breath, and a little flutter of panic swept
over me when I realized someplace in me was wishing he was
closer, pressing in and taking me whole.

He leaned up on his elbow and brushed back my hair. "So
are we going to have to worry about Ben ratting us out to your
parents?"

"I don't think so . . . I begged him to keep it between us. I
told him we're supposed to be friends and I would do the same
for him."

"Dude hates me about as much as I hate him, Samantha.
Don't think he's going to be doing me any favors."

"Maybe he likes and respects me more than he hates you."

Christopher quirked a grin. "Probably not. But I guess we'll
just have to deal with that as it comes. Your parents are going
to find out about us sooner or later, anyway."

Fear flickered in my subconscious, and I tucked it down. I
didn't want to face that day, because I really had no idea what
lengths they would go to in order to uphold their rules, and I

knew there was no way in the world I'd give up Christopher. No matter what they said.

Christopher silenced all those worried thoughts with a kiss, one that was long and slow, deep enough that I felt it all the way to my toes.

I released a tiny moan.

Things would be so much easier if he didn't make me feel so good.

Christopher grinned at my mouth, pecking his lips at mine, almost playful as he began to let his fingers wander just under the hem of my shirt. "Am I mistaken, or are we taking this slow?" he mumbled and teased at my mouth.

My stomach jerked as he slipped his hand around and palmed my backside.

"Y-y-yes . . . slow," I forced myself to say.

"How slow?" he asked as he kissed over my chin and down my neck.

"What if I said I wanted to wait until I'm married? What would you think then?"

Playful laughter rumbled in his words. "Then I'd say we're getting married really, really young."

A throaty giggle rippled through me, and my heart felt too full. I clutched at his hair, pulling him forward in the same second I tried to push him away. "Don't you know that's why all good girls get married young?"

He licked a path along the collar of my shirt, dipping just below it to the very top swell of my breasts.

I sucked in a shuddered breath.

"Are you a good girl, Samantha?" It came out on a gentle tease that lacked even an ounce of pressure, though I knew he wanted an answer, that he was taking his cues from me. How far was I going to let this go? And when?

My voice was thick with fear and anticipation. "Today I am. Probably tomorrow, too. But I'm not so sure I'm going to be when you're done with me."

"I'm never gonna be done with you." He swept his lips up to my ear, and goose bumps covered me with his promise. "Never."

TEN

Samantha

All week I'd procrastinated. A lot of that time I'd spent questioning myself. Questioning my motives. Weighing my options. I was torn between wanting to beg off and back out and praying for Saturday to finally hurry and arrive.

After work today, I'd gone straight to my parents', visited a little with my mom before I spent a couple of hours with Stewart in his room. Mainly we'd watched goofy videos on YouTube and joked around. I'd just needed to see him, needed a reminder of what was important, a reminder that all of these *issues* I thought I was having really weren't issues at all.

Not when compared to what my brother was going through.

Standing here tonight, though, trying to find the courage to talk with Ben, to tell him where I was going tomorrow night, and asking him to be there with me, didn't seem to come any easier than it had at any other time during the past week.

I pressed my hands into the cool granite of the kitchen

counter, scolding myself for being such a coward. I loved Ben. I really did.

No, it wasn't a passionate kind of love. But that was okay. I'd surrendered to the belief that some loves were better that way. The kind you didn't fall into. The kind that came with time. The kind that one day were just there because you didn't know anything else.

But what I hated was the fact that I'd allowed him to make me feel as if I needed to ask his permission to do the things I wanted to do. All of that was on me. I accepted it and I knew I was the one who had to change it. I'd gone into this relationship with such resignation, with such apathy, that I'd given little thought or care to the way I really felt or to what I really wanted.

I'd been too hurt, too overcome, too broken.

Mindlessly, I'd followed him. Let him sculpt me into who he wanted me to be, let him lord and rule, because after all, *Ben knew best.* At the time, I honestly didn't mind. I'd willingly given up control because I'd felt like such a fool, as if maybe I couldn't make my own decisions because they would only be faulty and dangerous.

Beyond that, my parents trusted him. They'd been so relieved that Christopher was out of my life that they'd had only encouragement for Ben, and found little concern in the fact that Ben was four years older than me. They'd wanted a real man there for their daughter, someone who grew up in their church, someone who'd been raised with their same beliefs.

They wanted me safe, and Ben had made me feel that way, because there was little threat of him breaking me.

But I was no longer that little girl he'd taken under his protective wing.

It was time I broke that mold and became an equal partner in our relationship. That pathetic period I'd slipped into, one where he constantly coddled and comforted me, had long since passed.

Drawing in a deep breath, I straightened, smoothed out my shirt, and walked toward the family room. I propped my shoulder up against the wall and looked down on where Ben sat on the couch, tapping away at his laptop.

Going for casual, I lightened my voice. "So you'll never guess who I ran into at Target."

I didn't bother to mention I was talking about something that had happened two weeks earlier. Some things he just didn't need to know.

He didn't lift his head, just muttered a disinterested "Hmm?" as his focus remained fixed on his computer screen.

My heart skipped a panicked beat before I remembered my mission. I was breaking chains. Reclaiming me.

"Aly Moore. Well, not Moore anymore. She's married and has a baby. Her name is Aly Holt now."

Ben's attention flew to me, his expression screwed up in disgust. I resisted the urge to roll my eyes.

Well, that got his attention.

"What did you just say?" he accused.

"I said her new name is Aleena Holt."

Anger burned across his face. Jaw ticking, he ground his teeth. "Aleena Moore?" His words were cold and one hundred percent an insinuation.

A surge of defensiveness rose in me, pressing full, because he said her name as if it was dirty. There was nothing *dirty* about Aly. I was certain she was one of the nicest, most genuine people I'd ever met. Insolence lifted my chin, and I crossed my arms over my chest. "Yeah. Aleena Moore. *Holt* now."

"You mean the sister of that bastard who took advantage of you? The asshole who manipulated you? Ripped you up and left you in a million broken pieces. His sister? That Moore? Is that who you're talking about?" None of them were questions. It was all formed as one long accusation, as if I was completely ignorant. Incompetent. Clueless.

Just like he always wanted me to believe.

So, yeah, I'd been naive.

That didn't mean I couldn't make my own decisions now.

"Um, yeah, *that* Moore," I said, my own anger oozing out.

God, he could be such a jerk.

"Well, I hope that interaction was short, because I don't want you anywhere near a Moore . . . regardless of what her last name is now." A disdainful huff bled from him and he turned back to his computer, banging at the keys as he spewed his own ignorance. "That girl must be just as clueless as you. Jared Holt wasn't any better than that punk-ass kid who thought he was going to use you up. You're lucky I was there to save you. Too bad she didn't get out so easily."

Tears pricked at my eyes, and I fisted my hands at my sides.

So easily?

Damn him. His assumptions pissed me off. Ben was the clueless one. I didn't think I'd ever seen a happier couple than Jared and Aly. Besides, I'd just wanted to have *one* normal conversation with him. One mature conversation. One time when he would listen to me and not talk over me or down to me.

That seed of hatred I'd always harbored for him threatened to sprout, trembling somewhere in the fragmented place in my spirit. Christopher had wronged me so deeply it was scored forever on my heart, a wound so deep I wasn't sure I could ever fully forgive him. But I knew just as deeply that Ben had taken advantage of the situation, taken advantage of me, swooping in when he knew he'd have little resistance.

Sighing, Ben pushed the laptop toward his knees. He rubbed

at his eyes with the pads of his fingers. He dropped them and stared across at me. "Just trust me on this, Sam. You shouldn't have stopped to talk to her in the first place." His expression softened into a plea. "The only thing in this world I care about is you, and I can't stand the thought of you getting dragged into old memories that can only hurt you. I was there, remember? And I know what you went through. Just forget that you saw her and I'll forget that you even mentioned it."

The last sounded almost like a threat.

I blinked away the brimming moisture in my eyes, and somewhere inside me, I felt resentment taking root.

My thoughts spun hard and fast, contemplating my direction, what I wanted to say. My heart hurt when I finally spoke. "It wasn't a big deal, Ben," I lied softly, quietly, because that was something I never wanted to be. A liar. But I didn't know how to go toe-to-toe with him on this. I really didn't even know where I stood. Every reservation I'd had about going back to Aly's surfaced, but it all floated on my determination to give this a try. Like Aly had said, I needed to let this bitterness go. To free myself.

And if this was a mistake? Then it was my mistake. One I would own. If Ben couldn't even allow me to get one sentence out without jumping all over my *stupidity*, then he didn't deserve to be a part of it.

"I just was telling you I ran into someone I knew from the old neighborhood," I continued, my tone lifting in nonchalance, as if that meeting hadn't marked a shift in my world. What that change would be, I still had no clue. But I felt that anxious anticipation proclaiming that things were never going to be the same.

He looked at me as if maybe he didn't trust me. "Just be careful, Sam."

I nodded and changed the subject. "So are you hungry? Do you want me to make something or do you want to go out?" I turned to head into the kitchen, then paused to look back over my shoulder, my mouth going dry. "Oh . . . and tomorrow night I'm going over to Cici's. My friend from work? It's her birthday and she's having her girlfriends over for a couple drinks." Guilt closed off my throat, and I quickly turned to head into the kitchen.

Christopher had always made me into a liar.

Guess I learned from the best.

Because in the end, that's what he'd turned out to be.

The most ruthless kind of liar.

Saturday evening I spent more time getting ready than was wise. Standing in front of the full-length mirror in my bathroom, I stared at my reflection. Maybe if I studied it hard enough, I would find some sort of clarity.

This morning I'd texted Aly asking if I could bring anything, what to wear, and what Courtney might like, since the last time I'd seen her she hadn't even turned ten.

Aly had instantly replied, and it was as if I could sense her warmth in the letters that made up the words of her text. And again, it had reaffirmed that I *liked* her, that I felt a connection with her that I had with few other friends. She made me feel as if I belonged somewhere, when usually I remained on the fringes, too cautious to ever step into the fray.

For the first time in such a long time, I wanted to get mixed up in it.

My phone buzzed with *that* tone, and I smiled as I grabbed it from the bathroom counter. I pressed down to accept his Snap.

Stewart's face was all lit up, superclose to the camera, his eyes bugging out as he widened them as far as they would go. Scrawled across them was, *What's up, Crazy Lady?*

My heart pumped true with affection.

In the full-length mirror, I snapped my own picture, a straight-up mirror selfie of my party-ready persona. So maybe I typically didn't go for all of this egotistical self-love. But I figured if anyone would appreciate my efforts, it was Stewart, the little nag, always telling me to get out more, even though there wasn't a chance in this world I'd let on to where I was really heading.

Aly had told me they were all dressing up a little to celebrate. Taking into consideration that it was hot, I picked out my nicest pair of black shorts, fitted around the waist and flared at my thighs, a silky, dark blue pullover blouse, the short sleeves all billowy and soft, and a pair of high platform wedges to set it all off. My hair was pressed into long sheets and my makeup was soft, my red lips coated in clear, shimmery gloss, pursed in their permanent pout.

I typed across my picture and pressed send.

Livin' it up tonight! #BirthdayParty

Instead of a Snap, my phone dinged with a regular old text.

Sexy bitch.

Ha, I tapped back out, unable to contain my grin.

Immediately, he texted back. *No, seriously, you look beautiful.*

The way I looked bolstered my confidence, even if my outward appearance didn't come close to matching the mayhem that was staging a frontline war in my mind.

But I felt as if this was my redo. A chance to go back to that moment that had changed me so drastically and start again. To prove to myself that I was strong. A survivor. But also, that I was full of forgiveness and I could stand in a room with the man who'd hurt me more than anyone else ever had and not look on him with bitterness and blame.

I wanted to be that girl.

One without regrets.

I doubted I could achieve all of that tonight. Finding that strength and letting go of all the pain I'd held on to would take effort and wouldn't come in a passing day. But it was a start, and I knew the first step was facing Christopher. Facing the way he made me feel. All of it—the chaos and confusion and uncertainty. The anger and the hate. The passion and the need and those flickers of a naive young love that had never dimmed or died.

It was time.

Another text buzzed.

Don't forget about little ol' me when the man of your dreams sees you and sweeps you off your feet tonight . . . We have a date tomorrow . . . My house. Noon. Expect the time of your life ;)

I shook my head, my fingers flying across the pad.

Um . . . Ben . . . remember?

His reply was almost instant.

Riiight . . .

I felt his eye roll from all the way across town.

Stewart had this overly dramatic, overtly romantic notion for my life. To Stewart, Ben didn't fit the bill. I was pretty sure the kid didn't even like him, and he'd get all bristly and quiet whenever Ben stopped by to spend time with him. Lately those visits had become few and even farther between.

I didn't quite get Ben. He'd been the one with that amazingly profound gesture for Stewart. But once Stewart got sick again, Ben seemed not to want anything to do with him at all.

When Ben admitted he was the one who'd written the letter that was responsible for the book that had become Stewart's most prized possession, I'd finally allowed myself to give in and let go. Ben and I had seemed inevitable, anyway, and if any one person could be that thoughtful, how could I continue to turn him away?

That was the kind of man I wanted.

A thoughtful one. Kind and considerate.

I'd once believed Christopher to be that . . . but as it's said, actions speak so much louder than words.

My response was simple yet somehow painful.

Ben is a good man.

Another Snap came through. I clicked into the message, and this time it wasn't my brother's face, but a picture of a girl being spun around in a field, her long hair flying behind her as she laughed toward the sky, held in her lover's arms. Across it in a pretty script, it read, *Every girl deserves to be swept off her feet.*

I didn't respond, because what could I possibly say? Christopher had swept me off my feet and then tossed me right on my ass. I couldn't have fallen any harder. Stewart couldn't understand that. I knew he'd looked up to Christopher so much, thought of him as the cool guy who'd joke around with him, make him laugh. Viewed him as someone who didn't treat him as if he was any different from everyone else. Loved him, even.

But it'd all been a front. A fucking game.

Was I crazy for wanting to forgive Christopher for that?

I glanced at the clock. I was already half an hour late.

Sighing, I walked to the front door.

Guess so.

Completely insane. Out of my mind.

I gathered the pink gift bag stuffed with glittery tissue paper.

A present for *Cici.*

Making up all these stupid lies made me cringe, but once you made up one, you had to keep up, and Ben had tagged along with me to the mall when I'd gone to buy a gift. The next came when I said another girl from work would be swinging by to pick me up, and yet another when I filled him in that she'd so kindly also be bringing me home.

Yep, I even had my own little fake DD. Ben had been all kinds of grateful for her. He said he wouldn't have to worry about me making it home safe. But really it meant he could have an unrestricted night out with the guys, and I wouldn't be putting a damper on his plans.

Funny how he always wanted me safe at home while he could go out and do whatever it was he did every weekend.

About thirty minutes earlier, he'd left with a quick peck to my lips and the instruction not to wait up, while he had the nerve to tell me not to stay out too late.

Resentment rolled through my consciousness. If he just had let me talk, he'd know where I was going. Maybe he'd even have been my date.

But my disappointment in him didn't come close to equaling my relief. I needed to do this on my own and without his interference. Strong and independent.

I flung the door open and squinted into the glaring light. Heat pulsed along the desert ground, the sun sagged low on the horizon, strewing glorious hues of colors across the desert sky as the endless blue canopy slowly darkened with the imminent night.

I pulled in a cleansing breath and locked the door behind me. I couldn't tell if I was more nervous this time or the last, my stomach flipping and my heart like a scatter of birds flapping at my chest.

Last time I hadn't known what to expect, whether I would see Christopher, and if I did, what I would feel.

If I was being honest, I guessed I'd hoped I'd feel nothing— that seeing him would mean nothing, that he'd faded into nothing but a distant memory. Forgettable.

Now I knew full well the violent impact he had on my senses. That dreaded anticipation ballooned, pressing and puls-

ing at my ribs. Still, I forged on with staunch determination set
in my feet.

Those confident steps faltered when I rounded the corner
and saw the cars lining the street. But it wasn't the number of
them that caused me concern. It was that ominous, unmistakable
black truck sitting right in front of Aly's house that stole my
breath and sent a rush of panic trampling through my senses.
The same one I'd nearly collided with last Sunday afternoon.

Foolish, foolish girl.

The thought struck me deep, driving a blade of awareness
into my soul. Within the confines of my house, I had such good
intensions, such profound resolutions.

But now, as I approached the door to Aly's house and the
sound of carefree voices and buoyant laughter beat at my ears, I
felt even smaller than that gullible girl who'd been curled up in
a ball on the bathroom floor at that party seven years ago, completely crushed. And like Ben had said, I'd been lucky he was
there. The desperate relief I'd felt that night when he'd scooped
me into his arms was one I'd never forget. Literally, he'd picked
me up. Then over the years, he'd pieced me back together.

Swallowing back the memories, I pressed a trembling finger
to the doorbell.

I can do this.

ELEVEN

Samantha

Ten excruciating seconds passed. Each of them was spent in contemplation, torn between running and staying, the coward's way out or the path of the brave. The most terrifying part was I didn't know which direction was which.

Just when I almost gave in to my fears and turned to escape, the door flew open to a smiling Aly. She surged forward and hugged me hard. "You came," she murmured at my ear, the sound of her voice filled with more restraint and caution than it had been last week when she'd casually dragged me inside. Tonight, her welcome was edged with tension. She pulled back, her face close to mine. "He's here."

Fear clogged my throat, and I fought against the urge to rock up onto my toes to look over her shoulder, to scour the room for the raging green eyes I knew I would find. "I know. Does he know I'm coming?"

Almost in sympathy, she nodded. "Yeah. He wasn't happy

about it, but he promised he would leave you alone and let you enjoy yourself. Are you going to be okay?"

I hefted out a breath. "Maybe I won't be tonight . . . but one day I will be."

It was a promise, a commitment to the friendship we had made.

She squeezed my hand. "I know you will." She reached for the gift and my purse. "Let me take those." She piled the gift in an overflowing mound against the wall and set my purse on a table collecting personal items. "Come inside. I want to introduce you to everyone."

My pulse picked up a notch. Was I ready for this? Warily, I peered inside. The one person I was searching for was nowhere to be found.

Exhaling, I let Aly take my hand and lead me in. She snapped the door closed behind us. "Hey, everyone," she called to the small circles of people chatting in groups in the great room of the house. "I want you to meet one of my very good friends, Samantha. Samantha Schultz."

It was as if she was making a declaration. As if I was important, my presence required. No doubt, Aly knew I needed the encouragement to stand here and endure the faces that turned my way.

A few of those who didn't know who I was came right up, shaking my hand and introducing themselves, telling me how they knew Aly and Jared. All of them were pleasant. Nice. Just like I'd expect any friends of Jared and Aly's to be.

"Hang on one sec." Aly lifted her index finger and backed away, disappearing into the crowd taking up most of the kitchen. Five seconds later she came out of it hauling a blushing blonde by the hand, the girl with the biggest smile smeared across her entire face. Her cheeks were lit up in a pinked glow that could give my constant blush a run for its money.

Aly had their hands woven together in a show of solidarity.

"This is my sister, Courtney, the birthday girl. Courtney, this is Samantha. I don't know if you remember her?" she prodded, and I was pretty sure Aly had already filled Jared's little sister in on who I was and the significance I bore, if it could be considered significant at all.

But to me, it had been *significant*.

That was the hardest part. Every second I'd spent with Christopher had felt that way, as if I was experiencing the most vital, meaningful moments in my life.

It cut me to the core that they'd turned out to be a sham.

I stretched out my hand, trying to keep it from trembling. "It's so good to see you again, Courtney. Happy birthday."

I thought it was adorable that Aly had claimed Jared's sister as her own, and from the timid joy that exuded from this beautiful girl I could tell it meant the world to her.

Instead of accepting my hand, Courtney stepped forward and hugged me. "I remember you." Her voice was soft and sincere. She pulled away and self-consciously tucked a lock of blond hair behind her ear, glancing up at me under lashes with a shyness I rarely witnessed anymore. "Wow . . . you are so pretty."

Quiet laughter trickled from me, and it was my turn to be self-conscious. "Not half as pretty as you."

Instantly, I felt a kinship with Jared's sister, could sense how real and unsure of herself she was. As if maybe she was almost as uncomfortable as I was with this whole situation.

I knew little about her, other than what Aly had filled me in on during coffee the previous week. After Jared's mother had died, she'd gone to live with her grandparents for close to two years. Their father had been in no state to take care of a little girl, too consumed with the loss of his wife.

But when Jared and Courtney's grandmother died, Courtney had gone back to her father, who'd immediately packed them up and moved them to California, while Jared had still been in juvie, estranged from his family. It had been only a few months since Jared and his father had reconciled, and he was just now reestablishing a relationship with his little sister.

No wonder she seemed so anxious, ill at ease, and yet still like she wouldn't want to be any other place in the world.

Seemed I wasn't the only one with her past catching up to her.

I let my attention glide around the room. Silver and black balloons and streamers were strung up all over the place, and laughter rang against the walls, echoed in from outside.

Clearly, today's celebration was about moving on and embracing the future. There was no question about it.

Hope blossomed inside me. My thoughts from earlier hit me. It was time for me to embrace my future, too, to finally let go of the past.

"Oh my God! Look who's here!" An enthusiastic voice rose above the crowd, and Megan cut away from the three people she was talking with near the sliding glass door that led to the back. She shot forward and threw herself into my arms. She squeezed and rocked me like I was her oldest friend and she hadn't seen me in years, and I was laughing when I hugged her back.

"It's good to see you, too."

Megan turned to Courtney. "*Now* you're officially having the coolest party in history, because all of the coolest chicks are here."

Courtney looked around the big, open space, all the rooms overflowing with people. "I know. I can't believe they did all this for me."

"And why in the heck wouldn't they?" Megan asked. "All Jared and Aly have been talking about is you finally getting here."

Courtney blushed harder, but the most heartfelt kind of joy gleamed from her ice blue eyes.

God. I wondered if it was hard for Jared to look at her . . . or for her to look in the mirror . . . because she looked almost exactly like I remembered their mother.

"Sheesh . . . I feel like an outsider over here with you pack of gorgeous blondes," Aly teased, holding on to Courtney's hand, swinging it between them, her grin bouncing around the three of us.

I exaggerated an eye roll. "Right. Because you're absolutely hideous."

Aly's laughter echoed around the room, and I couldn't help my smile. Comfort enveloped me and I was suddenly thankful I'd come, even though I knew facing Christopher without running for my life was going to be difficult. But somehow I knew it was going to be worth it. Aly made me believe this was where I was supposed to be.

Aly looked over her shoulder. "Come on outside. The steaks are almost ready and I need to see if Jared needs any help. Would you like something to drink first?"

Megan groaned toward the ceiling. "Oh my God, go for the punch that Karen made. Aly's mom is some kind of wonder bartender, and she made a huge bowl of punch to prove it. Best thing I've ever tasted. And believe me, it has a kick to it. Two glasses in and I'm already feeling it. I'm pretty sure you're going to need a very *tall* glass."

Was it that obvious I needed something strong to calm my nerves?

Considering I couldn't stop looking around the room, and I was sure it was totally clear what . . . or rather who . . . I was seeking, I guessed the answer was a resounding yes.

Ignoring the turmoil inside me, I let a grin pull at one side of my mouth. "Since you seem to be the connoisseur of all things alcoholic, I doubt you'd steer me wrong. I'll grab one and meet you out there."

Aly frowned in concern. "You sure?"

"Yes. Completely."

She hesitated.

"Go on." I shooed them with my hands. "I'll grab a drink and meet you outside."

"Grab me one, too," Megan called as she trailed Aly and Courtney out the back sliding glass door.

"Got it," I hollered, chuckling under my breath, still not understanding how it was possible that I'd found myself in the midst of such easy affection, with such good people who welcomed me right into their fold without a second thought.

Well, all except for the one who'd managed to wring me inside out. The one who seemed to matter above all else. Because no matter how hard I tried to minimize his importance, the idea of really facing him continued to pump and feed the agitation that stirred and stewed within me, like some unseen force was calling me deeper into the promise of the unknown.

I seemed all too intent on throwing myself headlong into it.

As I chewed at my bottom lip, my gaze again traveled the room, which was thinning out, everyone heading out back when Jared called that the food was ready and dinner was set up on a buffet table outside.

All of that anxiety that had followed me through the week had gotten all mixed up with the ease I felt every time I was in

Aly's space. Still, the one face I was so terrified and completely desperate to see was nowhere to be found.

That didn't mean I couldn't *feel* him here.

His overwhelming presence was strong. Tremors rolled through me as I made my way into the kitchen, my head downturned as I said a quiet *hello* to two guys from Jared's work who were on their way out.

I stood at the counter in front of the bar, staring down at the round slices of oranges floating in the glass bowl.

Get a grip. You can do this. You're strong.

Grabbing two clear plastic cups, I filled them with ice from the bucket, scooped the red punch into the ladle, and lifted it to fill a cup.

Liquid courage.

I felt my own smirk right before the breath hit me at the back of the neck, and I froze. Chills flashed across my flesh, drenching my skin in a ripple of delicious sensation that quickly gave way to a cold flush of dread.

I sucked in a staggered breath. With shaking hands, I set the cup aside and let the ladle slip so that it clattered around in the glass bowl. The cold granite was unyielding as I made a vain attempt at digging my fingers into it to keep myself from falling when my knees went weak.

Again, I'd thought I was prepared for the onslaught of emotion Christopher sent barreling through my senses.

But the truth was, there was never a time in my life when I'd been prepared for him.

Behind me, I could feel his body towering over mine, an inch away. Dark and consuming. One step back and I was sure I'd sink into the raging sea of this man and forever disappear. Right into a black hole of nothingness.

He edged forward and forced my stomach into the counter,

the length of his hard, hot body pressing into mine. I gasped and clung to the edge, his presence crawling over me, sucking me in with the intention of spitting me out.

I wanted to be strong, to turn and face him, to assert that he no longer had any control over me. To pretend as if every inch of my skin didn't come alive with his close proximity.

But instead I felt myself faltering, and fear seized my heart when I realized I was going to crumble at his feet.

I wasn't even strong enough to stand.

The sickest part of it all was that he had me pinned. Literally. This demon of a man was keeping me from falling to the floor.

He leaned in closer, brushing his mouth across my ear. Shivers raced through me, and I clamped down my mouth, trying not to inhale the potent nature of the boy who'd rocked my entire world. The one responsible for the huge, gaping crack in my foundation.

The fault.

And the fault was his.

I'd be wise to remember that.

His words were sharp and not in the least unexpected. But they stung nonetheless. "Thought I told you to stay the fuck away from me. You're not welcome here, Samantha." He drew out my name in a whispered taunt, coaxing me to look at his face, which felt like it was less than a millimeter from mine.

God, I wished I hadn't.

A sharp breath wheezed down my throat when our eyes locked, and I drew in everything that was Christopher Moore. My mind and body lit up in recognition when I was struck with his distinct, unforgettable scent.

But tonight, there was a hostility saturating it, more intense than ever before.

Pure sex bidden by a brilliant, raging fury.

Like he'd consume me and there'd be nothing left.

Ashes.

That's what had remained after he was finished with me the first time.

After he'd promised me forever.

Maybe I'd been that stupid, naive girl then, but I definitely wasn't her now, and I wouldn't allow him to reduce me to a stammering, blubbering mess.

Resistance lifted my chin in a firm set of defiance, my heart thrumming too hard and my stomach feeling as if it might spill over. I wrenched out of his grasp. I wanted to scream a million insults at him, to make him feel as small and foolish as he had made me feel, but I remembered my mission. This was about forgiveness. About regaining that part of me that had been lost to Christopher. About moving on.

"I'm here because *your* sister invited me. Because she came to *my* home and asked *me* to be here. I'm here because she's *my* friend and I've always considered her to be, even after you took her away from me."

Christopher blanched, and a surge of hurt flared in his searing eyes, before he recovered with a sneer. "I took her away from you?" He snorted. "Seems to me you have a pretty poor memory"—he leaned in close—"*Sam.*"

He said it hard, with an emphasis that drove another stake straight into my failing heart. So desperately I wanted to be courageous, but he knew my weaknesses. He knew I hated when he called me Sam. But even more, he'd hated when anyone else called me that.

It was a clear slap to the face.

Moisture gathered in my eyes, and I tried with everything in me to blink the tears back, but the first one fell, hard and fast.

I squeezed my eyes, looking away to the floor. I pressed my hands to my chest, trying to hide the way it heaved and shook, but the tremors just took over my body.

Could anything be more humiliating than this? Christopher watching me fall apart?

"Fuck," he cursed, and even with my eyes shut, I could almost see him shift, the way his body shrank and he fisted his hair. His voice lowered. "Goddamn it, Samantha, what are you trying to do to me?"

Tentatively, I cast a timid glance up at him, because there was nothing I could do to stop myself. He wore the most tortured expression I'd ever seen, his brow all twisted and his eyes the deepest forest green.

Why did he have to be so beautiful?

And why did I still have to love him so much?

He jerked his face away for two anguished beats before he leveled his gaze back on me. All traces of emotion had been erased. "Stay out of my way, Samantha. If you think you have a right to be here, then fine. Stay. But don't think for a second this means anything. You're *dead* to me."

My entire being quaked with a jolt of pain.

There should have been no surprise. He'd made that abundantly clear when he'd stared vacantly across that room at me all those years ago, the trace of a smirk on his face confirming I'd meant nothing to him at all. I realized once I got older that it'd probably gotten him off, giving him a sordid sense of pleasure attained only in my misery.

Every single promise he'd made me had been a lie.

And the one he'd just made?

That's the one I needed to remember.

I was dead to him. Nothing. I'd always been. All these years

I'd spent hurting and longing and wondering had been nothing but a waste.

I'd known it then and I knew it now.

Christopher Moore was a bastard.

When they found out I was with him, my parents had begged and pleaded with me to see reason, to open my eyes and realize the direction I was allowing my life to go, warning me I was conspiring with the devil.

As I stood there staring up at all his glorious beauty, the man outwardly too perfect to be real, his black hair unruly and chaotic, his green eyes vicious and cruel—and his body—his body an altar of temptation, I realized their warnings hadn't even come close to the truth.

I'd sold my soul to Lucifer himself.

TWELVE

Christopher

Swells of hurt pounded at my skin, a radiating agony slamming me hard and fast. One brutal hit after another. Those endless blue eyes I'd spent way too much time dreaming about were staring up at me like I'd just crushed her into a million tiny pieces, but then some sort of hardened resolution seemed to take hold of her features.

But that lone fucking tear streaking down her face had damn near been my undoing.

I'd been overwhelmed. Overcome with the need to grab her sweet face between my hands and lick it from her cheek.

Then proceed to lick every delicious inch of her body.

Most disturbing part? That urge didn't come close to just being about the physical. My spirit buzzed, consumed with this need to comfort her. To hold her and protect her. Exactly like I used to. I'd been about five foolish seconds from making all kinds of unsound promises that this girl wouldn't even want me to make.

Chances were, she'd slap me right across the face.

No matter how badly the fact tore me up, Samantha wasn't mine, and the voracious hunger gripping every cell of my being, the one begging me to reach out and touch her, to take her back, had to be crushed.

So I'd done what any man would do and put a stop to all those insane thoughts hijacking my brain.

Of course, that was after I'd rubbed all up on her, teasing myself with just a taste of what only this girl could make me feel. And damn if that little brush of our bodies didn't feel better than any of the thoughtless flesh I'd poured myself into over the last seven years, my dick straining painfully and my heart hammering so hard I was pretty sure it'd beat right out of my chest, spilling out in a bleeding, nasty mess on the floor.

Seemed fitting, 'cause it'd always belonged to Samantha, anyway.

My eyes skimmed down her body where she stood three inches from me, her hands balled at her sides, her smell and her sweet all up in my face, clouding my senses.

She was taunting me. I knew it. She knew exactly how to bring me to my knees. My gaze got locked on the bronzed, defined lines of her toned legs, tracing up and down. My fingers twitched, wanting to be the ones doing that tracing. She was wearing these supersexy short shorts. Not the kind the sleazy girls wore to the clubs that promised the first guy who walked up to them a good time. No. These were the *You can dream of me all you want, but there's no chance you're getting in these* kind of shorts.

Yes, they had a name, and Samantha wore them well.

And because the world hated me, the girl had to go and pair

them with the sexiest pair of shoes I'd ever seen, accentuating every sleek line of her sexy legs.

Did I mention sexy? Yeah, the girl was a fucking wet dream. Believe me, I knew. She'd starred in plenty of mine.

And here she was, standing right in my sister's kitchen like she belonged there.

When Aly told me Samantha was coming tonight, she made me promise to be on my best behavior, telling me Samantha was her guest and she wanted her to come. But the second I saw the temptress standing there, every oath I'd made to my sister flew right out the window.

Considering my best behavior wasn't exactly good, anyway, Aly should have known better.

The second I got close, it was all over. She'd always had this thing about her that made me feel like I was brushing up against something special, a treasure rarely found, and it'd always felt like when I touched her she cleansed some of the ugly from me.

And I'd wanted it. To feel good again. To feel like I mattered. I wanted to think if she'd let me, I could make her life better the same way she'd once made mine.

I wanted all of that just about as goddamned badly as I wanted to soil her, to taint this good girl with every dirty thing I'd learned since the second she left me with a battered, broken heart, wanted to get lost in that body, lost in that mouth, lost in her hands and her mind and those haunted eyes.

Logically? I knew she was taken. I couldn't have her. But the rest of my body didn't give a fuck.

I blinked hard, swallowed harder, trying to tear myself away from that gaze burning into me with so much pain and hatred I was sure she was going to dissolve me into a molten, boiling puddle right in the middle of Aly's kitchen floor.

Shit. It hadn't been my intention to hurt her. It was the last fucking thing in this world I'd wanted to do.

And here I stood, doing it again and again.

What the hell was wrong with me?

But the truth was, I hated her, too.

"Christopher." The word was low, thrown out like a caution flag, striking me from behind. I twisted to look over my shoulder.

My mom, Karen, stood there, her brown eyes knowing, soft, but filled with warning.

Just her presence broke up all the intensity, a flutter of awkwardness taking its place.

"I came to find you." She tilted her head. "I thought you were bringing me a drink. I'm dying of thirst out there."

I resisted the urge to roll my eyes. *Subtle, Mom.* God, she was so damned obvious.

"I was just telling an *old friend* hi." I let the sarcasm roll from my tongue.

A worried frown pinched up Mom's face as her attention darted between us. Samantha shifted in discomfort.

I knew Mom meant well, but fuck, none of this was fair. They just expected me to welcome Samantha with open arms. I swear, it felt like I was being ganged up on, all the women in my life hitting me from every side. Mom had been ecstatic when Aly told her Samantha was coming today, filling her in that she lived right around the corner.

All of my family was in love with the girl who'd torn me to shreds. Of course it was obvious Mom was assuming all those same things Aly had assumed, that I'd been callous and cold and had just tossed her aside when I was finished with her, when God's truth was I would never have gotten my fill.

Never.

I promised her I was *never* going to be finished with her. It was Samantha who'd *finished* me.

"*I* haven't gotten the chance to tell Samantha hi yet, either, so I'm glad to find you both in here." Mom settled her warm gaze on Samantha. "It's so good to see you. It has been far too long."

Samantha exhaled heavily, drawing my attention to her. She seemed to compose herself, forced a smile. "It's so nice to see you again, Mrs. Moore."

"Pfft." Mom waved her off. "You never called me Mrs. Moore before. Please don't start now. You're just going to make me feel old."

Mom straightened out her impeccable clothes, and I wanted to laugh. *Old* and *Karen Moore* were an oxymoron. She was the epitome of beautiful, that timeless kind of woman who never showed a sign of the passing years. She also had a heart the size of Texas, and even though Aly and I took more after our dad, with his dark hair and deep emerald eyes, I knew my little sister got all her sweetness from Mom.

Soft, submissive laughter floated from Samantha, and I felt it somewhere in my chest.

"Okay, *Karen*. It's nice to see you again."

"When Aly told me she'd run into you, I couldn't believe our luck."

Luck?

Right. Lucky me.

Samantha laughed a little deeper, a throaty sound that sent a fresh round of blood pumping through my veins, washing out that constant numbness and filling me with all the shit I didn't want to feel.

"I was honestly shocked when I first saw her . . . the baby and Jared and just everything." Affection softened Samantha's voice, and I was doing my all to block it out and somehow doing my best to feel it a little more.

Goddamn it. Was this what it felt like to lose your mind? Because everything I felt was at odds, wanting to shun every last thing and begging for more.

Mom chuckled lightly. "Well . . . she gave us all a shock, believe me. But everything works out like it's supposed to, doesn't it?"

She slanted a quick glance in my direction.

Oh, stealthy, Mom. I scowled at her, hoping she could read my mind. Didn't she know some other fucker had gotten my girl? He was the lucky one. And he'd damn well better deserve her.

For one second, Samantha cast her attention to the window behind her, out into the backyard, where Aly and Jared had gathered with family and friends, before she turned back to my mom, smiling. All the while she seemed frantic to avoid my gaze at all costs, the gaze that kept getting locked on her, desperate to read every emotion pouring from that expressive face.

Dead to me. I snorted to myself. *Right.*

"For them, it definitely seemed to. They seem so perfect together. I really am happy for them."

"So am I. There's nothing better than knowing one of your children is truly happy. That they're where they're meant to be." Mom's face flashed with something significant, then she threw out her arms. "Well, what are you waiting for? Get over here and give me a hug. I missed you like crazy. And oh my goodness, sweetheart, you've always been beautiful, but look at you now."

A soft stream of self-conscious giggles flooded from Samantha, and her face got all red while I got all hot. Samantha shuffled over to my mom and wrapped herself in her waiting arms.

I rubbed my hand over the knotted muscles at the back of my neck, torn between wishing I didn't have to witness their exchange and not being able to look away.

Because Samantha was clinging to her as if she'd been reunited with family, someone who'd been lost to her and was now once again reclaimed.

Fuck.

She'd always been good. So fucking good and sweet and kind. Selflessness was the very extreme of her nature. Her only crime had been me, her trespasses hinging on everything I'd pushed her into.

Until the night I'd pushed her too far.

Squeezing my hands into fists, I shifted on my feet, warring with the urge to rant and rave and yell.

Why was I the one who had to suffer through this? Why did she get invited back into my life when she'd forbidden me from hers?

It wasn't fair.

Not at fucking all.

Yet here I stood, trying to regain my cool. To pretend like nothin' mattered at all. Just like I always had.

Mom rested her eyes on me, all sympathy and love mixed with a wash of regret.

No doubt, she could see right through me. She always had been able to.

In discomfort, I dropped my attention to my ripped-up Vans and raked a hand through my hair.

"Samantha, why don't you go on out back and fix yourself something to eat? Jared made the call to dinner about ten minutes ago. You don't want your steak to get cold."

I chanced looking back up, and Mom had stepped away from Samantha, holding her by the upper arms.

Warily, Samantha looked back toward the kitchen. Sad blue eyes skimmed over me before they darted to the spot where I'd basically assaulted her ten minutes before. "Oh . . . well, I was supposed to grab drinks for me and Megan."

A small smile wobbled at the side of that mouth. That fucking mouth.

I itched, wet my lips.

Laughing, Mom patted her. "Don't worry about it. Christopher and I will handle it, won't we, sweetheart?"

"Oh, gladly," I drew out. Now I was getting her drinks? Tonight just got better and better. Apparently my mom loved to torture me.

Samantha hesitated, nodded. "Okay . . . that would be really nice."

Then the girl had the nerve to smile. Like really smile, her red mouth all twisted up like a bow, a present I wanted to tear right into, knowing all the joys hidden inside.

She didn't get to do this to me. She didn't get to make me feel alive under that smile that warmed me from the inside out, the one that had always made me lose my head and so easily captured my heart.

She didn't get to hurt me.

Not again.

Not with that gorgeous face and that perfect body.

And most definitely not with that sweet, soft spirit.

It was the most treacherous thing of all.

Samantha slipped around the island and disappeared out the back door. The entire time, I watched her go, my focus all wrapped up in her retreating form, her ass all round, her legs all sleek, the long length of her near-white hair swishing all down her back.

I suppressed a groan.

Mom snapped her fingers in front of my face, shooting me a

smirk that presumed too many things. "Punch bowl is behind you, in case you'd forgotten what you're in here for."

I gave her a mocking glare as I backed farther into the kitchen. "So I may not be the brightest of your kids, but I do think I know a spiked punch bowl when I see one. At least I have one redeeming talent," I said, the words dripping sarcastically from my mouth.

"Ha ... says the one who just graduated from ASU and within a month was partner in a business. You're *so* terribly worthless," she teased, rolling her eyes as she headed farther into the room. She came to an abrupt standstill in front of me. "Always thinking you're less than you are. And you're more than smart, more than capable, Christopher," she said quietly, her demeanor from seconds earlier shifting. Her brown eyes gleamed as she looked up at me, her expression pointed but filled with understanding.

I squirmed, and she set her hand on my cheek before she moved it down to settle it on my chest. "You just tend to think more with that heart you like to pretend doesn't exist."

I winced.

What the fuck was that supposed to mean?

She turned to the punch bowl and began filling four cups with ice. "It's high time you started paying attention to it," she said, not looking my way.

Scornful laughter rushed up my throat. "I'm twenty-three, Mom. You don't need to intervene. I dug my own grave and I'm content to lie in it. I'd appreciate it if you and Aly didn't go trying to dig it up."

She scoffed. "Content? You are many things, but content is definitely not one of them." She turned to look at me. "You want to know what I walked in on ten minutes ago?"

"No, I really don't."

Ignoring me, she continued on, "Two very confused, very hurt people. Two people who obviously need to forgive each other. Two people who are trapped somewhere in the past. You think I didn't know you were torn up over her, Christopher? You think I didn't see you change after the two of you broke up?"

"I changed when my best friend tried to kill himself and got himself sent away."

She huffed in disappointment. "That scared you, Christopher. Hurt you. What happened with Jared made you question everything in your life. It did that to all of us. But I know there was so much more to it than that . . . and I know it had everything to do with that girl outside."

Anger spiraled through me, and I rushed both my hands through my hair, hating that my mom had it, spot-on, when I'd thought I'd kept all of this shit tucked so perfectly inside.

My resentment boiled over. "It doesn't matter," I almost yelled, then quieted my voice to a harsh whisper and leaned in closer, hissing the words. "It doesn't fucking matter. She moved on, or did you miss that part? Even if I wanted her . . . even if she wanted me . . . she's living with some guy. And I promise you that I know Samantha well enough to know that's not a casual thing." I hated the way the words got all choked up, sounding like they just about killed me to say them.

But they did.

It fucking killed me to say it. To admit it. To think about Samantha crawling in bed with some asshole every night. To think about him undressing her. Adoring her. She wouldn't be with him unless she loved him. Completely and wholly.

And she was supposed to be mine.

Mine.

And I'd fucking lost her and I'd hate myself for the rest of my days for doing it.

And I'd forever hate her for letting me go.

Sympathy flashed across Mom's face, like she'd just read what had raced across mine, and she gently reached up and touched my chin. "Everything matters. Don't think for a second it doesn't."

Quickly she filled the cups with punch, grabbed two, and began to walk away. She paused before she got to the door and looked back at me. "And for the record, I never said a word about you getting back together with her. The fact that's exactly where your mind went should tell you something."

Clutching a cup, she lifted her hand, gestured to the two remaining on the counter. "Now, grab those and come out. It's time to enjoy your friends and family."

She ducked out the door, and I silenced a frustrated scream.

This was pure and utter torture.

I shifted my chair back from the table, stretched my long legs out casually in front of me, nursing a beer like I didn't have a care in the world, while I dealt with the clusterfuck of emotion raging inside me.

Searching for a second's reprieve, I looked up toward the invisible stars. Night clung to the dense sky, a thin sheet of clouds stretched across the endless expanse. Miles of city lights glowed against them to cast the whole of the backyard in a milky haze. Earlier in the day, Jared had had me help him string up strands of clear bulb lights, each draping across the yard to make it feel like the place was closed in.

Special.

Sanctified.

Helium balloons sat in clusters around the wall's perimeter, and the twinkling party lights and the haze from above made them glimmer with color, the entire backyard setting the tone for the perfect party Jared wanted nothing more than to give to his little sister.

It made everything seem closer. More intimate.

Now it was late and most of the party had cleared out. Just our closest friends and family remained—and, of course, Samantha. Four hours had passed in a blur, she and I partaking in some kind of forbidden dance where we weren't allowed to speak to each other, weren't allowed to look, which was about damned near impossible. We'd managed not to utter one word to each other over the rest of the night, acting as if the other wasn't there while somehow we were both involved in the conversations happening around us.

Soft laughter floated from the well of that sweet little mouth. In defense, I slammed my eyes shut, but there was nothing I could do, and they opened just in time to catch that bashful blush rush to Samantha's cheeks. She was all lit up, the lights from above making her appear angelic.

Unreal.

My chest squeezed.

Self-consciously, she tucked a lock of blond hair behind her ear, hair I wanted nothing more than to fist in my hands, mind you, and her soft tongue darted out to wet her bottom lip. She pressed her teeth to the plump flesh, fighting off a smile that only grew as she listened to everyone telling stories about their most embarrassing moments.

She'd gotten comfortable, settled into the casual vibe that had taken over the backyard, while I sat there feeling all the screws holding my sanity together coming loose.

Clenching my jaw, I gave it my all to look at my sister, who was currently numero uno on my shit list. I still couldn't believe she thought there was anything okay with inviting Samantha here.

Then I made a feeble attempt to look at my asshole *BFF* sitting snuggled up beside her. All night he couldn't seem to decide if he wanted to smirk at me or watch me with some kind of pitying smile that I wanted to knock right off his smug face.

My attention jumped around to the rest of our friends and family who sat around the long banquet table that had been set up in the middle of the yard.

But fuck me. I couldn't stop looking at her. I lifted a bottle of beer to my mouth. Ice-cold liquid flowed down my parched throat as I slanted my eyes back in her direction. I went for inconspicuous, but I was pretty damned sure she could feel the heat of my gaze, because the girl kept sliding her attention my way, catching me staring, before she'd get all fumbly and panicky and jerk away.

Megan laughed hysterically at my side, pulling my attention back to her. I cracked a grin, because she was funny when she was all liquored up, always kinda loud and obnoxious but completely sweet at the same time.

She kinda reminded me of me. You know, except for the sweet part and she wasn't a slut.

I was always giving her crap, teasing her relentlessly, because she didn't hesitate to give it right back just as good as I gave it. She was superhot, too. No question about that. Wouldn't touch that girl for a million bucks, though, no matter how much of that razzing might tell otherwise. She was one hundred percent friend material.

"Oh my God, seriously, you guys don't even know," Megan continued with her story, her expression brimming with exaggerated mortification. "There I stood in the center of the school playground, crossing my legs and trying to cover up the huge wet spot soaking my pants with my hands. The entire fourth grade class had made a circle around me, but the worst part of all was Tyler Adams standing there pointing and laughing at me, yelling, 'Look! Megan peed her pants.' Most embarrassing moment of my life *and* my first broken heart. He was supposed to be my boyfriend and instead he told me I was gross." She shook her head sadly, biting back laughter.

Aly and Samantha laughed like it was the funniest thing either of them had ever heard.

God, I needed a distraction, to quit letting myself get lured into that sound that was making me all kinds of crazy.

"You are gross," I tossed out, because like I said, Megan was an awesome target.

Megan pointed at me. "Shut it."

Bull's-eye.

"What?" I shrugged innocently. "I'm only speaking the truth."

"Ha . . . you want to start talking about gross? I have way too many stories on you to start talking *gross*, so watch yourself, dirty bird."

Ouch. Of course she'd go there.

From across the ten-foot space, I could feel Samantha's sudden discomfort, the way she shifted and her face dropped toward her lap, and I also knew from experience that Megan was way past capacity for her to keep her tongue in check. She loved ribbing me about my not so stellar history with the opposite sex. Usually I didn't mind—it was all fun and revelry—but not tonight. I'd once told Samantha I hadn't earned all of my reputation, but I sure as shit had earned it now, and with all joking aside, it wasn't exactly something that made me proud.

"Now, now, now . . . let's not get carried away," I cajoled, going for casual. "My mom *is* sitting at the table *right* next to you." The jerk of my chin at Mom was playful, but I saw her soft

brown eyes go that disappointed shade again, the way she always looked at me anytime the subject of me and girls was
brought up.

She'd always been the supportive type, quietly strict, rarely
getting upset when we got in trouble, instead responding with
insight and words that made us think.

But my lifestyle was a whole other issue, and she never had
any qualms expressing her displeasure about that.

Tonight, it was blatant. I totally got it. My mom wanted to
see me happy. She thought I deserved more than mindless sex
and endless bodies.

But I didn't.

She tsked to break up the tension that'd gathered thick, then
looked at Megan and lightened her voice. "Yes, by all means,
spare me. The last thing I need to hear about are the escapades
of either of my sons. These two . . ." She trailed off suggestively,
shaking her head. She shot an accusatory eye between me and
Aug, who was rubbing his neck as he looked toward the sky,
trying not to laugh, because my little brother was just as guilty
as me. "I don't know what I'm going to do with either of them."

Beside him, Courtney blushed a hundred shades of red. She
had to be one of the shyest girls I'd ever met. Hadn't seen her in
years, and damn, was she the spitting image of Helene. Fucking
beautiful, all serene and soft and with a kind of innocence that
had just about gone extinct.

I was pretty sure I wasn't the only one who'd noticed the
way Courtney and Aug had been sneaking glances at each other,
either. Jared was watching his little sister like a hawk, probably
just damned near as close as I was watching Samantha, but for
entirely different reasons.

Scratching the side of my jaw, I studied my jock of a younger
brother, figuring it was about time he and I had a little chat. I'd

learned my lessons the hard way. Guys like us didn't go getting
sweet on girls like that.

Megan gave me a little shove. "Fine, you're off the hook. But
only for Karen, since she loves me best," she taunted, glancing
at my mom with a wide smile before turning right back to me.
"And you better watch yourself or I'm letting loose."

"Heard you already were." My eyes went wide with the jab.

"Gah . . . I will kill you." She smacked me in the chest, hard,
and I laughed just as hard, leaning off to the side as she continued with a barrage of slaps against any piece of me she could get
her hands on.

I rubbed at the sting on my skin.

Totally deserved that one.

And yes, it was totally worth it.

I pinched her side, and Megan squealed, jumped, swatted
me again. "Christopher Moore! You are going to pay for that."

"Oh, is that a promise?" I waggled my brows, my words
pure innuendo, all play.

"In your dreams, dirty bird."

Like I said, easy target.

My dad huffed. "All right, you two, knock it off. Can we remember it is Courtney's *sixteenth* birthday? The whole lot of you
are terrible influences." Dad never said all that much. He was
the quiet type, always content to sit in the background until the
moment he felt it prudent to intervene.

Megan took in a deep breath, straightened herself out.
"Okay, okay. Truce."

"Truce," I agreed.

Smiling, my gaze drifted, drawn right back to Samantha, who
was fighting an amused expression, her blue eyes soft and light.

My heart took a stuttered beat, and for the longest minute,
I got stuck there.

God, she was beautiful, glowing with that radiating kind of beauty, the kind that's not just surface but real. Deep and pure and honest.

A lump grew thick at the base of my throat, and I tore my eyes away, swallowing over it.

Like she was giving a toast, Megan lifted her cup. "All right, Samantha, you are up! What's your most embarrassing moment?"

When all the attention landed on her, Samantha blushed just about as hard as Courtney had, minutely shaking her head as she again nibbled at that plush red lip.

Goddamn, what I wouldn't give to be the one doing that for her.

"Do I have to?" she almost pled.

She'd been sipping at that plastic cup all night, filled up with my mom's special punch, which packed a major *punch*, and I knew she was feeling good, the way her mouth seemed lax and her words hinted at a tiny slur.

So fucking cute.

I raked my palm over my face and over the top of my head, trying to break up the unwanted thought.

"Uh . . . yeah, you do," Aly supplied, giggling as she got cozy tucked into her husband's side. "The rest of us had to. Now, spill."

"Ugh," she groaned, this throaty sound that hit me low, dragging all my blood with it.

Awesome. The girl had the same effect on me as she did when I was sixteen.

"Mine's the worst. Believe me." For the flash of a second, her eyes darted to me, before she sucked in a huge breath, then released it slowly. "So . . . when I was seventeen my mom asked me to run an errand for her. I didn't have my own car, so I took my dad's. I drove to the Walgreens, parked right at the front, jumped out, and ran inside. When I came back out, I stood there staring at the empty spot where my dad's car had been. Inside, I was freaking out that it'd been stolen." She glanced around. "Then I heard this man yelling."

She bit back laughter, though it was swimming all over that pretty face. "I looked across the parking lot to where he was waving his arms in the air, his face beet red, screaming, 'Whose car is this? Whose car is this?' over and over again." Blue eyes went wide with emphasis. "Turns out, Dad's car wasn't stolen. Instead of putting it in park, I'd put it in neutral, and it rolled across the parking lot and crashed into a brand-new Lincoln. When he saw me standing there, the old man started screaming at me, demanding to know if this 'piece of junk' was my car, and I just shook my head no and walked away."

Clutching her stomach, Aly doubled over, cracking up. "No, you didn't."

"Oh yes, I did. Walked all the way home, three blocks in the middle of summer. I dumped the bag on the kitchen counter and went straight to my room. The most embarrassing part was my dad came in about a half hour later and wanted to know where in the heck his car was. When he finally pried it out of me, he drove me straight back in Mom's even crappier station wagon. He made me get out and apologize for lying and leaving the car there. Of course by then there were about fifty people gathered around *and* four cops. Let's not forget about them and the five-hundred-dollar ticket they gave me. They told me I was lucky they didn't arrest me for leaving the scene of an accident."

Jared howled, tipped the neck of his beer bottle in her direction like a high five. "Now, that is embarrassing."

"Told you. Most embarrassing moment in my entire life."

"But not the worst we'll hear tonight." Jared slanted his eyes at me. I wondered which of the billion dumb-ass things I'd done to embarrass myself as a teenager he was going to call me out on.

"Watch yourself, man," I warned, feeling the wry smile forming on my lips in the same second a smirk landed on his. I wasn't exactly *shy*. Hell, everyone around this table knew it, too. I just didn't need to prove what a dumb-ass I could be.

He cocked his head. "Oh, you're not getting out of this, my friend."

"I thought this was about telling our own stories. What makes you think you get to tell mine?"

"Uh . . . because there's no way in hell you'd ever speak this one aloud."

Jared looked around the table, gestured in my direction. "So when we were fifteen, our boy here decided it'd be an awesome idea to break into the school and go skinny-dipping in the team pool. In the middle of the night and with three girls."

"Oh, dude, you wouldn't dare go there," I warned, amusement growing thick in my chest.

He smirked. "Oh yes, I would, and I am."

Aly moaned. "Oh, gross. I don't want to hear anything about my brother naked. I was traumatized enough when I lived with him."

"See. What did I say? Gross," Megan shot out. Both of them fell right back into hysterics, all at my expense. "And with three girls?" Megan shook her head and pressed her hand to her chest, like it made no sense at all. "What on earth were they thinking?"

"That they wanted to see me naked." I added a drawn-out "Duh" for good measure.

"I give up," Dad said, throwing his hands in the air, and Samantha started chewing at that lip again, trying not to fall into the same fit of laughter Aly and Megan were rolling in.

Jared chuckled. "Without giving it a second thought, Christopher stripped down, tossed his shoes and all his clothes onto the bleachers, and jumped right in."

I just shook my head, scratched my chin, laughing at how crazy we'd been, what a great time Jared and I'd always had when we were young, back when we didn't care a whole lot about anything but having fun. It was the year before Samantha and I had gotten together. I remembered that night so clearly. The whole thing really hadn't been that sexual. I mean, I'd be lying if I said we weren't feeling on top of the world when those three hot girls willingly followed us out there, thinking we were about to get an eyeful of what we were dying to see, but it was more about being young and free.

"Dumb-ass didn't stop to take into consideration it was December. He surfaced, screaming and hollering that it was freezing. Two seconds later, all the outdoor lights flipped on, and there was Dale, the security guard, coming barreling through the field toward us. Christopher hauled out, stark naked, trying with his hand to cover up his junk that was all shriveled up from the cold. He just started running, yelling at us to get out of there. We all were right behind him, watching his lanky white ass sprinting across the parking lot and into the next neighborhood." He pointed at me. "Dude had to walk two miles home in the shadows while the four of us were laughing our asses off. Next day we show up at school and all his clothes are on display with the announcement that they were looking for the owner. Turns out Dale couldn't make out faces from the distance."

"Entire school knew it was me, but not a soul fessed up. Got away with that shit. Never got back my favorite shoes, though."

"Christopher, that's terrible," Mom admonished, wide-eyed and a little in shock.

"Oh, come on, Mom, don't tell me you never went skinny-dipping when you were a kid."

She laughed, flushed a little. "Well, I never broke into the school," she said, as if it made it any better.

Aug covered his ears. "Oh God. Please stop. Don't need those images in my head."

"Oh hush." Mom both frowned and smiled. "Don't you think your mom should have some fun once in a while?"

"Uh . . . no . . . not that kind of fun, and I most definitely don't need to hear about it."

"Well, Aly and I definitely have experience with skinny-dippers, don't we?" Megan said. "All our friends used to think stripping off all their clothes and diving into a pool was the highlight of the night." Megan grinned over at Aly.

"Ugh . . . yes," she groaned toward the sky. "I always stayed as far away from that train wreck as possible. Was not getting mixed up in that mess."

Jared hugged Aly a little closer. "See, Courtney, you should totally take after Aly here. Boys start taking off their clothes?" He pointed at her. "You get the hell out of there."

"Jared!" Courtney almost whined, almost rolled her eyes, but was too embarrassed to do either.

"What?" He shrugged. "The last thing I need is to have to take a trip out to California to kill someone."

Rubbing my hand over my mouth, I tried to contain my laughter. Dude was so overprotective it bordered on criminal.

Megan slanted me a coy smirk before she looked back at Samantha. "What about you, Samantha? Do you like peeling off those clothes to relish the cool water?"

Little bitch. She knew exactly what she was doing—taunting me, teasing me with fantasies that hit me hard and fast. Thinking about Samantha naked was about the last place my mind needed to go.

Scowling, I slouched in my chair, shuttering my brain from

going in those dangerous directions. But I couldn't stop my thoughts from going damned near haywire, blinking out as I visualized what that sweet little body would look like all glistening wet.

Goddamn.

As much as I didn't want to listen to Samantha's answer or watch her reaction to the question, there was nothing I could do to stop from latching onto the sight of that rush of heated embarrassment that flamed on her chest and rushed up her neck, splashing crimson all over her cheeks. They glowed red, almost as dark as the red on those pouty lips.

I sucked in a shuddered breath.

Keep it together, man.

"No," she finally said, hesitantly, before she quietly confessed, "I don't swim, let alone do it naked." She pushed out the last like a joke.

"You've got to be kiddin' me," Jared accused, grinning wide as he tipped a bottle of beer to his mouth, his foot propped up casually on the edge of the table as he rocked back. "You live in Arizona and you don't swim? There has to be something fundamentally wrong with that."

"She's scared of water." The words slipped from my mouth before I could stop them, and they weren't mean or hateful or filled with the vengeance I'd wanted to spew at her hours before. Instead I was remembering how intensely real her fear was.

An awkward silence filled up the backyard, everyone frozen when Samantha turned those shocked blue eyes on me. Something heavy passed between us. It wasn't beyond anyone here that those words were the first time either of us had acknowledged the other since we'd come out back.

"Can't believe in all these years you never got over that." I let the words come soft, because that's what I'd felt for her then, back before every place she'd once inhabited in me had been left hardened when she'd gone. Instantly, I wanted to steal them back, because for a flash she looked at me like she really saw me, like she recognized the person I'd once wanted to be.

I'd have done anything to be him. To be good enough for her.

"Some fears hold on forever," she whispered, and she swallowed hard, still clinging to my gaze.

A gentle breeze blew in, rustling through the trees and swaying the lights strung up overhead, a low howl uttered from the skies that whipped through her hair. I felt myself flailing within, a mayhem of nerves and memories of all the love I'd had for this girl that had turned sour, what had blackened my beliefs and slaughtered the only pure hope she'd bred somewhere in my spirit.

God, I wanted it back, the chance to prove myself to her.

Aly cleared her throat. "I'm going to go in and check on Ella."

Everyone around the table nodded, like maybe they were nodding away their discomfort.

My mom stood as Aly headed inside. "I think we'd better call it a night, too. It's getting late." She pulled Courtney up, hugging her close. "I am so glad you're here, sweet girl." She dropped an affectionate kiss to Jared's temple, then leaned in to brush another to Samantha's cheek. "Don't be a stranger."

"I won't," Samantha promised.

Mom rounded the table, hugged me and Megan, while Aug and Dad casually said their good nights. And I knew I should make my call, too, bail out and go find something or someone to pour my frustrations into, but I stayed rooted in my chair.

A thick quiet had taken over. The five of us who remained just sat there suspended in it, surrounded by it, comforted by it. Even though it was excruciating all at the same time.

Hesitating, I leaned my elbows on the table, picking at the

label on my beer. Finally I lifted my head, catching those blue eyes trained on me. It was like she could anticipate what I would say.

"How is Stewart?" I stumbled over the words that were filled with those fears and worries I'd been feeling since the second Aly'd told me he'd had a recurrence.

Blinking, she sucked her bottom lip between her teeth, fighting that same war we'd been fighting all night. Did she take the easy way out? Act like those vile words I'd spewed at her were the truth? That she was dead to me and I was dead to her? Or be the one to take a chance and whisper one solitary truth.

The expression that transformed her face was one I'd witnessed so many times, when she'd come to me at night and I'd hold her after she'd been holding Stewart all day, when all her fears had caught up to her and, just for a moment, she'd needed someone else to be strong for her. Her mouth trembled. "He's sick, Christopher."

No doubt she already knew I'd heard about Stewart. It was clear in my question. But her words weren't an answer. They were an admission.

That lump in my throat throbbed, and I rushed my hand over my face, my head inclined as I leaned in closer, whispered lower. "How bad is he?"

A phone chimed and buzzed on the table, the plate lighting up against the peace, bursting the secluded bubble we'd all been in.

I'd forgotten anyone else was even there, and I sat back uneasily, my eyes darting between the three others. Some kind of curious satisfaction spread on Megan's face, while a deep sadness had fallen over Jared's. The guy just always got it, even when I didn't want him to.

Cringing, Samantha grabbed her phone, swiped her thumb across it to reject the call.

"Everything okay?" Megan ventured.

Samantha shook her head, as if she were flustered and distracted. "Yeah . . . it was just Ben. He's probably just checking up on me."

Ben.

In a straight-up stupor, I blinked, a fog clouding my brain as the name pressed and pushed at my consciousness, vying for a way in. Finally it crashed through. Awareness settled hard and fast. A torrent of anger surged, a rogue rush of hatred pounding through my veins. Beating and battering until all I could see was red.

Ben.

My face pinched. "What did you just say?" I seethed, my voice coarse and ragged, filled with all the rage I probably didn't have a right to feel. But fuck, could anyone really blame me?

I wanted to crawl across the table and rip the phone from her hand, spew all the words at him I should have told him years ago, then smash that fucker into a million tiny pieces.

Him or the phone, I wasn't sure.

She jerked her head up. "What?" she asked, completely at a loss. Oblivious.

"I said . . . what did you just say?" It was nothing less than a bitter accusation, but I couldn't stop it from spilling out.

Eyes narrowed in confusion, she scrunched up her little nose, her head shaking the slightest bit.

"I said it was Ben checking . . ." She phrased it almost as a question, before she suddenly trailed off. Like it'd just occurred to her that this bit of information might matter to me. That it might fucking matter because that asshole had always wanted her, and I'd always known it, too. That slimy bastard was always playing the protective big brother when really all he'd wanted was to take what was mine.

"Motherfucker," wheezed from my mouth as I dragged my

hands erratically over the top of my head. Slowly, I shook my head, all those repulsive images I'd wanted to shun, the ones of Samantha with the man who'd taken my place assaulting me. Only now that man had a face.

My stomach turned and bile burned up my throat. All that fiery heat pulsing through me combusted, shooting me to my feet. I felt my insides curling, my skin blistering. Hot summer wind blasted across the yard. It scraped across my face and arms, rubbing everything raw, reminding me just how insanely bad loving someone can hurt.

I turned and slammed my fist into the closest inanimate object.

A fucking brick wall.

In fury, in agony, I screamed out, because I didn't want to pretend anymore. Didn't want to keep pretending she was dead when she'd been the only person who'd ever made me feel alive. Didn't want to keep pretending she meant nothing when she meant everything.

I stumbled back, right into Jared, who'd come out of nowhere and stood directly behind me. His voice was calm, placating. "Come on, man, let's go cool off."

Just then, the sliding door to the house opened. I saw my sister in the doorway. I felt her panic race along the lawn as she watched her carefully constructed plan crumbling to pieces.

"Oh my God, Christopher." Assessing the damage, her eyes darted around all of us. "What did you do?"

"What did I do?" I flung my arm out in her direction, all my hurt bleeding free. Yeah, she meant well. I got that. But goodwill didn't mean you had it right, and my sister had gotten this terribly wrong.

"What did I do?" I repeated. "What the fuck did you do, Aly? You did this. You brought her here."

Jared's hand fell heavily to my shoulder, gripping me tight. "Not tonight, man. We'll hash this shit out later. Right now I think you need a little breather. Let's go walk it off."

I glared around the yard at everyone staring back at me, all of them thinking I'd lost my goddamned mind, which apparently I had.

Everyone except for Samantha. No. She was watching me like she was fucking terrified of me standing here. Just as terrified as I was of her standing there.

I tore my arm free, shrugged him off, eyes still narrowed on Samantha. "Don't worry about it. I'm already gone."

THIRTEEN

Samantha

Harsh, hot wind whipped through Aly's yard, stirring leaves and howling through the trees. Overhead, the night felt heavy as dark clouds gathered thick, the city lights ominous against the descending summer storm. Lightning flashed, sending a ripple of energy streaking through the air. It skittered over my flesh like a warning, leaving me cold and agitated in the wake of Christopher.

In shocked silence, we all gaped at the vacant doorway where Christopher had just bolted from the party. I ran my hands up and over my arms in an attempt to chase away the chills.

What the hell was that?

Christopher gave me whiplash. One minute his tongue lashing, striking with severe, cutting words, the next that same mouth filled with soft concern for my brother, then shifting again, his entire body vibrating with hostility, his actions swift and violent and far too much for me to process.

172 A. L. JACKSON

My heart pitched and rolled, dislodged from its seat. It rose to my throat.

Shakily I stood, blinking. "I think I should go."

Aly approached, appearing beaten and guilty. "I'm so sorry. I really didn't mean for this to happen."

"I know you didn't. I'm fine. It's fine," I corrected, my smile weak.

"It's not fine."

No, it wasn't, but like I'd been saying for weeks, what was done was done, and there was no chance Christopher and I could undo all that hurt, no chance what Aly had in her mind for us could ever work.

I hugged everyone around the table, hugged Aly the longest. "Thank you for trying."

Resigned, she stepped back, and I knew she was letting go. Maybe not as my friend, but she was letting go of that crazy, insane notion she'd had that somehow Christopher and I could see past all the mistakes we'd made.

"Why don't you have Jared drive you home?" she offered. They shared one of those moments again, when they spoke a thousand words to each other without even the slightest utterance, both remorseful and disappointed, sharing in my pain, wishing there was a single thing they could do to ease it.

But all of us knew that was impossible.

I shook my head. "No . . . thank you. Honestly, I would prefer to be alone."

Aly nodded acceptance, walked me to her front door, and hugged me again. She squeezed me tight. "Good night," she said quietly.

"Good night," I murmured, forcing a reassuring smile over my shoulder as I stepped back out into the night, when really, I felt completely defeated.

Out front, it seemed darker, almost sinister, as the dense clouds encroached, building higher and higher, preparing to devour everything in their path.

I hugged myself, dropped my attention to my feet as I hit the sidewalk leading back home. My hair whipped around my face, and I succumbed and gave in to the tears that I'd fought all night, as I'd sat in that backyard and listened to his voice and acted as if it didn't wrap around me every time he spoke, as if he were just some guy and I was just some girl.

A gust of wind blew in low, sending a scatter of debris tumbling along the road. Lightning flashed overhead, a sheet of the brightest white, ushering in a clap of thunder right behind it, the storm chasing me down. Ducking my head, I increased my pace, knowing I was five seconds from getting caught in the grip of a monsoon.

Another flash of bright light lit up the night, streaks illuminating the dusty haze. I cringed, waiting for the strike, for the crash above that would surely give way to a torrential downpour of rain.

Awareness crawled over me as I noticed headlights growing nearer, the deep rumble of an engine close behind. Fear lifted the hairs at the nape of my neck, and shivers rolled in a cold wave of dread down my spine. My head screamed at me to run, all these clanging, blaring bells warning of the danger that lurked. But it was a familiar awareness that curled and pulsed, freezing my feet to the concrete below.

Slowly, I turned, blinded by the headlights burning from behind, though there was no mistaking the huge black truck that came to a stop twenty feet away. The door cranked open, lighting the cab.

And I knew I should run. Flee. Because I'd never been in greater danger than I was at that moment. His gorgeous face shifted from one dark expression to the next, his hair untamed, wild, as wild as the green eyes cutting me through as he jumped from the truck.

"Are you crazy?" I demanded against the wind, pounding my fist at my side, this man a raging contradiction.

Bitter laughter seeped from him while he glared across at me. "Crazy?"

Five excruciating seconds passed as we stood there, the storm gaining strength, gaining speed, beating at our senses. Before Christopher broke.

He closed the space in four long strides. Demanding fingers dove into my hair, pulling me flush against his body.

All defenses evaporated the second his mouth found mine. This wasn't a sweet kiss. It was rough and angry, his tongue commanding. His teeth bit and nipped. Those flames licked and jumped, fueling the fire that years ago he had lit, and my tongue sparred with his, fighting a war I knew I'd lose.

Frantic, his hands roamed, cupping my neck, sliding down my shoulders and arms, thumbs flicking across my breasts. My nipples hardened, and a moan raced up my throat. Christopher groaned and swallowed it down, then gripped me by the hips, lifting me from my feet.

He slammed my back up against hard, hot metal. Pinned to his truck, I gasped, his body towering, consuming, devouring me the exact way I knew he would. His erection strained against his tight, tight jeans, pressing between my thighs, pressing into my stomach. My body trembled with the idea of setting him free, the idea of what he'd feel like pulsing inside of me, taking me right here, in the dark against his truck.

He closed his mouth over my bottom lip, sucking it hard, a direct tether to my sex that clenched, begging for more.

"Fuck." The word reverberated like a moan from deep within

his chest, the urgency in his touch finally tugging at my common sense that had gone numb with the assault of his mouth.

And he felt familiar and right and totally, incredibly wrong, this man I didn't even know, because I never really had.

He rocked against me, and all those little pleasured places inside of me cried out in tortured relief as my spine grated painfully against metal. My legs tightened their hold on his waist, my hands just as desperate to feel and remember as my heart. But another part of me screamed to stop. To *remember.*

He threaded his fingers in my hair, gripping it tight, forcing my head back, his mouth running up and down my neck. His voice was a rumbled threat. "All I want is to be inside you, Samantha. To fuck you until you never forget who you belong to." He bit my jaw, then kissed it softly, rolled his hips again.

And my face felt wet, soured and soaked. I couldn't tell if it was from the tears I didn't know were still falling or the storm that had begun to pelt heavy droplets from the sky. Realization dawned, and my chest heaved with a moan as sorrow fell.

Christopher mistook it for want, just like the rest of my body did, because I couldn't stop myself from pressing back when he rubbed against me, brazenly shameless in the middle of the darkened street.

A street Ben could come driving down at any moment, the street where I lived, where I was supposed to be making a home—before Christopher again tore into my life.

My hands traveled to his chest, and I pushed him back. With my resistance, Christopher struggled to bring us closer. Memories of that night flickered, the stark reminder of the crazed need there was no breaking through.

"Please, stop," I whimpered, pushing at him harder.

Disoriented, he pulled back, like maybe he'd just realized what had gone down, what he'd done, what I'd allowed him to do.

Those whimpers grew, and a ragged sob tore up my throat. I pounded him on the chest. "No . . . no. You don't get to do this."

Releasing me, he stumbled away. My feet landed unsteadily on the ground. Lightning flashed bright, like a spotlight on what we'd done, and Christopher watched me with wide, wild eyes before thunder cracked right above. Energy sizzled through the air, and the heavens opened up and poured their fury from above.

"No," I whispered through a choked sob, the word drowned in the rain. I swallowed down my remorse, swallowed down the desire that blazed as hot and fast as the skies roiled. "I'm not a toy. You don't get to play games with me. Not ever again."

I forced myself to move, my four-inch wedges sloshing clumsily through the little rivers of water that gathered, running at the edge of the neighborhood street. I felt cold, chilled by his gaze that penetrated me from behind. I gathered all my courage, paused to look back at the man who held so much control over me, knowing it was time I took it back.

His hair was soaked, black locks clinging to his beautiful, furious face, his jaw clenched tight.

I found my voice. "You broke my heart once. You don't get to do it again." Then I turned my back and began to walk away.

His words hit me with the force of a two-ton truck. "You broke up with me, Samantha. Remember? I think it's time you admitted who broke who."

I looked back at him in disbelief, in my own indignation. Of course I remembered. I remembered every detail. I remembered what it felt like when he came to my room that last time. What it felt like to be terrified of the boy I thought loved me. Terrified that I didn't recognize him. Terrified that he wouldn't stop.

I remembered two days later at that party, standing there while Christopher stared at me with that vacant satisfaction on his face while he fucked another girl.

I remembered it all.

And now I realized clearly that I could never put myself in the position to feel that way again. Just this much of him was more than I could take.

"Stay away from me, Christopher." I tore myself away, crossed my arms protectively over my chest, and propelled myself into the driving rain, refusing to look back.

FOURTEEN

Samantha

January, Seven Years Earlier

Loud, raucous laughter lifted above the throb of music blaring from the party downstairs as it beat through the floor of the dimly lit upstairs room. It only accentuated the quiet within, the intensity of Christopher's gaze as he cupped my face with his hands, searching it with worried eyes. He wove his long fingers into my soaking-wet hair.

"Are you sure you're okay?" he asked with all the gentleness he could muster, though I felt the ferocity vibrating in his muted tone. He stood between my knees, a towel wrapped around my shoulders and my skirt bunched up around my thighs, the flowy fabric just as wet as the rest of my body. When he'd carried me inside, he'd set me on the bathroom counter, which opened up to a huge master suite.

I nodded through my tears, a shudder rolling through me as I choked down the last sob fighting to break free.

Jasmine had pushed me into the pool. Shoved me headfirst into my greatest childhood fear. Left me a sobbing mess that Christopher had jumped in to save, coddling me and shushing me and promising me I was okay when I was sure I was going to drown.

She'd played it off as an accident, just like she'd done when she'd dumped a full cup of beer down the front of my shirt an hour earlier.

Christopher gripped my chin, forcing me to look up at him, examining me more closely. Green eyes flashed with something dark, something protective and powerful, and it thudded my already hammering heart. "I swear to God, that bitch is lucky she's a girl, because I've never wanted to kick anyone's ass as badly as I want to kick hers."

With the corner of the towel, he dabbed at the droplets still dripping down my face. An inappropriate sound shot from me. It was half disbelieving laughter, half a cry filled with the remnants of fear that had taken me hostage when I'd been submerged in the dark, freezing waters, all of that twisted up with the mortification of being dragged from the pool by Christopher. I'd been panicked, choking and crying over the water I'd so stupidly drawn into my lungs. I'd never learned how to swim because I'd always been too fearful to even get in.

"Look at us," I whispered apologetically.

Christopher was as soaked as me, his threadbare shirt clinging to his wide chest, his dark jeans slicked to his skin. His hair was pieced and chunked, the black locks a shiny mess around his head.

God, if it was possible, he looked even more beautiful than usual, while I probably looked like a drowned rat.

His mouth pulled up at one side, and he slid his hand down to palm my neck. "Don't be embarrassed, Samantha. None of this is your fault. I shouldn't have brought you here. I'm so sorry. I should have known better than to have gotten you anywhere near that whore."

"I hate her," I admitted, dropping my gaze with the dirty confession. "I've never hated anyone before . . . but I hate her." Warily, I peeked back up at him. "I hate that you let her touch you. Hate that she's had you in ways I haven't."

For more than four months I'd been with Christopher. Countless times he'd snuck me out into the dark of the night, to the playground he'd first taken me to or to the seclusion of the little fort behind his house. We'd kiss for hours, touching, hands roaming over clothes, a few times wandering under, but we'd never taken things much further than that.

I was still his *good girl*, as he liked to call me, and it was always playful and sweet and a stark reminder that I wasn't sure I wanted to be anymore.

But I was scared.

Scared of giving myself to him that way.

Of him taking that part of me I could never get back, not sure if that missing piece would fracture me or if Christopher would hold on to it tight enough to hold me together, forever cherishing it the way I'd been taught it was supposed to be.

The way I wanted it to be.

Christopher gathered my hand and held it over his heart. "She means nothing to me, Samantha. Nothing. *She's* nothing, and she knows it. She pulls this shit because she's jealous. She sees how beautiful and sweet you are, and she knows she could never in a million years come close to being as amazing as you are."

"She's jealous of me because I'm with you."

Simple as that.

It was easy to see her hatred had very little to do with me, but rather with what I had.

And somehow, this boy was mine.

"Maybe. But it all comes back to who you are. I want to be with *you* because you are all those things. You are everything, Samantha. Everything. You know that, don't you?"

Awe filled my smile, this feeling that pulsed in my spirit and pressed at my ribs. "You make me feel that way."

He ran the back of his hand along my jaw. "That's because you are."

I burrowed my nose up under his chin. He shivered.

"You're freezing," I whispered against his cold skin.

I felt the force of his grin from my hiding place.

"That's because I just jumped into a pool in the middle of fucking winter with all my clothes on."

His hands roamed up my sides, and his voice grew deep as he moved to murmur near my ear. "You see . . . there's this girl who's on my mind every second of every day, and she drives me kind of crazy because I don't really understand the hold she has on me. But she has me in a way no one else ever has and more than anyone else ever will. And this girl . . . she needed me, and I didn't think twice about that jump, because getting in deep with her is the only place I ever want to be."

Emotion locked up my throat, and the chill coating my body warmed from the inside. "Thank you." I managed to pull him closer, let my words float out on a surrendered breath from my mouth. "Thank you for being crazy about me."

Wrapping my legs around his waist, he tugged me from the counter and carried me out of the bathroom and into the middle of the darkened bedroom. Slowly, he knelt and laid me down on the floor. It vibrated with the disorder below, heavy strains of music thrumming an intoxicating energy into the room.

He held himself up with one hand, hovering inches above me, the pads of his fingers gentle as he ran them down the angle of my jaw, then brushed them across my lips.

I exhaled against them, my mouth parting at his touch.

Light shined in from the bathroom, silhouetting this beautiful man in bold shadows, his profile sharp and strong.

Green eyes latched onto mine.

"Completely, crazy in love with you."

Time stopped. And I just stared. Enraptured by his words.

He looked at me intensely. Sincerely.

It was the first time he'd told me. But I'd been feeling it for a long time, falling deeper and deeper, losing more and more of myself to him.

My fingers whispered across his face. "Christopher." I murmured his name as if it were sanctified. "I love you with every part of me."

And I knew then that every piece belonged to him. I wanted him to hold them. Have them. Because I knew without a doubt he would cherish them.

With trembling hands, I fumbled through the top three buttons of my blouse. An invitation. A plea.

Christopher groaned as he watched me expose myself down to white lacy bra that had become transparent with the dampness that still coated my skin. My breasts felt heavy under his gaze, and they tightened painfully when he dipped down and nudged the material of my shirt wider, running his nose in a slow circle around the rosy bud of my breast, the only barrier that separated us a thin piece of lace.

My hands dove into his hair when he closed his mouth around it. "Make love to me," I breathed, the words emanating from somewhere in my spirit.

His moan was low, guttural, and he moved to adorn my skin with lush kisses, beginning between my breasts and trailing a path up my chest and neck and chin, until my mouth was being consumed by his. His tongue pushed through my lips and met mine in a tangle of need. A fuse lit, burning up my insides and pulsing between my legs. As if he felt the heat, he hardened, and I felt light-headed with the way his body reacted. I gasped when he pressed that hardness more earnestly against where I needed him most.

Clutching his shoulders, I arched up. "Please."

This time he moaned in frustration and ripped himself away. Leaning back on his elbows, he bracketed me, caging me in. His voice was rough, but somehow the words were soft. "God . . . do you have any idea how badly I'm dying to?" He rocked into me as if he needed to show proof. Sparks rocketed through my body. "How many times I've been alone with you and all I could think about was what it was gonna feel like when I finally got to be inside you?"

The shake of his head was filled with restraint. "But not here . . . not like this. Not when that bitch is downstairs. It's something we're both going to remember forever, and I don't want it to be here on this floor."

His eyes darkened with a hazy lust. "But I am going to make you feel good."

He dove in, his mouth hot and wet where he kissed under my jaw, then up behind my ear, brushed his lips to mine. "This mouth," he groaned, deepening the kiss. "You make me insane, Samantha."

Shivers flashed across my flesh, and I clung to him, lifting my hips, begging for a way to relieve the yearning ache.

He shifted to the side, and he suddenly slipped his hand under my skirt and cupped my mound over my underwear.

My shocked gasp echoed around the room, and I arched higher as he pressed harder.

He'd touched me there before, but only over my clothes. It'd always felt like a promise. A vow that one day he'd take me on a journey I'd yet to travel, that he'd elevate me to a place I was desperate to go. I wanted it to be him. For him to be the one to show me. To teach me.

He grazed his fingers over the fabric. "Is this okay?" he asked.

"Yes," I whispered.

Hooking his fingers around the edges of my panties, he sat back on his knees.

Slowly he dragged them down and spread me by the knees. All coherent thought escaped me when his mouth descended, and he kissed me in a way I'd only read about, in a way that I'd been taught was dirty and vulgar when really it had to be the most beautiful thing I'd ever experienced.

His tongue laved against my sensitive flesh. He singled out a spot that had me gasping, stifling these tiny cries of pleasure that kept working their way out. And it felt like too much, like too little, like I couldn't handle what was happening to my body.

Like I'd die if he stopped.

It built higher and tighter, and he kissed me more. Then he touched me deep and it sent something speeding through me. It broke in white-hot waves that rolled and pulsed and seeped and spun.

This time I was certain I was drowning.

But it was in complete and total ecstasy.

"Christopher," I whimpered, my body stretched taut as tremors rolled. Slowly he eased away, and he kissed me gently on the inside of my thigh. His breaths came out in short, heavy pants, like what he'd just done had affected him as profoundly as it had me. But I knew it couldn't be, because I could feel him pressed to my leg, harder than before.

And maybe I was just a naive little girl. Maybe I was a fool. But I didn't care because I knew what I felt for him was real. I shifted out from under him. Jolts of pleasured energy still zinged through me, and I wanted to beg him to do it again, but instead I pushed his back to the ground.

I tugged at the buttons of his still damp jeans, and those pants from his mouth came hard with anticipation.

"My birthday's in six weeks," I said, glancing up at him under veiled eyes, knowing he'd know what I meant, know what I wanted.

The memory I wanted reserved for my sixteenth birthday.

"Six weeks," he answered. He shot up and gripped my face between his hands. His eyes were wild and pleading and promising me all the things I wanted from him. "Six weeks and it's just you and me and forever."

Nerves raced through me, a shivered thrill and a flutter of anxiety, because I had no clue what I was doing.

All I knew was I wanted to do it.

Pushing him back down, I freed him from his underwear.

In awe, I touched him, watching his expression, the pleasured lines that dented his forehead, the parting of his lips.

When I took him in my mouth, it didn't feel weird or awkward like I'd expected, and Christopher uttered my name like a song of praise. He followed it with a sharp curse. His hands twisted in my hair, and I let go of every insecurity I had.

Everything that had transpired earlier suddenly felt like

fate—Jasmine flinging her drink at me, her cruelty when she knocked me into the pool when she knew I couldn't swim.

Like destiny welcomed.

Because it led to this.

Because instead of tearing us apart, she'd pushed us closer together.

Exactly where we belonged.

FIFTEEN

Christopher

Rain pelted from above, my entire body soaked, water dripping like a faucet from my hair and clinging heavy to my jeans.

What the fuck was I thinking, chasing her down?

But I couldn't stop the insanity she spurred in me.

I hadn't felt anything real in a long, long time.

But that kiss.

That kiss.

First real emotion in years. Of course it would come from her. And it wasn't bitter or angry. No. All I was feeling was light. The good. Even with her torment, I felt it, like I could seep inside her and feel that same sweet girl who'd knocked me from my feet years ago.

I watched her sloshing through the rivers flowing down the road, her head down, wrapping herself up in her arms as if it could shield herself from the pain I'd just inflicted.

I was so tired of hurting her.

Tired of her hurting me.

She'd been hurting me for fucking years.

I was tired of it all.

How'd I become enemies with the person I cared about most? Couldn't handle that anymore. Hating her. Blaming her. Just didn't know if there was any way for me to fix it.

SIXTEEN

Samantha

On the Wednesday after Courtney's birthday party, my students were gathered around me on the large play rug, their legs criss-crossed, enchanted by the story I read them.

The door cracked open. Cici popped her head inside. "Hey... psst... Samantha," she whispered as if she hadn't already disturbed the class. An excited smile crossed her face. "We need you up front."

I frowned and tucked a bookmark between the pages. "Everything okay?" Why I was whispering, too, I didn't know.

"Um... yeah... I would say so. Go on... I'll watch these little guys for a couple minutes."

Disquiet rippled through me, and shakily, I stood. "Okay, thank you."

"No problem." Cici stepped inside and retrieved the book. Her words were magnified when she sat in my chair in front of the kids and opened to the page I'd marked. "Oh, this is my favorite story ever," she said, winking at me as if to say *I've got this.*

She was one of the aides, her job one of the busiest in the school. She ran around doing everything from designing and printing parent flyers for the week to rushing toddlers who were about to wet their pants to the restroom.

I slipped out. My sandals echoed on the hard linoleum tiles as I plodded down the silent hall, everyone shut in their classrooms for afternoon activities. I clicked through the heavy door that led out into the front office, trying to quell the haunted feeling that slipped along the floor behind me. It followed me everywhere I went.

Since Saturday night, I'd barely slept. Exhaustion made my limbs feel heavy and weak, and my mind felt clouded by a constant fog.

It was really difficult finding sleep beside Ben after what'd happened with Christopher. Instead I lay there and listened to the deep, even breaths of his slumber, swimming in guilt while he rested completely at peace. Christopher had set off a bomb in the quiet sanctuary of my life that had left my world in shambles.

It blew through me constantly. His words. The accusation behind them.

That kiss.

God, that kiss.

Every time I closed my eyes, memories of it tore through me like a tempest, a savage, destructive force, fighting to eradicate every kiss Ben had ever given me.

Every inch of me burned.

It felt as if I were being incinerated from the inside out. All that hatred that had bled from him only scorched me deeper, winding me up in fear and trepidation and the sense that nothing was going to be the same.

Christopher Moore had always been trouble.

Now I knew he was dangerous.

I edged into the center of the office. Martin, our IT guy, rocked back in the office chair. He didn't turn to look at me, just continued to tap away at the keyboard. "Looks like someone's getting lucky tonight," he said, the tease seated deep in his words. "Why do some guys insist on making the rest of us look bad?"

My gaze landed on the bouquet that sat on the high reception counter just inside the door of the main office. Dread knotted up my insides, because I instinctively knew two things.

Those flowers had been delivered for me.

And they weren't from Ben.

Ben would have sent me a billowing floral arrangement, pink roses with garnishes and twists of white satin ribbon.

But this . . . this was as foreboding as the chaotic expression Christopher had worn on his face when he'd chased me down in his truck this last weekend. The bouquet was held in a tall, slender, cylindrical clear glass vase. Black calla lilies extended from the top in a regal arc, and at the center was a large white lily protruding above them all, as if the light were stretching up to keep all the darkness out. The stems were wrapped with a red silk ribbon, twisted in the simplest bow, though it somehow seemed the center of the arrangement.

It was simple. Graceful and mournful.

It felt like sorrow and hope.

Unease prickled the hairs at the base of my neck. His words tumbled through my consciousness. *You're dead to me . . . I want to fuck you until you know who you belong to . . . It's time you admitted who broke who.*

I sucked in an addled breath.

Everything he'd thrown at me four nights ago had been at odds with the other, his need and apparent hate, and I had no

idea what to believe. Somehow this arrangement seemed to sig-
nify them both.

"What? Are you going to stand there and stare at it all day
or see what your man has to say?" Martin asked when he looked
at me over his shoulder, perplexed.

Our head secretary, Lila, came bounding into the office. "Oh
good . . . you're here. I just about died when I saw the deliveryman come through the door. Of course I went and hoped that
my husband might have remembered our anniversary is this
week. Should have known better. Seventeen years and he hasn't
remembered once." She plopped into her chair and pushed her
glasses up her nose. "I signed for them and promised I'd get
them to you. Hope that's okay, honey."

"It's fine," I whispered.

She waved toward them. "Ben must really love you. Special
occasion?" she asked.

"No." My voice sounded raspy. That haunted feeling that
had trailed me for days slithered up my legs, wrapping me in
tendrils of fear.

And that was the truth. I was scared. Scared of the control
Christopher Moore held over me.

I mean, God, I'd basically allowed him to assault me against
his truck. I'd been close to begging for it. It'd taken everything
I had to push him away.

My stomach clenched, and I forced myself to walk around
to the front of the counter. There was a large envelope tacked to
the side of the arrangement, and my name was scrawled across
the front in a strong script. My pulse stuttered when I recognized the handwriting, and I was rushed with a swell of
light-headedness.

Christopher had personally written what was inside.

"You okay?" Lila looked up at me. "You don't look so good."

I ran shaky fingers over my sweaty forehead. "I'm actually not feeling that well. I probably got too hot out at recess with the kids. I think I'm just going to . . ." Awkwardly, I gestured behind me, trailing off when I realized I was a blabbering mess. Without another word, I took the bouquet, clutched it against my chest, and escaped back into the hall. I slipped into an empty classroom.

My knees were weak and I sank into a chair. Tremors rocked through me, and I fumbled with the envelope and pulled out the card.

It was blank on the front, and I almost anticipated the inside to be as well. But no. The note was made up of letters etched heavily into the page, the pen crushing through the fibers of the stock.

When your life is made up of more regrets than joys, you no longer know who you are.

You are desperate and violent.

You destroy what is good and go in search of what will destroy you.

You shun the light and welcome the dark.

You hate because it hurts too much to love.

You cross boundaries that should never be crossed.

Attempt to steal what is not yours to take.

You lie.

You curse.

When in truth, you are only cursing yourself.

And that regret hounds you, eating you alive.

Until it spits you from its mouth, casting you out onto your hands and knees.

And you're there, the hard earth piercing your skin, and you realize you're begging.

Wishing for a way to take it back.
Begging to be forgiven for what you've done.

At the bottom, I could feel the change, could picture Christopher's face as some of the intensity faded.

It seems like every time I see you things won't come out right. All that shit I said? Everything I did? None of it was okay. What I should have done was begged you for the chance to be your friend. I know I don't deserve anything more than that. Hell, I don't even deserve that. But I want it and I'm a big enough asshole to ask for it. Please don't walk away from Aly. Or from me. Stay.

I pressed the unsigned card to my chest. This is what I'd gone in search of. Forgiveness. To find a way to set free the pain of our pasts. But somehow Christopher's anguish only made me hurt more.

But was it real?

Or another game?

The most unsettling part was I wasn't sure how much he was asking me to forgive him for.

SEVENTEEN

Samantha

A horn bleeped from the street. I grabbed my purse and slung it over my shoulder. I was quick to lock the door behind me, and I rushed down the walkway toward the dark blue car waiting at the curb.

I ran around to the passenger side. An eager sigh gushed from my lungs when I plopped down into the seat and slammed the door. With a smile, I glanced over to find Aly grinning at me from behind the wheel. "Woohoo! Are you ready to party?"

I laughed. "Yep."

Ben was away for a week on a business trip, and we were going out.

Aly put her car in gear and flipped it around, and I turned to look in the seat right behind me. "Hey, Ella, sweetness. How are you today?"

Even though her car seat was facing away, I could see her little hands flail, and a coo erupted from her with the mention of her name. My heart pressed at my ribs, and I maneuvered to take her hand.

I'd fallen hard for this little girl. But really she was impossible not to love.

Aly glanced in the rearview mirror. "I can't believe I'm leaving her tonight."

"Are you worried?" I asked.

"Do I think something bad will happen to her?" Aly shook her head. "No." Then she lifted her shoulders in a helpless shrug. "But it feels wrong being away from her."

A soft smile edged my mouth, as I felt a little more awe at my friend. She was the kind of mom I hoped to be one day. "You and Jared deserve a night out, though, Aly. You both put her before everything, and it's okay for you to take care of yourselves sometimes, too."

She returned my smile. "I know . . . it's just hard leaving her for the first time. I haven't been away from her for more than an hour since she was born."

"I'm sure your mom is more than thrilled she's finally getting grammy time." I pouted at her. "You're kind of a hog, you know."

Aly laughed. "I know, I know. I can't help it."

Ella was already three and a half months old. Every time I saw her she seemed to be more vocal, more interactive. She was growing so fast.

I let my gaze travel out the window.

Three weeks had passed since I'd received the flowers from Christopher. And in that time, we'd become . . . friends.

Internally, I scoffed, knowing that was a coward's label. I knew friends didn't swim through stifling tension, continually aware of each other, dancing around a blatant attraction that we both were trying desperately not to acknowledge.

After receiving the flowers, I made the choice to really make Aly and her family a part of my life. I knew that meant welcoming in Christopher as well, just like I had before, but everything about it felt different now.

The first time I'd seen him after receiving the flowers was just in passing when I was leaving Aly's house. Our eyes had met tentatively, cautiously, as if he were searching mine for the response to his letter. I'd given him the softest smile, fueled by my own confusion. But the lump wedged in my throat came from the affection I still felt for him.

Since then, we'd kept it light, casual *hellos* and *how are yous* that fell very, very short of what needed to be said. We treaded lightly, because we both knew someday things would come to a head and we would have to lay it all out.

Truthfully, I wanted to get to the point where I trusted him enough to believe what he might have to say. I'd already accepted his flowers and letter as an apology for the way he'd treated me when we first saw each other, an apology for his brutal words and that ruthless kiss. More than anything, I wanted to finally forgive him for the past.

The more time I spent with Christopher and his family, the more distant I grew from Ben. At first I thought he'd started to change, but I guess I was coming to realize it was me who was changing. I was beginning to see things in a different light, and that light shined on the fact that he wasn't so much protective as he was arrogant and controlling.

It'd never been so apparent as when I'd ventured to mention Aly's name again, telling him I was meeting her for lunch. He'd exploded. Livid, he'd thrown his glass, smashing it against the kitchen wall, pointing a finger at my face as he warned me "one last time" to stay away from her.

Shock had frozen me, my mouth gaping and my eyes wide.

Immediately he'd recanted, hugged me, and promised he was
only protecting me, but that attack had set alarm bells off in me.
Yes, I cared about him. Deeply. I hated the idea of my life without him in it. But more and more I'd been questioning whether
he was really good for me.

Aly pulled into the apartment complex where Megan lived.
She was waiting for us at the curb. "What's up, bitches?" she said
as she leaned forward and kissed Aly on the cheek, squeezed my
shoulder, and then peppered loud kisses all over Ella's face.

Megan and I had become good friends, our relationship easy
and fun and a welcome relief from all the heaviness that seemed
to follow me through my life. She was constantly texting me
goofy stuff as if she knew I needed a reprieve from the stress of
the day.

"Ugh . . . just so glad the weekend is finally here," I said. "I
think the sun has fried all the kids' brains. They were completely out of control this week."

Megan released a sympathetic groan. "I can't imagine han-
dling a classroom full of five-year-olds. I don't envy you one bit."

Lightly I laughed. "Eh. It's really not so bad. But believe me,
they run me ragged by the time I leave at the end of the week."

Megan tugged at a lock of Aly's hair. "What about you,
momma? Good day?"

"Always." Then Aly shot her a glare through the mirror, the
corner of her mouth twitching with playfulness. "And for the
record, if my daughter's first word is *bitch*, I'm holding you personally responsible. That means free babysitting for the rest of
your life."

"Ha . . ." Megan buckled in, grinning. "Have you listened to
your husband talk or are you so busy staring at his body that
you can't hear a word he says? That man has the filthiest mouth

I've ever heard. And like I'd ever charge you to watch my baby girl . . . huh, Ella," she crooned toward her.

A giggle hitched in Aly's throat. "Oh goodness . . . don't I know it. He's working on it, though. I'm supposed to hold back all his favorite things when he slips in front of Ella, and believe me, he really doesn't want to go without them." She waggled her brows suggestively.

I clapped my hand over my mouth, trying to stuff the laughter back inside, but it just broke free, right along with Megan's.

"Right," Megan drew out. "I'm pretty sure that setup is one destined for failure. Neither of you can keep your hands off each other."

Aly blushed red, guilty, then went for the most aloof tone she could muster. "What? He's hot. If you had a husband that looked like mine, you wouldn't be able to keep your hands to yourself, either."

I could hear Megan's eye roll from the backseat. "Um . . . if I had a husband that looked like yours, I'd never leave the house . . . and neither would he. He would be chained to my bed."

Crickets.

Yep.

Total silence as all our eyes darted back and forth from one to another. Then we all busted up.

"Eww, Megan! Don't be making googly eyes at my man. That's just wrong and gross and I will kill you," Aly warned, pointing at her through the rearview mirror, trying to contain her laughter. "Speaking of, Jared wants me to swing by the job site really quick so he can tell Ella good-bye before I drop her at my mom's. Then we can hit the mall and go get ready, while Jared runs home to grab a shower before we head out."

Since it was their first night out, Aly wanted to start it with a fast shopping trip, something she hadn't been able to do since before she had Ella.

My stomach did a flip-flop in anticipation of tonight. This would be the first time I saw Christopher outside the safety of Aly's house. Yes, all of us were going out. Which meant I was *going out* with Christopher. Which also meant I was anxious and worried and much too excited. I'd chewed all my nails off, and I was suddenly all too thankful that Aly'd asked us to go shopping with her. I was in desperate need of some retail therapy. Therapy that promised I'd look my best.

Sick?

Yes. Yes. Very sick.

But I didn't care.

Aly programmed the address into her phone navigation and made a couple of quick turns into the neighborhood where Jared was heading up a complete remodel.

My stomach bottomed out when I saw Christopher's truck parked at the curb.

Aly slanted me an uncertain glance before she parked behind it.

Jared and a couple of his guys were in the front yard, unloading a piece of granite from the back of a work truck. The lot of them had shed their shirts in the overwhelming heat, and sweat glistened from the contours of their hard bodies.

"Good Lord," Megan mumbled, "I think I need to change professions." She poked her head up close to Aly's shoulder. "Ask Jared if he's hiring."

Out the windshield, Aly gawked, unable to tear her eyes from her husband, who caught her staring. He smirked at her, shouted out some orders to his workers, and began to make his way over. Aly opened her door and climbed out to meet him.

Figuring I didn't need to witness their reunion, I averted

my gaze toward the house. What I saw there sent me into a state of panic, my breath jumping out of my lungs.

Oh. My. God.

Christopher sauntered out the front door, raking a hand through his unruly hair. My mouth went dry.

Like the rest, he was shirtless. It'd been a lot of years since I'd seen him without one, and a whole lot had changed.

Swirls of color were inked in intricate patterns across his chest. The distance was too great for me to make out the design, but close enough to have my fingers twitching, wanting to trace the ink, to discover what the patterns meant. The tattoos rolled up and over his collarbones and slipped down over his shoulders, covering the entirety of one arm and a quarter of the other. Muscle rippled and bunched under rays of sunlight that streamed in to kiss his dark, tanned skin.

He was all sweaty and dirty and the sexiest thing I'd ever seen.

Fingers were suddenly under my chin, nudging my mouth closed.

Ruffled, I smacked at Megan's hand. "Stop it," I hissed, glaring at her in the backseat, and she laughed, her eyes twinkling.

"What? I'm just trying to help a girl out."

"I don't need any help."

Lured, my gaze drifted back to Christopher, who'd noticed Aly's arrival. The brightest smile lifted his face. Those places he'd singed with his kiss smoldered.

Which was pretty much every inch of me.

God. What was happening to me?

Megan chuckled. "Nope, doesn't look like you need any help at all."

When Jared released Aly, Christopher pulled her in for a big hug, then the three of them headed over to Ella's side of the car.

On instinct, I rolled down my window, catching Christopher's eye. For a flash, surprise flitted across his face, before a slow satisfaction took it over.

"Hey there, Sam," Jared said as he passed, yanking open the door behind me.

I twisted and grinned back at him. "Hi, Jared. You look . . . *hot*," I teased.

Jared winked. "You think so, huh?"

Aly rolled her eyes at me. "Not you, too."

"Oh come on, baby," he said, a ribbing grin slanted in her direction. "I'm sweating like a fucking dog. Sam's just worried I might die out here."

I liked Jared. He'd been a decent guy back in high school, even though he'd been pretty cocky, but he'd always had a good heart. Now he had a depth to him that hadn't been there before. But he was still playful. Fun. And he loved my friend perfectly.

Christopher tipped his head in a cordial tease. "Samantha." It sounded like silk.

I wanted to kick myself when a small giggle rolled out, but there was nothing I could do to stop it, because it seemed almost like he was trying to one-up Jared by using my full name.

He'd always insisted on it, and damn it, how I liked hearing it roll from his tongue.

Jared unbuckled Ella, his voice soft as he murmured to his daughter, while Christopher and I were locked in some kind of wistful stare.

Christopher shook himself off, tore his gaze away, and said, "My turn." Gently he took Ella from Jared's arms. He lifted her face up to his. Her tiny body curled up, and the sweetest smile pulled at her precious mouth. Christopher nuzzled her, whispering words and adorning her with tender kisses.

Again, my heart did that crazy, erratic thing. Except this

time it somehow felt soothed. There was no tearing my eyes from the man who for so many years I'd believed to be callous and cold, because there was nothing but love and warmth flowing from him as he adored his niece.

"That bad, huh?" Megan said, her voice completely void of the tease from a moment ago, quiet enough that no one else could hear.

I choked on her assessment. "Yeah," I admitted. I guess it really was that bad.

Four hours later, we had safely delivered Ella to her grandma, who was ecstatic to have her for the night, and spent way more money than we should have shopping, and now we were back at Aly's house getting ready. We'd opened up a bottle of wine, and music was blasting as we danced around Aly's bedroom, trying on all the different clothes we'd bought.

Megan insisted on doing my hair and makeup, telling me two girls weren't truly friends until they'd done each other's hair.

Okay.

I just laughed and played along, downing my second glass of wine.

Energy swirled through the room, the promise of a good time. How much had I needed this? Needed them?

I glanced at Aly, who stood in front of the mirror, trying on her tenth pair of heels, searching for the perfect ones to go with her new jeans. She and Megan were belting out a song, singing back and forth to each other like they'd done it a million times, Aly shaking her butt while Megan danced around behind me.

"Karaoke queens!" Megan yelled when the song ended with a fist pump in the air.

"Hell yeah!" Aly shouted back, grinning wide.

Megan caught my eye in the bathroom mirror, smiling and giving me a gentle squeeze on my shoulder. "There," she said, "all finished."

She'd curled my hair into soft waves, and it looked so different from my normally superstraight style. It was sexy and a little wild, and the makeup she'd put on my eyes made them smoky and dark.

She went to dab some lipstick on my lips, but I stopped her with a hand on her wrist. "I have a little addiction to this." I pulled out my clear lip gloss and waved it around. Okay, maybe not an addiction. A sick little obsession.

She laughed. "Rub it in that you have the most gorgeous mouth I've ever seen. How is it even possible your lips are so red?" She gasped. "Oh my God . . . that's it! You look just like Khaleesi from *Game of Thrones* but with blue eyes and, you know . . . without all the dragons and fire. She is my *favorite*," she exuded with a starstruck inflection.

"Pssh." I waved her off and hobbled on the four-inch red heels Megan had insisted I buy. "Not even close."

She looked me over. "Um, you are completely blind, my friend, if you don't think you look stunning."

I looked at myself in the floor-length mirror. Okay, so I had to admit, the way I looked made me feel good.

Beautiful and sexy and confident.

A loud knock sounded at Aly's bedroom door. "Are you all decent?" Jared called.

"Yep!" Aly shouted back, smoothing herself out just as Jared walked in.

He stalked over to her. "Goddamn, baby, you are a vision."

She blushed, pushed up on her toes to reach his mouth for a quick kiss. He'd already showered and shaved in the other bathroom. "Are you all about ready?" he asked. "I'm starving."

"Me, too," Aly said. "You two ready?" she asked.

"All set."

Megan and I followed them out just as the front door flew open.

Christopher was there, sucking all the air from the room.

He'd showered but hadn't shaved, his hair a completely perfect mess. He'd changed into black fitted jeans and a light blue button-down shirt. The sleeves were rolled up his forearms, tattoos exposed, and the first two buttons of the collar were undone, giving a peek at the tattoo on his chest.

Just looking at him shattered me.

He took a faltering step back when he saw me, his gaze raking me up and down, before he tore his eyes away and spoke to the rest in the room. "Everyone ready?"

No. Not even close.

EIGHTEEN

Christopher

Music pulsed heavily through the club. Lights strobed down on the dance floor, which was packed with bodies, the beat seductive and dark. Just off to the side, I stood watching. Girls paraded around, wearing next to nothing, begging for the attention that two months ago I would have been all too happy to give them.

But not tonight. Not anymore.

Samantha was the only thing I could see.

Honest to God, this girl must get off on tormenting me.

I lifted the bottle to my mouth, taking a deep pull from my beer, unable to tear my eyes away.

Samantha, Megan, and Aly were close to the edge of the dance floor, maybe ten feet away. They were facing one another in a small circle, dancing together the way girls do, all sexy and flirty and like they were having the time of their lives.

All night, they'd been slamming vibrant-colored shooters, the kind that taste like Kool-Aid and fuck you up faster than you

can say "cheers." With each one, they got a little more uninhibited, and with every passing second, Samantha wrung me a little
tighter.

Not one part of me was interested in any of the girls who
made their way over, doing their best to win my attention. Hell,
not one had managed it since the second Samantha had barreled
back into my life. She was the only thing I could see.

She lifted the hair from the nape of her neck and into a
messy pile at the top of her head, like she was trying to cool
herself off, but I was pretty sure the act elevated the tempera-
ture in the club by a hundred degrees. Her hands were at her
head, and she rolled her hips, dancing close to Megan.

That mouth twisted up in a sensual pout and I just about
came undone. Hunger roared through my body, my palms
sweaty and my pulse igniting in an all-out inferno.

Shit.

I scrubbed a hand over my face.

I'd been hard since the second I swung by Aly's with the
intention of following everyone over to the restaurant. The sight
of Samantha had nearly knocked me to my knees, and I'd come
damn close to dropping to them and begging her to take mercy
and put me out of my misery.

To douse the fire that had been raging since the second I felt
her succumb to my kiss before she'd pushed me away.

Tonight, instead of dousing the flame, she'd poured gasoline
on it.

She was in a pair of dark blue jeans that had to have been
designed just for her, because they were hugging those delicious
hips and that round ass perfectly. Her shirt was black and satiny,
all modest in the front and scooped superlow in the back to reveal a creamy expanse of bare skin. My fingers twitched, wanting nothing more than to trace the length of her spine. And just

because I was cursed, she went and paired all of that temptation with these sexy-as-all-hell red heels, so high they brought the top of her head up close to my chin.

I knew firsthand, too, because I hadn't been able to resist pulling her in for a hug after dinner, when she'd come up beside me and whispered a quiet *thank you* after I footed the bill. *It was my pleasure*, I'd murmured, yanking her to me, because it really was and there was no chance I could keep my hands off her for a second longer. She'd startled, then given in, and I'd just held her like I could forever. She'd shivered when I pressed my hands against that bare skin of her back that was threatening to drive me wild. For the briefest second, I'd buried my nose in her hair, filling up my senses with all that sweetness, so potent I was damned sure she'd made me drunk on it.

Because here I was, still nursing at my first beer, since I had to drive, and yet there was this fuzziness that eddied through my veins, and my limbs felt heavy and weighed down with want.

Clutching her hair, Samantha looked toward the ceiling. Red, blue, and green lights flashed against the smooth, soft skin of her face, her neck exposed, and she danced as if she'd just discovered what it was like to be free.

I jumped when Jared appeared at my side. He lifted a brow. "Figured you might want a fresh one." He offered me a new beer. "That one's gotta taste warm as piss by now."

I accepted the drink and set the other on the tall table next to me. "Thanks, man," I said, appreciating the cool liquid slipping down my throat.

We both turned our attention back to the dance floor. Jared sipped at his own beer, resting an elbow back on the table, his eyes sharp as he watched the vultures flock around the girls. Every douche bag in this place was dying to swoop their claws in, every calculated move they made bringing them one step closer.

"Hate these kinds of holes," Jared muttered on a grudging sigh. "Only reason any guy ever steps foot in a place like this is because he's looking to get laid."

If it'd been up to us? This would have been about the last place on earth Jared or I would have picked to bring the girls. But they made it clear real fast that this was *their* night, and their night meant they wanted to go dancing, and dancing meant getting cozy with these assholes who were circling around them.

I'd been that asshole plenty of times, and I knew exactly what scenario was playing out in their minds.

"You and me both."

Some dickhead finally got brave enough and made his move. Edging up behind Samantha, he swept a hand down her side like he had a right to touch her, then pulled her back against his front.

My jaw clenched just as tightly as the hold on my beer, my teeth grinding in my ears.

Apparently *dancing* meant rubbing his dick all over her ass.

I sent up a silent *hallelujah* when Samantha eased away and put some space between them, because this I could not handle. It was bad enough knowing she chose Ben, that somehow she'd ended up in his arms. But at least I didn't have to see that shit.

Which was just a blessing and a curse. The whole fact that Samantha was sneaking around, keeping it from Ben that she'd become friends with Aly. Quietly, almost as if she was humiliated about it, she'd mentioned she didn't want Ben to know she'd reconnected with Aly, and it became clear she was making up excuses to hang out with her and in turn to hang out with me. Really quick I'd surmised that he'd been a dickhead, like I knew him to be. He either gave her a hard time about it or she knew from experience that he would if he found out.

Plus side?

I didn't have to see the asshole with her.

But the last few weeks had left me with all kinds of questions. Was she really happy with him? Did she really love him? Was he good to her? Good for her?

Because if it was me, I couldn't stand the idea of my girl not being able to be honest with me.

Honestly, I couldn't stand the idea of her not being *my girl*, but I'd come to the place where I knew I cared about her enough that I'd accept them being together if it was truly what *she* wanted.

But then why was she doing this? A twenty-three-year-old woman having to lie about where she wanted to be? To a guy she wasn't even married to?

That was just uncool, wrong on a whole lot of different levels, and I hated the idea of her slipping back into the same kind of lies she'd had to spew in order to be with me back when we were in high school.

But we'd been left without options.

Was that her situation now? Was she being oppressed, shackled by others' beliefs, pushed into what others thought was right for her life?

Tonight, she most definitely didn't look *oppressed.*

She looked vindicated.

Liberated.

That same kind of beautiful that had knocked me from my feet when I was sixteen.

My spirit thrashed. That's what I really wanted. For this girl to be happy. For that light to shine. Bright and unrestrained.

Since the day I'd met her, she'd been held down. I'd put bets down that the same kind of bullshit was happening in her life now.

Ass bag behind her couldn't seem to take a clue, and he edged in like he was determined to get some of that for himself.

I shifted, trying to force myself to stand there and watch this when all I wanted was to rip his filthy hands from her.

Jared chuckled low, tipping the neck of his bottle in my direction. "Now you know what that shit feels like."

I scowled in his direction. "What the fuck are you talking about?"

He laughed a little louder. "Look at you, getting all pissed and fiery 'cause some punk-ass kid wants a piece of your girl."

"Not my girl," I growled.

"Yeah?" Jared challenged, the cut of his eyes angled in speculation. "And when'd that change? Because last thing I knew before I got my sorry ass dragged off to juvie, you couldn't imagine living your life without that girl. Seems to me I missed some important details along the way. Considering how you want to climb out of your skin every time she's around, I think it's about time you filled me in."

Regret and frustration blistered below my skin, charged by this guy groping Samantha. Dude was about five seconds from getting his arms ripped clean from his body.

"I happened," I spat out. I drained my beer, swallowed hard, my words bitter. "And I guess I haven't been doing a whole hell of a lot of that living since then, have I?"

"So you gonna change that or do you plan to keep fucking your way through the city?"

Incredulous, I glared over at him. My tone sharpened. "Pretty clear she's moved on, isn't it?"

He glared right back. "Is it? Because the only thing that's clear to me is there's some major unfinished business between the two of you."

I almost laughed. Yeah, Samantha and I had a whole ton of *unfinished* business.

Samantha chose that moment to flick her eyes over to me,

letting them slither down my body and back up in a slow wave. She rolled her hips. Dickhead behind her took that as an invitation, and he dug his fingers into her hips. She tried to maneuver out of his hold without making a big deal of it, but he made the mistake of tightening his grip.

That was it. I snapped. My feet moved of their own accord, my destination clear.

Not my girl? But she used to be, and I'd say in a situation as dire as this, that shit counted.

So maybe Jared would be giving me hell for the rest of my life.

She was worth it.

I pushed through the throbbing crowd, going straight for her. Her eyes registered shock as I shoved my arm around her waist. My hand hit the smooth, bare skin, and every inch of mine lit.

Goddamn.

I tugged her forward. Over her head, I shot the douche a look that warned him to back the fuck off.

Samantha floundered forward into my arms.

She smelled good, just about as good as she felt.

Then she giggled, reminding me of just how tanked she had to be with how much she'd had to drink. Wide, blurry eyes smiled up at me, a suggestion of a slur on her lips. "I think he liked me."

A quiet chuckle rolled from my tongue, my hold protective as I tucked her close, one hand secured to the small of her back, the other at the back of her head. She buried her face in my chest.

"Sweetheart, pretty sure everyone in this club likes you," I murmured at her ear, scrutinizing the crowd, gauging who I'd have to protect her from next.

She clutched my shirt, the words strained. "You, too?"

I sighed, feeling like the direction of this conversation was not one we should take when she'd drunk half her weight in alcohol. "Of course I like you," I whispered.

"I thought you hated me." Sadness poured from her strained statement, and I could barely hear her sweet voice above the music, but it was like I could feel the words emanating from her. They sank right into my bones.

"Never." It came out ragged. Hoarse. And my heart hurt a little more as I stood there swaying her in my arms. I hated that I'd ever given her that impression, that I'd been so callous and resentful that I chose to cut her down rather than facing the way she made me feel.

Totally off tempo, we swayed, the techno beat pounding a throb of energy through the pulsing crowd while we rocked slowly in our own little world, but I no longer knew how to let her go.

Who knew for how long we danced like that, because the music shifted and slowed, then sped again, and I finally realized Aly, Jared, and Megan had disappeared. They all came walking back over, my friend Cash in tow. I'd texted him earlier about showing up.

When she saw me and Samantha, Aly smiled unrestrainedly, her eyes warm and fuzzy but clearly filled with tenderness.

Reluctantly, I released Samantha, who seemed about as unhappy about letting go as I felt.

Aly's expression quickly shifted, and she stumbled a little on her drunken feet. She hooked her thumb over her shoulder. "Look who we found wandering around the bar. And he insisted on buying us girls another round of shots! Guess who's my new best friend."

"Hey." Megan pouted. "You're going to sell me out for a drink?"

"Oh, don't worry yourself, Meg," Jared cut in. "I'm pretty sure Aly here is going to be cursing Cash's name come tomorrow morning." Jared had a lemon-drop shooter in each hand. He waved one in Aly's face. "Are you sure you want another one of these?"

She took it with a grin. "Heck yes, I want another one of those. This is my one night out!"

Oh yeah, my sister was going to be hurting tomorrow. I didn't think she'd had more than a drink or two since Ella'd been born, and tonight she was tossing them back like water.

"All right." Jared laughed. A little affectionate smirk played at one side of his mouth. "But don't say I didn't warn you."

He passed the other to Samantha, and Cash started to hand one to Megan, but then he jerked it back and demanded a kiss for it. I laughed. Dude was such an asshole.

Megan slugged him in the arm and ripped the drink from his hand. "This girl can't be bought, buddy, so you'd better watch yourself before you get a whole lot more than that little punch."

"That's what I was hoping you'd say."

She punched him again.

Cash was always laying it on thick. The guy was larger than life, with both a giant body and a giant mouth. He'd had a pretty serious girlfriend about a year ago, but he'd gone and messed that up real quick. No surprise there. But we all knew he was just razzing Megan. They'd known each other for as long as I'd known Cash, and he messed with her just about as relentlessly as I did.

The girls all held up the tiny glasses rimmed in sugar. "To the best of friends," Aly said, glancing around at the two of them.

They both returned, "To the best of friends."

Glasses clanked and they tipped them back.

Samantha's face screwed up in the most adorable way, and

she clamped her hand over her mouth while she shook her head. "I think you two are trying to kill me!"

Megan laughed. "If we're going down, then you're going down, too. That's what friends are for, right?"

Samantha's face got all rosy, and she chewed at one corner of that bottom lip, murmured, "There's no one else I'd rather go down with," like having these friendships meant the world to her.

My heart squeezed, and I just stood there like watching all of this didn't affect me at all. And again I was wondering about her life, what it was like once she walked away and returned to Ben.

Aly stumbled and Jared caught her around the waist. "Watch yourself, baby," he cautioned her with a kiss to her temple.

She held her head. "Whoa . . . that one hit me hard."

Samantha giggled, making it pretty clear it'd hit her, too.

"I wanna dance," Megan demanded, jumping around, trying to yank Aly back onto the dance floor. But Aly was fading fast. The girl could barely stand.

"Pretty sure she's going to fall flat on her face if you drag her back out there," Jared said, canting his head to take in his wife. "What do you say we head home? Otherwise I'm going to be carrying you out over my shoulder."

She nodded, and he pressed his mouth to her forehead. "Okay, let's get you out of here." Jared wound his arm around her waist, attention darting between Megan and Samantha. "You two ready to go?"

"Nooo! It's still early," Megan insisted.

"Way early." Cash threaded his fingers through Megan's. "I'm game to hang out with you for a while longer. I'll give you a lift home later. Good with you?"

"Yeah," she agreed without thought. "Totally not ready to leave yet. You want to stay, Samantha?"

Samantha glanced up at me, and the sweet expression she

gave me twisted me somewhere deep. She looked back at Megan. "Thanks, but I think I'd better call it a night, too."

"Suit yourself." Megan dropped kisses to everyone's cheeks, then gave a little salute as she backed onto the dance floor with Cash. They were quickly swallowed by the crowd.

Jared began working his way through the throng of bodies, leading Aly out. I turned back to Samantha, who stood there looking a little lost.

What the hell, I said to myself with an inward shrug. Somehow the girl who once was my entire life had ended up becoming my responsibility tonight, so I wrapped her hand in mine. Every nerve in my body released a contented sigh, this thrumming satisfaction beating a path through my system. She snuggled in close, like she was seeking protection, like she wanted me to touch her and hold her and keep her safe.

Fuck.

What was I doing, setting myself up to get crushed again?

But I couldn't stop.

I squeezed her hand, slipping her a reassuring glance before I picked up a trail behind Jared and Aly.

We stepped out into the night. A gentle breeze blew through the overflowing parking lot, dull streetlamps casting a hazy glow from above.

Up ahead, Aly leaned heavily on Jared as he helped her to his truck, and Samantha stuck close to my side as we followed.

Jared clicked the locks, opened the passenger door. "Come on, love, let's get you home and into bed."

"You can take me to bed but you're coming with me," Aly contended, but it was all garbled, and she gave him a flirty, coy grin that was all kinds of sloppy.

Jared chuckled and gathered her hands in his, kissed her knuckles. "I seriously doubt that, baby, because I'd put good money down that your sweet little ass will be passed out by the time we get home, and I'm not into that."

She pouted, and Jared boosted her into the truck. She slumped into the seat, her legs dangling out.

I laughed. "Looks like it's sleepy time, Aly Cat," I teased.

She went for a glare, but it was weak and she could barely focus in on me. Jared hoisted her legs inside.

All of a sudden, Aly choked.

Jared's eyes went wide. "Oh shit, baby, are you gonna puke?"

Vigorously she shook her head, and tears started streaming down her face as she clutched her stomach. "I miss Ella."

I suppressed my laughter when Jared gave me a helpless look. He brushed back the hair matted to her forehead. "Baby, she's spending the night at your mom and dad's. Remember? We'll go over and pick her up first thing tomorrow morning." Under his breath, he tacked on, "When I can haul your hungover ass out of bed, that is."

Aly wailed, "But I need her now."

I chuckled. "See . . . this is why girls shouldn't drink, Aly Cat. They get all emotional and weepy, and then some sorry sucker like Jared here has to take care of her. There should be a law against this atrocity."

Samantha smacked at my upper arm. "Shh," she scolded, "she misses her baby. You don't know how upset she was to leave her for the first time. And if there aren't drunk girls, who in the heck are all those jerks inside supposed to hit on?"

I busted up. "All right, you've got me there."

"Please," Aly begged.

Jared rubbed a frustrated hand over his face, though his voice remained patient and soft. "Do you need me to take you over there?"

And that's why he'd always be my brother, thicker than

blood, good enough for my sister. He'd do anything for her, big or small. Minimally inconvenient or life changing. Didn't matter what it was, as long as he was doing it for her.

She nodded through big, fat tears.

"Shit," he grumbled, then his voice became soothing again. "What do you say we just have a sleepover . . . We'll snuggle up in your little twin bed back in your old room? That way you'll be right there when Ella wakes up in the morning and we won't have to wake up the whole house and drag Ella out in the middle of the night. Sound good?" He smiled softly, cupping her cheek. "Plus your mom would have my ass if I stole Ella away on her first sleepover."

"You'd stay there?" she asked hopefully, her eyes all awash with the awe she felt for her man.

A pang of envy hit me, that innate need to have someone look at me like that. I squeezed Samantha's hand a little tighter. My breath caught in my throat when she squeezed back.

Jared kissed Aly's forehead. "Of course."

He looked over at Samantha. "You ready, Sam? I'll drop you by your house before I head across town."

That little hand was still burning in mine, and I wasn't about to let go. "I'll give her a ride." The offer swung from my mouth as fast as if I were batting for a home run.

Jared frowned. A hint of suspicion. A trace of a warning. A whole lot of *Yeah, I bet you will.*

I lifted my shoulders in indifference, though I was still holding on for dear life, and Jared's deliberation dipped to our hands.

"I mean, if Samantha's good with it," I tacked on, praying to get a couple more minutes with her.

She hesitated, big blue eyes darting to me, then to her feet, and on to Jared, before she nodded forcefully. "That's probably a good idea . . . I mean, you should hurry and get Aly to Ella," she added quickly, like she was searching for a valid reason for me to be giving her a ride home.

Sounded reasonable enough to me.

I shrugged at Jared. "See? Not a problem."

He huffed knowingly, then shook his head like it wasn't his business. "All right, then."

Shutting Aly in, he took a step toward me. "Take it easy, man." His eyes were narrowed when he said it, and he clapped me on the back. He went in for a quick hug with Samantha. "It was great hanging out with you, Sam. I'm sure we'll see you soon."

"Definitely," she promised. "Call me if you need any help tomorrow."

"Sure thing." With a short wave, Jared climbed in his truck, started it up, and drove away.

We just stood there watching them go, our fingers all twined, Samantha's breaths palpable as she released them out into the heavy air.

I looked down at her in the same second she looked up at me. Emotion knotted my throat with regret and need.

God, why did she have to be so beautiful?

Softly, I smiled at her, then inclined my head into the distance. "I parked over in the back lot."

Silence wove around us like a blanket, and I basked in the comfort that came with saying nothing, just being in the same space with the sound of footsteps and panted breaths and beating hearts.

Samantha trembled when I helped her climb into the front passenger seat. Both my hands slipped to her waist to hoist her up.

She gave me the softest, questioning smile when I took the liberty of reaching across her and buckling her in, though she didn't make a move to stop me. The snap of the seat belt locking into place echoed in the quiet cab, and I froze when I pulled back and my gaze tangled with hers, her nose close to brushing mine.

"There," I whispered through the dense air, all that sweet filling up my senses, intoxicating. A fresh wave of lust clenched every muscle in my body.

"There," she agreed on a breath from that mouth I was dying to feel, to taste if it was still as sweet, that candied kiss that would bring me to my knees. Her eyes filled with something I hadn't seen in so many years, the trust she used to watch me with. Like she didn't get how hung up I was on her.

But I was.

Hung up.

Stuck.

I'd never had the strength or desire to move on. I was becoming pretty damned sure she was where I was supposed to be.

Tentatively, I reached out, wondering what in the hell I hoped to achieve when I let my fingertips trace along the line of her jaw. Because she'd made it clear we weren't going in that direction, but the signs she was sending me tonight had me itching to head there, and fast.

Shivers rolled through her, and her eyes dropped closed. Nervously, she swept her tongue across her plump bottom lip.

I bit back a moan, fighting the overwhelming urge to push past those boundaries again, to kiss that mouth like it'd never been kissed before, to mark and claim and declare what was mine.

But she was drunk and that would make me a bigger asshole than I'd already proven myself to be.

And I'd promised her a friendship. Promised myself I owed her the effort to earn back her trust. Promised my jaded heart I'd push back and make it through if she really didn't want me to win her back.

It took about all I had to pull away.

In slow surprise, her blue eyes fluttered open, a confused disappointment.

Groaning, I slammed her door shut and ran around to the driver's side.

I turned the key in the ignition, and the engine rumbled to life. The headlights splayed out ahead of us, like they were peering into the darkness of the vacant, empty lot next door. It reflected back some kind of eeriness, this strange sensation that we were waiting at the cusp, preparing to delve into the unknown.

I rushed a hand over my face and up through my hair, rubbing at my neck when I chanced looking over at her. This time she was smiling, like she'd broken through the wisps of smoldering smoke, no longer trapped in that haze of lust that had held us under.

"Thank you so much for the ride."

I threw the truck in gear and pulled out, laughing under my breath. "It's nothing, Samantha."

"Sure it is." She twisted a little in her seat to focus on me. "You hung out with us all night. Watched over us, made sure no drooling monkeys climbed up our backs and stole us away."

Out of the corner of my eye, I caught her wink, and I chuckled with a shake of my head.

Then she sobered a little.

"You could have . . ." She hesitated, chewing on that damned lip, her gaze dropping with the flush that reddened her cheeks. "Didn't you see all those girls looking at you? You could have taken any one of them home."

She looked back at me, seeking an answer. Wasn't it obvious why I hadn't? Why I'd rather be here than anywhere else? Did she forget that kiss?

Yeah. I'd told her I wanted to be friends, but the current passing between us exposed the lie of that promise.

I kept my attention trained out the windshield. "Didn't want to go home with any of those girls, Samantha."

My confession flared the tension. I could feel her eyes on me, probing, as if she was desperate for a way to see inside me. Silence stretched like a keening bow, all that unsaid shit that remained a barrier between us stealing the air, all that hurt and injustice screaming out like a burden I no longer wanted to bear.

Exhaling heavily, I turned into her quiet neighborhood, our few stolen minutes coming too quickly to an end, and I felt no more satisfied than when she'd turned her back on me the night I'd kissed her on this very street.

Samantha's raspy voice cut into the silence. "I don't want to go home."

Confused, I looked over at her.

"Please, don't take me there," she begged, a little panicked. She shut her eyes as if she was terrified to say it, but still the confession quietly bled free. "I hate it there."

My lack of hesitation when I flipped a U in the middle of the road should have been a warning. "Then where do you want me to take you?"

"Anywhere. Just not there."

I scratched at the stubble on my chin, contemplating how fucking ecstatic I felt. In the next instant, I felt like shit, sick at my own selfish happiness when this amazing girl had just admitted she hated her home. But that news was too good to my ears for me to pretend otherwise. I slipped her a sidelong glance. "Not a whole lot is open at this time of night."

She wrung her hands, then whispered, "Take me to your place." Her volume increased. "I want to know where you live . . . what it's like. Take me there." Curiosity and excitement widened her eyes, and she clapped her hands like she'd just latched onto the most brilliant solution.

Okay, maybe she wasn't just tipsy. She was pretty danged sloshed, and she'd made a quick flip to all cute and pleading, and my dick that had been misbehaving all night suddenly had ideas of being very, very bad.

"I'm not sure that's such a good idea."

"Please?" she begged, all eager and thrilled. "I've been wondering what it's like . . . where you'd live now that you're grown. Is your bedroom as messy as it used to be in high school? I bet your entire house is trashed." And I knew she was joking now, but I could feel it, her trying to tie me to that boy she used to know.

A strangled groan crept up my throat, and I cursed under my breath when I gave in and turned in the direction of my house. "Some things change, Samantha."

Her voice dropped. "For the good or the bad?"

"A lot for the bad," I admitted softly, knowing she needed to hear it, because the girl was no fool, and I knew she had a suspicion of the man I'd become.

Somehow I needed to prove I didn't want to be him anymore. Needed to find a way to make her understand that everything important had remained the same.

I pulled into my neighborhood. As I neared my house, I pressed the garage door remote, and it sprang to life.

"Oh my God." Samantha looked at me, those blue eyes all swimming with excitement again. "This cute little house is yours? Now, this I did not picture," she said as she leaned forward and peered through the windshield, taking it all in.

I eased my truck up the driveway and into the garage. I threw it in park and cut the engine, swiveling my shoulders to look over at her while I still held on to the wheel. "And just what did you picture?"

And how often and why were you picturing it?

She shrugged, biting back the laughter that rumbled around in her chest. "I don't know . . . something dumpier . . . like with peeling paint and dust covering the windows. Maybe with some of that yellow tape roping it off . . . HAZARDOUS WASTE stamped across it," she said, digging it in a little deeper.

"Are you kiddin' me?" I was doing my best not to bust up.

Laughter ricocheted around the cab of my truck when she set it free, and there was no stopping the force of my smile. I drifted on it, lost in the sound of the amusement rolling from her mouth. "I'm sorry!" she begged through an apologetic giggle. "You have to admit you were kind of a slob back then."

Back then, meaning back when I got to hold her and kiss her and make promises that had never come to be.

Tonight I was feeling like it was high time they did.

"Admit it!" she prodded, poking me in the side.

I wrangled out of her reach, grabbed her hand to block her attack. "All right . . . all right. I was a slob. I admit it. You win. But some things do change for the better. Come inside. I'll show you."

I jumped out and came around just in time to help her down. She rocked a little, and I steadied her. "Careful."

She rolled her eyes. "I know how to walk."

"Barely."

"Ha-ha-ha," she tossed over her shoulder, grinning at me as I followed, my fingertips just brushing the skin of her back.

At the door I stepped around her, reached in to flick on a few lights. "You ready?"

"Yep."

I opened it wide, allowing her to walk in ahead of me.

She wandered just inside, looking out over my living room and kitchen. "Oh my gosh, Christopher." She smiled back at me. "Some things really do change."

Everything was completely organized, sleek and clean, dark colors with bold lines, the quintessential man pad.

"Who taught you to be this clean? And who the heck designed this place?"

I laughed a little as I made my way over to the kitchen. "Well, Aly and I lived together for a couple years, and she wasn't about to clean up after me, so she trained me pretty quick. But all of this . . ." I gestured around the space, lifted a shoulder. "When I bought it, I figured decorating wasn't quite my thing, so I handed Mom a credit card and told her and Aly to have at it. Within a week, they had the entire house looking like something out of a magazine. Suits me, don't you think?"

She nodded, raking her teeth over her bottom lip. "Yeah. It's perfect for you." She arched a brow. "And you clean all this yourself? It looks like every inch has been scrubbed with a toothbrush."

I leaned my hands on the island countertop, grinning across at her. "Hey, I get on my hands and knees to clean this place. Wear gloves and an apron, too."

"Really?" she asked, this adorable look of disbelief crossing her face.

Shaking my head, I laughed. "No, not really. But the business with Jared is going great. Found myself with all this extra money that I have no idea what to do with, so I hired someone to come in a couple of times a week to keep the place clean."

"Oh, so you're saying you're spoiled," she assessed with a grin.

"Uh, no, not spoiled. I work my ass off. And before you ask, I do pick up my socks and underwear from the floor and every once in a while I even venture into doing my own laundry."

"Impressive," she drew out with all the sarcasm she could muster.

"Isn't it?" I winked and pushed off the counter. "Can I get you something to drink?"

Her eyes lit up and she walked into the kitchen. "Do a shot with me? We were drinking all night and you and Jared were all sweet and played DDs for us."

"Are you insane? You're already going to have the hangover of a lifetime tomorrow."

She shrugged. "Like Aly said, I don't get to go out all that much, and however terrible I feel tomorrow, it will be worth every second of tonight."

How could I argue with that?

I opened the cabinet, dug the vodka out from the other half-emptied bottles I kept in there. I grabbed two shot glasses, filled them halfway.

She edged in closer, and I could smell her vanilla, all the sweet emanating from her skin.

God, I was a fool to bring her over here. Having her this close and knowing she wasn't mine was pure agony.

On the island, I slid a glass over to her, lifted my own. "What are we drinking to, Samantha?"

She lifted hers, hesitated, averting her gaze before she gathered her courage and looked up at me. "We're drinking to tonight . . . to reconnecting with people we thought we'd forever lost."

I'd gladly drink to that.

Lightly, I clinked her glass. "To being found."

Her eyes darkened, and shakily, she tipped her glass back in the same second I knocked back mine. Fiery liquid burned down my throat, hitting my stomach hard.

Samantha forced hers down and pinched her eyes closed as she blew the air from her lungs. "Guh. That burned."

Quietly, I chuckled and didn't stop to question myself when

I softly brushed back a lock of hair that had fallen across her face. "Yeah. Not quite like those girlie drinks you've been chugging all night. You took that like a champ."

She grinned, her mouth falling lax. "Did that officially make me a dude?"

A warm, relaxed feeling slipped over me, and I found my thumb running up and down her jaw, my hand cupping her cheek. She leaned into it, and my head tipped to the side, my voice subdued. "Uh . . . no . . . that most definitely did not make you a dude."

Spellbound, I stared, before she quickly turned away. She wandered over to stand in front of the large French doors that sat between my kitchen and living room and looked out onto the backyard.

"It's beautiful," she whispered.

Out back, it was dark, but the pool light slowly changed from one color to another, and the landscaped yard glowed with the small lamps that jutted out from the strategically placed plants. The patio was set with comfy loungers and a matching table set.

I came up behind her, stopping just off to her left and a foot away. "That's my favorite part of the whole house. I love sitting out there at night, just listening to the city while I get lost in my thoughts."

Fingertips fluttered up to the glass pane, as if they were filled with a yearning to touch something they couldn't reach. "You have a pool," she murmured as if it were a secret.

I edged closer. My breath fluttered through the strands of hair that flowed over the delicate cap of her shoulder. "Does that bother you?"

Slowly she shook her head and drew in a long breath as if to steel herself. "Will you teach me?"

I felt the frown crease between my eyes, pull at my mouth. The memories of her fear were vivid. Like it had all happened yesterday—that day seven years ago that had felt like the last day I'd been alive because it was the last day she'd truly been mine. The words scraped up my throat. "Aren't you scared?"

She laughed with quiet irony. "Everything about you has always scared me. Maybe it's time I faced some of my fears."

Short pulses of awareness pinged between us, sending an upheaval of nerves pitching through my body.

"Not tonight," I whispered, "not when you've been drinking."

Definitely not when she had me tied up in a million intricate knots.

She swallowed hard. "What if I don't have another chance?"

"You'll have another chance. I promise."

Silence surrounded us. Tension stretched taut across the space. Energy surged, and all I wanted was to press her to the glass, to feel my body against hers.

Finally she shook herself off, regarded me over her shoulder. Her face was so close, my breath got all locked up in my throat. "Show me the rest?"

I offered her my hand, and she accepted it. I led her down the hall off to the left of the kitchen, showed her one bedroom that had been set up as an office, the other as a guest bedroom.

"Cute," she said, trailing behind me.

"Hey, there's nothing cute about my house."

She giggled. "Right . . . sorry. Manly," she corrected, grinning this grin that twisted around my heart, jolts of energy passing between our connected hands. I led her back into the living room and through the double doors that opened to my room.

"And this is the last . . . the master bedroom."

She squealed and blazed past me. I scratched at my head. Apparently that shot had hit her hard, because she was suddenly without an ounce of shyness. The girl just kept shifting from one extreme to another.

"Oh my God, Christopher, that is the biggest bed I've ever seen!"

Yeah, and about the only thing I wanted to see right then was her laid out across it.

She kicked off her heels and pretty much hurtled onto my bed and started jumping in the middle of it.

I rubbed my hand over my mouth, my laughter low and full of amusement. "What do you think you're doing?"

"What does it look like? I'm jumping on this amazing bed." She stretched her arms out, like she could fly, and a million questions spun through my head. It felt like I still got her, the way she used to say I was the only one who did. But so many years had passed and so much had changed.

Slowly, I crossed the distance, my footsteps calculated as I came to stand at the edge of the bed.

"You still go to church, Samantha?" I asked quietly, my chin lifted so I could take her in. Why that was the first question out of my mouth, I didn't know. But so much was wound up in it, that goodness that I'd loved about her, the belief and faith I'd never experienced myself somehow still apparent in her eyes and soft on her tongue.

I also knew the way she was raised in the church had a whole lot to do with why she hadn't been allowed to see me.

She slowed, bouncing softly, and she gradually lowered her arms. Her head tilted, and something significant flared in her eyes. "Yeah." She said it like she was surprised by my asking, but like she appreciated that I had. Now she was just bouncing on her toes, closer to the edge. "But I don't go to my dad's church anymore. I needed a place where I felt comfortable to be myself, where I wasn't the pastor's daughter. Because no matter how old

I got, everyone still expected me to act a certain way, you know?"

My hands found her hips, and hers found my shoulders. She blinked down at me, sucking me into her warmth.

From her back pocket, Samantha's phone chimed with a funky little song, and her eyes went wide with excitement, while mine went wide with dread. For a second, I'd almost forgotten about Ben, that she belonged to someone else. I'd put money down on it being him. The asshole was like a thunderstorm raining all over my own personal town parade.

But Samantha smiled too wide and dug into her pocket, squeezing my shoulder with the other hand. "Stewart."

Old affection tightened my chest, and Samantha flopped down onto her butt, pulling at my hand to haul me with her. On my side, I propped up on an elbow, and Samantha held up her phone so we both could see. Then she swiped into her Snapchat message.

When the picture popped up, affection squeezed me so tightly I was sure it had to be constricting all airflow. But in it was this jolt of crushing pain that not one thing in this godforsaken world could have prepared me for.

God, how much had I loved this kid?

Stewart wore a goofy smile, his bottom lip jutted out in a pout, the words *Can't Sleep* stamped across his forehead in the added font.

Fuck, I couldn't even begin to believe how much he'd changed, no longer that cute kid like I remembered. I could see even from the snapshot that he was almost a man. All traces of childhood had been stripped from his skin. But the sickness . . . it'd ravaged his body. He was drawn and worn and frail. His head was bald, and his sunken cheeks made his blue eyes stand out in stark contrast to the rest of him, his skin a pale, chalky gray.

Goddamn it.

Seeing him this way broke my fucking heart.

Samantha looked at me, like she got me the same way I felt like I got her. Sympathy and sadness deepened the lines of her face. She turned back to the image. The way she looked at it killed me, like she was cherishing something that was already gone. She ran the tip of her finger over it. "He's so sick, Christopher. I'm sorry I didn't warn you . . . I wasn't even thinking this is the first time you've seen him since he got sick again, and he's so much worse this time. I just wanted you to see . . . His messages always make me happy. I'm just so glad to be with him in any way." She whispered the last.

I touched the side of her jaw, and my damned voice shook. "Don't ever apologize for wanting to share something with me. I want to be there for you. I was just . . ." She looked at me, earnest and open, and I swallowed down all the emotion I didn't know how to handle. "Shocked. I'd half expected him to still be a ten-year-old boy." My mouth curved with a soft, sad smile. "Thank you for sharing this with me."

She nodded, laid back on the overflowing pile of pillows stacked against my headboard. She lifted her phone, twisted up into the silliest face, and snapped a picture of herself.

I chuckled. "He's going to know you're drunk. Those fuzzy eyes are a dead giveaway."

A soft giggle floated from her, and she tinkered around on her phone, talking while she added a frame and a message. "Well, I am drunk, so not much can be done about that. And I pretty much tell Stewart everything."

I glanced at the photo, Samantha looking like the angel she was as she posed for her brother. It read, *That's because you're missing me*, across the top. She pressed SEND.

Five seconds later, her phone buzzed with a regular text, and I snuggled in closer so I could read what he said. *Where are you?*

Samantha cringed. So apparently she didn't tell him *everything*.

She tapped out a quick response. *At a friend's.*

It took all of three seconds for him to respond.

In their bed?

Another quickly followed.

Who is this friend?

"Nosy little bugger," Samantha mumbled. A smile tipped the edge of her mouth. "I swear to God, he should write books. His imagination is off the charts. I'm sure he's imagining all kinds of salacious scenarios right about now."

She was swift to change the subject. *How are you feeling?*

Time stopped when she got his response. *Like I'm dying.*

She shook when she attempted to type out her answer, and I just lay there frozen, watching her denial, the shake of her head and the way her fingers frantically beat at the keypad as if she could force it not to be true.

"Why does he have to say stuff like that?" she begged through a pained whisper, looking at me helplessly, before she sent her reply.

No, you're not. You're not giving up, Stewart. I won't let you.

Two minutes later, her phone beeped again.

I love you more than anything in this world. You know that, don't you?

Her response was instant.

Yes. And YOU are what makes this world great. You know that, don't you?

She waited for his return, but when none came after a few minutes, she tossed her phone down toward the end of my bed and slumped back onto my pillows.

I pulled her by the waist to face me. "You okay?"

Contemplating, she slanted her eyes to her fingers that were twisting in my dark comforter, mixing in with the fabric of my shirt, her short fingernails grazing the material. Tormented eyes flicked up to meet mine, and they punched me with another shock of heartache.

Her voice trembled. "Not if he's not. I hate knowing he's in his room alone, in pain, pretending like he just can't sleep. I hate knowing he's suffering and there's absolutely nothing I can do about it."

"How could you think for a second you're doing nothing for him, Samantha? You've always taken care of him. Been there for him so he wouldn't feel alone. And after all this time? It's obvious you still do the same. Why do you think it's *you* he messaged in the middle of the night?"

Her brow creased in grief and hope.

"Because he knows he can count on you," I continued, taking her hand and weaving it in mine. "He knows you're there to listen when he needs you. That you love him with everything. You think that doesn't ease some of his suffering?"

"I'd give up everything for him, Christopher. Switch places in a heartbeat. I was so hopeful that I'd get to be a bone marrow donor for him, but I didn't match."

I heard the heartbreak quivering in her tone, and her eyes glistened with moisture, emotion thick in her throat.

And God, I didn't mean to let it, but a tear broke free and streaked down the side of my face. It fucking destroyed me seeing her this way, seeing him *that* way. I'd hoped with all the hope I'd had left in me that he'd be okay, that he'd grow up to live a normal life like he deserved to.

Samantha released my hand and reached out with her knuckle to gather the wet trail running down my temple, like maybe she was comforting me. "Why does it feel like you're the only one who really understands?" she asked.

I took her hand back, squeezing it, a soft puff of air huffing from my nose. "I don't think I could ever really understand everything you've been through. But I've always loved him, Samantha. I never stopped."

She stilled, biting at her lip, something fierce taking over her expression. "Have you? Have you really? You weren't just pretending?"

A frown cut between my eyes, and I shook my head in question. "Of course I loved him. He's about the coolest kid I've ever met. In all these years, don't think a day ever passed that I didn't think about him."

That I didn't think about you.

The doubt in her expression turned wistful, and a smile wobbled at the corner of her mouth. I realized how close we'd gotten, the lengths of our bodies pressed together, so close I could feel her heart beating beneath her shirt.

Rueful laughter slipped almost unheard from between her lips. "Do you remember when you took him skateboarding for the first time? He still says that was the best day of his life."

Quietly I laughed and tucked her closer. "I almost had a heart attack when he fell. Scraped himself up good. He was such a brave little man. Didn't want to cry in front of me."

Blue eyes glistened, shimmering in sorrow and love.

Was it possible for her to still feel some of that love for me? After all the shit I'd done?

I swallowed over the lump lodged in my throat. "And you," I said, my voice hoarse, "you took the fall for us all, telling your mom he tripped on the sidewalk when you were walking him home from tutoring."

She trembled a grin. "Tutoring I was supposed to get him to, but you had better plans."

Smiling, I swept her hair from her forehead, her hand still warm in mine. "Stewart thought it was a better plan, too."

"Yes, he did . . . and he still does to this day." Her voice deepened with meaning. "You were his favorite person in the world."

Emotion tugged at the edge of my lips. "He's always been real high on my list, too." On my fingers, I could count the people in my life who really mattered. Ella. Aly and Jared. My family. Stewart.

And the girl shivering in my arms.

"I'm so scared for him . . . scared of what my life might look like without him in it." Samantha could no longer hold it in, and she sobbed quietly into my shoulder, clutching my shirt.

Tears soaked through. I pulled her closer, wove one hand in her hair, cradled the back of her head. I'd give anything to take some of her pain away. "Shh . . ."

She struggled to get closer.

"I've got you," I promised, my touch gentle as I ran my fingers through the length of her soft-as-silk hair, threading them in.

I don't know how long she cried for, but eventually she took in a couple of gasping breaths, shuddering as the heightened emotion and alcohol in her system steadily drew her toward sleep. I kissed the top of her head, giving her whatever comfort I could.

She shifted, and her nose dug into my collarbone as if she were seeking a way inside. The words were choppy and rough, barely audible. Still they tore through me as if she'd screamed them in my ear. "I miss you."

She exhaled heavily, the smell of candied alcohol filtering over my face. I would have laughed had it not hurt so bad.

I held her close, listening to her breaths steadily even out, and this girl dragged me right along behind her, lulled me with the sweet smell of her hair, the slow rhythm of her heart, and the goodness in her spirit.

And for the first time in my life, I drifted off to sleep next to Samantha Schultz.

"Oh my God," Samantha gasped.

Blunted fingernails scraped against my chest. Disoriented, I shot up in bed in the same second Samantha scrambled off of it, ripping all her perfect warmth from me when she did.

Horror etched her face. In the muted light, wide blue eyes watched me with flat-out mortification and shame, and I jerked my attention down. Somehow I'd lost my jeans and shirt in the night. There was nothing worse than sleeping in your clothes, and I must have fumbled out of them in my sleep.

So there I sat, covered up by nothing but my underwear, trying to blink off the best sleep I'd had in years while Samantha gaped at me like she'd just realized she'd been kneeling at Satan's seat.

"Oh my God," she said again, tearing her eyes away from my bare chest, hands shaking as she began to search frantically for her phone in the covers.

"Samantha." I said her name, trying to break into whatever freak-out she was having, but I didn't make a dent.

"What did I do . . . what did I do?" she mumbled miserably, chanting it repeatedly like a petitioned prayer. She almost sobbed in relief when she finally found her phone. Clutching it to her chest, she darted around the bed, ducked down to grab her shoes, then broke out into a sprint as she ran from the room.

What in the ever-loving fuck?

Everything kicked into gear, and I jumped from the bed and dragged on my jeans. I didn't take the time to bother with a shirt or shoes.

By the time I made it out into the living room, Samantha was already flying out the front door.

I raced after her, tearing the door open when she slammed it in my face.

"Samantha," I hissed out, just barely above the dull drone of crickets, trying to get her attention without waking up the neighborhood. Terrified, she looked over her shoulder at me and increased her speed.

Barefoot, in the middle of the night, and she was running away.

You have got to be kiddin' me.

I was right behind her, and I grabbed her elbow in an attempt to talk some sense into her. She flung my hand off, held her shoes and phone to her chest like a shield of protection.

"Stay away from me."

"What the fuck, Samantha? You're going to walk home in the middle of the night without any shoes on? Are you out of your mind?"

"Apparently so."

I moved to keep up with her, hissing in pain when I stepped on something so fucking sharp I was sure it was now impaled in the bottom of my foot. Goddamn emotional women.

"Come on, Samantha. At least let me give you a ride home. It's not safe for you to take off like this."

"I'm not safe around you," she shot back.

I glanced back toward my house fading in the distance, then back to Samantha, who ran down the sidewalk, ducking her head with her shoulders hunched as if it would hide her.

I swung at the air, an aimless punch, confused and frustrated and straight-up pissed off.

Evidently, I couldn't do one single thing right.

But the one thing I was positive would be wrong was letting her stumble home in the middle of the night.

It took me all of two minutes to run back to my house, grab my keys, and jump in my truck. I tore out of the garage, the engine thundering when I threw it in gear and hit the gas, another thirty seconds to gain on the girl who was about to make me lose my mind.

Beaten down, Samantha limped along the sidewalk. Visibly she cringed when I pulled up beside her. I rolled down the passenger-side window. "Get in the truck, Samantha."

She shook her head emphatically, refusing to look my way.

"Come on, Samantha, this is absolutely ridiculous. You'd rather walk two miles in the dark than let me give you a ride that will take all of five minutes? You hung out with me all night. What could five more minutes hurt?"

She stopped, slowly turned her head in my direction. Her face was soaked with tears. "Everything hurts."

My heart squeezed and my stomach dropped, and I sighed in frustration. "Just get in. You know I can't leave you out here by yourself."

She averted her gaze to her bare feet, and I saw the second she gave in. Cautious and slow, she shuffled forward and climbed in my truck. She shut the door with a soft click, the darkness that always seemed the safest swallowing us up, just the muted green lights on the dash giving light to her face, that gorgeous silhouette I'd memorized so long ago.

I didn't want it to just be a memory anymore.

In silence, I drove to her house, pulled up at the street in front. I threw it in park but didn't cut the engine.

I could barely look at the home that outwardly was almost identical to Aly's, the walls that housed her life a place I'd never be welcome in because she shared them with someone else. Someone I knew in my heart was wrong for her, someone I couldn't help hating.

Because she belonged with me.

Anger and resentment burned through my blood, her reaction to waking up in bed with me tearing me in two. Those fucking sick visions assaulted me anew, the ones where I couldn't keep from picturing what happened inside this place, the tragedy of this girl being touched by hands other than mine.

I fisted the steering wheel.

Samantha just sat there, staring at her lap.

I bit back the bitterness and leaned toward her, my head cocked to the side in an attempt to get her to look at me. To *see* me.

She seemed to be gathering her courage. Cautiously she looked my way, worry and guilt snuffing out all the light.

And that shit pissed me off, too.

Her tongue darted out, making a swift pass along her bottom lip, the plump flesh glistening with moisture.

Hunger pelted me, my straining cock cutting off all sensible thought to my head.

What the hell was happening to me?

I didn't know up from down because this girl had twisted me inside out.

"D-d-did we . . . ?" Samantha stammered the words as if they were her dirtiest, darkest secret, her blue eyes all awash with a girl so full of loyalty it meant she shunned what she really wanted.

Because it was there, too . . . longing. Like somewhere inside she was hoping it was true.

My dick jerked, and I shifted close enough so my face got all up in her space, so close I could taste each of her panted breaths.

"Do you have no recollection of what went on tonight? What was said?"

She swallowed, and my eyes darted to watch the movement along her delicate neck. "I remember being at your house, talking about Stewart, lying in your bed." Her brow cinched in sadness. Then she slipped right back into that nervousness that bounced her knee. "But then I blacked out."

A groan of anger and sexual frustration rumbled in my chest, and I inched even closer. I clutched the back of her neck, my fingers in her hair and my thumb running along the angle of her jaw. The words were raw, abraded. "After everything that happened tonight, the parts you do remember, you honestly believe that I'd turn around and take advantage of you?"

My voice dropped like a threat. "I can promise you one thing, Samantha." I leaned in close to her ear. "When I fuck you, you're damned well going to remember it."

On a gasp, she made to pull away, but I held her tight, forcing her to look at me.

"You didn't black out. You fell asleep. In my arms." I fingered the neckline of her shirt. "These clothes you're wearing . . . they never came off. I'd never hurt you like that."

Her expression hardened, the same as her words. "Wouldn't you?"

Shame sliced through me, cutting me in two as she threw the biggest mistake of my life in my face. "That person wasn't me, Samantha. Back then . . . everything was being taken from me, everything important stripped away. Most importantly you. I lost it. But I never would have—"

She cut me off. "I trusted you." Like a barrier, her eyes dropped closed, and she shook her head. "I'm not sure if I can ever fully trust you again."

"Are you in love with him?"

She jerked with the change of subject, her eyes flying open. "Ben respects me. Cares about me."

"That's not what I asked."

But I didn't need an answer, because I saw it all over her

face, saw it in the way she looked at me like my question caused her physical pain.

He was nothing more than a security blanket. Something easy when she didn't want to face all the important shit that was hard.

She'd never stopped loving me, and I'd bet that she'd never come close to really *loving* him. Not the way she did me.

She just refused to acknowledge it.

She unlatched the door, fisting the handle. "I already told you, you don't get to do this to me. I told you we could try to be friends, but I don't know if I can handle all of this." Agitated, she gestured between us. "What you did . . . what I *saw*. That can't be erased and that hurt can't be undone. It scarred me in ways I'm not sure you can ever really understand."

Confusion knitted my brow as the deepest hurt swam in her eyes. "What in the hell are you talking about, Samantha?"

Disbelief coated her coarse laughter. "You can be a real asshole, you know that?" She climbed down from the truck, stood there with the overhead light shining down on her face, her lips pressing into a hard line.

My confusion thickened, and I raced back through every memory, trying to get to the one she was talking about. *What she saw?*

She continued, uncertainty and affection woven in her tone. "Then you go and show me you can be the sweetest man. How do I know which one's real?"

"Let me prove it to you."

"I have a boyfriend, Christopher, someone who was there for me when you weren't."

"Let me be there for you now."

Shaking her head, she backed away, like she was drawing an invisible line. "I don't think I can be anything more than friends with you. And sometimes even that seems impossible."

Impossible.

Now, that I agreed with.

But I wasn't about to concede to what she was saying. That she couldn't tolerate being in my space.

"I can't deal with any more tonight," she finally said, cutting off my dissent. "My head hurts and I just want to lie down."

I gave her one terse nod, because I was pretty sure tonight she wouldn't accept anything I had to say, and she shut the door and ran up her sidewalk to her house, glancing back once before she ducked inside.

Movement rustled at the side of the window, her silhouette blanketed in the sway of the sheer drapes as she peeked out at me. When she dropped them, I threw my truck in gear and forced myself to drive away.

Five minutes later I was pulling up the driveway of my house. The faintest hue of light threatened at the horizon, the last minutes of the night clinging to the darkened sky. Without her in it, the house echoed back the loneliness, the stifling quiet more than I could bear. I went straight for the shower in the bathroom adjoining my room, turned it on high as I peeled off my clothes.

I half sighed, half grunted when I freed my erection that had been raging all night.

With my eyes closed, I stepped into the spray.

I could still smell her, hear her, and that mouth was smiling as I imagined her dancing just for me.

I banged my forehead against the cold tiles. "Fucking Samantha," I groaned.

Fucking Samantha.

She made me insane, tore me to shreds, and I knew she was the only one who could piece me back together.

I gripped myself, making hard, punishing strokes up and down my length.

Since the night I'd kissed her, I hadn't touched another girl, and I came fast, moaning her name toward the ceiling.

The entire time, I imagined just what it was going to feel like when I finally got to make love to her for the first time.

We'd been robbed of it. Something that was supposed to be special. Just for us. What no one else could ever have.

A promise of firsts and lasts, because we were supposed to be forever.

Standing there, panting like a teenager, I made another promise.

This time I promised her God I was taking her back.

NINETEEN

Christopher

January, Seven Years Earlier

Samantha slid up my body and draped herself across my chest. Uncontrolled, my heart hammered, my racing pulse skipping beats, a thunder of love and devotion pounding through my veins.

I'd never imagined I could share something so intense with another person.

Feel so close to someone.

Like we were connected on another level.

And we hadn't even had sex.

Did I want to? Did it just about kill me to stop when she was offering herself up?

Hell yeah.

But I respected her way too much for that.

But this? Maybe it was even better.

Telling her I loved her for the first time and knowing she trusted me . . . knowing I could trust myself with her . . . made me feel like someone different. Like someone I wanted to be.

Gentling my fingers through the locks of her still damp hair, I kissed the top of her head. Contentment seeped from between those lips that had been my complete undoing. "I love you," I murmured quietly, reiterating the admission that had come so naturally.

I'd finally realized it when the worst kind of fear had torn through me when I saw her floundering in the pool. It'd been a physical type of pain. Gripping. Suffocating. There'd been zero hesitation, and I'd jumped in after her.

I hadn't come close to understanding just how severe her fear was until I'd dragged her out. Weeping and trembling and completely in shock, Samantha had fallen to pieces in my arms. It'd killed me seeing her like that.

What I really wanted was to kill the person who was responsible for it.

I squeezed Samantha protectively.

Jasmine.

That fucking bitch.

I'd never met anyone so vile. So vicious. Every chance she got, she was in my face. Unrelenting. Acting like a temptress when really she made me want to puke. She was so delusional she believed she could somehow lure me away from the best girl in the world.

Not a chance.

Samantha had nailed it.

Jasmine had made her the target of her jealousy because somehow that bitch had her sights set on me, like she thought me different from any of the other guys she'd gotten on her knees for.

Her mission had become making Samantha miserable.

But even I couldn't believe what Jasmine had pulled tonight.

Soft fingers trailed along my collarbone. "I love you so much," Samantha whispered, peeking up at me.

"You're my world, Samantha. Everything I do, from now until the end of time, I'm going to be doing for you." I leaned in, kissed her with all the tenderness I felt for her. And that was the thing with this girl. She made me feel *good*, like just being around her made me part of something greater. Something bigger than all the empty, frivolous ambitions that fueled the thoughts and actions of most of the people I hung out with.

What used to fuel me.

Samantha had all these beliefs that there was something greater than just this world that I'd never given much thought to, permitting little time or credit to ideas that seemed so ambiguous. But she had this light about her that I was drawn to, and I saw it in her little brother, too, something different and unique that I'd come to crave. I wanted to see it glow in Stewart when I did or said something that brought him joy, to watch it burn in Samantha when she just sat and appreciated the sky.

I found myself wanting to contribute to it. Be a part of it.

Guess there was something in her that made me want to believe.

She made me better in all those places inside me I'd never really liked. I'd always been a selfish kid. A punk who liked stirring up trouble just for the fun of it, getting a rise out of the people around me purely for my pleasure. Didn't want to be like that anymore.

I hugged her again. "We'd better get you home."

She nodded like she really didn't want to go, but she let me help her stand. I resituated her clothes. The deepest blush rushed all over her face as her thoughts so obviously strayed back to ten minutes earlier when we were partaking in things that weren't all that *innocent*.

But this girl was mine and I was hers, and I couldn't find one thing wrong with that.

I threaded my fingers with hers. "You ready?"

Nervousness flitted across her face, and she squeezed my hand. "I think so."

"I won't let her hurt you ever again, Samantha. I promise you."

Nodding, she snuggled up to my side. "I know you won't."

I led her across the room, unlocked the door, swung it open.

Ben Carrington stood on the other side, his fist raised like he was getting ready to pound on the wood. A sneer transformed his face when he saw me standing there.

The fiercest swell of possessiveness rose inside me, squeezing my lungs about as tight as I squeezed Samantha's hand. I edged in front of her, like I could cut off the asshole's view. "What are you doing here?"

His brow creased and he cocked his head to the side. "What am I doing here? I think the better question is what is Samantha doing here?"

"She's with me."

He scoffed. "Yeah. And do her parents know that?"

Samantha wriggled out from behind me, still clutching my hand but moving toward Ben. I wanted to yank her back. "Just . . . don't, Ben. You always make things a bigger deal than they are. Christopher was just taking me home."

"Really? Because it seems like a pretty big deal to me when you're at a party, locked in a room with this piece of shit, when you're supposed to be at home asleep in your bed."

Panic shook her, and she took a pleading step forward. "Please, you can't tell them."

Frustration billowed from the sigh he released toward the

ceiling, as if he were dealing with a disobedient kid. He set his hands on his hips. "Did I make you a promise, Samantha? I told you before I wouldn't tell them. And I won't. But what I won't tolerate is you sneaking out with this asshole. I can't even believe you're here. I'm really disappointed in you."

She hung her head in shame, chewing at her lip while she stared at her feet.

My fist curled. I wanted nothing more than to mash the guy in the face. He knew nothing about her, nothing about her dreams and desires, that she needed a little freedom to figure out who she was and what she wanted to be.

So no, bringing her here wasn't my best idea.

But he was acting like she'd just robbed a bank.

"She's fine." The words came out with a challenge.

"Doesn't look that way to me." He gestured with his chin to Samantha, whose clothes were still all damp, her hair tangled, more from my fingers twisted in it than anything else, but he sure as hell didn't need to know that.

"I was just taking her home."

He shook his head. "Wrong. I'm taking her home."

I bristled and took a step forward, just hating the bastard. What it was about him, I didn't know, but he rubbed me wrong in every kind of way. The way he treated Samantha like a little girl but looked at her like he wanted to eat her. Nah, he wasn't all that much older than us, but something about him was off. Like he got off on her cowering to his will.

I smiled when this time she didn't. "No, Ben, you're not taking me home. Christopher is. And we're leaving. I'm tired and I just want to go home."

In irritation, the corner of his mouth twitched, and he gulped down whatever thoughts he was having. "No more of this," he warned her, but his tone was soft, like he was trying to convince her of what was best for her. "You don't belong here, and I don't want to hear about you sneaking out with him again."

She nodded, then pulled at my hand.

Every part of me wanted to turn around and put him in his place. But Samantha didn't view him the way I did. Clearly she revered him on some level, respected his position with her family, appreciated his words.

I didn't trust him for a second.

I slipped my arm around Samantha's waist, glanced back at Ben right before we hit the top of the stairs. Smug, he stood there with his arms across his chest, like he held a straight flush and had just laid down his hand.

Protectively, or maybe it was just to rub it in, I pulled Samantha closer, and she buried her face in my side when we hit the stairs. That protectiveness lifted and rose, rumbling like a storm in my chest as I led her back down into the depravity of the scene where I never should have brought her.

I could give Ben that much.

Samantha didn't belong here.

Beauty shouldn't be exposed to trash like this.

With my free hand, I guarded her face when we were met with all the curious stares. Jasmine leaned against the wall. When we walked by, her mouth coiled with a satisfied smirk, making her look like the snake she was.

She didn't dare say a word, because I was pretty damned sure she knew from my expression I would have snapped.

Outside, the night had grown deep, the air crisp and cool. Chills flashed across Samantha's skin.

"Damn it." I wrapped both my arms around her in an effort to get her warm. "I should have found you a change of clothes before I brought you back out."

She smiled up at me, her face aglow, illuminated in the half-moon. "I'm perfect, Christopher." She turned her face toward it. "Even after everything, tonight was kind of amazing, wasn't it?"

I chuckled, dropped a kiss to her forehead. God, yes. Fucking incredible. "You're amazing."

"You just love me, so you're blind," she teased, knocking her hip into mine while she walked.

I hugged her close. "Not blind . . . but the love thing you got down pat."

I helped her into my car and drove the two miles to her neighborhood. I parked at the head of her street, cut the lights, and went around to meet her at the door. Our footsteps were subdued as we made our way toward her house so I could sneak her safely back through her window. Same way I'd done what felt like a million times before.

But tonight the lights weren't all dimmed. Every light in the house blazed through the windows. Samantha gasped when she saw her mom standing on the sidewalk in her robe, her arms crossed over her chest, clinging to herself as if she were trying to protect herself from an outcome she didn't want to face.

"Mom." Samantha started to run for her, her sandals smacking on the pavement, fear in her voice. "Is Stewart okay?"

Her mom jerked her head up. Relief flashed across her face, which had already been stained with tears. "Yes, yes, Stewart's fine. Thank God you're okay. I've been worried sick about you." She hugged Samantha, then pushed her back, holding her by the tops of her arms, and that relief twisted to anger.

Five feet away, I stopped. Panic surged.

"Do you have any idea what I've been through tonight? I went in your room and you weren't there . . . I . . . I thought something terrible had happened to you." Her mouth trembled. "Don't you think we have enough stress, enough worries with your brother? And you're going to put us through *this*?"

"Momma," Samantha begged with desperate apology in her voice. "I wasn't trying to hurt you."

The front door opened, and her father stepped out behind them. He shut the door with a low click. Probably an inch or two shorter than me, he was still tall, but he was also thin, his build unthreatening. Even the way he carried himself was unassuming, modest and simple, his head held in a permanent bow.

But it was the silent rage brewing in his eyes that told me I had every right to be scared.

Shit.

I wet my lips, having no idea what to say, because I'd just been caught red-handed with his daughter. Samantha had lied up and down about the two of us, swearing we were nothing more than friends so I could get into their house and have those few hours with Stewart in the afternoons, so I could be at her side, tortured with not being able to touch her, but satisfied in knowing I'd be alone with her soon.

It was blatantly obvious there wasn't a lie in the world that could get us out of this.

Her father's voice was cold. "Go inside, Samantha."

"Dad," she pled, reaching for him.

He stopped her with a disappointed hand. "Do not argue with me, Samantha. There is nothing left for you to say. Now, go inside and to your room. You're going to be in it for a very long time."

Dread knotted in my stomach, and I chanced a step forward. "Please, Mr. Schultz. It was my fault."

His attention jerked to me. "Yes, I completely agree with you. This is one hundred percent your fault. My daughter was always obedient until the day she started spending time with the likes of you. You think I haven't seen the way she's changed in the last few months? All of it's your fault."

Samantha's mom heaved out a sob and her hand flew to her mouth. "Have you been drinking?"

Flustered, Samantha frowned. "What? No, of course not."

I saw the second it dawned on Samantha's face. The fucking beer that slut had dumped on her had soiled her clothes with the stink of alcohol.

This just got worse and worse.

Samantha's mom clearly mistook the shift in Samantha's expression as some kind of guilt. "I'm done with all the lies, Samantha. No more. It ends now." She pointed between me and Samantha. "All of it. It ends now."

Stumbling back, Samantha shook her head in short, furious jerks. "No."

Her father answered for her mother. "You have no say in this. You've already proven you can't be trusted. You made the choice to disobey and now you have to face the consequences."

She swung around, her fist pounding at her chest. "What choice? You never gave me the choice! You give me no freedom at all . . . no room to experience life, no room to make mistakes. This isn't fair!"

I took a step forward, my hand extended toward her, knowing she was only making it worse. "Samantha . . . baby, don't."

Mr. Schultz pushed her behind him, his angry words directed at me. "She's not your concern."

He was completely wrong. She was my only concern.

He looked at his wife. "Sally, take her inside and see that she gets changed into some warm clothes."

Mrs. Schultz nodded and shuffled forward, nudging Samantha toward the door. In yearning, Samantha looked back at me. Fear and worry were etched all over her sweet face.

And it hurt watching her disappear inside, because I knew

with every fiber of my being, nothing was ever going to be the same.

Frantic, I pushed Samantha up against the hard brick wall.

She hit it with a grunt. Frenzied hands slipped down my sides and under my shirt, almost as fevered as my hands that sought out every exposed inch of her skin.

I plastered the length of my body against hers, desperate to feel her. "God . . . I miss you."

What I wouldn't give to kiss her slowly. To savor that sweet mouth I craved like nothing else. To have the time to tell her she meant more to me than anything else in this world.

But we didn't have time.

We had five fucking minutes.

And I wasn't slowing down.

I assaulted her mouth. Every piece of me was coming un-hinged, this consuming want tearing through my senses.

"Christopher," she cried when I pulled back a fraction, and I descended on her with more intensity than before.

In the last two weeks, I'd barely seen her. Glimpses of each other were all we'd been given, shadows and seconds stolen in the hidden corners at school. Her parents had even made her transfer out of the one class we shared.

It was complete bullshit.

But Samantha's sin was spending time with me, and they were seeing to it that she repented.

Two minutes earlier, when I saw her walking out the cafe-teria doors, I'd hauled her behind the building, the area ob-scured by tall, thick shrubs.

"It's going to be okay," I whispered harshly at her mouth, unsure who I was promising.

I just knew it had to be.

I deepened the kiss, my tongue slipping between her lips. Warmth skimmed my insides when she returned the kiss, but in a tender, soft way, with a sadness that weakened my knees. I cupped her cheeks and eased away, this time promising her. "It's going to be okay."

Anguish brimmed in those blue eyes, and she swallowed like she didn't want to speak. "No . . . it's not."

I kissed her harder. "Yes, it will."

She began to shake her head. "No, it's not." Tears streaked down her face and into the palms of my hands. "We're moving."

I jerked back. "What?"

She chewed at her bottom lip, and for the first time the act didn't send my thoughts straying toward sex. Instead I wanted to weep. "What?" I asked again, a rock sinking to the pit of my stomach.

"My parents put our house up for sale. Stewart is officially in remission. They said they want to make a fresh start."

Anger and resentment ballooned in my chest. They accused Samantha of being dishonest? Of being a liar? *Right.* There was no doubt in my mind that this had nothin' to do with Stewart. This was all about stealing this girl away from me.

"They're taking me away from you, Christopher." She knew it, too.

"Where?" The word dropped from my mouth like a stone.

"Somewhere across town. They haven't decided exactly yet."

Distorted relief pelted me. Across town. That I could handle, and I needed to hang on to something. I forced a hopeful smile, brushing my thumb across her bottom lip. "Hey, that's not so bad. We can figure it out."

"Why are they doing this to us?" Her voice was a pained whisper.

I dropped my forehead to hers. "They're just trying to protect you from what they don't understand, Samantha."

From what I really didn't understand.

"There's not anything that will keep me away from you," I said, the frenzy silenced, and instead I pulled her into my arms, hugged her, refusing to let her go. "Nothing."

"Nothing," she whispered back.

When you're young, you think the world is yours to take. When in reality, the world is just lying in wait, holding out for the perfect opportunity to show you that it's going to *take* everything from you.

It takes time to build something good. Effort. That effort I'd been so shocked I wanted to put in when I first started things up with Samantha.

But it takes only one second to destroy it all.

Over the last four months, I'd watched while everything important to me was stripped away.

While I sat helpless.

Fucking powerless to do anything to stop it.

When it rains, it pours, and all that shit.

But it hadn't just poured.

It was a torrential flood.

One week after Samantha told me she was moving, I got a call from my dad to come straight home.

I was busy being a punk, figuring out how the hell to get alcohol for the party we'd been planning all week. If I didn't get to spend time with my girl, then at least I'd had this to look forward to. It was supposed to be something special for my best friend, who was turning sixteen.

For months, I'd given him crap that he was just a kid, fifteen, teasing him that I had to drive his sorry ass around.

Of course, he'd turned around and tossed it right back at me, rubbing it in that my girl was younger than him by four weeks. If he was nothing but a kid, then that made me some kind of creepy perv for touching her.

We both knew those three months really didn't matter.

But what we didn't realize was how much one moment did.

All it took was one moment to change everything.

Ruin it all.

Jared was driving back from getting his license and cut in front of an oncoming truck.

His mom, Helene, was killed. Jared was critically injured.

For an entire week, I'd sat beside his hospital bed, silently begging him to live and wishing Samantha could somehow be at my side. I'd needed her there, to let me know everything was going to be okay the way I'd promised her it would be. Needed her to let me know I wasn't alone. That no matter what shit we had to make it through, we'd *make* it.

But Samantha never came, and even when Jared recovered, he never really woke up. Yeah, he breathed and his heart still beat, but guilt had robbed him of everything else.

Inside, Jared was dead, and somehow that managed to kill some part of me.

Helene had been like family, my mom's best friend, our families best friends. When we lost her, everyone and everything fell apart. My parents became distant, not because they didn't care, but because the wind had been knocked from them. Depressed, my mom had struggled to find her own feet, to figure out how to breathe again, and my dad was desperate to help her find her way.

All that time I had to sit and watch the guy I considered my brother, *my best friend*, lose himself. He tried to hurt himself in every way, his self-loathing evident for all to see. Before long, he was using. The only time he wanted anything to do with me was if I was up for going and getting high with him, but he'd gotten himself in much deeper than just smoking a bowl now and then. He'd done nothin' but stare straight through me when I'd gotten up in his face, first threatening him, then pleading with him to stop.

Every day he faded farther away.

Did it make me a bastard that after all of this, after everything my family was going through, the hardest part was watching Samantha slip through my fingers?

Her parents saw to it that she had zero contact with me.

Being without her got harder and harder. I was trying to hold on, to find some kind of confidence in what we had, but every day I became more uncertain.

Loneliness had become my constant partner, this hollowness I couldn't shake. It made it hard to breathe, difficult to get out of bed. My grades sucked, and I was one missed day away from flunking out.

Sad part? Not one fucking soul was there to notice.

So here I sat at another lame party I didn't want to be at, drowning in my very own personal pity party.

From the corner of the room, my glazed-over gaze wandered the riot overtaking Marcus' living room. Everyone was laughing, talking too loud, people making out, living like nothing mattered. This was the same house I'd brought Samantha to that fateful night, the night when upstairs I took the plunge, told her I loved her—and then everything fell apart.

That hollowness throbbed.

I lifted the bottle to my mouth.

Why did it feel like she'd deserted me?

I knew it wasn't her fault, but it sure as hell didn't feel like she was fighting for us. All she was doing was letting her parents win.

Her sixteenth birthday had come and gone. That day, I'd never even seen her. Didn't get to kiss her. Didn't get to tell her how much I loved her and missed her and wanted her.

I definitely didn't get to make love to her, and that shit sucked.

But I'd wait. I'd wait forever because that's how much I loved her.

Going to Samantha's window at night was no longer an option. Her parents kept her under lock and key, and Samantha said trying to sneak by them wasn't worth the risk. The only time I ever saw her was in those quick interludes at school, like when we'd sneak behind the cafeteria.

But that was never enough, and I knew that, too, would soon be coming to an end when she moved across town and switched schools.

Now the FOR SALE sign in their front yard boasted a SOLD sign beneath it. Only three weeks and we'd lose the little contact we had.

It left all these broken, aching places vibrating inside of me.

Hating life.

Hating everyone.

Especially Samantha's parents.

How could they do this to us?

"There you are," Jasmine purred. The stupid slut tried to crawl onto my lap.

I pushed her off, didn't give a fuck that she stumbled back and knocked into the wall. "Stay away from me," I warned, knowing my voice was slurred and filled with all the loneliness that seemed magnified in my heart tonight.

She laughed. "You sure that's what you want? Looks like you could use some *company*."

I sure as hell could, but not from her. "Fuck you."

She laughed again. "Whatever. You let me know when you give up on that little tease of yours and decide you want someone who can take care of you."

I sneered. One side of her filthy mouth curled in satisfaction, before she sauntered away to join her pack of bitches at the other side of the room.

I lifted the cheap bottle of tequila, chugged the quarter that remained, and let the darkness close in.

Because all that perfect light dimmed, narrowing as it thinned, flickered as it threatened to completely blink out.

God, how desperately did I miss it?

The tortured sounds of my mother weeping echoed from behind her closed bedroom door. I stood on the other side of it at the end of the hall, reeling, my head spinning with the magnitude of what'd happened tonight.

Three months ago when Jared had caused that accident, I'd thought it impossible for my life to get worse.

I'd been wrong.

How could he?

I pressed my hand against the wall to hold myself up.

How could he?

Jared had been granted a second chance at life.

And he'd tried to take it.

From the depths of my soul, I *knew* it.

The two deputies from the sheriff's department who'd sat on our couch asking us questions had left fifteen minutes before, insinuating that my best friend was nothin' more than a drug addict, a junkie after his next fix, breaking into the neighbors' house, tying up the owner, and stealing his car. They were charging him with all these bullshit crimes instead of realizing he'd just been crying out for help.

They'd found the car in flames in the lot where we used to play, the place that was so special to us growing up, where I'd taken Samantha just because I wanted to share a part of it with her.

Somehow Jared was no longer in the car, and they'd found him on the ground beside it.

Overdosing.

I gripped my hair, swallowing down a wave of pain.

They'd found a shit ton of heroin on him with all the paraphernalia to go along with it. Of course, I already knew about that, but like an idiot, I'd never said a word because I'd been trying to protect my friend. Even when he'd gotten busted at school a few days before, I'd tried to pretend like I didn't know how bad it'd gotten.

Now I'd give anything to go back and take the title of snitch to save him.

Because when they mentioned the gun he'd stolen from the Ramirezes' house, I knew.

I fucking knew.

Asshole was trying to take one more thing from me.

How could he?

How could this even happen?

The overwhelming urge to punch something rose within me. To destroy something. My forehead dropped to the wall, and I panted against it as I listened to my mother's torment on the other side, my dad trying to convince her of all this bullshit, telling her Jared had earned whatever he got. My hand fisted against the wall, and I wished I could break through it, push all my anger out, rid my body of all this insanity.

But that anger only flared, this prowling hatred bounding through my spirit, filling me up and forcing everything else out.

What happened to the God that Samantha believed in? The one I'd started to trust?

Was he missing in all of this?

Or did he just not exist?

Because not one thing about this was fair or just.

I sensed my little sister, Aly, slowly approaching from behind. Shaking, I turned around to look at her. I'd always thought of her as so young. Innocent. But there was a profound horror in her eyes, this deep sorrow of someone who understood. I wanted to go to her, hug her, tell her everything was going to be okay.

But I knew it wasn't going to be.

Everything was ruined.

Jared was getting sent away.

Samantha was going away.

And I was finally going to lose it all.

I clutched Aly's shoulder when I passed, hoping to give her some kind of comfort when I had none to give.

"Christopher," she pled, reaching for me.

I said nothing, just shook off the hand that landed on my arm, fumbled to my room and grabbed my keys, and ran out the door.

All I wanted was Samantha. For her to make it all go away.

But I couldn't have her, so instead, I headed out to one of those parties where I didn't belong but that were the only places where I really felt welcome.

And I tried to convince myself that I didn't give a fuck anymore.

What good was it anyway? Caring? Wanting more?

What bullshit.

It took me all of half an hour to get shit faced. Good for me. I'd become a fucking pro.

It took Jasmine even less time to start in.

She crawled onto my lap, her disgusting hands all over my

chest. Nausea rolled in my stomach, bile burning in my gut and rising in my throat.

And everything hurt.

My head.

My heart.

I tossed Jasmine off, stumbling as I staggered to my feet and outside, gasping for air.

Marcus came up beside me, clapped me on the back, and like the fucking awesome friend he was, he gave me something foreign that I swallowed down, two little pills I so clearly *needed*. For two minutes I stood there trembling with remorse, knowing I was giving myself over to the same bullshit Jared had, but then this sensation came rushing in, coursing through my veins, clouding everything out.

Everything except for Samantha.

Samantha.

I rubbed my hands over my face, trying to focus, realizing suddenly I was standing at the end of her street, my brain spinning when I ended up at her window.

I shouldn't have been all that shocked. My soul knew that was the only place I wanted to be.

My vision blurred, and I struggled to stay upright, my knuckles begging at her window, rapping at the pane.

A surge of grief tore through me, pressing through the numbness, tugging me in places I didn't understand. It nearly brought me to my knees. I doubled over, feeling sick, all those threads of sanity being snipped away one by one.

God, I almost wept when I saw Samantha's face appear on the other side of her window, and I let that sanity go, no longer clinging to anything else, because she was the only thing I needed.

Slowly, she cracked the window open an inch, and I shoved it wide, crawling over the windowsill and into Samantha's arms.

"Christopher." My ears pulsed with her voice, but it sounded distant and fading.

I needed her closer, wouldn't let her go.

"Samantha . . . oh my God, I need you. Fuck. Need you."

And her skin felt so good under my hands, like warmth and comfort.

I'd gone without it for too long, and there was nothing I wanted more. Nothing could touch this despair except for her.

Her mouth was even hotter, my tongue pressing in, searching for that balm, for a way back to what we'd been, before she'd been stolen from me.

She was on the floor, and I was over her, on her, seeking. My hands were frantic, tearing through our barriers.

I thought maybe I was dying, this suffocating suffering. Only Samantha could give me breath.

"Samantha." I felt her name whimpered from somewhere within, like a plea, a cry, and I struggled to get her closer.

I could hear her calling me, too, this reflection of pain that echoed through her room. And that pain was palpable, tangible as it cut and clawed into my skin. Fear pounded through my chest, and somehow I knew it was hers. Her voice sliced through the haze, breaking through the tortured numbness.

Something sharp.

A vicious sting.

My own fear clogged my throat, and I scrambled back, squinting to see her in the darkness of her room.

She was curled into a ball, rocking. Rocking. Praying to her God to make me stop.

Her top was torn wide open.

And I wanted to cry when this awareness fell over me, this sickness when I realized what I'd nearly done. The top two buttons of my jeans were undone, and my fingers shook uncontrollably when I reached up to my face. Blood coated my fingertips from the deep scratches her nails had slashed across my cheek.

What had I done?

On my knees, I slid my hand along the carpeted floor in an appeal. "Samantha . . . please . . ."

I wouldn't have. I would have stopped.

Wouldn't I have?

She flinched, curling up tighter. Her mouth shook, and she silently cried, her face turned toward the ceiling, like she couldn't bear to look at me. I could barely hear her when she spoke. "Please, go."

I fumbled forward, keeping myself low, as if that could wipe out the disaster of my actions. "I just need you . . . please . . . listen . . . I wouldn't have . . ."

She choked, her voice an anguished whisper. "I don't even recognize you anymore. Please . . . just go."

"You promised me . . . you promised me we'd make it."

She lolled her head in my direction. Her expression alone destroyed the last good thing in me. Because I knew it was done.

"I trusted you," she said, the words breaking as they scraped from her throat. "My parents were right to protect me from you."

I swallowed over the heartbreak. My chest burned with it, this fiery anger as I stared down at the one person who I always believed would have faith in me.

Instead she looked away.

I tried to climb to my feet but fell back to my knees. Like the cursed, I slid along the floor on my belly, grunted as I hoisted myself up and over the windowsill. I landed on the dirt ground with a hard thud.

Two days had passed. Two days since Jared took those extra steps to ruin his life. Two days since I'd turned right around and ruined mine.

Riddled with shame and bitterness, I sat back on Marcus' couch and lifted the bottle to my mouth.

No, I wasn't getting so fucked-up that I could hurt anyone else. Not ever again. When I'd woken up the previous morning with my head splitting in two, I'd sworn never again. I'd never allow myself to lose that kind of control, my mind nonexistent in the abyss of all that blackness.

But my heart was already broken, and the bottle I clutched in my hand worked just fine with that kind of pain. So I chased that numbness, the dulled sense of accepting that nothing mattered.

Nothing mattered because there was nothing left to fight for, and I was giving in.

Yesterday I'd tried. I'd sucked it up and made one last valiant attempt. With my heart lodged in my throat, I'd dialed Samantha's home number.

On the first ring, it'd chanted that three-beat chime, the one that warned I'd reached a number that had been disconnected.

And now that's all I wanted to be.

Disconnected.

To pull the plug on every one of these emotions wringing me tight.

It hurt too bad, and I didn't want to feel anything anymore.

That afternoon, I'd sat in the quiet of my room and poured my heart onto paper, sifting through myself for the remnants of her light, dug deep for the few things left within me that I still cared about. I'd ended up with three letters.

One was for Jared.

One for Stewart.

The other for *her.*

I'd sealed them up in envelopes, same way I sealed off my hemorrhaging heart. I took two out to the mailbox and hid the other away.

Now I sat on the couch, draining an entire bottle of Jack. I slumped back, and the empty bottle slipped from my fingers and hit the floor. Muddled faces floated through my vision, the party loud and obnoxious, but somehow I felt as if I was watching it from above.

Detached.

Hands slipped over my chest, a warm body pressing firm at my lap, a hot mouth on my neck.

I groaned, and my cock reacted. My fingers dug into skin as a distorted pleasure reverberated through my body.

She laughed, and the tip of her nail trailed down my chin to the neck of my shirt. She clutched it and tugged. "I told you one day you'd come to your senses."

I laughed in her face, an incredulous, crazed sound, because she couldn't be further from the truth.

I'd lost every last one of them, all except for the physical need to let it go, to give in and take the one thing within my reach that would let me feel good.

Jasmine pulled me to my unstable feet.

My parents were right to protect me from you.

I let her lead me upstairs and into the dimly lit room.

How she knew I'd follow, I didn't know. Maybe I was bleeding defeat.

And I hated her as much as I always had. But I hated myself more.

She kissed me and I kissed her back, but it didn't feel anything like the kisses I gave Samantha. It felt empty, and the hollowness inside screamed out.

It clashed with the nerves shooting across my skin where her hands touched me, rushing up and down, spurring the coil of lust that fisted in my stomach.

Samantha left me.

Numbly, I helped her undress me, watched idly when she stepped back and undressed herself. She pushed me back onto the floor, the same floor where Samantha had promised herself to me, where I'd told her I loved her and I'd given in to the delusion that somehow all of our firsts would belong to the other.

But that was nothing but a stupid fantasy. I was never good enough for her. Somewhere inside, I'd always known it. Known I was only going to hurt her, and hurt her was exactly what I'd done.

I didn't stop Jasmine when she straddled my legs. She moaned my name when she lowered herself onto me.

And it felt so wrong, but everything had gone wrong a long time ago.

She rode me and I just lay there, wanting to erase every memory. Hate filled me up so full I wanted to vomit. Hate for Jasmine. Hate for myself. Hate for Jared for being so selfish.

Most of all, I hated that Samantha had given up on us so easily.

She'd said she loved me.

She'd said we were forever.

I'd fucked up . . . but I'd thought . . . I'd thought that's what love was supposed to be about, finding a way through those faults, making them right and ensuring we never committed the same sins.

Turned out what I'd done was unforgiveable.

Or maybe she'd just never really cared all that much.

I turned my gaze from Jasmine, couldn't watch the victorious expression on her face.

Instead I looked off into the distance and let the physical pleasure consume me.

A destructive reprieve.

Even still, I couldn't rid my mind of Samantha's perfect face. She was all I could see, that beautiful, sweet girl, all that blond hair and those blue eyes. A sad smile tugged at me when I thought of that mouth.

And God, I wanted to picture her happy, like she used to be, but she was standing there drowning in all the sadness I'd caused her. The tears and the hurt. The girl falling to pieces over her own broken heart.

Softly I smiled, somehow hating her and still wishing there was a way I could take away all her pain.

But there was not one fucking thing I could do. So I shut it off and turned back to Jasmine. I grabbed her hips hard and fucked her like she'd been begging me to for months.

And for a few mindless minutes, skin was the only thing I felt.

TWENTY

Samantha

Rattled, I stood staring at the closed door.

I was tempted to run back through it.

On the other side, I could hear the low rumble of his truck when he shifted into gear.

I wanted him to stay.

I needed him to go.

To say my emotions were a mess was a gross understatement. I was a wreck.

I'd woken up next to Christopher Moore. And God help me, the first few disoriented seconds were complete and utter bliss. The smooth, inked skin of his bare chest under my cheek, the steady thrum of his heartbeat beneath my ear, and what felt like an endless expanse of rock-hard abs twitching under my roaming hand.

Intoxicated, I'd buried my nose under his jaw, gorging myself on his smell, a lust-inducing euphoria clouding my head, coaxing me to drift into the warmth of his body.

But all of that had only drawn attention to the excruciating need in mine, this undeniable burn seated deep between my thighs promising me everything would be just fine if I got a little closer.

Awareness had come crashing in.

Me curled up in his arms. In his *bed*. With a gaping blank spot in my memory.

And he'd been aroused.

Very glaringly so.

At the memory, my stomach dipped and clenched.

Right. And there was that.

It had been enough to send me straight into panic mode.

Ha. Panic mode. More like deranged-and-irrational-drunk-girl mode. So maybe Christopher had been joking when he was giving Aly crap that women shouldn't drink, but I was beginning to think there was some validity to his statement.

Bottom line, I shouldn't.

Not like that.

Not when I was with him and vulnerable, liable to fall into all sorts of foolishness. Not when the sweet boy I'd thought I once knew had come out to play.

Especially when I was no longer sure it was just an act.

Because I'd felt it tonight. Heartbreak. Christopher's when he first saw Stewart, this true and genuine concern that had come rushing from him uninhibited. And for those few moments, I'd felt as if I could rely on him the way I used to. I used to believe he was the only person who really understood how I felt. The only one who'd allow me to fall apart and then patiently put me back together.

Tonight it'd felt the same.

Every rational side of me knew I should be terrified of Christopher. His big hands could shred me.

The truth of the matter was, I had been. That night when he'd come into my room, I hadn't recognized him. Seeing his face at my window? I'd been inundated with relief. Finally he was coming to save me. Finally he'd come to prove to me that everything he'd promised about making it through was the truth. He wasn't giving up, no matter what obstacles we had to face.

Because I'd been losing hope.

After what happened with Jared, something had changed in Christopher. He was no longer carefree. No longer full of life. He was distant, going out and partying all the time, and insecurities had begun to wind themselves through my heart, choking out the confidence that he truly loved me.

But I'd hung on.

Instead of bringing relief when he'd pushed through my window, his presence had stolen all the air and filled it with fear. Terror had trembled all the way to my bones when I realized he was really going to force me.

My first time and he was going to force me. And it wasn't even the physical that broke my heart. It was the fact that he could treat me that way.

The sad thing was I would have given myself to him.

Right there, on my bedroom floor, if he'd have stopped long enough to look at me. To show me that he saw me and he wasn't seeing right through me.

But I'd been so caught off guard, the desperation in Christopher's touch and in his words hadn't processed. The next day we were moving, and I'd already been withdrawn from school, so it wasn't until two days later that I'd heard the gossip about Jared, the boy who'd spiraled so far he'd finally hit bottom.

As soon as I had, I'd been struck with overwhelming grief. Christopher had *needed* me. Just like he'd said. He wasn't looking through me. He wasn't able to *see* at all.

So I'd gone to find him.

To hell with my parents and all their rules.

I didn't care.

We would run away.

But when it came to Christopher, I'd always been just a foolish girl.

Turned out I had no idea about broken hearts until that night when I found him.

It had destroyed me.

It'd all been a joke.

A cruel, sick joke.

And with *her*.

It had to be her.

Thank God Ben had been there. I was scared of where I would have ended up had he not.

And here I was all these years later, standing in the middle of my living room, listening to the roar of Christopher's engine as he accelerated and drove away. All those things I knew I should never want suddenly felt like they were missing. All those resolutions I'd made didn't seem so solid. And the commitment I had to Ben didn't feel so real.

Yes. I was terrified of Christopher Moore.

Physically? No. It was a sad, sick twist of fate that in his arms was where I felt safest.

I was terrified of what he could do with this burgeoning heart.

When I walked into my classroom on the Tuesday morning after I'd woken up in Christopher's bed, there was an envelope on my desk. My name was pressed into it with the familiar heavy-handed script, and it was wrapped in the same red ribbon that had adorned the bouquet the month before.

I cast a suspicious glance around the room.

How had he snuck it in here?

Drawing in a calming breath, I inched across the room and sank into my chair. Finally I gathered the courage to pick up the letter. My fingers shook as I pulled the ribbon free. It dropped to my lap and I slid the card from the envelope.

Again the front was blank, but this time I had no delusions that the inside would be. My eyes blurred as I read the words.

> *What does it take to delete the past?*
> *A thousand apologies?*
> *A million regrets?*
> *A litany of prayers?*
> *If I shouted them, would you hear?*
> *If I whispered them, would you believe?*
> *If I fell at your feet, would you forgive?*
> *If I asked, would you start again?*

Blinking away tears, I clutched the letter to my chest as if it could blunt the ache inside.

Would I?

Could I be brave enough to accept what I really wanted? Could I forsake Ben and shun everything my parents ever wanted for me?

Above it all, could I ever forgive Christopher for what he'd done?

TWENTY-ONE

Christopher

Slipping my key into the lock, I knocked lightly at Aly and Jared's front door before I turned the knob and poked my head inside. "Hello?"

Shrill cries rattled from down the hall, and I chuckled a little with the sound of Samantha's frazzled voice. "In the nursery."

Yeah, I knew she was babysitting.

And no, I couldn't stay away.

I strode in, flinging the door shut behind me as I headed straight for Ella's room. Samantha was at the changing table, struggling with Ella's flailing legs as she tried to dress her in a fresh diaper. Samantha gave me an exasperated look. "For one of the sweetest little girls in the world, she sure hates getting her diaper changed."

I laughed outright as I crossed the room, loving every step that brought me closer to these two girls who absolutely owned me. Funny, their paths never should have crossed, and here I was, standing watching Samantha loving on my niece.

"Are you giving Samantha a hard time, princess?" I asked as I palmed the top of Ella's head. She pushed into the movement, her tiny round head sliding back to look up at me with those big ol' blue eyes. Distracted, she gave me her biggest smile with that adorable mouth and cooed against the fist she suddenly decided to start trying to eat. Samantha took the opportunity to quickly afix the tabs on her diaper.

"There," she said with all kinds of affectionate pride in her voice.

Yep, man card no more. That fucker had been permanently revoked the night Samantha had fallen asleep in my bed, because between these two girls, I didn't even recognize myself anymore. It'd been a month since Samantha and I had really reconnected, since she'd opened up to me about her brother, and in those moments I knew where we belonged was together. Sure, she'd flipped right the fuck out when she woke up next to me, but I knew that was only because she was feeling it, too, and she didn't know how to reconcile all the shit I'd done with the obvious bond we shared.

We'd fallen into a tenuous *friendship*. The entire month of September had pretty much passed in a blurry whirl that had the two of us dancing through all the tension and pretending like we both didn't want to decimate the boundaries that'd been set in place. We hung out a ton with Jared and Aly, but we'd also started texting a bunch, laughing over the inane bullshit that made up our days. Joking and messing around.

Crazy thing? It didn't feel like we were getting to know each other in a new light. It was like we were remembering who we once used to be. I was doing my best to keep it cool, trying not to be so blatantly transparent about how badly I was dying to touch her. Because even though I'd resolved she was again going to be mine, I knew that shit was going to take some time. But the more time I spent with her, the harder that got.

Samantha pulled a clean outfit out of the drawer for Ella and began to dress her. "Would you do me a favor and get the bottle that's in the warmer on the kitchen counter?"

"Sure."

I grabbed the bottle in the kitchen while Samantha settled on the couch with Ella. She'd begun to fuss and cram her hand in her mouth with a little more vigor. I sat down close to them, couldn't help the chuckle rumbling at the base of my throat when Ella began to kick when she caught sight of the bottle. Shouldn't like this scene so damned much, but I did. "Somebody's anxious, huh?"

Samantha accepted the bottle from me and situated Ella on her arm in a good position to feed her. Ella latched on like she'd been drowning and finally caught a breath of air. Samantha slanted me a smile filled with all kinds of yearning. "She's the sweetest thing, isn't she?"

Soft affection huffed from my nose, and I traced the pad of my index finger along the intense lines dented across Ella's head as she voraciously sucked down her lunch. "Yeah, she really is. Never thought I'd fall in love with anything the way I did with her." It was something pure and honest. No greed or selfish intentions.

Samantha hummed, a sound that seemed both agreement and a question. "I love kids. That was the main reason I wanted to be a teacher."

"You gonna have any of your own?"

The second I asked it, I regretted it. That was the problem when I was with Samantha. Couldn't keep my damned mouth shut.

She shrugged a delicate shoulder, that pretty face pinking up, but it didn't seem in embarrassment. It was rather in more of the longing she always seemed to watch my niece with. "Hope so." She lifted her shoulder a little higher and peeked over at me. "When the time is right."

Agitation sifted through me, and I drove a flustered hand through my hair. *Brilliant.* Going there. Knowing it'd rip me apart.

And what did assholes like me do when they got all edgy and disturbed? They lashed out, and damn it all if I didn't know better, but I couldn't keep the scornful words from whipping from my tongue like a flog. "So where's dickhead this weekend?"

Samantha winced and averted her gaze, discomfort fortifying all those walls that I wanted to break down.

On a regretful sigh, I flopped against the sofa back. "Damn it," I muttered quietly as I scrubbed my face. I rolled my head to the side and caught Samantha peering at me warily. "I'm sorry. I shouldn't have said that."

Really, I wanted to say a whole ton more, to berate the asshole who I knew in my gut had always had it out for me, but what good would it be taking it out on Samantha?

"It's fine," she whispered with a short shake of her head. "I know you weren't exactly his biggest fan."

"And he wasn't exactly mine."

She laughed. "No. Definitely not." She smiled over at me, and it was sad and small and like a confession. "Honestly, he can be a real asshole."

Anger tightened my chest, a swell of protectiveness that had me wanting to wrap her up and never let go. "Does he know you're here?"

"No." She looked at me as if she was truly wondering if I wanted the truth.

I lifted my chin toward her, urging her to go on.

"He'd flip out if he knew. The couple of times I've mentioned Aly, he just about came unglued, and I really don't want to deal with his judgment."

"You scared of him?" The words were strangled, and I wasn't sure I could handle the answer.

She swallowed hard. Blue eyes that had me all itchy and anxious settled on me. "Not like that." Her voice lowered with the confession. "I'm scared that he's not right for me. Scared that I'll never love him like I should."

Relief pounded another beat of hope into my heart. I'd known that night when I took her home that she didn't love him. And now she sat five inches away, admitting it to me.

I struggled through a heavy breath and shifted to the edge of the cushions so I could face her. She was so close that she was filling up my breath. Drawn, I scooted forward. All I wanted was to eat her up. Consume her. Make her realize that she was always going to belong with me.

But there was this nagging inside me, her parting words from a month ago haunting me day and night. There was a piece of Samantha that was scared of me. Terrified really. I saw it there in the shift of her eyes, the way they flared with want and need, but darted away when she'd be hit with a flash of fear.

She sucked in a sharp breath when I pushed to standing and leaned over her. Her head dropped back, and I took that gorgeous face between my hands. Held it gently like the fragile treasure it was. "I need you to know something, Samantha."

She blinked, and there was no missing the tremor that rolled through her body. I hovered close, my nose an inch from hers.

"These hands." I squeezed her a little with the significance. "They won't *ever* hurt you."

That sweet mouth dropped open a fraction, the plump red flesh the greatest damned temptation I'd ever faced. But this wasn't about lust or my fucked-up need. This was about a girl I'd done wrong. "That night I came to you? I stopped because I *felt* you. Even through the haze of my mind, I *heard* your heart, Samantha. I realize that now. I never would have pushed you over that line."

A strangled sound worked its way up Samantha's throat, and all I wanted was to swallow it down.

"The night last month in my truck?"

She gave a tiny nod of acknowledgment, still remaining in my firm hold.

"What did you mean, what you saw?"

Her expression immediately hardened, and I nearly jumped out of my skin when the front door suddenly flew open to a giggling Aly. She came to a standstill just as fast as she'd stumbled in, breaking through all the intensity that hovered thick in the air.

Shit.

In surprise, Aly looked between me and Samantha, who'd jerked out of my hands as if she was being branded by fire. She turned all her focus back to the little girl who'd fallen asleep in her arms. Aly cocked her head in question, and I glared across at her.

Perfect timing, little sister.

She shrugged and mouthed, *What?*

Over her shoulder, Jared smirked at me, scratching at his temple with his index finger, thinking he knew all too well what he'd walked in on.

If only it were that simple.

I turned back to Samantha, tucked my finger under her chin, and lifted it so I could latch onto those tentative eyes. "I mean it," I said, not caring that we had an audience. "Wouldn't, Samantha. You gotta know that's not me."

And yeah, we had a shit ton of unfinished business. So much that needed to be said and resolved. But if this was the only one we ever tackled—and we never got a chance to work through the rest of it? This was the one I needed her to know.

I'd never hurt her.

I cast her a pleading glance as I backed away.

Never.

TWENTY-TWO

Samantha

I tried not to skip out of my boss' office. But the second the door closed behind me, it was on. I raced back to my empty classroom, my feet barely touching the ground. I threw the door open to the darkened room, and it slammed closed behind me.

Squeezing my hands into the tightest balls, I squealed and ran in place, my knees nearly knocking into my chin. Like a thirteen-year-old girl who'd just found out her favorite boy band was coming into town.

It wasn't pretty.

But I couldn't find one hidden place inside me that cared.

"Yes! Yes! Yes!" I screamed below my breath, my hammering heart pumping an erratic elation through my veins.

I couldn't wait to tell him.

Dancing around like a complete spaz, I grabbed my phone from my purse, unable to contain the grin plastered across my face. My fingers flew across the screen as I texted Christopher.

Guess what?!?!

He answered almost immediately, as if the hours had passed too slowly like they had for me and he couldn't wait to hear the news. *You got it?!*

Yep! They offered me a full-time, permanent position. You're looking at a for-real teacher ;)

They'd kept me on after the summer session ended because they ended up being short staffed when the school year started. It was halfway through October and I was still working per diem, even though I was supposed to work only through the end of August. When my boss had asked to speak to me in her office during the lunch break, I'd been praying it was for this very reason.

Three seconds passed before my phone buzzed.

God, Samantha. That's FANTASTIC. I'm proud of you. Really proud. But are you surprised? They'd be insane to let you go.

I almost snorted. He dug those types of sentiments in constantly.

But they'd become his thousand apologies.

His million regrets.

And I'd found myself whispering my own litany of prayers, searching above and beyond for the correct path.

Fear kept me from taking that leap of faith. When he promised me at Aly's house two weeks ago that he'd never hurt me, every part of me had wanted to believe him, but it was that last inkling of doubt that kept me from fully giving my trust to the only one who had the power to destroy it.

But I knew I couldn't continue like this for long.

Christopher had quickly become my everything.

The only problem was he wasn't really mine.

My phone buzzed again. *And for the record, I'm not looking at you. But I really wish I was.*

You wish, I shot back.

Uh, yeah, clever girl, that's what I said. Wait, are you sure you're qualified to be a teacher? Now you're giving me second thoughts.

With a short laugh, I shook my head. *Such a punk. Anyone ever told you that?*

His response was immediate. *That's why you love me ;)*

God love him and damn him all at the same time. Yet somehow, my smile only grew.

I had another text from him before I had time to reply. *When do I get to see you again? We need to celebrate.*

My conscience vibrated with guilt. I hated sneaking around to see Christopher. No matter which way I looked at it, it was wrong. No old emotion could warrant the number of lies I had told.

But I didn't want to stop.

Home had never felt so close.

And it wasn't as if I was cheating.

But I recognized how lame that excuse was. I might not be having sex with Christopher, but who had I called with my good news?

Seven years of my life had been consigned to Ben. Would I really give that up? Hurt him when he'd always been there for me? I hated even the idea of it. I wasn't that type of girl, one who'd trample another's heart for the benefit of her own.

But the idea of losing Christopher again crushed me. I cherished him as a friend. But I felt a crossroads approaching. A fork in the road. One direction or the other, because I couldn't travel both.

Would I risk it all on a boy who was the ultimate risk?

Because no matter how close we grew, there was no erasing what he'd done.

My phone buzzed again.

Let me take you out. Can you get away tonight? I need to see you.

I squeezed my eyes shut, and with every part of me I wished that things were different.

I can't tonight. Dinner plans. I left out the part that they were with Ben. *This weekend?*

Ben left Friday for a meeting in L.A. and wouldn't return until Sunday, and here I was again, feeling all kinds of relief about it.

How can I steal you away before then? I'm not above bribery.

Don't think that's going to happen. I lifted my phone and snapped a picture. So maybe I added what I hoped was a sexy pout. Sue me. *This will have to hold you over until then.*

My knees got all wobbly when I looked at his return message, my eyes glued to the image on the screen. He was patting his heart, his mouth twisted in that wicked grin, green eyes gleaming back at me.

Kill me now, the man was unjustifiably beautiful.

Tingles raced through every inch of me, like the devil was at their heels.

I shook my head.

I was in so much trouble.

Later that afternoon, Cici popped her head into my classroom, clutching the side of the door. "Hey, you."

"What's up?" I asked, cleaning up the last of the mess left behind by our art project. All of the kids had gone home and I was spent. But it was a good kind of spent. The kind attained in the satisfaction of hard work.

It'd been a good day.

Being offered a full-time position here had been something I'd been hoping for basically since they brought me on part-time. It was honestly a little surprising how much I loved it here.

But there was something else.

Something greater simmering below the surface that buzzed beneath my skin and hummed in my spirit.

Cici pushed the door wider and gestured down the hall. "That man of yours is at it again . . . the delivery guy stopped by a few minutes ago." She smiled softly. "What a sweetheart."

A flurry of nerves scattered through me.

Sweetheart.

Crazy how fitting that sentiment was.

Of course Cici had no clue who really was the *sweetheart*, how dark and dangerous he seemed on the exterior until he let you reach down deep into the middle, to what was hidden inside. Somehow I knew I was the only person he'd allowed to touch him there.

"I'm just finishing up," I told her. "I'll be out to grab it in a minute. Thanks for letting me know."

"No problem." She started to retreat, then paused. "And congrats, by the way. It's going to be great having you around here permanently."

I smiled at her. "Thank you. I can't tell you happy I am to be a part of the school."

She nodded as if she completely understood how truly thankful I was, and with a small wave she let the door drop closed behind her. I rushed through the rest of my cleanup, stuffed some paperwork into my messenger bag, then slung both it and my purse over my shoulder, all too eager to race down the hall and into the office.

I pushed open the heavy door, and my pulse ratcheted up a hundred knots at the simple bouquet waiting on the high counter. It was just three white lilies wrapped in that same red ribbon, tied in a soft, delicate bow, but to me it felt like another piece of my world falling into place.

The office staff had cleared out for the day, leaving me alone in the silence with my thrashing heart. But this time my heart wasn't pounding with fear. It was thundering with hope. My hands were shaking as I plucked the envelope from the holder, my name once again scrawled across the front in his powerful script.

I tore into the flap, holding my breath as I flipped open another card with a blank front.

Missing were all the pleas for atonement, the desperate words of Christopher's regret.

Instead they were simple words of encouragement.

> *Few people deserve the gifts of this world.*
> *But then there are some who are the gift.*
> *Those are the ones who step into a room and suddenly*
> *it's a better place.*
> *Those are the ones who stand in the shadows and*
> *somehow still reflect the sun.*
> *Those are the ones whose smile chases away the dark-*
> *ness and whose laughter heals the soul.*
> *Don't ever hide your light, Samantha. Let it shine. Let*
> *it burn bright. Because you? You're everything in this*
> *world that's right.*

Tears stung my eyes, and I wiped away the emotion that came like a rush of deliverance. Gathering the arrangement, I hugged it close and slipped out the front door, feeling lighter than I had in years. I made sure the door was locked behind me before I headed for my car parked across the lot.

Evening approached, the late afternoon air still, noise from the nearby thick traffic filling the air.

All my attention was trained on my feet, and I yelped when a hand landed on my forearm. I whirled around to find Christopher standing before me and grinning. He pressed a finger to his lips and made a little *shh* sound as he began to haul me behind the cover of a tree.

I struggled to catch my breath, laughing as I chastised quietly, "What are you doing here?"

He pulled me to face him, searing green eyes darting all over as he studied me up and down. It seemed whatever he was looking for and he clearly found filled him with relief. He captured a strand of my hair that in the lazy breeze had whipped haphazardly around my face. With an easy grin, his head slowly dropped to the side and he tucked the chunky piece behind my ear.

My insides went gooey. God, he was beautiful and perfect, and his presence made me a little dizzy.

His smile widened to show a big flash of teeth.

Okay, a lot dizzy.

"I couldn't wait until the weekend to tell you congratulations, so I figured if you couldn't come to me, then I would come to you."

I shook my head, chewing at my lower lip that slipped right into a self-conscious grin. "You really are crazy, aren't you?"

Christopher just laughed, before his expression transformed into something unfathomable. "You have no clue, Samantha."

He glanced down at the flowers held fast in my arms before he moved his gaze up to meet my own. The air seemed to crackle around us, a charged awareness taking hold. Christopher hesitated before he finally reached out to cup my face in the frame of his hands. He stared down at me. "Hope you know every single word is true, Samantha."

And I knew he was referring to the words scrawled in the cards that were now tucked away in a drawer that housed my most precious possessions: accolades from school, an heirloom ring passed on from my great-grandmother, letters from Stewart, sweet pictures my first students had drawn.

Now Christopher was there—with what I cherished most.

Green eyes searched my face and his thumbs skated across the apples of my cheeks.

Realization crawled over me in a blanket of shivers.

I wanted him to kiss me.

Silently I begged him to make the move, to turn me and press me up against his truck like he'd done all those months ago. But this time I wouldn't stop him. This time I would welcome him.

Instead he dropped his mouth to my forehead. His lips lingered there for the longest time, his hands stroking up and down my jaw, my heart a complete shattered mess because I knew without a doubt he now held it in the palm of his hand.

Because I no longer wanted to be afraid. No, it wasn't that. What I wanted was for my fear to no longer hold me back.

I wanted to trust because I was certain this amazing man had earned it.

Reluctantly, he pulled away, and God, did it make me a fool that I wanted to beg him not to?

"I'll see you on Saturday," he said. He squeezed my hand when he stepped away, like he didn't want to let me go any more than I wanted him to. He didn't release his hold until our arms were stretched out between us, our fingertips hovering in the air to get one last brush of skin before we parted.

"Saturday," he said again, although this time the promise was clear.

It was the promise of something more.

A loose thread of uneasiness was still woven through the fabric of my being. But it was thin and quickly fraying. I no longer wanted to be controlled by my fears, and I no longer wanted to settle. I no longer wanted to lead Ben on and I no longer wanted to push Christopher off.

Because as I stood there watching him climb into his truck, I knew.

I wanted to belong to him.

Candlelight glowed from each of the linen-covered tables, the quiet ambiance of the room making the restaurant feel even more intimate.

Ben sat across from me, filling me in on every inane detail of his day at work. I'd barely gotten in little more than two words edgewise.

Never had I felt more uncomfortable in my life. Fiddling with the corner of the linen napkin on my lap, I let my eyes wander over his masculine face. My eyes narrowed in on his jaw, the way it flexed and clenched as he took a bite. He took a sip of wine and swallowed, giving me a tight smile when he set the glass back on the table.

I made myself focus on him. He was attractive. Not like Christopher, though. Not even close. But clean and strong and proud, a cookie-cutter cutout of what should equate to every girl's dream man. And I searched everywhere inside myself, seeking out even the tiniest spark. For a small flicker of something *more* to emerge. To feel an ounce of what I should feel for Ben.

Because I'd cared about him for so many years, but I knew that care had never come in the capacity it should.

He cut into his steak. "So how was your day?" he finally asked.

"Well," I began, leaning into the table, "I actually got some really great news today."

"Yeah?" He glanced up, and I felt a timid smile materialize on my face.

"Yeah. The school offered me a full-time position. I get my own class starting next week. Second grade."

Pride filled up my chest. A deep joy that I could feel burning from the inside shining as it made its way out. I was a little shocked by how much I'd wanted this.

Midcut, Ben stilled, his utensils poised over his slab of meat. He smiled, but it faltered in his eyes. I watched the bob of his Adam's apple as he swallowed. "That's . . . wonderful, Sam," he said, though everything about his congratulations felt forced. Turning back to the task of sawing through his steak, he eyed me with the lift of his brow. "And what did you tell them?"

"I accepted it of course."

Slowly he nodded, contemplating. "Are you sure that's the best direction right now? Things are really beginning to happen at work for me. If I cinch this account in L.A., which I will"—he gestured between us with his fork—"we'll be set. There's really no need for you to work at all."

I felt the deep frown creasing my forehead, and I blinked rapidly. "I just finished school. Why would I want to stop working? I'm only getting started."

He sighed as if he were trying to reason with a petulant toddler, quietly set his utensils aside, and reached across the table for my hand, which was clenched in a fist at the side of my plate. He squeezed it in what I could only assume was supposed to be affection.

All it made me want to do was yank it away.

"It's time to start thinking about the future," he said. In emphasis, he squeezed tighter. "Our future. Settle down . . . begin thinking about starting a family."

Nerves barreled through me at full force, panic and anxiety and an all-out defiance. My knee began to bounce. "You know I'm not ready for that yet, Ben."

Did I want a family? I always had, and Ben knew it, too. But I never thought he'd use that desire as leverage.

And somehow, I knew that's exactly what this was.

In some way, I guess I'd always known he used my every want against me. I'd just been too caught up in dwelling on all my terrible choices to admit it.

His voice took on that soothing, placating tone, and he rubbed his thumb in circles on the back of my hand. "Trust me on this. I only want what's best for you, and getting into some long-term contract with that school isn't going to benefit us."

Right. The only person it wouldn't benefit was him.

I sat back, meeting his eye. "I *am* taking this job, Ben. You should be happy for *me*."

Pushing out a breath, he rubbed his forehead, and his voice softened as if it could change the impact of his words. "Of course I'm happy for you. But it's not a good time to go making huge changes in our lives. Not when I'm this close to everything I've worked for."

Anger exploded through me. "Isn't that what you're asking of me? To change the direction of my life to satisfy you? After everything *I've* worked for?"

With a feigned smile, he backpedaled. "It was just a suggestion, sweetheart." In pure condescension, he patted my hand, like I didn't know he never intended it to be anything close to a *suggestion*.

"What do you say we not make any decisions tonight?" he continued. "Wait and see what happens after this trip? Then we can decide. Deal?"

Though I nodded in acquiescence, my decision had already been made.

TWENTY-THREE

Samantha

Why aren't you here yet?

Redness climbed up my neck to my cheeks, and I chewed at my lip. Why I was blushing from a simple text, I didn't know. But whatever the reason, it felt really good.

Can't you tell time? I teased. *You're the one who said 5. That's not for another 40 minutes.*

Immediately, my phone buzzed. *Can't wait that long. Come now.*

With a wry smile, I shook my head, as if he could see me. Thank goodness he couldn't. *Not ready yet.*

Drop everything & walk out the door. I'm finished waiting.

Bossy.

Grinning like a fool, I tapped back a message. *Um . . . that could be embarrassing and quite possibly a felony. I'm not exactly dressed.*

He didn't miss a beat. *Even better.*

Okay, definitely blushing. *You're impossible, crazy boy.*

And you're perfect, Sweet Samantha. Throw something on and get your ass over here.

Sweet Samantha. Affection pulsed at my ribs, and suddenly I couldn't wait to get to his door. *I'm on my way.*

I tossed my phone to the counter and got ready faster than I had in all my life.

Twilight whispered at the edge of the shimmery October sky. Tall, lush trees grew high overhead, and the vast lawn below us was perfectly manicured. The brutal summer was finally giving up its hold on the city, and a soft breeze blew through, ushering in a gentle warmth that hung in the air.

I glanced in his direction. A rush of shivers rolled through me when I caught him looking down at me.

God, I was in deep.

A genuine smile curved his mouth, that face so beautiful I found I no longer knew how to look away. The sum of them was enough to plunder the breath right from my lungs.

Guess that was exactly where I wanted to be.

I felt him place his hand at the small of my back.

"Let's see if we can find a good spot." He scanned through the people milling around the vendor trucks and booths, across from those who were gathering in small groups hoping to find a place on the grass to watch the show.

A jazz festival.

This might have been the last place I'd have expected Christopher would take me. But at every turn was another surprise, every new corner we rounded just another reminder of how thoughtful I'd once believed him to be.

While he searched for an open spot, I took the opportunity to look at him.

To really *look* at him.

My gaze traced along the defined contours of his strong jaw, covered in a thick coat of dark stubble. His profile was strong and his demeanor proud. Predatory. That troublemaking teenager my parents had been so terrified of had evolved, manifesting into an all-around menacing physical force. A beautiful type of intimidation. Too pretty to touch and too dangerous to approach.

For so long I'd believed him evil.

Cruel and vile.

My spirit thrashed in protest.

Impossible.

So much time had been wasted questioning myself. Wondering if I'd just been a blind, naive little girl. I hadn't given myself the chance to believe.

But I realized it now. I did. I believed the words he'd poured onto paper for me. I believed his smile and the emotion held fast in his eyes.

Christopher slipped his hand all the way around to grip my side. Every inch of my skin came alive.

He pointed off to the left. "How about over there?"

"Looks great to me."

He led me by the hand past all the vendors and up a small hill. My dress flats squished into the damp lawn as I followed close behind. With a squeeze of the hand, he released me and spread the blanket out over the side of a small incline that faced the stage. The spot he picked was a little more private, back away from the crowds that were situated right up close under the stage, but close enough that we had an excellent, elevated view.

"This is perfect," I said, unable to keep from chewing at my lip. Excitement bubbled beneath my skin. I loved getting the chance to be this free with him. Just Christopher and me.

Us.

Inside, that ball of anxious anticipation flared, that warning of impending change. But this time it lacked even an ounce of dread.

Christopher frowned, though somehow it was a smile, dents of curiosity striking across his brow. "What are you thinking about?" He tilted his head to study me.

"This just . . . feels . . . good," I admitted quietly.

Okay, way more than good.

Amazing and perfect and everything I'd ever imagined it could be.

A rush of shyness hit me with these thoughts, and I chewed at my lip, coated in that yummy gloss, wondering how in a few short months, everything inside me could feel so radically different.

Christopher reached across the short space between us and took the errant strand of hair blowing around my face between his fingers. He brushed it away, and a small smile lifted at one side of his mouth as he let his fingers slide down my neck.

I shook beneath the feel of his fingertips and the weight of his spirit.

Finally he turned back to catch my gaze. "Every second I get to spend with you is *good*, Samantha. Don't doubt that."

And I didn't. Every second I'd spent with him had slowly eradicated those doubts.

His voice came out rough. "Thank you for coming out here with me."

Gratitude shook my head. As if somehow I was doing him a favor? "This . . ." I shook my head a little harder. "You don't know how much I needed this. How much it means to me that you'd bring me out here. That you'd take the time to celebrate something so small as my new job."

"Small?" He took a step forward, erasing all the space between us, tipping my head back to meet his gorgeous face. "Nothing small about you achieving something you worked for,

Samantha. Don't want to ever hear you implying that something's not big enough or good enough when it's important to you. And if it's important to you, then it's important to me. You understand what I'm saying?"

It sounded hard, almost angry, and it struck me deep, in those places that I'd kept locked up and reserved for him, the places that I thought were just a fantasy, about a boy who understood me and believed in me. My fingers were somehow twisted in the hem of his T-shirt. "Yes," I barely got out, the word catching in my throat.

"Good," he said firmly. Then he shot me one of those wicked smiles that I liked far too much, although it was more intense than I ever remembered. He touched the pad of his thumb against the corner of my mouth. "Tonight's yours, Sweet Samantha, so let's make it what you want. Yeah?"

A shiver trickled down my spine. "Yeah," I agreed through a whisper.

He stepped back and looked over my shoulder at the vendors behind me. "Why don't you save our spot and I'll grab us something to eat and drink?"

"I can do that."

"What would you like?"

"Um . . . aren't you supposed to drink beer at these things?" I asked.

Christopher scratched at the back of his head, chuckling. "Uh, I think you have about as much of an idea as I do. Can't say I've ever been to one before. But a beer sounds pretty damned good right about now."

"Beer it is, then."

"Don't move." He pointed at me. "I'll be back in a few minutes."

I settled down on the blanket, kicked off my shoes, and pulled my knees up to my chest. "I'm not going anywhere."

"That's my good girl."

A blush rushed to my face at the old sentiment Christopher used to wrap me in, the way he said it like praise, like a promise of what would be.

I couldn't tear my eyes away as he sauntered off toward the slew of vendors set up in the distance. Every few seconds he'd look back at me, this expression on his face that had me hugging my legs, holding myself close, wishing it was him holding me instead.

What had he done to me?

Another band struck up, and I relaxed back on my elbows as I listened to the strains of music that floated across the park. The air was perfect and the atmosphere was even better. I'd just thrown on some worn skinny jeans and a wide-necked sweater, and I felt totally comfortable under the emerging night.

How much time had passed, I didn't know, but it was as if I was drawn to glance over to the side, where I saw Christopher approaching, balancing two beers in his hands. Food was stacked up against one arm held close to his side.

I giggled under his towering shadow, grinning up at him. "It looks like you could use an extra hand. Why didn't you have me come help you?"

He handed off a beer to me, kneeling down on one knee so he could lay out the food he'd purchased on the blanket. "Because tonight I'm taking care of you."

Oh.

I grinned a little harder. I couldn't help it. I hadn't felt this happy in a long, long time.

Releasing a contented sigh, Christopher settled down beside

me on the blanket and casually drew a knee up to his chest. He looked out toward the stage and took a sip of his beer. I watched the bob of his throat as he swallowed, and all these little sparks lit inside of me.

He was so beautiful, his presence so powerful, so big and overwhelming.

Too much.

But somehow I wanted more.

He glanced at me. "This is kinda cool, yeah?"

"Completely. I've always wanted to go to one but never seemed to get around to making plans to do it."

Christopher unwrapped the mess of food he'd brought back for us, hamburgers and brats and tacos. We both dug in. Our laughter and voices were subdued as we talked, ate, and enjoyed the music. We immediately stumbled into this casual rapport. Everything between us felt completely natural. Instinctive.

Not light.

No.

There was a weight in every word we spoke, an importance neither of us could miss. But everything about it felt right. The band playing in the distance had wrapped us up in ease as the night fell deeper. All of it had somehow drawn us closer.

I finished eating and balled up my wrappers. Christopher gathered everything and went to dump it in a trash bin. I drew both my legs up to my chest, hugging them, and when he returned, he settled down even closer than before.

"So tell me about this new job," he said as he knocked his shoulder into mine.

Self-consciously, I shrugged. I tipped my chin up so I could look at him, his arm pressed along the length of mine. "They offered me a three-year contract and they've assigned me to the second-grade class. They said they think I'm the perfect fit for that age-group and they'd be honored to have me there."

I hesitated. "It felt good," I finally said quietly. I turned away and looked out toward the lit-up stage as I let the admission bleed free. "My whole life, I've always done what everyone else has wanted me to do. I just..." I peered up at him. "I wanted this. I just want to make a difference in these kids' lives. Even if it's small... that's what *I* want."

He reached out and placed his hand on the back of my neck. He brushed his thumb along my jaw. A coaxing caress. Warmth spiraled through me.

His voice came near my ear. "I'm so proud of you, Samantha," he whispered, speaking only to me. It was as if he had the power to inject the words right into my spirit. "So fucking proud. Those kids are going to be the luckiest damned kids in the world. They get to have *you* in their lives... get to have you teach them all the shit they have to learn. But the most important thing? They get to look up to you. They get to see firsthand what it means to be good and kind."

Christopher stared at me, those green eyes flitting all over my face. I got lost there. And I never wanted to look away.

Slowly, he shook his head. "Can't believe you're sitting out here with me."

My heart skipped, then sped, and I could feel the heat burning at my cheeks, the fire that had always belonged to Christopher setting up a soft glow that warmed my insides. I wet my lips, my words grating with honesty. "I can't believe it, either. Do you know how many times..." I trailed off, not sure I should say it aloud.

"So many that I'd thought I'd lose my mind," he supplied, as if he was filling me in on his own truth.

A truth that perfectly matched mine.

Heaviness strained between us, all this emotion and regret that I wasn't sure either of us knew how to handle.

Christopher cleared his throat and lifted his plastic cup between us. "But you're here now," he said, "and that's all that matters. And tonight is about you. So, my Sweet Samantha, let's toast you." He shifted closer and lowered his voice. "May you always find joy in this life. May you reach out and take whatever it has to offer. And may it offer you everything you deserve."

I touched my cup against his. My voice was small as I laid myself bare. "And may I do it without fear, but with faith."

I'd lived in fear for so long, a prisoner to all the what-ifs that held me back, letting myself fall into a safety net that had served only to snuff the life out of me.

There was no amusement on his face, only this brazen hope and something that looked like his own fear. "Amen," he murmured so quietly I could barely hear. A testament rumbled out into the descending night. Like this man could somehow understand my prayer.

Chills raked across the surface of my skin, and my body shivered.

"You cold?" he asked, his tone turning worried.

"A little."

But I wasn't. Not at all. I just needed to be closer to him.

"Come here." He set our drinks aside and took my hand, guiding me to crawl between his legs. He pulled my back against his chest. He wrapped me up in his strong arms and hooked his chin over my shoulder. I rested my head back next to his. "Better?" he asked at my ear, his nose running down my neck.

Goose bumps erupted across my flesh, and I gasped a short breath. Nestled in his arms was the best place I could ever wish to be. I was helpless to do anything but nod and sink further into his protective hold.

Music played on as the atmosphere progressively became subdued. A deep comfort rippled through the crowd, tranquility and peace and calm. A breeze rustled by, whipping through my hair.

Christopher nuzzled his nose deeper into my neck, running his thumbs in delicate circles on my belly over my shirt. That shock of unruly hair brushed along my cheek. I turned toward it, inhaling, clouding my senses with the intensity of this man, the inundating flood of sex and lust and everything I'd always believed I shouldn't have.

But I wanted it.

Wanted him.

His lips were at my shoulder, leaving a whisper of a kiss as he dragged them across my bare skin. One arm tightened across my stomach while his other hand slowly slid up my torso. I shuddered as he drew it up between my breasts and to the center of my chest. He held it there, and I could feel my heart beating a thousand emotions against his palm.

Christopher's mouth parted against my jaw.

I whimpered.

God, I just needed to see him, to make sense of what was happening. I twisted out of his hold to face him and sat back low on my knees.

His expression was fierce, his eyes frantic as they darted all over my face.

With a trembling hand, I reached out and ran my fingers through his hair.

Eyes dropping closed, he snatched me by the wrist and pressed the underside to his lips. He gentled a kiss across the sensitive skin. "Samantha," he mumbled, almost pained.

Chills skated free and fast. "What is this?" I forced out, the words shaky.

He grasped both sides of my face, bringing us nose to nose. "This is *unstoppable*."

Christopher threaded his fingers in my hair, and I could feel the tension wind through him, the coil of strained muscles that bunched and flexed as he held me an inch from his face.

"Samantha," he murmured again, before he leaned forward and captured my bottom lip between both of his. All that soft fullness closed over mine, the kiss a sweet assault of gentle tugs and pulls of his mouth that danced right through my soul. He kept the kiss slow but brimming with emotion, so full I wanted to weep.

It reminded me so much of that first tentative kiss, the one back in the park years ago that had swept me off my feet.

Succumbing, I uttered a tiny moan, my lips pushing back, brushing his, welcoming more.

Hungry hands cupped my neck, before he ran them over my shoulders and down to my waist. I rose higher on my knees, my hair falling down around us as I fell into his kiss.

Beneath the slow exploration, all those smoldering ashes lit. A furor of flames licked and jumped.

I never wanted it to end.

The kiss remained gentle, almost a contradiction to the intensity brewing between us.

Fingers dug into my sides when I pressed closer, needing to feel more of him, and his tongue slipped into my mouth, a controlled chaos that would be my complete undoing.

"Christopher," I breathed, and he burrowed his fingers deeper. There was no mistaking his blatant want. Every inch of this beautiful man was hard and straining and as desperate for me as I was for him.

He ripped himself away. "It's time to go."

I almost laughed at the madness of it all, this crazy boy who held me in his hand, the one who made me feel as if I could fly, the same boy I'd follow wherever he wanted me to go.

When had I forgotten?

He helped me to stand, then gathered the blanket in a ball. He tucked it under his arm and guided me away with the other. Our breaths were labored with intent as we wove behind the vendors and deeper into the night, traipsing through the grass to the parking lot where we'd left his truck. Christopher said nothing as he helped me in, then rushed around to his side to get in the driver's seat. He slammed his door shut.

A stark stillness took us over as the overhead lights dimmed and cast us in shadows.

Even then, I could feel the severity of his gaze. His voice was gravel. "If I take you back to my place, it means you're mine, Samantha. You understand what I'm telling you? Otherwise I'm taking you straight home."

Unable to form words, I nodded.

"Then tell me now, what's it gonna be? Because I refuse to share you with that asshole."

The decision scraped up my throat. "You. It's always been you."

It was never really a decision to make.

No matter what happened between me and Christopher, the relationship I had with Ben was a charade I could no longer keep up. Maybe it had everything to do with Christopher. I didn't know. But what I did know was Ben never had my heart. It'd always belonged to Christopher.

He started his truck, threw it in gear, and tore out of the lot. We said nothing as he drove the short distance back to his house. We just let all our unspent emotion build up between us.

He didn't even touch me.

But I knew I was his.

He pulled into his garage and cut the engine. Overhead, the chain ground against the metal wheel, and the large garage door slid shut behind us, making it feel like the two of us were the only ones that existed in this world.

I sat in frozen anticipation as he made his way around to my side.

Was this really happening?

I was shaking when he opened the door. He reached across me to release my seat belt. Stealing all the air. Filling me up with his own.

Grasping me by the hips, he pulled me into his arms. He hiked me up high on his body, my head above his. I wrapped my legs around him, my urgent hands clutching him at the back of his neck.

Oh God. I might lose my mind if I didn't get him closer. After all this time, after everything we'd missed, I didn't think I could ever get him close enough.

"Sweet Samantha," he uttered and those green eyes flashed with desire. He stared up at me and twisted his fingers through my mass of hair, bunching it in his hand, the other bracing me around his waist. "I was a fucking fool to let you go. Won't ever do it again."

Never breaking our gaze, he carried me into his house and toward his room.

I clung to his shoulders, knowing all those beliefs about forgiveness that my father had ingrained in me held all the power they promised. What happened in the past no longer mattered. I only needed to be assured of one thing. "Promise me something."

"Anything," he said as he carefully laid me out in the center of his bed.

I lay there staring up at the beautiful man towering over me. Desire coursed through me. A magnetic energy that coated my veins and pulsed through my nerves. Palpable. Real. My chest heaved with strained breaths, an open display of everything I wanted to give him.

"Promise you'll never lie to me," I pled through a pained whisper, and deep inside those old wounds flared.

It was Christopher who held the power to extinguish them.

Emotions moved through his expression, lines of remorse and devotion scoring his face.

Slowly, he climbed onto the bed. Never breaking his unyielding gaze, he nudged my knees apart to make him room. He planted his hands on either side of my head. Muted lights glowed from high up in the recessed niches outlining the far wall behind him, casting us in shadows.

He cupped one side of my face. His words were earnest and sincere. "I promise."

Acceptance swallowed me whole.

A soft smile curved my mouth, and I reached up and fluttered my fingertips along the side of his face. "I've missed you so much."

Christopher gathered my other hand and drew it up between us. In the darkness, those severe green eyes locked to mine, a silent fury stirring in their depths. "Not one fucking day went by that I didn't think about you. Miss you. And these last few months . . ." His tongue darted out to wet his lips, and he shook his head. "It was torture having you so close and knowing you weren't mine." He blinked a long blink. "I am still so in love with you, Samantha. Completely, crazy in love with you."

My heart stumbled at the same words he had uttered so long ago. It was a memory that had haunted my years. A promise of forever I'd thought would never come to pass.

"I love you with every part of me, Christopher. I never stopped."

How could I have?

A wistful smile edged his mouth, his brow drawn tight. "It was supposed to just be you and me."

I gentled my fingers across his bottom lip, giving myself over to that old sorrow that now was replaced with so much hope. "Just you and me and forever."

"Forever," he said. Something passed through his eyes, before he descended to capture my mouth in a kiss. Coaxing. A constant ebb and flow, a needy push and pull of his lips as they played fervently against mine. He lifted up on his hands. His shoulders tensed as he dipped down to nip at me with his teeth, before his tongue dove in to tangle with mine.

And I kissed him with everything I had. With everything we had lost. With everything I had left to give.

It was that same war of pent-up need, tongues and teeth and desperate hands.

One I no longer wanted to win.

This was surrender.

Christopher moved to lavish my neck with openmouthed kisses. I lifted my chin to grant him more. Chills skimmed across my skin and I whimpered.

Could anything feel better than this?

"Samantha," he murmured, trailing lower, across the exposed skin on my chest. "Baby, I need you so fucking bad. You have no idea."

He rocked against me, his erection pressed to my center, and all those pleasured places cried out for him, begging for relief.

I drove my fingers into his hair, and my back arched when he closed his mouth over my breast, which was covered by far too many layers of clothes. "Oh God, Christopher. Please," I begged. "I've never needed anything as much as I need you."

My voice almost sounded foreign to my ears, but at the same time it was so clear. I'd never been more certain of anything in my life.

Hot and desperate, his hands slipped beneath the hem of my sweater. I shivered under his touch. He tugged it over my head, and his mouth went right back to my neck as he pushed his hands under me to unclasp my bra.

He sat back on his knees and slowly drew the straps from my shoulders.

A rush of cool air bit at my flesh, and the buds of my breasts pebbled as I lay there exposed to this man, who stared down at me as if he'd just been handed the world.

And I felt no urge to cover myself the way I normally did. No force of that modesty and discomfort that had haunted me for the last seven years.

I wanted him to see me.

Because I belonged to him.

He exhaled a weighted breath and brushed his fingertips up my belly.

I jumped and squirmed, every nerve alive.

"You're gorgeous, Samantha." He flicked through the buttons on my jeans. He leaned back, his eyes hungry and hot as he slowly dragged them down my legs. He left me in nothing but my panties, and I felt like I'd burst into flames when he swept his gaze down my body. "So fucking gorgeous."

He looked back up at me, swallowing hard. "Do you have any idea? Any idea at all what you do to me?"

Redness blossomed across every inch of my skin, and my heart hammered an unsound beat, filling up all those places that had been empty for so long. Desire pulsed as a tortured throb between my legs, and my hips bucked in anticipation, spurred on by his stare.

Christopher pulled his shirt over his head and tossed it to the floor.

My attention went straight to the intricate colors that adorned the entirety of his chest. It swirled up over his collarbones and shoulders, spiraling down both arms, an expanse of delicate art imprinted on his skin. An intonation of hope and light.

All of it was mesmerizing, this dangerous man who'd marked himself with grace.

"You're beautiful," I said on no more than a whisper. I sat up and placed my hand over his thundering heart. "Somewhere inside, after everything, I always believed it. You're beautiful, Christopher. Inside and out."

He grabbed my face between his hands and shook his head. "No, Samantha. You just make me better. You can't see all my ugly when I'm surrounded by your light."

My gaze trailed down the defined planes of his stomach. I kissed his chest, and my shaky hands slipped down his sides to fumble through his belt. I struggled with his buttons, too anxious and nervous to get my fingers to cooperate.

A tender smile pulled at his mouth and he eased off the end of his bed.

Everything about this moment was Christopher. *My Christopher.* The boy I'd come to love and trust and know when I was just a girl.

Slowly, he worked through the rest of his buttons and rid himself of his remaining clothes, never taking his eyes off me as I watched him undress.

I only shook more when he nudged me onto my back and pulled off my panties.

Nerves hurtled through me, desire and need and a flicker of fear.

And I understood the risk, that my heart was again in his hands. Exactly where it'd always been. But this time it was more vulnerable than before, just as vulnerable as my naked body that quivered as he slowly climbed back over me.

He could break me so easily.

Because I was giving him everything.

My heart. My future. My trust.

Christopher kissed me, a passion-fueled kiss that left me light-headed and almost frantic for more. I panted, digging my fingers into his back while his hands explored. I jerked when he ran the back of his hand down between my thighs.

"You okay?" he asked, turning his hand to run just the tips of his fingers back up through my slick folds.

That fire raged.

"Yes." The word fluttered from my mouth. More than okay. "Perfect."

The faintest smirk pulled at his mouth, and he lifted up on just one hand. He focused on my face as he pushed two fingers inside. I gasped and he groaned. "Samantha . . . baby. Been dyin' to touch you this way."

Frenzied, my fingers scraped over his chest and shoulders.

He turned and kissed the inside of my elbow, the sweetest brush of flesh, and he whispered across the sensitive skin, "Love you . . . so fucking much."

He sought out that tiny pleasured place with his thumb. He circled it as he pumped his fingers. Little sounds whimpered from my mouth, an incoherent utterance of his name, and shamelessly I writhed, feeling as if I might die, as if I finally could live. "Please . . . make love to me."

Christopher stilled, searching my face, before he leaned over and grabbed a condom from his nightstand drawer. Sitting back, he ripped it open. I watched in awe as he rolled it down his length.

He was so big and beautiful, every inch of him, and I trembled beneath his brazen, hungry stare. Desire swelled between us, sparks of energy igniting in the air. But it was more than lust. Heavier. Denser. Fuller.

All consuming.

He lowered himself, his breath at my ear. "It was always supposed to be you." He fisted his hands in the sheets at the sides of my head, his body straining over me as his erection nudged at my center. My eyes went wide as he slowly spread me.

Fire and light.

Heaven and hell.

The most exquisite kind of torture.

And I couldn't see.

Could only feel.

Christopher filling me. Taking me whole.

"Fuck," he grunted. Then his words slipped into a strained whisper. "So good . . . so fucking good."

My lungs felt strangled as he scored deeper into my body, marking me in my darkest places. In places I had no idea existed. Places that had been created just for him.

Uncontainable, tears broke free as all the love I'd kept shored up inside spilled over. I squeezed my eyes shut, unable to process the magnitude of it.

It was stunning.

Staggering.

His voice was suddenly at my ear. "Shh . . . baby . . . don't cry." Christopher dragged his lips over the flood of emotion I couldn't hold back, kissing me all over my tearstained face. He

lifted my arm and draped it around his neck, and his hand
slipped under my back to bring me closer. He pulled back so he
could look at me. "No more tears. It's just you and me."

He withdrew slowly, and then rocked into me, hard and fast.

I released a gasp, and those intense green eyes watched
mine, pulling me deeper into them, and I lost myself a little
more. He drove into me again and again, lifting me higher, this
boy who'd always made me feel as if I could fly.

And they fluttered around my consciousness, frantic wings
of pleasure that twisted up my insides. My stomach tightened.
"Christopher." It was a plea from somewhere in my spirit.

His movements became jerky, and he shifted, striking me
deep. The base of his erection hit that sensitive spot and I knew
I couldn't take much more.

He clutched me tight, the action purposed and strong when
he did it again.

White-hot light burst behind my eyes. Blinding. As hot and
blinding as the tremors that shot through my body as the most
acute pleasure erupted in my core. A torrent of it rushed just
under the surface of my skin, taking me whole, my entire being
lifted to the highest high.

Ecstasy.

I floated on it for what felt like forever, while my walls
clenched around him, gripping him tight while Christopher
jerked and cursed. His body went rigid when he came.

Panting, I clung to him and buried my face in his heaving
chest as I tried to regain my failing senses.

But the only thing in this world that made sense was him.

It took him the longest moments to come back down. Tremors vibrated his stomach when he cautiously eased out of me and
fell onto the bed at my side. On a heavy exhale, he pulled the

condom off and tossed it in the trash, and he came right back for me, kissing the top of my head before he palmed it and ran his hand down the back, nestling me in the crook of his arm.

Little pleasured pulses still tingled through my body, and I pressed against him, reveling in the way his muscles ticked and jerked beneath my hands.

Contentment settled fast, the two of us saturated by bliss.

I traced along the colors on his chest. "I love you, Christopher," I whispered.

He grabbed my hand and pulled my fingertips to his lips. "Not letting you go. Not ever again."

"Never," I agreed.

He drew the covers over us and tucked me close in the middle of his enormous bed.

He brushed a soft kiss to my forehead. "Sleep, my sweet girl."

And I did, so easily drifting off into the sweetest kind of sleep.

Because nothing in this world could touch us.

TWENTY-FOUR

Christopher

Daylight blazed through the edges of the window blinds. Groaning, I rolled to my back and blinked away the sleep.

Samantha.

The thought of her slammed me hard.

Like a fucking vise, my chest tightened when I realized she wasn't lying at my side. Frantic, I shot up in bed. I heaved out a sigh of relief when I heard someone rattling around in the kitchen.

Shit.

I rubbed at the sore spot right over my suddenly frenzied heart. The girl had me wound so tight I couldn't breathe.

And if last night hadn't undone me, nothing would.

All right. So maybe I was *undone*. In the most fucking phenomenal of ways. Hadn't ever felt so good. Not in my whole life, because my *life* was finally here. Filling up all that dead space that she'd hollowed out when she'd gone.

I rolled out of bed and snagged my boxers from the floor. I pulled them on and ran a hand through the disaster on my head, all too eager to go in search of my girl.

Yeah.

My. Girl.

Still couldn't quite catch up to the fact that it was true.

Quietly, I slipped through the bedroom door. The air got all locked up in my throat when I found Samantha standing in my kitchen in front of the coffeepot. She was just pressing BREW.

Feeling a rush of satisfaction, I leaned my shoulder up against the wall, observing her from the side, and there wasn't a single thing I could do to look away.

She wasn't wearing anything but the T-shirt I'd been wearing last night, the fabric brushing her thighs. She was barefoot, and her blond hair was all mussed up from where my fingers had been buried in it all night. Rays of sunlight slanted in through the living room window.

My girl all lit up in a halo of light.

Like the woman she'd always wanted to be had finally worked its way out.

I swallowed hard, and she glanced over at me when she realized I was standing there. I watched the redness crawl to her face, and she chewed at that damned lip that I was already wanting to devour. She took a step back to face me, fidgeted with the hem of the shirt she was wearing, my shirt.

Lust curled my insides, right where it got all messed up with the love I had for her.

God, she was going to be the death of me.

"Good morning," she whispered, seeming unsure of what to say.

"Morning," I said, pushing from the wall. I took a step toward her, an irresistible need to be closer taking me over.

We fumbled through an awkward beat of silence, like neither of us knew exactly how to act after what we'd shared last night, those hours powerful and profound.

"Woke up and thought you left," I admitted finally, fucking hating the way it sounded grating up my throat. But hell, told her I wouldn't lie to her. Figured the shit she'd worked up inside me counted.

Her gaze dropped to the ground, before she tilted her head up and to the side, staring across at me like she was searching for an answer. "Where would I go?"

Relief gusted through me and took that second's unease with it.

Good answer, sweet girl.

A smirk twisted up the corner of my mouth. Couldn't do anything to stop it, either. I lifted my chin in her direction. "Nice shirt."

She reddened more but shocked the shit out of me and did this cute little curtsy thing, dipping her knees and holding the shirt out to the sides.

I just about fell to mine.

Fuuuck.

She was so sexy it hurt.

"You like it?" It was all flirt. Pure tease.

I rubbed my fingers over the smile forcing its way out. "A lot," I said, my eyes raking up and down, not even trying to hide it, because this girl needed to know exactly what she did to me. Finding her in my kitchen this way.

Best. Morning. Ever.

"You wearing anything under it?" And I tried to keep it a tease. But shit. Could anyone blame me for really wanting to know?

For a flash, those blue eyes widened in embarrassment.

Then she smiled another coy smile as she lifted the hem, just enough to let me peek at the edge of the black lace panties she'd been wearing last night.

And damn, if I didn't love the playful tone that just took over our mood, if I didn't love waking up to her in my house, if I didn't love every damned thing about this moment.

Fuck.

I just loved.

Simple as that.

Taking another step toward her, I cocked my head to the side. "Now, that is a complete and total shame."

"Oh, is it?" she challenged, blue eyes flashing with amusement. I stalked toward her. Because not touching her? That was no longer an option.

She backed up against the island. And the girl was fighting this huge-ass smile, teeth clamping down on that lip, trying to contain her laughter.

With a grin, I grabbed her by the back of the hips and lifted her. She squealed in surprise, throwing her arms around my neck.

"Christopher." She swatted at me, and I laughed.

"What?" I asked with all kinds of feigned innocence.

She wrapped all that soft, toned flesh around my waist and locked her ankles at my back.

Every inch of my body hardened.

"You're going to drop me."

"Not a chance."

I set her on the edge of the counter, and she pulled back to look at my face. It was her smile that got all tangled and snagged in my heart.

She looked so free.

Happy.

It made me happy, too.

I reached out and traced my fingertips along the rim of that mouth, the red candied bow that had been my torment for so many years. My voice dropped low. "You make me insane, Samantha."

Self-conscious laughter quietly rolled from her, and she shook her head. "That's a good thing . . . because I'm not feeling so sane myself." The words softened. "I still can't believe I'm here. It feels like some kind of a dream. One I'm terrified I'm going to wake up from."

I ran my hands up and down the outsides of her thighs, enjoying the feel of the creamy skin way too much. I leaned in close to her ear. "You're right where you're supposed to be."

Contentment bled through a throaty sigh, and a smile fluttered across her face.

I teased a kiss across her lips.

That mouth.

This girl.

So sweet.

A tiny moan slipped up her throat, and she threaded delicate fingers in my hair.

And she kissed me like I wanted to be kissed.

She kissed me like she was free.

On a growl, I dragged her closer and pressed her tight up against me. Need vibrated through my entire body, passing through to her, passing through to me. Every emotion one. Me and this girl the same.

Belonging on another level.

Because she'd always belonged to me.

My hands wandered her legs, all the way back to where her knees were locked tight to my hips, slipping back up to her waist. Samantha kept sighing as our tongues dipped and played.

God, it felt so good.

My fingers flitted around the hem of her shirt, before I bunched it enough to run the tip of my finger under the leg of that black lace.

A shiver rolled through her.

"Think we need to get rid of these." I gave them a little tug.

Samantha giggled, shy and seductive, and I felt that sound way down deep in my chest. "You do, huh?"

"Mm-hmm. I think we really, really do." I stepped back far enough to begin to peel them down her legs.

She shivered more.

"Gorgeous," I hissed. Every curve. Every inch.

I glanced up at Samantha's face. Eager blue eyes watched me with all that modesty. With all that goodness. But completely open, all the same. She helped me by twisting her feet out of her panties.

Desire fell like a storm, a billow of love and lust and devotion building strong.

Still, there was something about this moment that felt light.

Like all that weight I'd been carrying around for years had been lifted from my back.

It was so different from what we'd experienced last night. Last night we'd finally hit the edge. There'd been no more room for denying what we meant to each other. Resisting it was no longer possible.

Last night I'd given myself to Samantha in a way I'd never given myself to anyone else before. I'd fucking loved her. Cherished her. And all the vile numbness I'd drowned in for years had evaporated. Erased with her touch. For the first time in seven years I'd allowed myself to feel everything.

Every emotion. Every ounce of pain that lingered in her tentative touch. Every fragment of remorse.

Last night was a commitment. A promise.

But this morning? This was freedom. About the fact that we just got to belong.

I dropped the little scrap of lace to my kitchen floor, and as much as I liked my shirt on her, it had to go. I lifted it over her head, and her hair fell back down around her shoulders and over the swell of her breasts. Perfect tits peeked through the flowing strands, nipples puckered and hard. Samantha moved to rest back on her hands, and I grabbed her by the knees.

And there she was, all spread out on my kitchen counter.

Shit. I raked a hand over my face, about two seconds from coming unglued.

"You're the best damned thing I've ever seen."

A flush covered her heated body, her words thick. "You're the only one I ever wanted to see me this way."

She shifted forward and hooked her index fingers in the band of my underwear. She gazed up at me as she began to slowly work them down. "But I want to see you more."

My cock was fucking straining, and my entire body clenched when she groaned, looking down when she freed me. It was a needy sound that came from deep in her throat.

She pushed my underwear farther down my legs and I kicked them aside.

She was shaking when she reached out and trailed her fingertip around the defined ridge of my aching head, everything tentative and unsure when she slipped her hand around and gripped me soft, then squeezed me tight.

My stomach jerked and I rocked into her hand. "Baby . . . fuck . . . that feels good."

She looked up at me, her blue eyes all unsure and perfect as she began to stroke me. Without breaking her gaze, I riffled through the top drawer next to her to find the stash I kept there. I tossed it to the counter beside her.

With a little quirk of her brow, she frowned, fighting with the overt want seeping from her pores and all that sweetness she kept locked up inside. "You keep condoms in the kitchen?"

So maybe our worlds had traveled in different directions, far and fast, and I knew she'd never come close to understanding how dark mine had gone. The shit I'd done. Guess it was wrong I found some depraved satisfaction in it. Didn't ever want her to know how ugly my world had got.

Still, we'd ended up right back in the exact same place. Samantha shining all that light on me. Washing me in good. While I led her out to the shoreline. Coaxing her to dip her toes in a little of my world.

"What else is it good for?" I murmured. I dipped down to take one of those pert nipples in my mouth, rolling it with my tongue.

Yeah, that was sweet, too.

She groaned and arched, drove her fingers in my hair. Her voice was shaky. "Um . . . I don't know. Cooking. Eating."

"That could be arranged," I murmured as I traveled along her belly, kissing her, making her jump and squirm as she jerked and pulled at my hair. Grabbing her by both knees, I spread her wide.

I just needed to taste.

I swept my tongue through the bare, heated flesh. She was so fucking wet and tasted so fucking good. Better than I even remembered, that one memory I'd been desperate to ingrain in my mind not coming close to doing this girl justice. I sucked on one lip, probably too hard. I knew I'd mark her, and a sick, twisted part of me wanted it all the same. I turned to the other and repeated the action.

Samantha gasped and writhed. "Christopher . . . wha . . ."

She fell silent when I changed course, focusing all my attention on her clit, and any objections turned into all these mewls and moans, little *yeses* and a multitude of pleas.

I kissed her senseless, lapping then sucking that little bud, nipping at it with my teeth, sucking some more.

"Christopher." She fisted my hair, and I pressed two fingers inside her warmth, added another as I pumped them in and out of her body.

Her entire being shuddered as she came against my mouth. I lifted up, slowing my fingers as I watched her ride out her orgasm.

It was single-handedly the sexiest thing I'd ever seen.

She was still panting and trying to catch her breath when I tore open the condom. I kept watching her as I began to roll it on my cock that was raging, this violent need to get lost inside her almost overwhelming.

"I love you, Samantha," I said, and all that light from earlier no longer seemed to apply, because I was feeling frantic. My hands shook when I palmed her thighs, digging in to drag her closer to the edge.

I positioned myself at her center. "Already dying to be inside you again," I mumbled, trying to get a handle on the way she made me feel.

Sucking in a breath, I slipped my throbbing head an inch into that needy warmth. I floundered around inside myself, looking for some restraint, not able to fathom how one girl could control me this way.

I pushed a little deeper, and her tight, tight walls gripped my cock. I drew a sharp shot of air into my lungs.

Blunt fingernails dug into my shoulders, scratching, digging. Samantha seemed to be fumbling for the same. "Oh my God . . . Christopher . . . that feels so good."

"Supposed to feel good, baby." It was a ragged grunt, my body fucking shaking as I filled her whole.

She was still clutching me. "Let's just say I finally get what all the fuss is about."

My gut clenched, and I bit back the urge to fuck her wild, not for a second able to tolerate the idea of this girl being in someone else's hands. Instead I pulled all the way out and eased back in to the hilt.

"Christopher . . . please."

I pulled out, rocked into her again. "Yeah?" I asked, almost taunting, needing more.

"Yeah . . . yes . . . you." It was a jumble of words, all of them for me, this girl mine.

My hips rocked out and this time I slammed back into her.

The force pushed her back toward the counter, and she cried out, then she met me, pushing back. Our bodies colliding. Heaving. This surging mess of limbs and bodies.

She was panting, struggling.

Struggling just as much as me.

Her gaze latched onto mine, that storm of emotions that sucked me right under.

Pulling me deep.

Deeper.

Until I was sure I would drown.

I'd thought this would be playful. But I should've known better. Should've known the way this girl affected me.

We were nothing but liquid steel, melding, blending, one, when Samantha cried out again. She shattered all around me, her trembling body held firm in my arms. She dragged me right with her. The back of my thighs tightened. Pleasure ripped through every one of my nerves.

I shouted her name as I came. All this bliss pouring free.

I gasped for air, drawing it into my vacant lungs. Samantha had her face buried in my chest, doing the same, her fingers still planted deep in my shoulders.

My fingers rushed through her hair, and I kissed her temple, my exhale heavy and relieved as I whispered at her skin, "Samantha . . . my sweet, good girl."

She giggled a little, though it was all breathy, and she pulled back to look at my face. She scratched her fingertips along my stubble. "I don't think I qualify anymore."

Soft, incredulous laughter floated from me, and my words got all serious when I cupped the side of her face. "You being a good girl has never been about sex, Samantha. It's always been about who you are. What I've always loved most about you."

Her expression shifted and she nodded, and she pushed up to press a lingering kiss to my mouth.

Yeah, I could get used to this.

My thumb grazed her cheek. "So what do you want to do today?"

Pretty sure I wasn't ever going to let her out of my sight again.

Gentle fingertips trailed down my neck, tracing across my chest. Unsure eyes peeked up at me. "I'm going to go and visit Stewart like I do every Sunday. Then I'm going to go back to my place—"

It was uncontrollable.

The rage that built up, bursting at my ribs, bristling across my skin.

Squeezing my eyes shut, I clutched her sides, refusing to let go.

She touched my cheek. "Hey . . . look at me."

Reluctantly, I met her gaze.

"I'm going back to my house so I can end things with Ben. He'll be home this afternoon and I'm going to lay it all out. After that? It depends on you, Christopher. I'm leaving him one way or another. What I told you last night? I meant it. It's always been you."

I released an apologetic breath, guilt shaking my head. "I'm sorry, baby. I just . . . Fuck," I swore, driving a hand through my hair, trying to keep all these turbulent emotions in check. "Thinking about you and him makes me fucking crazy. I can't even stand the idea of you being around him. Not ever again."

Understanding softened her expression, but there was something resolute in it, too. She brushed her fingers through the flop of hair on my forehead, meeting my eye. "I was with him for seven years, Christopher, and he helped me through the worst time in my life."

Remorse fisted my heart, and I struggled to get her closer. God, I'd give up anything to take it back, that night on her floor, that mistake that had haunted me for seven fucking years. To take back all the pain I'd caused her. To stop the progression of shit it'd left in its wake.

I didn't even know how to be angry with Samantha for cutting me loose anymore. It still hurt, but I knew I'd been the catalyst. The one who'd set everything in motion.

"At least I owe him an explanation. An apology. All these months . . ." Pained, she swallowed and dropped her gaze to the floor, before she looked back at me. "No matter how much I tried to deny it at the time, somewhere inside me, I wanted it to lead to this. Every time I saw you, Christopher, I *ached*, and every time you left I missed you a little more. All of that only confirmed how much I still loved you . . . how much I wanted you. I mean, God, I packed a bag last night hoping I'd be waking up here *after* I sent a text to my boyfriend, telling him I'd be at home reading a book. What kind of person does that?" Her expression was pleading. "No matter what you think of him, I am still the one who betrayed him. And I never wanted to be responsible for something like that because I know how much betrayal hurts."

I started to protest, but she pressed her fingers against my mouth. "But I don't regret it. I don't regret us. I refuse to. But that doesn't mean I'm not guilty or that I didn't go about it all wrong. Because of it, I have to hurt him."

Resigned, I nodded against her touch. "I get it. I do. Doesn't mean I have to like it. You belong here. With me."

She lightened her voice, eyes shining. "Does that mean you want me to come back here after?"

"Haven't I already made that perfectly clear?" I rubbed up against her. "The only place I want you is right here . . . in my bed."

"That sounds tempting." It was all tease, just as teasing as her fingers that started fluttering down my abs.

"Not tempting. Mandatory."

She smiled a soft smile, and then she cringed and chewed at her lip. "I think maybe we should take some time to talk tonight?" Almost pleading, she tilted her head. "About what happened to us? You hurt me, Christopher, and I have to get it all out before we can really move on."

Fuck, I wanted to bury it all. To forget it. But I knew she was right. And the truth was, she'd hurt me, too. "Yeah, that's probably a good idea, but I promise you right now, Samantha, I'm not ever gonna hurt you again."

"I know," she whispered, her palms flat on my sides, high up on my ribs. I could feel the force of my heart beating against them.

I kissed the top of her head, bringing her back to hug her, changing the subject. "You excited to see Stewart?"

I felt her smile against my skin. "I can't wait. Even though it's hard every time I see him. But he needs me, you know?"

"Of course I know." I pulled back and tucked a lock of her knotted-up hair behind her ear. "I'd like to see him sometime. You think he'd be okay with that?"

This smile lit her face, the kind that punched me right in the center of my chest, the one that shouted out I was home.

"I think he'd love that," she said. Then a shadow blew in. "But you're going to have to give me a little time . . . let this settle in with my family."

Resentment flared. Part of me hated Samantha's parents. Hated what they'd done. They'd been guilty, too. "They're not gonna be so thrilled about us, are they?"

Dropping her gaze, she shook her head. "I don't know. Probably not. But it doesn't matter." She gathered my hand between both of hers, kissed across my knuckles while she clutched it. "What matters is what we want."

Samantha squeaked when I swept her off the counter, one arm under her back and the other under her knees, bride-style. *Yeah.*

I carried her toward my bedroom. "And the only thing I want is you."

TWENTY-FIVE

Samantha

At five minutes past noon, I pulled up to the curb in front of my parents' quiet house and cut the engine. I sat in silence, trying to gather my wits, which I was pretty sure I'd lost somewhere around six o'clock last night. Right where I'd left them at Christopher's feet.

No doubt, I'd been grinning like a fool the entire drive over, all this happiness bubbling up and over.

I flipped down the sunshade to peek at myself in the mirror. Bright, wide eyes stared back at me, brimming with excitement and an overwhelming joy there was no chance of bottling up, my cheeks rosy and flushed. I rummaged through my purse in the passenger seat and pulled out my shiny clear gloss and lathered it across my lips that were all puffy and swollen and just about as sore as I was between my thighs.

God, how obvious was I? I was pretty sure the second I

walked through the door my mom would see straight through the casual facade I was trying to front.

Right to the expression hidden underneath.

You know the one.

The one that screamed, *Your daughter's just been thoroughly sexed up by the baddest boy you never wanted to meet. And oh, by the way, she's madly in love with him, too. And yep, you guessed it, she's just about to throw away that seven-year relationship you were all too keen to tie her to.*

Yeah, that one.

Thank God it'd be just her and Stewart. Dad would still be over at the church, chatting and mingling with his congregation after Sunday services.

Truth was, I really didn't want to have to hide it. I wanted to shout it. But I wasn't about to let any of them in on this until I'd ended things with Ben. Not until I could bring Christopher here, stand at his side, and proclaim it all.

Would they be angry and disappointed?

Definitely.

Would they try to talk me out of my ignorance?

No doubt.

But it made no difference at all.

Because this time, I wasn't letting Christopher go.

Shaking my head, I forced myself out of my car and into the warmth of the balmy day. I headed up the sidewalk, truly anxious to see Stewart. I warred with the sadness that engulfed me when the picture of his face hit my mind. He'd progressively gotten sicker. Weaker. Thinner.

I hated it, but I pinned a smile on my face, unwilling to put any sort of damper on our visit.

With a quick tap on the wooden door, I twisted the knob and

stepped inside. "Mom?" I called. I eased into the silent house, walking through the foyer and stepping into the family room.

"Congratulations!"

I stumbled back in shock when a chorus of cheers rang against the walls. Stunned, I stood at the edge of the room, my mouth gaping as I took in all the faces smiling back at me. My mom and dad, and Sean and Stephanie were there, too. Stewart was on the couch, surrounded by a mound of pillows, tucked under a blanket.

My gaze glided back around the room to take in the balloons and streamers, the place decked out for a celebration. It trailed over to my aunt and uncle, who had my younger cousins in tow.

"What is this?" I asked, my chest feeling all light and fluttery, and my mom stepped forward.

"Oh, sweetheart, today we're celebrating you," she said.

Gratitude filled me to the brim, pressing full at my ribs, and tears welled in my eyes. I hadn't wanted to admit it, but it'd hurt when I'd received little recognition when I told my parents about the job. I'd felt it a brush-off, a dismissal of something that had been so important to me.

Still, with everything they were dealing with, I completely understood.

But this?

This was so much more than I expected.

"Sam." The deep voice assaulted me from off to the right, behind me, just out of view. Chills skated across the nape of my neck, lifting the delicate hairs. My stomach lurched when Ben approached from where he'd been hidden in the back corner. His mother and father stood behind him. Profuse, exuberant smiles on their faces.

Ben was so sure as he rounded me, as he dropped to his knee and pulled a black velvet box from his pocket.

Oh God.

Realization sunk like a rock into my consciousness.

No.

I couldn't deal with this.

Not today.

Not ever.

I could feel my head shaking, my entire body vibrating with the sentiment.

No. No. No.

This could not be happening.

My body leaned away, repelling the situation, desperate for a way to be saved from this humiliation.

But I was stuck, a soundless scream locked somewhere in my throat as Ben took my hand, our enthusiastic, expectant audience urging him on. Breaths bated, hands clasped at their chins, as they awaited the most romantic of gestures.

There was nothing romantic about this.

This was coercion.

Brown eyes flashed up to mine and he clutched my trembling hand, and he and I both knew it. I saw possession flare in his eyes, the zealous violence in the clench of his jaw.

Subtly, I tried to pull my hand away, silently begging him not to do this. Almost painfully, he squeezed my wrist.

And I stood there feeling like the most foolish little girl. Like the pitiful pool of despair that he'd found on that bathroom floor years ago because I had no idea how to make my mouth work as he slid the huge ring on my finger.

He didn't ask me.

And I never said yes.

Because I wouldn't.

And I was sure there was some part of him that knew it.

Part of him that *knew everything* even though he had no idea at all.

"There," he said, his mouth screwing up into a smug smile, his voice dropping low enough that only I could hear him. "All mine."

Hot, angry tears broke free. Tears my family misinterpreted as happiness. They broke out in applause.

I couldn't believe he was doing this, right here, in front of our families, but another piece of me wasn't surprised at all. I wanted to scream, *No! Never!*

But that guilt flared. What I'd been doing was wrong. Immoral. And despite where my heart lay, Ben had been my rock for a lot of years. There when no one else had been. It would be cruel to humiliate him in front of our families, and I needed to give him the time he deserved and end this the right way, if there ever could be a *right* way to end things.

But one thing I knew was I needed to do it without an audience. Without the disappointment and questions such a scene would be sure to inspire.

As excruciating as faking my way through this afternoon was going to be.

My mother rushed forward and pulled me into her arms, her words low at my ear. "Oh, sweetheart, I am so happy for you." She met my eyes, respect reflected in hers. "I'm so proud of the woman you've become." She turned and reached down, softly cupping Ben's cheek. "Thank you for allowing us to be a part of this moment."

She looked back at me, admiration steeped in her tone. "When Ben called me late Wednesday night and asked for my help putting this together, I was ecstatic. We even got your sister out here from California in time."

I wanted to puke.

Wednesday.

After our dinner.

Numbly, I stood there while our families filed forward. People who only loved me and cared and had no clue of the real nature of the man who pushed up from his knee to stand at my side, a self-righteous expression embedded deep on his face.

God, I really was a fool.

The only one who didn't come up to offer congratulations was Stewart. He remained on the couch, watching us, disappointment and disgust spread out over his pale, pale face.

I spent the rest of the day pretending.

Now I was sitting through the most torturous meal I had ever experienced, one that seemed to go on forever, one I was sure both my mother and Ben's had slaved over for hours, hoping to provide us with a perfect yet simple engagement party. Everyone tried to involve me in wedding plans, talk of dates and budgets and cake.

The bile wouldn't recede from my throat.

The entire time, Ben held my hand shackled in his on the top of the table, as if he'd won a prize.

While I had the most unladylike urge to spit in his face.

He'd orchestrated this just like he'd maneuvered me into the house he'd rented. Bending me to his will. Breaking the broken little girl just a little more. Molding me into who he wanted me to be.

But I no longer fit.

Could no longer conform.

Over my shoulder, I watched the movement from the couch. Stewart climbed to his unsteady feet, braced himself on the arm of the couch. "Hey, Ma, I'm going to go lie down on my bed. I'm not feeling so great."

Heavy emotion washed over her, but she forced a smile. "Sure, sweetheart. I'll come check on you in a bit."

He shot me a meaningful glance before he shuffled down the hall.

Pushing back my chair to stand, I finally reclaimed my hand from Ben's overbearing grasp. "I'm going to go spend a little time with him." Apologetically, I let my gaze bounce around the faces at the table. "Sunday afternoons are usually ours. I want to make sure I get to spend some time with him. Thank you all so much for coming today."

Nods from everyone, a scowl from Ben, confusion from my mom.

I rubbed at my forehead as I turned away.

God, Ben just had to pick today. He had to go and make it a hundred times worse. Make me break another oath that I'd not even given. Make the explanations even harder than they would have been.

I tapped at Stewart's door in the same second I pushed it open, casting him a soft smile as he pulled his covers up to his chin.

"Hey," I said.

A half smile flitted around his mouth, stark blue eyes bugging out at me. "Well, if it isn't the soon-to-be Mrs. Ben Carrington."

I cringed and crossed his room to brush a kiss to his forehead.

When I pulled back an inch, those blue eyes rolled and he smiled a playful smile. "You look thrilled, by the way. Just your typical, ecstatic blushing bride."

That was the thing with my little brother. It was he who could see right through me. He who knew me best. Facing away, I sat down on the edge of his bed. "That obvious, huh?"

"Uh . . . yeah. Horror was written all over your face. So why don't you go ahead and clue me in to who has your panties all wet, because I know it's not Ben."

Mouth gaping, I jerked my attention over my shoulder. "What is wrong with you, Stewart? You're so gross," I hissed, feeling all that redness I'd worn the last twenty-four hours flood right back to my face.

And how the heck did he know?

Chuckling, he shrugged innocently. "What? If I die without having sex, at least I get to make fun of you about it."

"Don't say that." God, he was always so morbid.

"Hey, you always say you want me to be completely honest with you. Think it's about time you were honest with yourself."

His words were pointed, like a double-edged sword driven straight into my heart, all the truths I needed to accept in my life, ones I wanted to welcome and those I wanted to reject.

Words muted to a whisper, Stewart leaned forward. "Now, tell me about this guy who has my sister all spun up. I want to know who had your eyes smiling before that asshole out there stepped in and stole it all away."

In shock, I stared back at this gentle boy, who held more insight than he should.

My phone took that opportune time to buzz. I had it clutched in my hand, and I discreetly glanced down to catch the message that lit up the screen. Christopher's name flashed across the top.

My heart did that erratic thing again, but this time I recognized it. An extra beat that accelerated toward perfection. A blip of a moment that spanned farther and farther, stretching to reach that place where I ultimately belonged.

"Who is it?" Stewart asked, trying to peek.

"No one."

The one.

I could feel the mischief ooze from my little brother, and he shoved his hand out, eyes teasing as he watched my expression. "Give it to me."

"No."

He grabbed it and tried to yank it from my hand.

"What in the world is wrong with you, Stewart? I told you it was nothing."

It was everything.

But would Stewart understand if he knew?

He didn't back down. "You wouldn't wrestle a cancer patient, would you?"

"Today I just might," I shot back, everything between us both light and heavy.

His expression shifted from playful to serious, sympathy and understanding filling up the well of his vivid blue eyes. "Please, Samantha. Let me see."

Hesitantly, I lessened my hold, nodding, giving it up, knowing Stewart was asking me to trust him. I gulped around the knot in my throat as he slid his finger across the plate. Stunned silence took him whole as he remained fixated on the message for the longest time.

Finally he looked up to find my anxious, unsure gaze. Stewart blinked through a million questions. "Christopher?" he finally asked, quiet and cautious, looking back down at the text Christopher had sent.

How is Stewart today? God, wish I could be there. This is torture, missing you. Feels like this is the longest day of my life.

I nodded again, this time fighting tears. "Yes."

It'd always been Christopher.

A soft smile edged his mouth. "You know the greatest wish in my life?"

The tears I was fighting won. They broke free and streaked down my face.

Stewart continued. "That you'd find happiness in yours."

He reached out and touched the side of my face, and I had the intense urge to hug him, to beg him to promise me he'd never leave me, to demand that he find the same for his own.

So I did.

He held me tight while I mumbled my pleas all over him, and I could feel his tears wetting my temple, mingling in my hair. His voice was rough and low. "Love you so much, Samantha. More than I think you could ever know. Thank you for always putting me first, for loving me and sacrificing for me. Now it's time for you to do that for yourself. Don't settle. Not now. Not ever."

"You're my happy place," I whispered, my hands in fists where they were twisted in his shirt.

His voice was still raw, but he chuckled, his response woven with suggestion. "Oh, I think I have a pretty good idea about your *happy place*."

"Ew." I smacked him lightly.

He laughed more, hugged me as tight as he could, even though he felt weak and feeble below me.

"Love you, Stew."

"Love you more."

"Not even possible," I said.

The door swung open. "What's going on in here?"

All that anxiety came barreling back, and I straightened myself to look back at Ben standing in the doorway.

"Oh, you know, just bonding with the big sis," Stewart said and he lifted a sarcastic brow. "Giving her all the congrats in the world for finding the love of her life."

I bit back laughter, but a short shot of it escaped and I clapped my hand over my mouth.

Stewart cast me a knowing smirk, while Ben just frowned.

Then he set his focus on me. "It's getting late. We should get out of here. Head home."

Yeah. It was time. As loath as I was to do it. But somehow I didn't feel quite as guilty as I had this morning.

"Sure. Give me a second."

He lifted his chin and shut the door.

I stood and leaned over Stewart, a good-bye kiss to his forehead, squeezed his hand. "Get better, Stewart. I need you well."

He cast me a somber smile. "Good-bye, Samantha."

I left his room and went around and told our families good-bye, giving thanks that I would just have to turn around and throw in their faces. I promised Stephanie we'd spend the rest of the day together tomorrow after I got off work before she had to return to California, and left my mother with an apologetic glance that she couldn't yet understand.

Then I got in my car and followed Ben home.

Ben pulled into the garage. He didn't spare me a glance when he climbed from his car. He just left the garage door open and went inside.

I parked my SUV behind him on the driveway. I wouldn't be staying, so there was no point in pulling into my spot.

In an attempt to gather my courage, I sat in the car, battling with the guilt that churned in my stomach. Resentment and bitterness only agitated it. All of it was mixed up with the joy that Christopher's touch had brought back into my life.

It was difficult to put my finger on any one emotion, this distorted loyalty at odds with what every part of me wanted to claim as my own.

I hated hurting Ben. But it was clear I'd come to the crossroads. So yeah, maybe I'd already taken a sharp right-hand turn, and there was no doubt I should have handled things differently.

Even then, I was one hundred percent certain that no matter if Christopher had come back to me or not, I still would be in this exact same spot getting ready to do the exact same thing.

It was time to put an end to what never had been there in the first place.

Night had fallen, the sky dark and quiet when I climbed from my car and headed inside. At the edge of the front room, I came to a stop when I found Ben standing in the middle of it, facing away while he held on to the back of his neck with both hands.

I knew he knew I was there, no words spoken, but somehow the silence said it all. Hostility ate up all the air in the room, leaving us flailing in this limbo that pushed against my resolve.

"Ben," I chanced, taking a step forward, his name sliding off my tongue like an apology.

He whipped his head around, brown eyes hardened with anger. "Are you trying to make me out to be a fool?"

Caught off guard, I stumbled back. "I . . ."

What could I say?

"I'm sorry." It held a finality Ben clearly didn't want to hear.

He spun all the way around, his head cocked to the side as he slowly approached.

My heart rate ratcheted up by a hundred knots when he released a maniacal laugh. "You're sorry? That's it? *You're sorry?*" He laughed again, this time incredulous. "All these years, I've protected you. Taken care of you. And this is the thanks I get? You making me look like an idiot in front of our families? You think they couldn't tell you were acting like an ungrateful bitch?"

Anger ate up my insides, and I flung my hand in his direction. The cut of the diamond glinted off the lights. "Is that what you think this is? Protecting me?" Fisting my hand at my side, I shook my head. "This isn't love or protection, Ben. This is you trying to force me into what you want. Did you forget our dinner last week? I told you I wasn't ready." I blinked across at him, hoping he'd understand I'd never be ready, and I lowered my voice. "I don't want this. I'm sorry, but I don't want this."

But my softened tone did nothing to calm him.

"You mean you don't want me." He scoffed, his hands propped on his hips as he swore toward the floor. Then he redirected his disgust back to me. "What is it you think you want to move on to, Samantha? Someone who doesn't give a shit about you? Are you so ignorant that you don't see what else is out there waiting for you?"

I squeezed my eyes shut against the assault.

Wow. So I knew he could be a jerk. This might have been the first time I realized he was a straight-up asshole.

He didn't stop or hesitate, just spat more of his contempt at me. He sneered. "Ever since you ran into that Moore bitch, you've been acting crazy. Did you let her fill your head with lies? With stupid, foolish ideas?" He inched closer, tilting his head with each step. "Did you see him? Is that what this is about?"

He stood up taller, intimidating, with the intention of making me feel small. "All these years, I've protected you. Do you know what from? From assholes like him. You want to know what the real world is like, Samantha? You want to know what guys like Christopher Moore do when you're not watching?"

Ben almost smiled. "He wasn't just sleeping with Jasmine behind your back. I could never bring myself to tell you before, but I think it's time you knew. Every party, Samantha . . . every party and he was fucking someone else. Long before your parents even found out about the two of you, back when you had some little girl's fantasy that you'd found your soul mate. He had you so unsuspecting you never even picked up on what was right under your nose."

A flood of insecurities came pouring in, and I shook my head. "No."

"Yes." He took another step forward, backing me into the wall. "You belong here. With me. Don't think for a second you'll ever find anyone better, because you won't. No one could care about you the way I do. No one will love you like me. Definitely not someone like Christopher Moore."

Confusion billowed through me, and I was shaking, unwilling to accept his words, but unable to erase them all the same. They blistered beneath my skin, a sickness that ambushed my heart and mind. I forced them aside.

"No," I said again, but it was an anguished whisper. And I hated Ben, hated his words, hated his voice. I didn't want to hear. I just wanted to escape.

The ring on my finger felt like it weighed a million pounds. So incredibly wrong. I was a rattled mess when I grappled for it, fumbling as I tried to work it over my knuckle. The gold band was too tight. A strangling noose I had to rid myself of before it snuffed out my last bit of hope.

I refused to honor Ben with the truthful explanation I had planned to give, couldn't even look at him as I shoved the ring I had clenched in my hand against his chest. "I don't want this," I said again. The last word cracked.

He squeezed my hand in a crushing grip, the diamond cutting painfully into my palm. "Doesn't matter if you take that ring off, Samantha, you know you belong to me. Pull yourself together and get over this childishness. You're just embarrassing yourself."

My breath left me on an exhale filled with all my disbelief. Arrogant prick.

I jerked my hand from his grasp and opened it out between us. The ring dropped to the floor. "That's where you're wrong. I never belonged to you."

I held my tears until I made it to my car. I didn't mean to cry, didn't want to, but I couldn't hold them back. I drove to Christopher's house, clutching the steering wheel the entire time, trying to see through all the bleary anger and hurt Ben had spewed my way. A flicker of that old, nagging distrust was trying to reassert itself, the one that was born the night I'd found Christopher with Jasmine. I didn't want those fears to rule me, but they wouldn't be silenced quite so easily.

I just needed to see Christopher and everything would be okay.

I skidded to a stop at the curb, yanked at my keys in the same second I threw it in park. I ran up the sidewalk. I just needed to see him. Feel him. Be reassured that all of that was in the past.

Because I already knew. I already had the burden of carrying the most vile of memories. Christopher fucking the one girl whose life's goal had been making mine a living hell. Closing my eyes to see the image that had been forever ingrained in my mind was torture. But I'd forgiven him. Accepted the past for what it was, anticipated the future for all I expected it to hold.

Believed in Christopher for who he was today.

Impatience had me hammering on his front door, and it flew open with all the intensity I'd pounded into it. Relief gushed from me when I saw him standing there, and it only made the tears pour faster down my face.

That was all quickly replaced by Christopher's panic. "Samantha . . . baby . . . what's wrong?" He grabbed me by the outside of my shoulders, dragging me in the door. He kicked it shut, his hands running all over me as if he were searching to find out if I was hurt. "What did he do . . . what the fuck did that asshole do? I swear to God, I will kill him, Samantha. What did he do?"

"He . . . he was at my mom's. H-h-he had a ring." I could barely speak, the words tumbling out in a mess of embarrassment and shame. "He didn't even ask . . . *he didn't even ask.* Everyone was there, Christopher."

"What?" Christopher's hold tightened. "He didn't even ask you what?"

"To marry him. In front of everyone he got on his knee and put it on my finger."

His attention flashed to my finger, barren of the evidence of Ben's coercion. Frantic, Christopher pushed me up against the wall, half-crazed, half-demanding. "I won't let him have you, Samantha. He can't have you. You're mine. You've always been."

By the waist, he lifted me, pinning me to the wall with the hard planes of his body. I could do nothing but wrap my legs around his hips. He rocked against me, the friction of his jeans igniting that fire, the threat of Ben fueling those flames. He buried his face in my neck as if he didn't want to see, his bite aggressive as he turned to nip at my jaw, at my chin, moving to my lips. "Told you I wouldn't let you go. Not ever again."

His frenzied voice ached with regret.

"Never," I told him, grinding myself on his erection that was pressed tight between my thighs. I felt desperate to erase the distance Ben had tried to wedge between us.

Christopher seemed even more fractured over it, unable to fathom the idea of what Ben had tried to force on me.

"I just got you back and he's trying to take you away."

"I'm here . . . I'm here."

"Here," he said as if a demand, tearing at my clothes, overwrought as he rushed to palm every inch of exposed skin. My shoulders were pressed to the wall, my chest heaving with harsh breaths. He pushed up my shirt and dragged off the cups of my bra. My breasts felt heavy and full as he looked on them with a stuttered groan. He splayed his hands across my back, dragging me forward, and his hot mouth was there, drawing my nipple into its warmth, sucking hard before he turned to the other.

I bucked, my hands fists in his hair.

He wrapped an arm low around my waist, his body leaving mine for a fraction of a second, and without setting me down, he dragged my shorts and panties from my legs. Fumbling, he pushed his jeans and underwear down around his thighs.

Without warning, he thrust into me.

I cried out from the perfect invasion.

No condom.

No heed.

Christopher took me completely.

Recklessly.

I clutched his shoulders while he drove into me, every pitch and roll of his hips possessive and demanding. My back slammed into the wall with every relentless, earth-shattering drag of his body.

And I knew he was fucking me like he'd promised all those months ago. Marking me. Ensuring I would never *forget*.

Emotions strangled me, my love endless and overflowing. Without question. At the same time, some piece of Christopher's love seemed just out of my reach, doubt Ben had spurred infiltrating the space that had seemed so solid when I walked out the door this morning.

Jumbled words left me as Christopher pounded harder and faster. Declarations of love and need and an inkling of the fear that Ben's words held an ounce of truth that had chased me back here to his doorstep.

My fingers dug deeper into the muscles that bowed and flexed on his shoulders as he devoured me. Taking me whole.

I refused to let go.

Christopher gripped my hips, and his hands slipped around to my bottom. He spread me wide, burying himself so deep I was blinded. No longer could I discern what was light or dark. What was inside or out. What was right or wrong.

Because he was everywhere.

I was fractured by the orgasm that tore through me, a cutting bliss that sliced open every last insecurity that had been bred in me, every doubt and uncertainty I'd ever harbored ripping free.

Christopher jerked and cried out, his body going rigid as he pulsed inside me. Every barrier down. Every wall destroyed.

He gasped for air, clutching my sides. He pressed his mouth against mine, the words ragged. "I love you. I love you so fucking much." His forehead dropped to mine. "So fucking much." The last sounded like an apology.

And I was stripped bare, overwhelmed and exposed in all my vulnerability. It all overflowed, the emotion that had sent tears streaking down my face gathering as a knot in the center of my chest. A sob raked up my throat.

"Did you want her more than me?" It killed me to ask, but I had to know. "All the time you were with me, did you want her?"

Christopher stilled and pulled his head back an inch. Confusion clouded his expression. "Who?"

"Jasmine." God, it hurt just to say her name. And I knew how much more it was going to hurt to hear him say it. But we had to get it out in the open. Confront that past, or, just like I'd told him that morning, I could never fully move on.

Her name seemed to jar him, striking him like a physical

blow. He jerked back, his hands moving to the outsides of my thighs. "No. *Never*," he swore. "Damn it, Samantha, I'd *never* touch that bitch. Not ever."

But his voice cracked, and the admission of deceit passed so vividly across his face. Those green eyes flashed with some kind of morbid dishonesty, something terrible hidden there that he didn't want me to see.

My eyes slammed closed to shield myself from it, and the pain inside became physical, so heavy I was sure it would crush me. I struggled to wring myself out of his powerful hold.

He held on tighter. "Samantha . . . baby, look at me."

Violently, I shook my head, refusing his call. With another smothered sob, I pushed against his chest, and he finally yielded, allowing me to slide down his body and onto my feet. But they were weak, just as weak as my knees and my heart, and I swayed with a rush of dizziness. I bent over at the middle, trying to hold the pieces together before I crumbled at his feet.

"Samantha," he whispered, his voice urgent and raw.

Nausea swirled through my stomach, and I bent down to gather my shorts and underwear from the ground. Humiliation burned up my insides, lashes of unbearable shame that licked at my skin when I fumbled and tried to pull them up my wobbly legs.

God, I must look pathetic.

I kept my face downturned, unable to look at the man I'd chosen to trust.

Foolish, foolish girl.

I should have known. I should have known.

When I heard him zipping up his pants, I winced, mortified by the fact that I'd just let him come undone inside me when I really didn't know him at all.

I gulped over the reality.

Because I did.

All along, I'd known him. When I'd first seen Aly, every self-preserving bone in my body had screamed at me to run. To stay away. To protect myself from the one who had the power to destroy me.

The one who had gladly watched me burn to ashes.

That malicious boy who'd just grown into an evil man.

"Fuck, Samantha, would you look at me?"

Finally I lifted my chin, meeting his gaze that jumped all over my face, but somehow didn't want to meet my eye. I choked over the disbelieving laughter that bubbled up. The sound was wet with regret and shame and all the hurt he continued to pile on me.

"What do you want me to see, Christopher? Do you want me to see the lies written all over your face? Or is it that you really just want to see the pain written on mine?"

"What the hell are you talking about? Of course I don't want to see you in pain."

"You know, Ben tried to stop me from going in the room that night. After I heard about what happened to Jared . . . I . . ." I couldn't hold any of this in any longer, even knowing it made me more vulnerable than I already was to tell him everything. "I was *heartbroken* for you, Christopher, heartbroken for Jared, and I thought I understood what happened the night that you came to my window. I went looking for you. I had some stupid fantasy that we'd run away together."

Christopher took a step back, his face warping with confusion.

That old anguish shook my head. "I was stupid enough to think you needed me. I believed you were just desperate and never intended on hurting me. But you had every intention of it, didn't you? You just stared right at me while you fucked that slut who *hated* me. Did you like it? Seeing me humiliated and broken? Do you like it now?"

All the color drained from his face. It only accentuated the lies he'd tried to hide. I watched the bob of his throat as he swallowed down my words, and his hands went to his hair. "No, Samantha . . . *never* . . . I *never* meant to hurt you. That was . . . I was out of my mind. *You* broke up with *me*. That night I gave up and gave in."

He ran his palm over his forehead, his attention toward the floor. "Shit." He looked back at me. "I'm so sorry. I didn't even know you were there, and I swear I never did it to hurt you. I couldn't see straight . . . couldn't feel anything but the misery that was eating me alive. Fuck, baby, I didn't know you were there. Please . . . you can't believe I would do that to you."

Never.

There was that word again.

Never.

The lie had slipped from him so easily.

I'd never touch that bitch. Not ever.

But he lied.

He lied.

Because he had.

He took a pleading step forward, dipping his head down to try to catch my face. "I've never felt worse than after that night. I never touched Jasmine before or after that night. Never. And I most definitely didn't know you were there. I would never do that to you. I thought I'd lost you."

Never. Never. Never.

The bile that had been lodged in my throat all day throbbed.

"Liar." The word oozed from my mouth. "Ben told me everything that night . . . when he had to pick me up and carry me out of that party. All those months I was missing you, holding on to the belief that we would find some way to work it out, all that time I *prayed* for a way for us to be together, you were with her. Tonight he told me about the rest of them, too. I *know* everything."

My own disappointment and sorrow wrapped around the words. "And here I was, naive enough to forget all of it if you really loved me now. Because I never stopped loving you, Christopher. Even after knowing you cheated on me all those months, I *never* stopped loving you."

Never.

There it was again.

But this time it was my truth.

I began to back away, trying to put space between me and what I wanted most, while Christopher seemed rooted to the floor, his expression shifting through a million dark shadows.

At the door, I stopped. "Laugh all you want, because you win. You finally broke me."

Just a pawn in his sick, twisted game.

I turned the knob. The sound of metal scraping pinged around the room.

"Motherfucker." Christopher was suddenly there, pulling at my arm. "He lied. He fucking lied, Samantha. He always wanted you. I knew it. I fucking knew it."

I yanked my arm away. "Don't touch me. You don't get to do that anymore. Not ever again. You lied to me . . . looked me in the eyes just now and swore you had never touched Jasmine. Not ever. How quickly your story changed when you knew you were caught. I'm done with it. I'm done with you."

"No . . . fuck, Samantha . . . would you just listen? You said we needed to talk. Talk to me."

"How can I talk to you when I can't believe a single word you say? I asked one thing of you, Christopher. *One thing*. I just wanted you to be honest with me. I was willing to forgive you for everything else."

I turned and flew out the door.

He was right behind me, fingers trying to touch, words trying to penetrate. I ran faster, pushing farther.

Desperate for space. Desperate for breath.

"There weren't any more. I swear to you. And I swear it was just once. I lied. Yes, I lied. I'm an idiot, Samantha, but I couldn't bear for you to know what I'd done. I've hated myself for doing it for so long. I'm so sorry. I was just trying to protect you."

I was sick of men trying to *protect* me.

I clicked the locks to my car, a rash, wild need urging me to get away.

"Samantha, baby, don't do this. Listen to me. Please, give me a chance."

I flung the driver's door open, rushing to get inside. "I already gave you a chance."

I slammed the door shut, fingers fumbling to lock it. Christopher pounded a flat palm against the window, yelling my name. My hands shook as I tried to get the key in the ignition. I gasped out in relief when I finally found the slot. I turned the engine over, threw it in gear.

And I left Christopher screaming for me in the middle of the street.

I refused to look in the rearview mirror, not that I could see through my tears anyway.

Refused to hear, even though I wanted to listen.

Refused to stop, because I knew the only choice I had was to go.

Loud sobs broke free, and I wept as I was struck with this consuming grief. Frantic, I tried to clear my vision with the back of my hand.

Sad thing? I had nowhere to *go*.

Nowhere I belonged.

Not when every piece of me belonged to him.

TWENTY-SIX

Samantha

May, Seven Years Earlier

I paced the kitchen. My hands were shaking. Shaking. I gripped a handful of hair, trying to shut down the quivers of anxiety that nipped at my already frayed nerves while I listened to the phone ringing on the other end. I really didn't want to call him. But where else could I turn?

"Hello?"

Relief sprang from my lungs when he answered, words flying off my tongue with a speed to match my hammering heart. "Oh, thank God, Ben, you answered. It's Samantha. I need your help."

"Whoa, slow down, sweetheart. What's going on?"

"Have you seen Christopher? I need to find him."

Ben's disappointment traveled through the phone, or maybe it was annoyance, I couldn't tell. "You know how I feel about him."

"I know . . . but I need to find him. I don't know what else to do. I tried his parents' house, but no one is picking up there." I lowered my voice to a plea. "It's really important, Ben. Please."

How bad did it suck that I couldn't give him details? Ben was my friend, but there was no chance I could trust him with this. He would never understand. I just hoped he cared about me enough to help.

"Sam . . . you're moving," he said delicately, as if he were trying to infuse the idea into my mind. Like I hadn't spent the last four months agonizing over it. "Why don't you give this up? He's only going to hurt you, and I can't stand to see that happen. This is your chance to get over him."

But Ben was wrong. Somehow I knew I was the one who'd hurt Christopher. I should have recognized it, the sorrow in his eyes and the grief in his touch.

"Please."

There was a long pause, an even longer sigh, and I could almost see him rubbing his temples in frustration. "Even if I wanted to, I can't help you, Samantha. I haven't seen him tonight. I'm sorry."

My own frustration knotted somewhere in my chest. I sucked it down and forced out a polite response. "'Kay. Thanks anyway."

I ended the call, tapped the phone against my palm, searching through my brain for any possible numbers I could remember. It didn't help that my parents had canceled my cell phone. My mom was going to be completely pissed off when she saw all the calls I'd made on her cell.

My friend Lydia had stopped by the house today to tell me good-bye before we left for the new house tomorrow. She'd told me all the rumors swirling around the school about Jared, that she was pretty sure they were true, that Christopher hadn't been at school in the last two days.

That fearful broken heart Christopher had left me with two nights ago had suddenly transformed, amplified with a need to get to him. To set things right. I desperately dialed what seemed like an endless slew of numbers trying to find him.

Damned the consequences.

I didn't care anymore.

As far as I was concerned, my parents had lost their right, had lost their say, because what they had done was wrong.

Five minutes later, my mom's cell rang in my hand.

Ben.

Fumbling, I answered it, probably a little too eagerly. "Hello?"

"God, Samantha, I'm going to regret doing this, but I'm at a party . . . at the same house I saw you at a few months ago? Do you remember?"

Of course I remembered.

That house. That pivotal night.

It had set about a change in direction that had woven Christopher so deeply in my heart, when he'd whispered his love and I'd admitted mine. When we'd confessed and I'd completely succumbed.

"Yes, I remember," I said, holding my breath.

Ben released his in a huge exhale. "Christopher just walked in the door. He's asking about you. You better get down here."

"Oh my gosh, I want to hug you! Thank you so much," I gushed, excitement bursting from my mouth. "I'll be right there."

I tossed my mom's phone on the counter and scratched out a note.

I don't know when I'll be back. Please don't worry, but I have to do this. I'm sorry.

Then I ran. Ran as hard as I could, the rubber soles of my canvas shoes slapping against the concrete. The steady beat echoed out against the deep, dark night. It took me all of ten minutes before I was standing in front of the two-story house tucked far back in a cul-de-sac, away from prying neighbors and passersby.

It was all lit up, lights blazing from the windows, the thump of music vibrating from within. Voices shouted, laughter sang.

And I kinda wanted to sing, too.

He'd never have treated me with disregard. I got it now, felt it deep in my spirit, and the boy I thought I had lost now suddenly seemed closer than he ever had.

I ran up the sidewalk and flung the door open wide. It clattered against the inside wall. I didn't stop to care that half the people in the room turned to look at me as if I were some kind of deranged person.

Someone who'd lost her grip on reality.

Not when I'd come to reclaim mine.

From the side, Ben grabbed my arm.

"Hey," I said, and I could feel the force of my smile as I turned toward him, felt it falter just as fast when I caught the sympathetic concern on his face.

Under his breath, he muttered, "I knew this was a bad idea."

I blinked, fighting the welling of panic that jumped up in me. "What are you talking about?"

Ben shook his head, seemingly talking to himself. "I wanted to give him the benefit of the doubt . . . hoped he'd changed and realized what he had, but I should have known better."

A shiver of foreboding slithered down my spine. "What are you talking about?" I repeated.

"Let me get you out of here and away from that asshole, Samantha."

I tore my arm from his grasp. "I'm not going anywhere until I talk to Christopher. Where is he?"

Ben's attention flicked to the staircase. "I can't let you go up there."

I didn't hear anything other than *up there*, and I was on the move, pounding up the stairs as fast as my feet could take me. Somehow I felt drawn to that room, the place where Christopher had seen me at my lowest low and then elevated me to my highest high.

I had to see him. To make this right.

A sense of dread clamped down on my spirit, and I paused at the door. My hand was shaking when I lifted it to the knob. I turned it, and the door swung open.

And I felt the fissure, the jagged cracks that splintered as my world crumbled from beneath me.

Over the last four months, since they'd caught me sneaking home in the middle of the night, my parents had done their best to pound their beliefs into me. To plant them so deeply in my psyche there was no possibility other than for them to take root. To mold their little girl back into who they'd raised her to be.

I'd rejected it all, steadfast in my own belief, a fortress of protection built up around my consciousness, the impenetrable walls made up of the love I had for Christopher and the devotion he had for me.

But this . . . this scene before me demolished it.

Every naive conviction was blasted away.

Devastating me.

A silent cry roared from my lacerated heart, this unbearable pain that sliced me in two.

As much as I wanted to run, I was frozen, locked in horror.

Jasmine cut her attention to me. A vicious sneer curled up her mouth, lipstick smeared, her naked body one with Christopher's. She exaggerated the roll of her hips and looked back down at a man I had no clue could be so cruel and vile. My gaze dropped, both terrified and desperate to see his gorgeous face— the one I'd thought held so much beauty, meant only for me.

His head lolled to the side. Through a rush of tears, I watched a disdainful smile spread, green eyes glued to mine, as if he were delivering a message.

One I heard loud and clear.

Then he turned away and drove his fingers into her too-skinny hips.

My gut twisted inside out, and I clapped my hand over my mouth to keep from puking all over the floor. Somehow I managed to tear myself from the doorway, and I staggered down the hall, my hand pressed to the wall for support. I barely made it to the bathroom, and I dropped to my knees at the toilet, purging all the turmoil that wrecked my body.

But there was no expelling this devastation. No balm or medicine or cure. I felt as if I was on fire, incinerating from the inside out. Those flames Christopher had lit, the ones that had once warmed me, were now burning me alive.

And I wept, wept as I retched and wished that I'd never followed him out my window that first time, wished I hadn't let him fill me with hope and love and belief when none of those things had ever existed.

Wished I hadn't been such a fool.

I hated that all the warnings my parents and Ben had given me were right.

"How could he do this to us?" I mumbled through the pain.

"Shh . . . Samantha, sweetheart." Ben was on his knees beside me, his hand soothing on my heaving back. "I'm so sorry. So sorry you had to see who Christopher really is. I thought I could spare you. He's not worth it, Samantha. He's evil. Evil. He's been with her for months, and when I saw him earlier, I thought maybe . . ." He squeezed the back of my neck, massaging, trying to give me comfort when none could be found. "Goddamn it," he swore, "I just wanted to see you happy. I know you've been struggling so much. I shouldn't have called you. You shouldn't have come here."

He pushed back the hair clinging to my sweat-drenched forehead, placed a gentle kiss at my temple. "I've got you, sweetheart. I've got you. He can't hurt you anymore."

And I felt so light when Ben scooped me into his arms. Weightless. Because I'd been burned to nothing.

Ashes.

I should have known. Should have listened. My parents had pled, warning me of the immorality I was being tempted into, the spiritual death that came with those sins.

And that's exactly how I felt.

Like a piece of me had died.

Something vital.

Something right.

A piece that would always belong to him.

TWENTY-SEVEN

Samantha

For hours, I drove.

Aimless.

Over near deserted streets, passing by vacant parking lots, storefronts closed down for the night, I roamed through all the disorder that had taken over my heart and mind. Exhaustion threatened to pull me under, my eyes puffy and red and unable to see far enough into the mess that had become my life.

When I could go no farther, I pulled up outside the slumbering house, cut the lights and the engine.

God, what was I doing? Funny, how after everything, this was the one place I felt I could go.

Resigned, I stepped from my car and stumbled up the sidewalk. Above, the night was dense, the trees still and the air full. I drew in a heavy gulp of it and wiped my soggy face, knowing I had to look a total mess. Nothing to be done about that. Like they wouldn't clue in that something had gone horribly wrong when I showed up at their house at three in the morning, anyway.

Softly I knocked on the door.

Movement rustled from the other side and the door cracked open to a sleepy, frowning Jared. "Sam?" He stepped back, opening the door wider, scraping a hand over his face to wake himself up. He wore only his boxers, obviously drawn from bed.

God, could I feel any worse for doing this? I peered up at him, tried to conceal the torment in my words, but it just leaked through like water through a sieve. "I'm so sorry for waking you up, but I didn't have anywhere else to go."

His frown deepened, but not in annoyance. "Hey, don't worry about it for a second. You know you're welcome here anytime."

"Thank you," I said, and he ushered me in. Subdued lights from the kitchen illuminated the space, and Aly emerged at the end of the short hall that led to their bedroom. She squinted at me. "Samantha?" In sleep shorts and a tee, she shuffled forward, craning her head. "Are you okay?"

"No," I admitted. And I thought I'd cried myself dry, but when I saw her face fall in sympathy, I broke.

Quickly she crossed the room and pulled me into her arms, shushed me and soothed me while I quite literally cried into her shoulder.

Jared stepped back, giving us space, but still there with unwavering support.

And in spite of every emotion I'd been wrung through today, or maybe because of it, I finally truly understood what friendship meant, what I'd been missing for all those years.

Little muffled cries stirred up from Ella's room.

"I'm so sorry for waking you all up," I apologized profusely, wondering if either of them could even understand what I was saying through my trembling voice.

Aly stepped back and rubbed the outsides of my upper arms. "No apologies." She squeezed in emphasis. "Jared and I both told you before, you belong here, with us. If you need help, we're here, night or day. Understand?" She gave me a warm smile. "Besides, Ella was due to wake up to eat any second."

Sniffling, I nodded. "Okay."

"Why don't you go sit on the couch and I'll make you a cup of tea. Sound good?"

"Yeah."

She turned to Jared. "Would you get Ella?"

"Glad to." He headed down the hall. The echo of his muted, tender voice filtered down the hall from his daughter's room.

Slipping off my shoes, I took a seat on the couch and drew my knees up to my chest, hugging them, searching for some kind of comfort that seemed impossible to find.

Still, being here?

It helped.

I rejected another call from Ben while Aly flitted around in the kitchen, quick to return with a steaming cup.

"Thank you," I said, accepting it. I blew at the hot liquid before I brought it to my lips to take a sip.

Aly settled at the opposite end of the couch, crisscrossing her legs in front of her. Jared sauntered in, swaying Ella in his arms.

"Mommy time," he said softly, easing that sweet baby girl into Aly's arms. Ella wiggled and grunted, little legs flailing as she was situated against Aly's chest. Jared ran his hand over the back of Ella's head and dropped a tender kiss to Aly's forehead. She lifted toward it, her eyes dropping closed as she relished his affection.

"Love you," she said.

"Love you." He glanced over at me, his expression uneasy,

questioning, before he tipped his attention back down to Aly. "Why don't I let the two of you talk?"

"Thank you," she whispered, smiling a smile reserved only for her husband.

Awkwardly, Jared stepped back, slipped around the couch, and walked toward their bedroom. We both watched him over our shoulders as he went. He paused just before he disappeared into their room, eyes earnest when they locked on mine. "I know Christopher can be a complete idiot." He shook his head. "I mean, we all can. Messing shit up every turn we take when it's the last thing we want to do. But I think you should know I've only seen him spun up over a girl twice in his life." Hand propped on the doorframe, he hesitated, then said, "Both times, that girl's been you."

Gratefulness and sorrow hit me full force. I flinched but tucked his words in deep. He dipped his chin before he disappeared into his room.

For a few minutes, Aly and I sat in silence while she situated Ella to feed her. We drifted on the charged quiet, Aly running her fingers through the thin strands of Ella's dark hair, looking down at her tiny cherub face. It was such a gentle scene of pure, unadulterated love.

It filled me with a yearning unlike anything I'd ever known and strangely comforted me at the same time.

Aly glanced over at me, turned back to rub the bottom of Ella's foot. Ella grunted in satisfaction. "I'm guessing it was my brother who put that look on your face?" Aly ventured.

Air filtered regretfully from my nose. "I think he's the only one who's capable of it."

"So . . . are you two . . ." She trailed off, confusion and question in her tone, like she was trying to catch up to the events that had led us to this place, when the truth was, I was having a hard time keeping up with them myself. I kept replaying and replaying everything Christopher had said, the pleas and the explanations I didn't know how to piece together with what I'd seen that night.

"Yeah," I finally confessed. The word was raw.

Well, we *were*.

Her face was downturned, but I didn't miss the flash of a smile that quirked at one side of her mouth.

"Are you really grinning right now?" I accused, trying to keep back the incredulous, confounded laughter that seemed to want to work its way out.

God, I had to be losing my mind.

Here I was, sitting on a couch in the middle of the night with the sister of the man who had yet again broken my heart. And she was making me laugh. The same way she always did, with that uncanny ability to dive below the surface, to reach out and pluck the positive from every situation that seemed entirely hopeless.

"What?" This time she let her smile widen, slanted it over at me, full and on display, her shoulders up to her ears. "Shouldn't I be excited that my friend finally got that screw loosened that had her wound up so tight?"

She winked, just accentuating the horrible joke, and this time I barked out a laugh that was hoarse with all the tears I'd shed. "Aly, you're terrible. Terrible." I cast her a trembling smile. "Thank you," I said again, this time quieter, letting her know how much I appreciated her.

"Seriously, Samantha." She sucked in a breath, as if she was trying to gather her thoughts. "You and Christopher . . . when you're in the room together? There's no question where either of you belongs. I'm not sorry that it makes me happy that you found each other." She blinked hard. "But what I am sorry about is that it led to this. You want to tell me what happened?"

Starting at the beginning, I told Aly everything, how much I'd loved him and how much I'd believed he'd loved me. My parents and all the rules they'd imposed with the intention of snuffing our love out. I tried my best to describe how horrible it'd felt to find him with Jasmine, how it'd wrecked something in me that I'd never thought could be repaired. I left out none of the sordid details, exposed myself in that time's innocence and the lessons I'd learned the hard, hard way.

And to be honest, it felt good to have it revealed.

Yeah, Ben knew all about it. He'd been there. But for years, he'd held it over my head as a fault to belittle my judgment, pouring continuous salt in that forever festering wound.

Nervously, I picked at the hem of my shirt. "The worst part of it all was finding out someone I thought was committed to me wasn't at all. I lost so much faith that night, seeing him with her and then Ben breaking it to me that he'd been with her all along. It killed something inside of me, Aly."

Regret slowly shook my head. "But being with him now? That part felt alive again . . . like I could really breathe again for the first time in seven years. How pathetic is that?"

Aly shifted in her discomfort for me. "Not pathetic, Samantha. It means you love him. Wholly. That he's a piece of you and when he's missing you feel the vacancy. You can't blame yourself for loving someone."

She swallowed and continued. "I'm so disappointed he put you through this. No matter what the circumstances or how difficult the situation, there's no excuse for him sleeping with her. He knew how miserable she made you. And I know my brother is prone to making all kinds of terrible mistakes. But I also know he's not a terrible *person*. I see the way he looks at you, and if one thing is obvious, it's the way Christopher feels about you."

I chewed at my bottom lip, fidgeting more, and a confused, hopeless sound worked its way free from my throat. "Tonight he told me Ben lied. He said he'd only been with her once. Of course, that was after he lied to me about ever being with her in the first place."

She paused, seemed to consider my words as she stared out into the darkened room. She turned to look at me, her chin tipped up in intensity. "Do you believe him?"

"I don't know. He sounds sincere, and every part of me wants to believe him. But my greatest fear is that desire is just another weakness . . . wanting him so much that I'm willing to delude myself into believing he really cares about me. All these months, I fought my feelings for him because I didn't trust him. Then the second I give him my trust, he turns around and crushes it again. The ironic thing is nothing in the past even mattered to me anymore, Aly. I was willing to forgive him for everything, if he'd just *respect* me enough to be honest with me." I pressed both my hands to my chest. "If he'd just love me and respect me and tell me the truth. That's all I asked of him, but he couldn't even give me that."

Slowly, she exhaled. "I'm no expert, Samantha, but one thing I've learned is men tend to take the worst paths to try to protect whatever means the most to them." She laughed lightly. "Stupid and destructive, and it doesn't make it okay, but it's the truth."

For the umpteenth time tonight, my phone lit up, and I groaned toward the ceiling when Ben's name appeared on the screen. Both he and Christopher had been calling incessantly. I pounded at the screen to silence it, tossed it to the middle cushion between me and Aly.

"God, I wish he'd give it a rest tonight. You'd think after twenty rejected calls he'd get the message that I don't want to talk to him."

Aly gestured to the phone with her elbow, now cuddling Ella against her chest. "If things don't work out with my brother, will you go back to him?"

"No." With pursed lips, I shook my head. "No matter what, that's over. I love Christopher, and going back to Ben wouldn't be fair to either one of us."

Five seconds later, my cell rang again. "Grrr . . ." I pressed the heels of my hands into my eyes, reclining my head against the back of the couch. "Which one is it?"

If all these calls were any indication, Ben wasn't going to just give up. I'd have to go back and give him the truth I'd intended to tell him earlier today. Even if he didn't deserve it, he would get my honesty. But it'd no longer come at my expense. No longer would I allow him to talk down to me or over me.

No more.

"Neither. It's your mom."

"Ugh." I dropped my arms, shaking my head. "I'm sure Ben called looking for me and has her completely worried. Things didn't go so well when I ended things with him earlier tonight."

"Why don't you let me answer it? I'll just let her know you're safe and you're staying at a friend's."

"Yeah, that's probably a good idea. Thank you . . . for taking care of me." I gave her a soft smile.

The smile she returned was knowing, filled with sympathy and all the support I didn't realize how much I needed until now. "I told you a long time ago I felt like we needed to be friends. Now I know we do."

She grabbed my phone and accepted the call. "Hi, Mrs. Schultz, this is—," Aly started to say, before she was overtaken by my mom's hysterical voice on the other end. But her worry wasn't for me. All I heard her screaming was "Stewart!"

Stewart.

Stewart.

Stewart.

The coldest chill slid down my spine, the empty feeling swooping in as if it'd drained all my blood with it. Hollowing me out.

No.

God, please, no.

Aly went pale, her voice so quiet I could hardly hear. "Okay," she whispered. She pulled the phone from her ear and shakily passed it across to me. "You need to take this."

TWENTY-EIGHT

Christopher

I raked my hands over the top of my head and looked toward the ceiling.

"Fuck," I swore, dragging them down and scrubbing my face, trying to clear my vision. I felt frantic.

Shock had knocked me stupid when Samantha had said Jasmine's name, and that fucking lie had slipped from my mouth without my brain having the chance to consider the consequences. Jasmine represented every obscene choice I'd made in my life, and I wanted to protect Samantha from the knowledge of the vile person I'd been.

But I knew the second it hit the air I'd done Samantha wrong. She deserved the truth. What I had no clue about was the fact that she already knew.

God.

She fucking *knew.*

She had seen me when I'd been too lost in my own destructive world of self-loathing and hatred to even know she was there. She'd come back for me. She had loved me then, despite everything.

I finally got it. Why she'd been so terrified to start things back up with me when it was so clear she knew she belonged with me, the resistance she met me with at every turn.

It hadn't been Samantha who'd given up. It'd been me. It didn't matter that she'd told me to leave that night I'd stumbled into her room. I'd still belonged to her and she'd still belonged to me, and I'd just thrown myself away, didn't wait or work or strive to make it right.

Didn't put in the *effort* she deserved.

Samantha believed I'd betrayed her.

And I knew in my gut the reality was that I had.

I figured there were few things that could have been more hurtful for her than finding me with Jasmine. Still, she'd somehow found it in that forgiving heart of hers to give me a second chance. Of course, because I couldn't help but be a fucking ignorant dickhead, I'd gone and screwed it up again.

I dug my phone out of my pocket and called her for what had to be the hundredth time since she'd fled out my door four hours earlier. My chest squeezed so fucking tight I could barely breathe when I listened to the sound of her recorded voice. It beeped, and I spoke, basically leaving the same message I'd been pleading all night. "Samantha . . . baby . . . please listen to me. You were never a game. Ever. Please . . . call me back. I can't lose you again."

Ending the call, I rubbed my forehead, trying to piece together everything Samantha had lived with as truth for the last seven years. I wasn't surprised for a second to find out Ben had been feeding her his own lies, pumping her head full of deceit as another way to bend her to his will.

What I wouldn't give to be able to go back and do it all over again. Tonight. The first time I saw her back at Aly's house. Jasmine. Maybe even go back all the way to the night her parents had discovered we'd been sneaking around.

Do all of it over.

Love her the way only a girl like Samantha deserved to be loved. Fight for her. Show her and everyone who cared for her how much she meant to me, that I was dedicated, and that what I felt for her wasn't just some teenaged crush that would fade. And no, maybe I'd never be good enough for her, because I doubted there was a soul in this world who was, but I wanted to prove I'd always be striving to be that person, striving to love her so much that maybe it'd make up for all of my inadequacies.

Relief pelted me when my phone rang in my hand.

"Damn it," I muttered under my breath when I saw it wasn't Samantha, but my sister. In a flash I realized that of course Samantha must have sought refuge there.

I accepted the call and lifted it to my ear. "Aly," I said hesitantly, bracing myself for the attack I knew I deserved.

"Christopher." She said my name with none of the anger I'd expected, but instead in a voice steeped in sadness.

My gut twisted. "What's going on? Is Samantha there?"

"She was."

Was.

In my panicked pause, she kept talking, her voice a strained whisper. "I know things fell apart between you two tonight, but while she was here, she got a call from her mom about Stewart. I don't really have any details other than he was taken to the hospital. Samantha went straight there." She softened. "I thought you'd want to know."

Fear curled through my senses, and I pressed the heel of my hand into my eye, trying to tamp down the emotion that spread like a flash fire. "God," I wheezed on a pained breath.

Not Stewart. Please.

I heard my sister swallow, could feel her hesitation and questions bleeding from across the distance. "She told me everything, Christopher. She was heartbroken when she got here. You know how much I love you, how much I want you to be happy, but I need you to be honest and tell me if you're just playing with her."

I pushed out a breath. "I fucked up, Aly. Really bad. But I love her. I always have."

A reassured sigh slipped from her, and she inhaled before she continued. "I won't try to make you feel better by saying what you did was okay, because it's not. But I get why you did it."

Did she?

"I knew the second I ran into her that there was a reason for it. She loves you. So much. And I'm worried about her. I've never seen anyone as distraught as she was when she left my house twenty minutes ago."

Frustrated, I paced in front of my front door, gripping a handful of hair. "God, I need to be there for her."

"I know, but I'm not sure she's in any condition to deal with what you put her through right now."

I exhaled in frustration. "You think I don't know that, Aly?" I was pretty sure her parents still didn't have the first clue about what'd been going on between us. Showing them now? All that would do was bring her more trouble . . . hurt her family more, and God knew they had enough to deal with right now. Plus, I didn't even know if Samantha would want me there. If my presence would cause her comfort or bring her pain . . . But shit, I couldn't just sit here, either.

"Do you know what hospital he's at? I just need to be nearby."

If she called? Needed me? Then I'd be right there.

Aly told me the name of the hospital, and I grabbed my keys from the counter and hit the garage. "Let me know if you hear from her, would you?"

"Yeah, of course. I love you, Christopher."

"Love you, too."

As if my life depended on it, I flew through the night, across the deserted streets, desperate to be there. Fifteen minutes later, I pulled into the visitor parking lot, which was only sporadically dotted with cars. Immediately, I spotted Samantha's parked right at the front, and my spirit churned with the need to go to her.

Instead I forced myself to hide at the far end of the lot, my truck backed in so I could keep an eye on the door but stay far enough away that I wouldn't draw attention to myself.

That desperation I'd felt to get here turned torturous as I sat for hours and waited. Agony for Stewart wrapped around me like an ill-fitting coat, squeezing me, burying me in the worry I felt for Samantha. All of it damned near had me making more bad choices, agitation bouncing my knee as I had to force myself to stay in the cover of my truck when all I wanted was to go to her.

Tall streetlamps illuminated the quiet parking lot. Off to the east, the intermittent drone of cars flying down the freeway just added to the overbearing stillness.

Exhaustion pinned my head to the headrest, my eyes heavy and burning as the first hint of light pressed at the horizon. But my heart and mind remained frantic, churning with regret and fear.

Rays climbed higher in the sky, blazing brighter, chasing away the night. Darkness slowly gave way to day. I scrubbed my palms over my face, trying to break up the tension contending with the emptiness doing its best to suck me under.

Goddamn it.

I blew out a breath.

My phone buzzed with a text and I rushed to grab it.

Aly.

Samantha texted me. Stewart's organs are shutting down. They are doing what they can to make him comfortable. I'm so sorry, Christopher.

Grief constricted my throat, and I slumped back in my seat, completely gutted.

Why did life have to be so fucking unfair?

Hours passed while I sat vigil, my sight glued on the hospital's front doors. At just after five p.m., they slid open for what had to be the millionth time that day. But this time . . . this time it was Samantha and her family.

I shot forward, gripping the steering wheel. Samantha's father held her mother around the shoulders as he led her out, Sally Schultz's face buried in her husband's chest. I felt jarred by the fact that her brother and sister, Sean and Stephanie, were there, too, the past years also having stripped them of all their youth. Their faces were pale, lost in a foggy stupor as they emerged from the hospital in a daze.

But it was really only Samantha who I saw. She came out last, in the distance appearing so fragile and broken. She hugged herself around her middle, her shoulders drawn up to her ears and her head bowed. The rest of her family shuffled out into the parking lot. Just at the edge of it, Samantha paused, holding herself while she lifted her face toward the sky, her face that was soaked with tears and a sorrow I'd give anything to rid her of. Blond hair whipped around her, like her movements commanded a raging storm.

My throat got all gravelly and my eyes burned.

I could feel it—the severity of her pain, the agony that vibrated from her bones, surging out on endless waves. They slammed into me, one by one.

Not going to her had to be about the most excruciating thing
I'd ever endured. Sitting here, my fingers curled into the leather,
I drew on all the restraint I had to force myself to stay still.

The selfish part of me was begging her to look up. To *feel*
me the same way I was feeling her. Begging her to call out to
me to come to her so I could hold her, so I could make her promises that she couldn't help but believe.

Because every single one of them would be the truth.

Instead I jerked when I noticed the movement off to her
right. That bastard Ben strode up to her, his head craned to the
side as if he was trying to get her to see him the same way I was.
He took her by the shoulders. I watched as her mouth dropped
open in shock, and I got as antsy as all hell when he tried to
wrap her up in his filthy arms.

A fierce swell of possessiveness started in my gut and spread
like wildfire, a savage blaze scorching my limbs, flexing my
hands into fists on the dash. I kept squeezing them, trying to
keep myself in check.

He'd *lied* to her, and because of it Samantha had spent years
harboring hurt over some shit that had never gone down. No
doubt, the douche bag had taken it into his own hands to slant
the catastrophe that had become our lives in his favor.

All of his protective big-brother bullshit.

He'd just been lying in wait, ready to strike when the opportunity hit, and the second I'd fallen he'd been right there to bury me.

I wondered how long it'd taken him to coerce her into bed.

She finally shoved him off, and it sucked that I felt some sort
of corrupted atonement in her rejection of him. Even though I
knew I deserved it, the idea of her running back to him after
what I'd done just about killed me.

Then I watched anger seem to seize him, the way his body
tensed as the good-guy act was peeled away to reveal the ass-

hole underneath. He curled his fingers at the outsides of her arms and shook her.

Fuck no.

That piece of shit was not going to get away with that.

My tongue darted out to wet my dry lips, and I shifted in agitation, knowing there wasn't much more I could take before I snapped.

Samantha's dad slowed, looking back, and then finally turned fully to walk their way. I could sense his own surprise at the heated exchange, and I couldn't help but wonder how little her parents really knew about what had been happening in Samantha's life and what she really wanted from it.

Ben flung his arm out in Stephen Schultz's direction, and Stephen shouted something back.

What the hell?

Narcissistic douche bag. Did he not get what Samantha and her family were going through right now?

I raked a flustered hand over my face in an attempt to battle the voice screaming in my head, demanding that I get involved. But I was pretty damned sure that would only make matters worse.

The rest of Samantha's family stood there in shock, her mother appalled at whatever was being said. Stephanie went to her mother's side and wrapped her arm around her waist while Sean edged forward, encroaching on Ben.

Ben turned back to Samantha, who had tears flooding down her face, but there was no mistaking the anger there, too. Her mouth curled up in hatred when she spat words in his direction.

Then it was as if the world stood still as I watched that piece of shit lift his hand and slap her across the face.

For two seconds, no one moved, time stopping as everyone seemed to process what was happening in front of us. Then

Samantha reared back, her face distorted in horror. Her shaking hand went up to her flaming cheek.

And then time sped.

Her father lunged for Ben, and there was no longer anything in this world that could hold me back. I threw open my door and hurled myself out of the truck. I couldn't even feel my feet slapping against the pavement as I flew across the lot.

The only thing I felt was myself coming apart at the seams. All the hatred I'd harbored for so many years rose to the surface. A suffusion of rage stormed through every last one of my senses. My love for her was bright. Blinding. The knowledge of the huge hand Ben had played in stealing her away from me vivid.

Still, every single one of those intense feelings was eclipsed by that fact that he'd hurt her.

In that moment, it was the only damned thing I could see.

I launched across the space and my body collided with Ben's in a force I felt all the way to my bones.

Samantha's father stumbled out of the way as I took Ben down. We crashed to the ground. I scrambled to pin him down and I cocked my elbow back. Trying to break free, Ben lifted his upper body, and I rammed my fist so hard into his face that his head rammed into the pavement. A sick sort of satisfaction fell over me when I felt his nose crunch beneath the force.

I didn't even give him time to register the hit. I landed another punch, this time to the temple. A garbled sound spluttered from his throat. It was another insult. More abuse targeted at Samantha. More lies. More accusations.

"So *he* is what this is all about?" he demanded, spewing hot hatred in Samantha's direction, his body bucking up, trying to knock me off. "This piece of shit is the reason you're leaving me?"

And I felt myself slipping, sucked beneath the crashing waves by this powerful undertow.

Somehow the asshole got lucky and clocked me on the side of the mouth, and my head rocked back. All that did was fuel the force of my next blow, which connected under his jaw.

I clutched him by the collar of his shirt, lifting him, then slamming him back down. "You touch her again and I will end you. Do you understand what I'm telling you?"

"Fuck you," he slurred, grappling at my wrists as he tried to throw off my hold. "You think you can just waltz back into her life and fuck with her head? Take her from where she belongs? You're nothing but garbage."

Where she belongs?

I rammed him down and pressed my forearm up under his chin, against his throat, my nose almost touching his as I growled in his face. "She belongs with me, asshole, and you saw to it that she was taken from me, didn't you? All these years, you led her to believe I'd been messing around on her." I increased the pressure. "Never. I'd never do that to her. And now she's hurting . . . hurting worse than she ever has, and you're going to make this day about *you*?"

A heavy hand landed on my shoulder. "Enough." I jerked to find Samantha's father frowning down at us. "Enough," he said quieter, when it was clear he'd broken through the craze that had taken over my mind.

Reluctantly, I released my hold and pushed to my feet, and Ben wheezed as he inhaled a sharp breath.

I dabbed with my tongue at the tiny cut at the side of my lip, tasting the rusty flavor of blood.

"You okay?" Samantha's father asked, tilting his head to the side, his eyes dropping to the cut like he was worried about my condition. He was panting, and there was no missing how rattled he was. Here the guy had just had his world turned upside down, and me and this bastard Ben were scuffling in the fucking parking lot like a couple of dumb-ass kids. And that shit sucked, but there was no regretting standing up for Samantha.

"Yeah," I mumbled.

Ben rolled over and propped himself up on both hands, coughing toward the ground. He glared up at me. "She was just fine before you came back. We were just *fine.*"

Her anguished voice hit me harder than Ben had. "*Fine?* You think I was fine? All those years you were lying to me, knowing how much those lies hurt?" She bit back a sob. "You have always decided what you thought was best for me. You don't get to do that anymore, because those decisions were never in my best interest. Every direction you ever tried to push me? You did that for yourself! I told you last night I don't want to be with you anymore. And after today . . . what you did? I don't ever want to see you again."

Ben struggled to standing and rubbed the back of his hand under his bleeding nose, smearing blood across his cheek as he looked to Samantha's father. "Stephen . . . help me talk some sense into her. Tell her what a fool she's being."

Turmoil radiated from Stephen's rigid movements, a jumble of disappointment and agony. "We lost our *son* today . . ."

I flinched at the sorrow contained in his words, and my insides twisted in two when the jagged cry left Samantha with her father's statement. All I wanted was to rush to her, to wrap her up, to promise her it would be okay. But out of respect, I averted my gaze to my feet, because I wasn't sure either she or Stephen Schultz would want me a witness to their pain.

His tone took on an air of disbelief. "And you come out here, making demands of my daughter." His voice tightened in emphasis. "Then you *strike* her and you have the audacity to think I'd take your side?" In disgust, he shook his head. "Go. Just like Samantha said, I don't ever want to see you near my daughter again."

"Stephen—"

"Go," Stephen cut him off.

Ben's attention darted around at everyone who was staring at him. With her hand pressed to her mouth, Samantha's mother quietly cried, and Stephanie clung to her side while Sean took on a defensive stance that warned he'd be all too happy to jump in if needed.

As if they were all scum under his feet, Ben lifted his chin like the cocky asshole he was, boastful pride filling up his expression. One that left me itching to knock it off his face. With a sneer, he looked to Samantha. "Your loss."

Then he turned and stalked away.

A muddled sob escaped Samantha, a mixture of relief and sorrow and confusion. Tortured blue eyes landed on me.

So much for playing it cool, hiding in the shadows, because I'd just dragged all our shit out into the open.

"God, Samantha, I am so sorry," I whispered, hoping she'd hear all the pain and regret in my words. For Stewart. For all the pain I'd caused her. For Ben doing her so wrong.

"You lied t-t-to me," she stuttered through the tears streaming down her face, clutching her chest. "You lied to me," she choked. "And my brother . . ." Her tone was hopeless, distant and full of denial.

Grief squeezed the air from my lungs, and my face pinched up with remorse. With the loss. "I'm so sorry," I said, the words coarse and choppy. "I know this has gotta be the worst day of your life." Warily, I looked around at her family, and I tripped over my words when I met with all the suffering pouring from their eyes. "The worst day of all your lives. And God, I never intended to make it worse." Grimacing, I turned back to that sweet girl, that girl who was so good and perfect and beautiful it fucking pained me to look at her and not be able to touch her.

"Please understand I just needed to be nearby, here for you if you needed me." I drove an anxious hand through my hair. "And when *he* showed up . . . when he *hit* you . . . I couldn't stand aside and do nothing. I'm sorry if I hurt you more . . . any of you . . . It's the last thing I want to do." I inhaled deeply, drawing air into my vacant lungs. "I am so tired of hurtin' you, Samantha. Don't want to do it anymore."

Her mother blinked through her confusion, trying to catch up, but it was clear from her father's expression that he was already there.

Dropping her eyes closed, Samantha whimpered before she chanced looking back at me. "How can I ever believe what you say, when every time you turn around, you lie to me? I thought . . . I thought this time it was real."

Real.

And it didn't matter that we had an audience. I took a step forward and laid myself bare. "You don't think what we have is *real?* Falling in love with you? That was the best gift I've ever been given." I swallowed over the lump that throbbed in my throat. "And losing you? For me . . . it was a tragedy. I condemned myself to a life of nothing, refusing to feel anything *real.* I cut myself off from feeling for a whole lot of years. Not a care in this world, because I just had lost the capacity to *care.* Aly . . . Jared . . . Ella Rose—each of them took a part in beginning to lift me from it. But, Samantha . . . you coming back? You rescued me from it. Because you're *real* . . . and when I'm with you, you make me that way, too."

But it came at a cost.

Loving someone. Caring about someone more than you care about yourself. The selfishness that reigned supreme no longer wearing its crown.

I knew it and accepted and wanted it.

No longer would I run from it.

"I love you. I love you so much that I'm willing to let you go if that's what you really want. But I'm never going back to that place of feeling nothing, because you've reminded me what it feels like to live. To really live. Not just for myself but to live because there's something greater out there that I should be living for, something bigger than all of us." Taking a single step back, I tipped my head to the side. "And I know I messed up . . . But every second with you? It was *real*. Don't ever doubt that."

I retreated further, feeling myself ripping apart as I gave her the space I knew she needed, the time I knew she deserved. Her mother walked to her side, winding her in supportive arms while Samantha looked on me with so much confusion and need it almost dropped me to my knees. I flattened my hand over my pounding heart. As I continued to walk backward, I cast her a sad smile and whispered the words I knew her heart would understand. "Just you and me and forever."

And fuck if it didn't damn near destroy me when I turned and left her.

But I had to go, because this was no longer about me. Not about what I wanted and what I was desperate for.

This was about a girl.

One I'd wronged.

One who was in pain.

One who needed to be set free—free from coercion and the chains that held her down. Free from pressures and compulsions and expectations.

Free to love.

For once, completely free to decide.

The sun shined high in the endless desert sky, bright and glaring and warm. It was a stark, blinding contradiction to the dark veil that covered the somber gathering. Discomfort shifted my feet, and I tugged at the black tie that felt like a noose made for the sole purpose of strangling the life out of me, constricting my throat, which bobbed heavily with emotion. Emotion so overbearing it clenched my teeth and burned in my eyes, a physical weight to my limbs and a burden to my failing heart.

God, it hurt.

And any sorrow I was feeling? It paled in comparison to what Samantha was feeling. What her family was feeling. A shock of grief and sympathy slammed me when I let my mind wander to what she had to have been going through for the last four days, since Stewart had passed.

I hadn't seen or talked to her in all that time, giving her the space she needed though every part of me wanted to be there.

I almost didn't show my face today, either. But this morning Aly had insisted that Samantha would want me here, even though she wouldn't give me a straight answer about whether Samantha had asked for me or not.

Either way, I knew in my gut I needed to come, that just like that awesome kid had touched every life here, he'd also touched mine. In a profound and undeniable way. In a way that had always made me better, even if for too many years of my life, I'd tried to ignore it, what it'd meant and by extension, what he'd meant.

I held back at the fringes of the sea of black, masked by the shade of a massive elm tree that stretched for the heavens, and something about it felt like a flagrant symbol of Stewart's life. Solid and bold and beautiful. Strong. Even though a disease had made him frail and weak, he had the strongest spirit of anyone I'd ever met. He had made his mark on this world, and there was no amount of time that could erase it.

I tried to keep it inconspicuous as my gaze roamed the faces, desperate to see the one who held me hostage, heart and mind. But I never caught so much as a glance, and I knew she'd be sitting in one of the two rows of chairs that were set up close to the casket, reserved for family.

A soft, broken voice drifted over the assembly. Samantha's mother stood at the podium, speaking the words that were in my own heart about the imprint that a beautiful soul had permanently etched on her.

"Even if I will never see his face again here on this earth"— she touched her chest—"I will forever feel him here."

And it was like you could see her words weave through the crowd, the way everyone swayed with the impact of them, like they, too, were tucking them away, fortified by this woman's bravery and belief.

When she began to cry, Samantha's father came up behind her and helped her down.

God, this was brutal.

Prayers were said and a haunting hymn was played as the casket was lowered. I fisted my hands, trying to ward off the grief of it all, the sadness that felt all encompassing. An invitation was made for everyone to attend a reception held at Samantha's father's church, and the crowd began to disperse.

I remained in the shadows, waiting, because I couldn't force myself to leave.

Aly and Jared emerged, the two hand in hand, my sister in a black skirt and sapphire blouse, Jared looking just about as uncomfortable and awkward as me in a dark suit.

Aly came right up to me and hugged me to her. "I'm sorry, Christopher."

I nodded, knowing I was owed no sympathy, but understanding what my sister implied all the same. "I know."

Jared put his hand on my shoulder, the gleam of his blue eyes knowing, because dude knew exactly why I was all spun up, how important all of this was, though I'd done my best to convince him otherwise. "Let us know if there's anything we can do."

I gave him a short nod. "Yeah. Thanks, man."

They headed toward Jared's truck. The crowd thinned, and I tensed when Samantha's parents appeared, flanked by both of her siblings. Sally Schultz lifted her face, lines cutting across her forehead, set deep at the corners of her eyes. I swallowed hard when they approached, suddenly feeling like it had been a really bad idea to show up. The last thing I wanted to do was show them any disrespect, to make this day any harder than it already was.

When they began to pass just a few feet away, I dropped my gaze to my feet. I startled with the soft hand that squeezed my biceps and looked up in time to catch the mournful smile Mrs. Schultz cast my way. "Thank you for being here." She cleared her throat, met my eye. "Go to her . . . She needs you."

Then she dropped her hold, Stephen Schultz gently leading her away. But not before he clapped me once on the back.

And I knew there was a whole ton left unsaid between us. Years of hurt and misunderstandings and bitterness.

No, there was no chance it'd be fixed in a day. But I also recognized their need to support their daughter, that the decisions they'd made in our past had never been out of spite but out of care for their daughter.

Slowly the area completely cleared out, until only she and I remained. She stood facing away, staring down at the black casket, which had been lowered into the ground, hugging herself in much the same way she had four days ago when she'd left the hospital. The long length of her hair whipped around her, her spirit protesting what was laid out in front of her.

Every inch of my body tightened as I silently edged for-

ward, my insides all tangled and coiled with sorrow and remorse and this hope that I refused to let go.

Four feet from her, I stopped, though there was a part of me
that felt at one with her, a partner to her pain, to the torment
that both twisted her up and broke her down.

What felt like an eternity passed, one we shared. Through
the space, I held her while she lifted her face to the sky, and I
knew she was saying good-bye.

My chest squeezed when she finally turned to look at me
from over her shoulder, her beautiful face laced with sorrow. "I
can't believe he's really gone," she murmured.

"It seems impossible," I whispered. All those pictures Samantha had been showing me were still vibrant behind my eyes,
impressions of memories that had taken hold. "I hate it . . . hate
it for you . . . hate it for your family."

Pain lashed across her face, everything exposed, completely
laid bare. Her hands clenched and unclenched at her sides. Like
she was lost in some anxious anticipation.

Like she knew after this moment nothing would ever be the
same.

"Do you love me, Christopher? What you said outside the
hospital . . . Tell me it's true, and don't make me a fool for believing it." It was a plea straight from her heart. Transparent and
vulnerable.

I took one tentative step toward her, then another, and Samantha slowly turned to face me as I got close enough to slip my
hand up to cup one side of her face, prepared to lay myself at her
feet. I grazed my thumb along the sweet swell of her bottom lip.
"The first time I caught sight of this mouth? I'm pretty sure
there was a piece of me that fell in love with you, because once
you hooked me, you never let go." My hand trailed down along
her delicate neck, and she shivered when it came to rest over the

thunder pounding in her chest. "But I *knew* it as soon as you showed me this amazing heart."

In a rush of relief and surrender, she collapsed against me, and I didn't hesitate to scoop her into my arms when her knees buckled beneath the weight of this unfair world.

Clutching my shirt, she choked over a sob that swam with sorrow and brimmed with hope. "Stewart always told me I deserved to be swept off my feet."

I exhaled heavily with the relief and joy of her words on such a sad day, and I pressed my face to the top of her head, making a silent promise to carry her wherever she wanted to go.

A breeze blew through, and I felt it deep, that fucking awesome kid who'd shined all his light, just a smile, and the world was a better place.

And I could hear him whispering for me to take care of her.

Not because she needed it.

Not because she was weak or naive.

But because she deserved to be loved in the same way she loved.

With everything.

Samantha buried her face under my chin, her voice hoarse but sure. "Take me home, Christopher."

TWENTY-NINE

Samantha

Soft rays of morning light roused me as they streaked through the windows, nudging my awareness as I was drawn from one of the longest, deepest slumbers I'd ever experienced. My heart's misery had kept me awake for days, and yesterday the severe exhaustion had finally caught up to me.

Here, I'd found respite.

I rolled to my back, taking the huge mound of covers with me. I felt so small lying in the middle of his ginormous bed, buried in a heap of blankets and sheets and pillows.

Deeply, I inhaled, pressing my face into the blanket and pulling that perfect warm scent into my lungs. A breath of the morning's freshest air. But still something else entirely intoxicating that belonged to Christopher alone. Sex and lust and everything I'd ever wanted but had been deluded into believing was too dangerous to have.

But I was no longer afraid.

Off to the left, the door creaked, and my head rolled to the side to find Christopher edging it open. A flop of black fell across his forehead, one eye peeking through the crack. Even though most of it was obstructed, I could see his entire face smile when he found me awake. But it was a soft smile. Tender and adoring and promising more than I had ever hoped to fathom.

As he slipped inside, I clutched the blanket to my chest. Emotion pressed so full I thought I would burst. Bare feet ghosted silently across the carpeted floor as he approached, his head dropping to the side to take in the sight of me bundled up in his bed.

His knee hit the edge and he slowly climbed up to my side. On his knees, he twisted his torso so he could press his hands to the mattress on either side of my head. He dropped down lower, to his elbows. Bracketing me. Holding me without touching me at all. Stealing all my breath.

He got close enough to bring us chest to chest, although we were separated by the pile of bedding between us. A wistful smile edged his mouth, and he brushed back the mess of hair from my forehead. Kind green eyes crinkled at the corners when he stared down at me.

Here I'd been, mere months ago, convinced I'd sold my soul to Satan himself.

Now I was certain I'd been sent a gift I'd been too blind to recognize.

"Mornin', beautiful," he murmured slow, drinking me in.

Overwhelmed, I chewed at my bottom lip. "Hey," I whispered. My eyes roamed all over his gorgeous face. Memorizing this moment. The moment I woke up to the man I loved, sure he really was mine.

The day Stewart passed had changed everything inside me. Broken up all the pieces I'd held on to so firmly and left me with a shattered hope that my brother would survive and live out a full life.

Somehow, Christopher had found those pieces and picked them up, as if his admission that afternoon had the power to cure my grief, touching all that was broken with a silent support. A support that never promised I wouldn't hurt but with a vow that he would be there to see me through.

Four days I'd spent in a daze, mourning my brother, slowly accepting the fact that he was gone while another part of me was slowly accepting the truth in Christopher's words.

He loved me and he always had.

And no, that love didn't come without mistakes and wounds.

But that didn't mean it wasn't real.

"You sleep okay?" he asked.

Yesterday afternoon, I'd fallen asleep in his truck. My mind had barely broken through coherency when he'd scooped me out of the passenger seat, carried me inside, and laid me here. The hazy memory echoed back, Christopher carefully undressing me, soothing hands paring me down to my panties and under-shirt before he buried me in the comfort of his covers. Stripped down to his boxers, he'd crawled in behind me, pulled my back to his chest, and murmured, "Sleep, sweet girl."

It was familiar and perfect and the last affirmation my spirit needed to know this was really where I was supposed to be.

I swallowed over the heaviness I feared would forever be lodged in my throat. "I don't think I've ever slept so hard in my life." I grimaced. "I haven't really slept much the last week."

He kept running his fingers through my hair. "You needed it. You were exhausted, baby."

"Yeah," I admitted. "It's been a rough week."

Understanding filled his features. "I know."

I made a vain attempt to lift the covers, but they only

budged an inch considering I was pinned under him. I grunted. "Come here. I need to feel you."

On half a grin, he dropped a sweet kiss to my nose. "Was thinking I'd feed you. You want breakfast?"

I gave a short shake of my head. "No. What I really want is for you to show me how much you love me, Christopher. Show me you need me as much as I need you."

Brows cinched, eyes searching, his fingertips traced along my jaw. "We have all the time in the world for that. You need to rest. Eat. Sleep. Then we need to *talk*."

That fullness in my throat throbbed. Because none of us ever knew what all the time in the world was going to mean, how long that would be, how many days we'd be granted. And I wanted this one to count. "This *is* what I need. I need to be close to you." I moved to whisper in his ear. "To feel your hands and your mouth and your body on mine." I scraped my nails down both sides of his neck, and he lifted to it, his chin drifting higher as he blew out a breath between clenched teeth. "I need this connection with you. I need time that is just about *us*. To feel how *real* we are. Then we'll talk."

He tipped his attention back to me, his expression flitting through a million emotions. This time none of them were dark. There was no evil, no malice or spite. All those false impressions that had burned and seared and left me in ashes were no longer my truth.

Because I believed in him.

"You're my world, Samantha," he whispered, shifting to the side as I lifted the covers so he could crawl inside. "My entire world." The rough of his jeans scraped my bare thighs as he settled between them, his heart beating strong with mine as he sank further into me. The covers were thick and warm and heavy, locking in all that heat.

That burn that he lit.

God, it felt so good, and I sighed out in contentment, then inhaled a jagged breath of need.

Christopher reached to the back of his neck and pulled the plain white tee he was wearing over his head. Tossed it aside. "Every second." He pressed his hands under the hem of my shirt, his touch hot on my skin, and pulled that off, too. "Every day."

Then he sank in deeper. "Don't wanna ever be without you," he whispered as he fell even closer. Skin to skin. Elbows caging. Spirit loving.

Beneath the covers, he kissed me. Long and slow. Tongue and mouth and body and soul. And I felt it. Far beyond the lies that were bred to protect. Ages past the ones that were built to destroy.

The honesty of what we were.

I gripped tightly to it, refusing to ever let it go.

He pulled back just enough to slide out of his jeans and boxers, and in less than two seconds, he was back, hovering over me, hands at my hips, helping me shimmy out of mine.

Christopher pushed up, his weight on his hand and the light bend of his knees. The pad of his thumb raked across my bottom lip, and he smiled when it curved against the touch. "This mouth," he said. "Can't tell you the number of times I thought of it . . . imagined this smile . . . the way it makes me feel. Wish you knew, Samantha."

But I did. I wholly grasped it now, what I meant to him now, what I'd meant to him then.

I arched toward him, and Christopher set to tracing me, drawing a pattern over my jaw and down the slope of my neck.

My lips parted on an exhale, and he breathed it in. Locking his eyes on mine, he dragged me with him, urging me to follow his gaze as he trailed it down my body. Fingertips tapped across my breastbone, the drum of a silent song that beat with my thundering heart. He played it soft and slow, letting those unsaid words resonate deep. Seep into my skin. Soak into my spirit.

His hand went to cup my breast, and he watched me closely as the buds tightened in a pleasured ache as he swirled a single finger around one nipple, then the other. He continued his exploration down my belly, tickling across my hips, over the jut of my pubic bone.

He led my sight lower, to the brush of his fingers descending between my thighs. They nudged between my folds, where the skin was fevered and wet and desperate, and something urgent left me on a cry when he pushed two inside. "Christopher."

"Samantha," he returned softly, "you need me to show you?" He slicked his fingers out in a slow drag of blissful torture. Making me gasp. Making me writhe. Slowly he pressed them back in.

A frenzy of nerves lit, a buzz beneath my skin. Growing fast.

"You see, baby?" he grated. "I've never touched anyone like this. Never touched someone because I loved them. Because I cherished them. No one but you."

He was whispering words to pull my attention to his face, green eyes fierce but sincere, brimming with love and need and devotion. "Do you see it? Do you know? Do you have any idea how much I love you? It just about killed me when you thought I didn't, Samantha. Killed me to think you walked out my door last week believing there was ever a day every part of me didn't belong to you. Killed me that all those years you thought that *this* was nothing but a game."

Christopher withdrew to spread me wide, his hips moving to take up the extra space, his beautiful body held in restraint two inches from mine. Our attention went to his cock, the length heavy and full and hot. My mouth went dry, and my stomach clenched in desire.

When I looked back to his face, I swallowed hard, shocked by the pleading look he was giving me.

"I'm clean." His words came hoarse. Like an apology. And I knew his thoughts had reverted back to five nights ago. "Would never hurt you like that, Samantha. Never. When you stepped back into my world? I knew there was no more living the life I'd been. Knew if I was going to be with someone it was going to be with you. Haven't touched another girl since I found you in the hall of my sister's house, and I went and got tested, knowing one way or another, I was leaving all that shit behind. Would never hurt you in the ways you thought. In the ways Ben led you to believe."

I curved my arms around his back, pulling him closer. I was met with the sweet feel of his length gliding between the folds of my sex and the frantic thunder of his heart against my chest.

"I trust you." I breathed my admission into his ear, and I knew that was the only thing this man needed to know. He pulled back a fraction, and the head of his erection caught.

He pulsed inside me in one strong thrust.

So sure.

So perfect.

He held my head in his hands, fingers woven in my hair. Nose to nose, breath to breath. Never breaking his gaze, he moved in me. With me. For me.

Loved me.

Cherished me.

Worshiped me.

He took me to those promised places.

Lifted me to that highest high.

A place high enough that my consciousness touched the stars and I glimpsed the future.

A future that belonged to him.

One he'd share with me.

Then together we fell.

A free fall of blinding lights and perfect pleasure that spun and spiraled. The two of us one. And when we landed, it was on a different level. One that belonged only to us.

His breaths heaved and his body shook, and I hugged him close and he pulled me even closer, pressed his ear between my breasts.

My fingers played through his hair, twisting through the ends as I worked to find an even breath.

I stilled when he spoke. "Every truth belonged to you, Samantha. And every lie? All those were yours, too. Whether I told them to keep you or told them to protect myself from hurting so bad after I lost you, every single one belonged to you."

Emotion clutched me by the throat, and I nodded, my chin hitting the top of his head.

"I need you to understand something . . . about Jasmine," he grated out.

I tensed, but he smoothed it away, hand gliding down my side. "I didn't want you to know about her. Not because I was trying to get away with something. But because of what she represented. That night when I came to your room?"

I nodded again, remaining silent, letting him talk.

"There's nothing in this world that could ever excuse what I did, but I need you to understand the dark place my mind had gone that night. I'd just found out about Jared, and . . . I . . . I was higher than a fucking kite. Everything about that night was so fucking wrong. Should've known better, but what made it even worse was that I went to you that way. I was completely broken up over Jared, broken up over you. Inside, I knew I was losing you. All those months your parents were trying to keep us apart, it felt like you were just giving in, letting them win when we were supposed to be fighting to stay together. But the second you opened your window? All this relief came barreling in. But it was distorted." He squeezed me tighter like it hurt to go back there. "Warped and perverted. And touching you felt like the only thing in the world that could make any of the shit we were going through right. I *never* wanted to hurt you. Ever. I'd rather die."

A remorseful breath left him. "When I realized what I was doing and you told me to go . . . I was fucking demolished, Samantha. Crushed that I'd hit such a low that I'd hurt the one person who meant the most to me. Still, I'd heard you that night, Samantha, *felt* your fear, and I stopped because that's a line my heart wouldn't let me cross. The next day, I gave it one more try and tried to call you, but your phone was disconnected, and I just . . . cut myself off from any hope. Completely lost myself."

My heart stuttered through empty beats, caught up in the knowledge that he hadn't just disappeared out my window and into the night, out of my life. That I'd been right when I'd been gripped by grief for him. Over Jared. Over the loss.

Christopher shifted his chin to my chest, peering up at me as I continued to run my fingers through his hair.

Forgiveness ran fast and deep, penetrating everything, erasing it all.

Still, I knew we needed no secrets between us. No more barriers to keep us apart.

And I knew Christopher needed to get it all out.

He met my eye. "Sleeping with Jasmine . . . it was like I was giving myself over to that depravity," he continued. "Letting myself slide right down that path of destruction, because there was nothing good left for me to live for. The girl who had me all spun up, the one who had me crazy in love and wanting something better for my life, was gone. What better way to bury that hope than to fuck it all away with the one I hated most?"

He laughed, but there was zero humor behind it. "Sick part? I lay there thinking about you. Wishing it was you and hating you at the same time because you cut me loose, hating myself because I knew it was my fault. No surprise, I was fucked up again, my mind detached and my body vacant. And it was like I could hear you crying, and I was picturing you somewhere, hurting just like me."

He buried his face in my chest. "I promise, Samantha, I didn't know you were there. Fuck, you gotta know I'd never do something like that to you. And no, that doesn't come close to gaining forgiveness for me sleeping with her. That was my choice and a fucking terrible one at that, but it was never done to hurt you."

He lifted his face. "The other night . . . when I lied . . . I know it was wrong, but that lie came out because I didn't want to be that person anymore. Didn't want to be the guy who fucked his chances away. I wanted to be the guy with a hope and a future and a forever. I couldn't stand the idea of that bitch tearing us apart, not after everything we'd already been through. Turned out she already had."

He moved to lean up on his elbow, eyes searching mine. "All these years you thought I cheated on you, and you were still willing to take me back?"

I looked up at Christopher as he looked down on me. "I fell in love with you then, Christopher. Completely. And that love nearly ruined me. But these last few months? I've loved you for who you are today. Loved the man I thought you'd finally become." Softly, I touched his face. "Turned out you'd been him all along. What hurts me most now is knowing we were robbed of so much time. Of so many memories. Of our *firsts*." My eyes softened in sincerity. "And I understand you needed me to know all of this. And what I need you to know now is I forgive you, Christopher. Completely."

He snatched me by the wrist and pressed my palm to his mouth. He kissed it, then slid it back to his cheek, covered it with his as he held it close. "Thank you."

I gave him a soft smile, and he set an adoring kiss against my lips. When he pulled back, his eyes flashed with something natural, something easy, a playfulness reserved just for us. "So now that I showed you just how fucking much I love you, told you how much, I think it's about time I fed you."

I giggled, warm satisfaction filling me up. "That sounds nice. I don't think I've really eaten much this week." The quiet agony of Stewart was wedged deep in my heart, slowly becoming a permanent piece of me. Still, I felt joy. A completeness I could find only in the love of Christopher.

He sat up at the side of the bed and bent down to grab his jeans from the floor.

I gasped when I saw the inflamed skin on his side. Skin I hadn't seen when we'd been buried beneath the covers. Skin inked with new words that hadn't been there five days ago.

It was a bold script that ran up the length of his side, over his ribs, beginning at his hip and ending just under his armpit.

Never stop believing in magic.

Confusion spread across Christopher's face when he looked back at the shock on mine. I sat up, holding the blanket to my chest as I leaned across and traced the tips of my shaking fingers along the beautiful words. The same words that flared across the front page of Stewart's most prized possession.

His survivor's prize.

Christopher cast me a sad smile, a sorrowful twist to only one side of his mouth. "That's for Stewart," he explained, raking a hand through his hair and emitting a soft, soft sigh as he looked toward the floor. "He just . . . he was always talking about this book . . . his favorite book. Every time I went over, he'd go on and on about it, wishing he had that same kind of magic. After I lost you . . . lost him . . . I thought maybe if I could leave him with one good thing, it would be a memento of that."

He shook his head as if it were stupid. "I wrote the author like fifteen times in a period of two days, pretty much begging her to send him a signed copy. I asked her to tell him to 'never stop believing in magic.' Told her how much he deserved it and how much he needed to believe it. I knew it'd never happen, but I had to try."

In contemplation, he looked back at me, with hope, while inside I was absolutely coming apart.

That book. That book.

The one that had filled Stewart up with peace and pride.

The one that had prodded at my broken heart.

The one that had won me over.

The one Ben had claimed.

Tears slipped down my cheeks in an unstoppable rush of love for this man. "It was always you."

It was always him.

He frowned, and I laughed through my disbelief, through my thankfulness, through my joy, through the gut-wrenching pain.

"What are you talking about, sweet girl?" he asked, brows pinched as he shifted around to face me, and there was nothing I could do but throw my arms around his neck.

"I just . . ." I swallowed, my mouth smiling with affection when I pulled back. "That book has been sitting on his shelf for the last seven years, Christopher. It's . . . I don't think you could ever understand how much it touched him. The hope it gave him." Those tears just kept falling. "I can't believe it was you. *It was you.*"

Surprise blew across Christopher's features before it transformed, settling into a deep satisfaction, his own joy, his own hope. He slid onto his knees on the floor, facing me. Big hands burrowed under the covers to palm me by the outsides of my thighs, pulling me to the edge. He swept away my tears and moved to hold my face. "It was my prayer for him then and it's my prayer for him now. Even if he's not here . . . in this world . . . I have to believe he's out there somewhere, that he's smiling down at us . . . still believing. That now he has that magic. And you gotta know . . . it was *you.* Because of all that beauty you shine. The good you give. The love that glows with everything you touch." He rose higher on his knees, this gorgeous man stealing my breath the same way he'd stolen my heart. "Because of it I see something bigger. Something better. When I'm with you? That's what I want to be. Better. You get it now, don't you? *With you,*" he emphasized, "that's the only place I want to be."

EPILOGUE

Samantha

Nine Months Later

The sun held high in the sky, Phoenix in the fierce grip of the long, hot summer. Heat waves pressed down, infiltrating everything, saturating the air, radiating from the ground. I lifted my face to it, basking in its warmth as I stretched out on the pool lounger in my backyard.

Contentment swamped me.

Yeah.

My backyard.

Or rather, *our* backyard, and I had to be honest. I liked that description the best.

That night nine months ago when I asked Christopher to take me home, he'd automatically brought me here, without question, without hesitation.

And I'd never left.

Even through our separation, something inside me had always known it was with him where I belonged, just like Christopher had known the same with me. I understood it now, how when I first reconnected with Aly, when I held her baby girl, when Jared had welcomed me into their home, I'd felt an immediate bond. The demands of this need never allowed me to shut them out, as if I was being drawn in their direction, that vacant place in me vibrating with the longing to be filled.

Something inside me knew they would fit perfectly.

Because they were an extension of Christopher. And in turn, that made them an extension of me.

I'd just never known how important they would become, how all these people would change the landscape of my life, how they'd lift me and fill me and adore me in the same way I adored them.

God, I guess I'd just never known how good life could be until I'd finally allowed Christopher to love me.

One of those perfect pieces came tottering toward me after her dad hoisted her out of the pool, Aly right there to help their daughter safely to her feet. Black hair soaked, the tips of her cute little pigtails dripping, big blue eyes filled with all that childlike innocence.

My heart pressed so full it almost hurt. The tiny girl wore a pink bathing suit covered in butterflies, her little legs chubby, almost as chubby as her adorable cheeks. Distracted by the puddle her body made, she stopped to jump in it, giggling wildly when she splashed droplets of water everywhere.

"Look at you, big girl," I cooed. "Did you go swimming with your uncles and your daddy?"

She nodded emphatically, then hopped the rest of the way over to the edge of my lounger. I was all too happy to scoop her up. Her cool body met with my sun-soaked skin, and she curled her arms between us, snuggling closer to get warmed up. She burrowed her face at my chest.

"Tee-tee," she attempted as she peeked up at me, her grin spreading wide, four tiny teeth visible in her heart-wrenching smile.

She couldn't say *auntie*, but the erratic beat of my heart knew exactly what she meant.

Joy lit Aly's face, and she bit at her bottom lip. Obviously she couldn't stand just how adorable her daughter was, either. She ran a gentle hand over Ella's head. "Yes, you did, didn't you, princess?"

Aly cast me a soft smile and sat down on the lounger beside me. She squeezed the water from her ponytail. "Pool feels amazing. You should put your feet in," she suggested.

I cuddled Ella. "This sweet little thing is keeping me cool enough, aren't you, love bug?" I said, hugging her tight.

She squealed and wiggled out of my hold. "Daddy . . . pool?" With the question, she pointed to him with her tiny finger, intent eyes going to her mommy.

We were just beginning to understand the words she struggled to form, and her little voice was about the most precious thing I'd ever heard.

"Yep . . . your daddy is in the pool acting like a big ol' kid, isn't he?" Aly teased, tossing her husband a flirty grin.

Jared splashed her and she squeaked, and Ella burst out laughing like it was the funniest thing she'd ever seen.

"Oh, you want daddy to splash you, too?" Jared turned his playful warning to Ella, sidling up to the edge of the pool, his smile so consuming and full of love as he looked at his daughter that I couldn't help but feel it right in the center of my chest.

My gaze automatically slid to Christopher, where it seemed to be endlessly drawn, and my heart stuttered when I found him watching me with an expression akin to Jared's, all this adoration and affection blazing just for me, like seeing me with his niece undid something inside of him.

Those flames licked and danced in my belly, anticipation and need.

Augustyn jumped on Christopher's back, and Christopher laughed a boisterous laugh as he flung him off, diving down to tackle his younger brother. Jared jumped in, the three of them uncontainable. Loving life. Living it. Enjoying every second of their days.

My mom appeared at my side and handed me a glass of ice water. "Here you go, sweetheart."

I accepted it. "Thanks, Mom."

"No problem." She turned to Aly. "Can I get you anything?"

Aly relaxed back on the lounger. "I'm perfect, but thank you, Sally."

This was how we spent most Sunday afternoons, hanging out with our families, slowly merging them together.

My and Christopher's dads were over at the grill, none too interested in getting trapped up in the dangers of the pool, where the younger guys were a bit on the rowdy side. Conversation between them consisted of few words, but they seemed to get along just fine. Christopher's mom had her legs submerged in the water, sitting at the side of the pool, watching her boys play while my mom cautiously eased over to sit beside her, their friendship at first tenuous and questioning, but blossoming into one my mother had needed long before she realized it.

She'd needed an outlet, a place without criticism or judgment.

That was something my mother and I had in common that I'd never understood before. She had also always felt as if she had to live up to everyone's expectations just like I had, I the pastor's daughter and she the pastor's wife. That mutual confession had gone a long way in helping us understand each other, and it definitely had brought us closer.

Above that, she needed a reprieve, someone to laugh with, to cry with, to help her whittle away the effects of a life spent in a self-imposed solitude, tormented with her worry for Stewart.

Bottom line, she needed a friend.

Of course, it was no surprise it'd taken some time for my parents to warm up to the idea of me and Christopher, although they hadn't been entirely surprised, either. Mom had opened up and told me her greatest worry when I was a teenager had been the intense connection she witnessed between Christopher and me. She said all those afternoons when he'd waltz into our house and we'd pretend like we were only friends, she'd so easily seen through those pretenses, right to the powerful attraction that was palpable underneath.

She'd worried about my age. About the clear differences in our beliefs. What had scared her most was the way Christopher looked at me and the way I looked at him.

She'd been shocked and concerned to learn of the way Christopher had once again worked his way into my heart and life, how for months I'd snuck around behind Ben's back so I could spend time with Christopher. Because in hindsight? I knew the entire time where it would lead.

But our devotion had risen above all of that, Christopher's love for me a testament, the care he took of me a cure. It wasn't long before I felt the shift in my parents, in their belief, in their support of me, which in turn had ushered in their support of Christopher.

I glanced down at the ring on my finger. Inconspicuously, I waved the diamond through the rays of light, watching as the bevels glinted and shined.

Christopher had proposed to me on my twenty-fourth birthday. He'd said we missed that milestone on my sixteenth and it was high time he rectified the situation. He no longer wanted to remember the date of my birth as something he'd missed but instead something he had gained.

It didn't even take a beat for me to agree.

My gorgeous dress was hanging in my mother's closet, right next to all my bridesmaids', Aly, Stephanie, and Megan set to wear the beautiful gray silk. Ella would walk the aisle, that sweet little one standing up as our flower girl next month. Or probably more accurately playing on the stairs of my father's church, stealing all the attention, but we were okay with that, too.

Stewart would be there, too. His spirit living on. Strong and beating in our hearts. Just like Christopher's prayer, I knew Stewart had to be out there, watching over us. Shining more of his beauty and positivity into our lives.

"All right, time to eat," David Moore called, holding a platter of food he'd pulled from the grill.

"'Bout time, old man," Christopher shouted, shooting a wink at his dad.

Dave Moore pulled up half a grin. "Watch yourself there, son. You don't want me to have to jump in there to teach you kids a lesson."

Aug laughed, swiped the dripping water from his face. "Better listen, man," he warned his brother, nudging him. "Dude took my ass out when we were playing football the other day. Dad's no joke."

"That's 'cause you're a pussy." Christopher smiled wide, messing with his little brother.

"Ass," Aug returned, punching Christopher in the arm.

Their dad waved his spatula. "Need I remind you two that we have little ears here? The lot of you are bad influences." And there their dad was again, the moderator, keeping his boys in line.

I giggled toward Christopher, and he cut me a sly smile.

Everyone climbed out of the pool, gathered to eat at the outdoor tables, the afternoon passing in that easy, content way. When everyone jumped back in the pool to cool off, I hung out at the edge, every once in a while getting brave enough to dip my toes in, that childhood fear still chasing me into adulthood.

But as I dragged my toe across the water, setting it in a tranquil sway of ripples, I no longer felt the slither of fear travel down my spine, but rather that anticipation of what was to come.

That my life was on the cusp of change.

But that anxiety was no longer one of dread, and it no longer instilled me with worries and questions, instead wrapping me in a fresh blanket of security.

Just as the sun was setting, our families bid us good-bye. Hugs were given and well wishes for the week. Certainly, I'd see Aly and her family, the three of them as constant in our home as we were in theirs. It was a rare day when I didn't see them or at least talk to Aly on the phone.

The rest of them I might not see until the next week, when we'd all gather again, coming together to share in this life.

I snapped the side gate shut behind them and turned to face Christopher, who was still in the pool, his head bobbing just above the water at the deep end.

Slowly, I crossed the yard, coming to stand at the shallow end, just at the start of the steps. A soft smile pulled at his mouth, and he swam forward to the middle of the pool and settled on his feet. Water lapped at his chest, his hair wet and gleaming. He flicked it back, and the little drips slid off the locks of his midnight hair and onto his shoulders, trailing down his dark, toned skin.

God, he was a vision, and looking at him still knotted me tight with desire, our love thick and unending.

I drew in a gulp of air, held it in my tightened lungs, and dipped my toes in above the top step.

A flash of a frown dented Christopher's forehead when I propelled myself forward, crossed that line that had always held me back. Fear pounded for a frantic beat, but I pushed it aside and focused on the man who I knew would guard me with his life, and I instantly found myself wrapped up in the comfort that washed through his eyes.

"What are you doing, beautiful?" he asked, edging forward. Ripples skated across the top of the pool as he came near, his body slowly exposed as he eased into shallower waters, his body that made me dizzy and his smile that made me weak. He stopped before he hit the bottom step, and I took another brave step, submerging both my feet to my ankles.

I shook, standing on the top step. Chills skidded across my flesh, and I breathed in, breathed out, found my voice. "You came back to me when I was filled with fear. When I was riddled with bitterness and hurt. One glimpse of you and I was thrown into a terror. One made up of everything you stood for. I knew how easily you could break me, how you'd wrecked me and destroyed me, and I was terrified that you still affected me the exact same way you did when I was a fifteen-year-old girl."

I took one step deeper, and the cool water crawled up my calf and landed just below the well of my knee. "But that fear owned me only because I gave it power . . . but it was a power that couldn't hold." My other foot came down to rest beside the first, and Christopher just watched my actions, silently coaxing me near, the man in tune with my goal.

"Letting go of those fears was so difficult, but when I finally did, the greatest joy was unearthed"—I touched my chest—"and my broken heart was repaired at your touch." I let the sole of my foot slide over the sharp curve of the step, and I sucked in a steeling breath as I sank to the third step. Water swallowed up my thigh. "I don't want to hang on to false fears anymore, Christopher, and this one . . . it's been hounding me for a long, long time. I want to face it with you." My left leg followed, and I stood in front of Christopher, submerged to midthigh, my eyes a head above his.

He tipped his head back and his hands came up to embrace me at my hips. "Samantha," he murmured, his expression cautious, his movements even more so. I so clearly saw the understanding flicker in his eyes, the warmth contained there, and I knew he knew this was about so much more than what most would consider a silly childhood fear. Because for most of my life, it hadn't felt silly in the slightest.

It had been crippling.

Debilitating.

But now? Now I wanted to run.

To fly.

To do it with this man.

Gentle hands slid further around my back, encircling me in a show of support, all the strength and security I needed to face this fear.

To face this life.

"Are you ready?" he asked.

"More than you could imagine."

He lifted me off my feet, bringing me flush to him, skin to skin, and I wrapped my arms around his neck as he allowed me to slip farther down, until we were face-to-face. Slowly he edged us back, sinking us deeper into the waters, the sun sliding away, diving toward the horizon, as Christopher took me deeper.

Past all those places where I was afraid.

Because with him I was free.

Free to love.

Free to dream.

Free to be me.

Out in the middle of the pool, he stopped his descent, and he pulled me close as he spun us in a slow circle, never insinuating the possibility that he'd even consider letting me go.

He was with me to the end.

"You're swimming," he whispered, dancing with me in the cool waters, my feet nowhere close to touching the bottom, my shoulders dipping down in sync with his.

I choked over the emotion. "And I'm not afraid."

One hand threaded through my hair, holding me at the back of the head. He caressed his thumb just under my jaw. "You have nothing to be afraid of, baby. Always gonna be right here for you. Whatever you need, I'm here."

I held him closer, breathing him deep into the well of my lungs. Contentment seeped back out on my sigh. My mouth was near his ear as he continued to sway me, hold me.

"I have something to tell you," I whispered, so low I knew he more felt the words than heard them, the same way I could feel the spike in his heart rate.

"Yeah?" he asked, hugging me closer, both hands splayed wide across my back.

"Yeah. And it's big, and I know our lives together have just begun and now everything's going to change again, but I want to dive headfirst into this with you."

I could feel his smile emerge where he rested his face on the side of my head, the man catching on. "Yeah?" he asked again, prodding for more.

"Yeah," I repeated, pulling back to look at him, releasing my hold enough so I could reach out and flutter my fingertips down the side of his face. "I didn't think I'd be scared, but I am."

But this wasn't a debilitating fear.

This fear was liberating.

This fear spoke of the future.

Of every hope.

Of a life filled with even more love.

I'd thought loving any more than I already did would be impossible. The love I had for him. For my family and for his.

I'd thought I'd been full.

Little did I know I had so much more to give.

I'd stopped taking the pill two months before.

We were supposed to use condoms.

We didn't.

Somewhere inside I think we both knew we were ready, the way Christopher had looked at me, asking me for silent permission to fill me whole, to take me skin to skin, knowing full well where we were likely to land.

"You got my baby?"

Clutching him, I nodded, feeling the force of a soggy smile break through the heavy emotion gripping my face. The way he said it with so much yearning just about annihilated me, burning through me, but how quickly I'd learned those flames supplied my breath.

"Are you happy?" I murmured against his neck.

He exhaled into my hair, brushing his fingers through it, before his big hand moved to hold my head in a firm embrace, his mouth at my ear as he murmured tender words. "Nothing in this world could make me happier, Samantha. Watching your belly grow with my baby. Claiming you as my wife. Having someone call me Daddy. It's all I want, baby . . . to spend this life with you."

I burrowed deeper, inhaling his warmth, the tears welling in my eyes slipping free. "I love you, my crazy boy."

Christopher captured my mouth in a kiss that rocked through me with its intensity, the man loving me in the middle of a pool, holding me up in my fears. He pulled back, green eyes staring right at me. "Completely, crazy in love with you."

A NOTE FROM THE AUTHOR

Dear Reader,

I'd like to thank you for reading *Come to Me Recklessly*! Christopher and Samantha's story was such a joy to write. If you enjoyed their story, I would LOVE your review on Amazon or other book retailers. I appreciate your helping to spread the word!

Don't miss exclusive excerpts, giveaways, and all my latest news! Sign up for my fan-only newsletter here: http://aljackson author.us3.list-manage.com/subscribe?u=a8a103f4006182d475 c20ad39&id=3a5ab5faac

If you prefer short, quick updates, you can subscribe to receive text-message updates by texting "jackson" to 96000.

If you haven't had the chance to read Jared and Aly's story in *Come to Me Quietly* and *Come to Me Softly*, I invite you to dive into their love story. It's one of my favorites and I hope it becomes one of yours! Keep reading to get a special peek at *Come to Me Quietly*.

Happy Reading!

Xoxo ~ Amy

Read the beginning of Aly and Jared's story
in the first book in A. L. Jackson's
Closer to You Series,

COME TO ME QUIETLY

Available now from New American Library

PROLOGUE

Dashed lines blur until they become a solid line. My bones vibrate from the thousands of miles I've spent straddling this leather seat, the muscles in my right arm screaming from the hours my hand has been locked on the throttle.

But I don't stop. I can't, and I don't know why. Something in my gut spurs me forward. I plow ahead.

Hot air blasts my face and my hair thrashes in uncontrolled chaos.

I bite back a bitter laugh.

Uncontrolled chaos. That's exactly how they described me.

The desert sky goes on forever, an ocean of the deepest blue. The city rises like a beacon in the distance. Because I am drawn.

What am I doing?

There is nothing here for me. I know it. I've already destroyed it all. I destroy everything I touch.

Still I can do nothing but press on.

ONE

Aleena

I was propped up on my bed with my sketch pad balanced on my bent knees. Megan was doing her best not to laugh from where she sat cross-legged at the end of my bed, bouncing.

"Hold still," I commanded, biting my bottom lip as I attempted to get her mouth just right. The shading was difficult, and I wanted it perfect. Megan had the most genuine smile of any person I'd ever met. I refused to mess it up.

"But I have to pee," she whined. She bounced a little harder. She couldn't hold it in any longer, and she released this hysterical laugh as she rolled off the edge of my bed. "I'll be right back."

With a groan, I tossed my sketch pad to the bed. "You're such a pain in my ass, Megan," I called after her as she ran out my door and across the hall to the bathroom. She'd gotten up to pee at least three times in the last hour. The girl could not sit still to save her life.

"That's why you love me so much," she yelled back.

The bathroom door slammed behind her, and I picked the pad back up to study it.

Megan's striking face stared back at me, smiling, her normally long blond hair traced in shades of charcoal, her normally blue eyes wide and black.

She'd been my best friend since she'd moved here from Rhode Island during our sophomore year of high school almost five years ago. I loved drawing her because she was so different than the typical model who offered herself up. She was short, just shy of the five-two mark, wore her curves well, and had a unique face. It was somehow both sweet and curious, this constant expression that made me think of innocence trying to work itself out.

She still lived with her parents in the same neighborhood where I'd grown up, just two streets over from my old house where my parents and younger brother still lived. She hung out here a lot at the apartment that I'd shared with my older brother, Christopher, since I'd graduated from high school two years ago. Christopher and I both went to ASU, and our apartment was near the campus. I was going to school to be a nurse, but God, sometimes I wished I could do something with my art. I knew it was absurd, that there was little chance that anything would come of it. That didn't mean I didn't want it.

She was grinning when she came back less than two minutes later.

"Feel better?"

"Oh yeah." Climbing back onto the bed, she crawled forward to steal a peek.

I hid the pad against my chest.

"Let me see." She reached out and tried to grab it.

I shook my head and held it closer. "You know the rules."

"I know, I know." She sat back. No one ever got to see. No one except for me.

From the floor, Megan's phone rang in her purse. She leaned over to dig it out. When she rose back up, excitement had transformed her expression. "It's him," she mouthed to me as she accepted the call and brought it to her ear. "Hello?"

Turning back to my sketch, I tried not to smile while I listened to her talk to Sam. She'd been chasing that guy for the last month, ever since she'd hung out with him at a party our friend Calista had thrown in May to celebrate the end of last semester. One kiss and she was hooked. I wasn't so sure he felt the same.

"Yeah . . . we can come . . . okay, see you there."

She dropped her phone to the bed and squealed.

Oh God. Megan didn't squeal. She was in trouble.

"Sounds like you have a date tonight," I muttered, my attention trained on the motion of my hand.

"Not me, we," she countered. "Sam is having a party tonight, and he wants us to come. I can't believe he actually called," she said, obviously talking to herself. "Two weeks and no word from him. I was beginning to think he was going to ditch me."

Beginning to?

So maybe I was a little protective of my best friend.

I hopped off the bed and went to my closet, dug through until I found the little black skirt I'd tucked in the back. I yanked it from the hanger and tossed it to her. "Here . . . wear this. It'll look a lot better on you than it does on me. You know it was those legs that tripped Sam up in the first place. I think the guy literally stumbled." I pointed at her. "And you better make him work for it."

"Oh, he's definitely going to have to work for it. You know me better than that." Megan held up the skirt to inspect it. "This is really cute." She looked up with a grin. "Maybe you should wear it. You know Gabe's gonna be there." The last she said in that singsong voice that she only used because she knew it annoyed the hell out of me.

"Pssh," I huffed under my breath, and she laughed because she of all people knew Gabe wasn't really that much of a draw. Gabe was my kind-of boyfriend. By kind of, I meant he was a guy who wouldn't leave me alone or take no for an answer. But he was unbearably cute and sweet in a boy-next-door kind of way and I didn't really know how to cut him loose without hurting his feelings.

And he was safe.

She lowered the skirt to her lap. "You should really quit stringing that guy along. It's kind of sad." Her tease turned serious, her blue eyes sober as she looked up at me from the bed.

I tossed a pair of shorts to change into on my bed. "I'm not stringing him along, Megan. He's the one who's strung himself to me."

"Whatever, Aly. You just keep telling yourself that. You always do."

I could see the concern pass over her eyes, could almost hear the argument pass through her lips, *the lecture.*

"Just don't, okay?" I said.

She blinked a couple of times, as if doing that would clear whatever picture she saw in her mind. "I just don't get you sometimes, Aly."

The party was mellow, just a few people hanging out on a Thursday at the house Sam shared with a couple of other guys. Most of us were out back, sitting around the pool drinking beer. The yard lights were off, the area cast in a muted glow from the lights shining through the bank of windows inside Sam's house. Megan was curled up with him on a lounger at the far end of the pool, their voices hushed and relaxed. Behind me flames rose and crackled from an in-ground fire pit, and a few people sat around in the chairs that circled it.

Leaning back on my hands, I dipped my feet into the pool. Water rippled out over the surface, the ridges illuminated above the shadows as they lapped across the pool. Even at eleven o'clock at night, it was still hot. Summer in Phoenix was my favorite. It always had been. Heat saturated everything, radiated from the concrete and pavement, pressed down from the sky. Bugs trilled and birds rustled through the trees. I loved that I could be in the middle of the sprawling city and still feel like I was out in the wilderness. Peaceful. There was no other way to describe it.

I wasn't surprised when Gabe settled down beside me. We'd chatted a little throughout the evening, but for the most part, I'd avoided him. He was shirtless and only wore a pair of white swim trunks. "You want to join me?" he asked, inclining his head toward the pool in invitation.

"Nah. I'm good," I said, even though the thought of the cool water was incredibly appealing.

Tilting his head back to get a better view of me, he almost smiled. Strands of his light brown hair flopped to the side, and his dark brown eyes swam with something I wished I didn't see. "You're missing out," he said.

I laughed quietly and shook my head. He was so obvious.

"I am, huh?"

One side of his mouth twitched. "Yeah, you are."

"Fine," I said.

What can it hurt?

Or I guessed the more appropriate question would be, why did it hurt? It was stupid. Childish. But I didn't know how to let it go.

Forcing myself to my feet, I pulled off my tank top and slipped out of the little shorts I'd worn over my green bikini.

Gabe's expression lifted with slow appreciation.

Embarrassed, I turned away and jumped in. My body sank to the bottom of the pool. I floated, weightless, the length of my black hair spreading out and drifting away. It was cool, invigorating. The water blocked out the voices and the noise of everyone else, and for a few seconds, I reveled in the solitude. When my lungs grew tight, I propelled myself up to the surface. I sucked in a huge breath of air as I flung my hair back from my face.

Gabe was already waist deep in the pool, smiling at me. "You have to be the most gorgeous girl I've ever seen, Aly," he murmured as he edged forward.

Lights from inside cast his face in shadows, but I could see the beauty in his silhouette. And I wanted to want him, wanted to somehow get back the part of me that I'd given away that night so long ago.

I didn't say anything, just stared at Gabe as he inched forward. I didn't stop him when his hands found my hips and didn't stop his kiss.

It felt nice.

But there would always be something missing.

TWO

Jared

Everything had changed even while everything seemed to remain the same. I rode the streets, searching. For what, I didn't know. In the six years I'd been gone, the city had crawled out past its boundaries, but the old neighborhood appeared as if it'd been frozen in time, like a snapshot I looked at from afar. A picture I'd been erased from.

I pulled onto the dirt off the main street, directly across the street from where I'd grown up. Every memory that ever mattered I'd experienced here. They were only that. Memories. I propped my booted foot on the ground to hold my bike up while I just stared. Cars flew by, my vision blurred in the flashes of metal.

What the fuck was I thinking? That this was a good idea? Because it was most assuredly not a fucking good idea.

I'd been back in town for almost a week. It'd taken me that long to even build up the nerve to get this close to the old neighborhood. Maybe I just wanted to torture myself, to make myself pay a little more, although no amends could ever be made. I'd already tried to pay the price, but fate wouldn't even allow me that.

As if I were anchored to the past, I couldn't force myself to leave. I could almost see us playing in the middle of the quiet street, hiding, chasing, laughing, running through the vacant land that backed the neighborhood. If I strained hard enough, I could hear my mom's voice as she leaned out the front door and called me to dinner, could see my father pulling in to the driveway at the end of the workday, could picture my little sister's face pressed against the window as she waited for me to return home.

All of it was an echo of what I had destroyed.

My chest tightened, and I fisted the grips on the handlebars as the anger raged. Aggression curled and coiled my muscles and I squeezed my eyes closed. A twisted snarl rose in my throat, and I bit it back and held it in. My eyes flew open as I gunned the throttle and shot down the street. I wound through cars and pushed myself forward. I had no idea where I'd end up because there was no place I belonged.

I just rode.

Hours later, I sat with my elbows propped up on the bar, my boots hooked over the footrest on the stool. I took a long drag from my bottle of beer, eyeing Lily from where she watched me with a coy smile from behind the bar. The girl'd had the nerve to card me, and we'd been fast friends since.

At least I hoped we were. A mild grin lifted just one side of her mouth before she shook her head and turned away to lean over and restock some beers, giving me the perfect view of her tight little ass.

Ice-cold liquid slid down my throat, and I breathed out a satisfied sigh. I'd forgotten how fucking hot the summers were in Phoenix.

When it felt as if I traveled every street in the city, I'd pulled in to the parking lot of this little bar. I was starving and in dire need of a beer. The place was pretty packed, filled with guys who appeared to be looking for a reprieve after a long day at work, there to unwind and catch the game, mixed in with some groups who were probably college students, dotted with a few like me.

Lily disappeared into the kitchen and reemerged with my burger. She set it down in front of me. She leaned across the bar on her forearms. Pieces of her chunky blond hair fell to one side as she tipped her head. "So, are you going to ask me for my number or just stare at me all night?"

I raised my brow as I took another drink of beer. "I figured I'd just wait here until you get off." I wasn't one to go through the motions or humor girls with pretenses.

She laughed with a hint of disbelief. "Pretty sure of yourself there, huh?"

I shrugged as I polished off my beer. I wasn't, really. I just didn't care. If she asked me back to her place, cool. But I wasn't going to be all torn up if she didn't. I'd find someone else. I always did.

Lines dented her forehead as she turned her attention to my hands, and she reached out in an attempt to trace my knuckles.

My heart sped, my hands fisting as I drew them back, my jaw tightening in warning as I lifted my chin.

She frowned when she looked up and found the expression on my face. She rocked back before she appeared to shake off the jolt of confusion she felt at my reaction. "You want another beer?"

"That'd be good," I said, my tone hard. It was always the same. They always fucking wanted to touch, to know, to dig. I didn't go there. Ever.

She nodded and turned away.

With an elbow on either side of my plate, I wrapped my hands around the huge burger and leaned in to take a bite. It tasted like heaven. I suppressed a groan. It'd been way too many hours since I'd had something to eat. I popped a fry in my mouth and went in to take another bite when in my periphery I sensed someone come to a standstill. He started to pass, but hesitated again before he stopped. Out of the corner of my eye, I kept a watch on him. All I could see were his hands clenching and unclenching at his sides, like he was trying to make a decision about something. I didn't acknowledge him, just focused on this fucking delicious burger and hoped the dude got some common sense and walked away before he got his ass beat.

He came in closer to the bar and cocked his head around to look at me. "Jared?"

My head snapped up to take in this guy who was really fucking tall, and even though he was lankier than shit, it was pretty clear he could go a round or two. His black hair was wild and sticking up all over the place, and his dark green eyes were wide with shock. He dropped onto the barstool next to me, staring at me like I was some sort of apparition.

I was pretty sure we were each having about the exact same effect on the other. For a minute every muscle in my body froze, my mouth gaping, before the shock wore off. Then I laughed and grabbed a napkin and wiped it across my mouth as I spun my stool toward him. "Well, shit, if it isn't Christopher Moore. How the hell are you, man?"

A thousand memories pushed to the forefront of my mind. I could see them all there, too, flickering across his face.

Christopher and I had been thicker than blood. He'd been both my best friend and the brother I never had.

A smile erupted on his face and he shook his head. "I'm good . . . really good." He blinked as if he still couldn't believe I was there. "How have you been?" His tone shifted, grew heavy as he leaned with one elbow on the bar, facing me. His attention shot from my face to my hands fidgeting on my lap and back up to my face again. He sat back, his brow pinching together. "Where have you been, Jared? I mean . . . I haven't heard from you in years. Why . . ." He wrenched his hand through his hair, unable to complete the question, his voice trailing off.

What the hell was I supposed to say? Christopher had written me all these bullshit letters saying none of it was my fault, that everything would be okay, that he *got* it, but he got *nothing.* How could he? I was the one who lay in my cell at night with the pictures of what I'd done burned in my mind. When I closed my eyes, they were the only thing I saw. And it was most definitely *my fault.* I never returned any of his letters, never called, never let any of them know where I went once I was released. I didn't need Christopher or anyone else to feed me lies, to try to convince me one day I'd heal or some fucking garbage like that. Maybe my heart beat on, but I died the day *she* did.

I trained my voice, acted casual. "I've been working up in New Jersey the last few years. I was able to save up some money, so it's been good."

He pressed his lips together. "And when did you get back?" he asked, although I heard the question. *Why are you back?* I was glad he didn't ask because I didn't fucking know.

"About a week ago."

Lily showed up in front of us with a fresh beer and began wiping down the counter. Her gaze landed on Christopher. "Can I get you anything?"

"No, thanks, I'm good." He waved her off and turned back to me. "Where are you staying?"

I sipped at my beer. "I've been staying at this shitty motel while I look for an apartment . . . across town."

For a second he worked his mouth in consideration. He released a breath and cocked his head to the side. "Why don't you come stay with me while you look? It'd be cool to catch up. It has to suck to be living in a motel."

"Nah, man, I couldn't impose like that."

"It's not imposing. You're like family."

Internally I cringed at his assertion. Yeah, maybe I'd been like family once. Not anymore.

Christopher reached over, grabbed my beer, and drained half of it. I stifled a laugh. The guy hadn't changed at all. Christopher was notorious for *borrowing* stuff. If I was ever missing anything, I knew where to find it.

"Help yourself," I muttered as I waved my hand at my beer, and he just smirked.

"Anyway . . ." He tipped the bottle in my direction as if in thought, working something out. "I have a place I share with Aly. It's just a few miles away. You'll have to sleep on the couch, but it's got to be better than living out of a motel. This is really cool. . . ." He nodded as if he were trying to convince himself this wasn't a really bad idea. "I'm glad you're back. It will be good to catch up . . . ," he rambled on before he slowed. He must have read the surprise on my face.

Aly is his roommate?

"Our parents and Augustyn still live in the old neighborhood, but when Aly decided to go to ASU, we figured it'd be cool if she lived with me since we're going to the same school. She moved in a couple of years ago . . . right after she graduated from high school," he added as if to clear up my confusion.

If anything, it grew.

He just laughed. "Jared . . . she's twenty years old."

I tried to work it out in my head, the little black-haired girl who'd followed us around like we were the greatest things in the world while we teased her relentlessly. Still I would've killed for her. A grin fought for release when I thought of her knobby knees and buckteeth. By the time she was twelve, she was so tall and gangly she could barely stand on her two awkward feet. The last time I saw Christopher's sister, she must've been about fourteen, but that year was just a blur. I couldn't even picture her at that age.

I smiled lightly and shook my head. "No shit?"

"Man, you've been gone for six years. What'd you expect? To come back here and everything would be the same?"

I didn't know what I expected.

Christopher let me off the hook with an easy grin. "It's really good to have you back, Jared." He stood and tossed a twenty on the bar, then clapped me on the back. "Thanks for the beer. Now go grab your shit. You're coming back to my place."

Christopher gave me his address, and I rode across town to the motel to get the few things I had, then headed back. It had to be getting close to midnight. Traffic was light, and the trip took me less than ten minutes. Their apartment was in Tempe right near ASU. I turned right into their driveway and up to the gate, then entered the code Christopher had given me. It swung open, allowing me entry into the huge complex. Large three-story buildings were situated around the property, and sidewalks surrounded by trimmed grass and small shrubs lined the walkways. I didn't get impressed by material shit, and it wasn't like this was the foothills or anything, but it was a thousand times better than the hole I'd been staying in since I got into town a week ago.

Why I let Christopher talk me into coming here I wasn't sure. I'd come to Phoenix without intentions, without expectations, only with the few meager belongings I could strap to my back and this foreign need in the pit of my stomach.

I no longer understood joy, but I had to admit, it was good to see his face.

I had some money saved up from the construction job I'd somehow landed back in New Jersey. I'd been a supervisor and made good money. No one knew me from Adam there, and my records were sealed since I'd been a minor when everything went down. The day I turned eighteen, I was released, and I'd hitchhiked my way across the country, putting as much distance between this place and myself as I possibly could.

Funny how I ended up right back here again after running so far.

I was going to have to find a job soon. I wouldn't run short of money for a while, but I'd need some kind of employment to put on my application if I wanted to get my own place. I couldn't stay with Christopher forever.

Really, agreeing to come here at all was a train wreck waiting to happen.

He'd hate me before I was gone.

I'd bet on it.

Winding around to the back of the complex, I parked my bike in one of the visitor spots in front of his building. I hiked my bag farther up my back and tucked my hands in my jean pockets as I ambled up the stairs to the second-floor landing. There were only two doors. Apartment 2602 was on the left. I rapped on the metal door.

Two seconds later, Christopher opened it. Cold air blasted across my face from the air conditioner, and I welcomed it as Christopher widened the door to let me in. "Come on in."

"This is seriously cool of you," I said as I stepped inside and took in my surroundings. It was a big, open room, the living area off to the left and the kitchen with a small, round table to the right. The two were separated by a low bar with three barstools sitting in front of it. The couch was in the middle of the living room. Behind it, a large sliding glass door led out to a small balcony.

Christopher gestured toward the couch. "Make yourself at home. Aly and I are pretty casual around here. I'm not doing much of anything this summer but sitting on my ass because I figure my senior year is going to be brutal, and Aly's working at a little restaurant while classes are out for the summer."

"Oh yeah? What are you studying?" I asked. Christopher had never been much of the studious type. I felt bad for even thinking I was surprised he'd made it that far in school.

He shrugged. "Just getting a bachelor's in business administration. I have no clue what I want to do with it, but shit, my parents saved all that money for me to go to college. I figured I'd better make good on it."

"That's cool. I'm sure you'll figure it out."

"Thanks, man. I hope so." It seemed like he wasn't so confident. He ran a hand through his messy hair and heaved the air from his lungs. "Listen, let me grab you a blanket and pillow."

He headed down the hall, tapped his index finger on the first door on the right. "This is Aly's room. Off-limits, obviously." He craned his head back. "She's kind of private and pretty much keeps to herself. You two probably won't run into each other all that much since she's working a lot while classes are out for the summer."

He touched the door on the left. "And this is Aly's bathroom. I don't think she'll mind if you use it." He said it as if it didn't really matter that much, but I couldn't imagine a girl wanting to share her bathroom with a guy she didn't really know.

"My room's at the end of the hall. There's a bathroom in there, too, if you need it."

"Thanks, man." I dropped my bag on the floor next to the huge black leather couch. It faced a large black TV stand with a flat-screen sitting on top of it. Controllers for a game console were stuffed inside a drawer with the wires sticking out.

I inclined my head toward it. "You still play?"

I kinda wanted to laugh because I used to have to drag his lazy ass outside to play or ride bikes or whatever the hell I wanted to do because Christopher always had his nose in a video game. He'd been the scrawny kid. When we were growing up, I'd kicked an ass or two in his name. Nobody had messed with him after that.

I hated fighting then, hated even the sight of the tiniest amount of blood. But I did it for him.

After everything went down, fighting was pretty much all I did. When the pressure built, *the anger*, it had to be released. Fighting served as the perfect outlet—the way the adrenaline spiked, the way it rose until it cracked me open, then flooded through my muscles and wept free from my veins, draining everything until I felt nothing.

Those were the only nights I could sleep. They probably would've let me out earlier if they weren't constantly pulling me off some kid who got in my way. Of course assholes to beat on in juvie were in no short supply. The population there was just a constant string of punks who deserved to get their asses kicked anyway.

Christopher laughed as he opened a closet in the hall. "Nah, I don't play all that much, but it's cool to unwind every once in a while." He tossed me a blanket and pillow. "You're welcome to stay as long as you want. I set a spare key for you on the coffee table." He pointed to the silver key before his hand fluttered in

the direction of the kitchen. "Aly and I share food. Just be sure
to chip in or whatever when she goes to the store."

"Yeah, for sure." I dropped the blanket and pillow on the
couch, sat down, and unlaced my boots to pull them off. Midnight approached, and I felt wasted, worn, but I doubted I'd
catch much sleep tonight. Anxiety was my constant companion,
and it'd grown since I'd gotten back into town. A disquiet rumbled somewhere deep inside me, the same feeling that had urged
me onto my bike and out onto the street little more than a week
ago. I hadn't even made a conscious decision to come.

The last four years since I'd been out of juvie I'd been focused, but without a goal. I showed up at the job site every day,
worked hard, fought a little, and fucked a lot. A pathetic substi-
tution for life, but it was all I had. And I'd had no intention of
ever changing it.

Then nine days ago I got up in the morning and got on my
bike and just rode.

Christopher pulled his cell phone from his pocket. "I'm going to give Aly a heads-up that you're here. I don't want her
coming in and freaking out that there's a strange guy sleeping
on the couch."

Nodding, I kneeled down and unzipped my bag. "Thanks
again. I'm going to grab a shower and call it a night."

"Sounds good. Clean towels are in the hall closet." Christopher hesitated at the end of the hall, then finally said, "I'm glad
you're back, Jared."

My jaw tightened, but I lifted it in his direction. "Yeah,
me, too."

The shower felt awesome. I kind of felt bad to have my naked ass surrounded by all of Aly's girlie shit, like I was some
kind of unwilling voyeur, but there was nothing I could do about
it. I grabbed a bottle of body wash and squirted a mound into

my palm. Coconut. I lathered it over my body with my hands and rushed it over my face. Damn, it smelled good.

Shaking my head, I resisted the urge to laugh because this whole thing was insane.

I toweled off, pulled on some boxer briefs and a clean pair of jeans.

Wandering out into the main room, I rubbed the towel through my damp hair and glanced over at the microwave. Already twelve forty.

Okay, so not really all that late, but was it weird Aly was still out? If I were Christopher, I wasn't sure how I'd deal with it, a sister out at all hours of the night. If I thought I couldn't sleep now . . .

My little sister's face hit me before I could stop it. *God.* I hadn't seen Courtney since she was nine. Not since the day she'd gone to live with my grandparents three weeks after I'd destroyed our family.

In the months that followed, my grandparents had wanted me to go with them, too, like maybe if they took me out of the house where my father drank away his days, they could save me from the downward spiral I was on. But I'd refused. There was nothing they could do to help me.

I was so much older than Courtney that I really hadn't ever known her all that well. I wondered what she looked like now—what she was like—if she was happy or if I'd ruined her life, too.

I flipped all the lights off except for the one that glowed beneath the microwave, spread the thin blanket out over the couch, and sank down onto it.

It was as comfortable as it looked.

Tucking the pillow under my head, I stared up at the darkened ceiling. Cold air pumped continuously from the vents, keeping out the suffocating heat outside. Everything felt incredibly still and silent. I could barely hear the muted passing of cars out on the main road and the quiet hum of insects in the shrubs outside.

Minutes ticked by as I lay alone with my thoughts. Nighttime was the worst, when the memories were so vivid, the images so graphic I was sure if I could just reach out far enough, I could stop it. Change it.

Fix it.

I'd do anything to be given that chance.

When I could stand it no longer, I let my eyes drift closed. They started as flickers, small blips in time. My heart sped as the sickness I kept down all day clawed through my veins and pounded in my ears. Nausea surged and I draped my arm over my eyes, squeezed them tight, wished for anything that would blot it out. Heat seared me from the inside out, and sweat broke out across my forehead and down the back of my neck.

Pain slammed me as everything closed in.

And all I wanted was to die.

Photo by Ali Megan Photography

A. L. Jackson is the *New York Times* bestselling author of *Take This Regret* and *Lost to You*, as well as other contemporary romance titles, including *Pulled* and *When We Collide*.

She first found a love for writing during her days as a young mother and college student. She filled the journals she carried with short stories and poems used as an emotional outlet for the difficulties and joys she found in day-to-day life.

Years later, she shared a short story she'd been working on with her two closest friends, and with their encouragement, this story became her first full-length novel. A.L. now spends her days writing in southern Arizona, where she lives with her husband and three children. Her favorite pastime is spending time with the ones she loves.

CONNECT ONLINE

aljacksonauthor.com
facebook.com/aljacksonauthor